T0340977

Murder in the Heart of It All

Murder in the Heart of It All

Michael Prelee

NORTH STAR PRESS OF ST. CLOUD, INC.
St. Cloud, Minnesota

Copyright © 2017 Michael Prelee
Cover art © Adobe Stock

ISBN: 978-1-68201-063-1

All rights reserved.

This is a work of fiction. Names, characters, places, and incidents are the products of the author's imagination or are used fictitiously. Any resemblance to actual events or persons, living or dead, is entirely coincidental.

First edition: May 2017

Printed in the United States of America.

Published by
North Star Press of St. Cloud, Inc.
19485 Estes Road
Clearwater, MN 55320
www.northstarpress.com

For Tina, who loves a good mystery.

Prologue

Kathleen Brimley heard the little mail truck slow down at the end of the driveway, brakes squealing a bit as the letter carrier stopped beside her mailbox. She looked out the window and saw the young man flip down the door, quickly put the mail in and pull away. She set her knitting down and got up from the wingback chair near the picture window. Red and orange maple leaves danced across the front yard, gathering in small piles and then dispersing again in the wind. They were falling early this year, she thought, with it only being mid-September. She would have to call the Clarkson boy up the road soon to have him rake them down into the hollow beside the house.

Robert's old denim work jacket still hung on a hook near the front door, and she pulled it on. Two years after his death, she could still smell his pipe tobacco. The thought brought a smile to her face.

The air was crisp and the sun was deceptively bright. It was one of those days where the outdoors looked inviting from inside but, once outside, the air had bite. The gravel driveway still had a few puddles from the rain of the last few days. She stepped around them and made her way to the mailbox.

She looked through the stack of mail as she made her way back to the house. It was the usual junk: a furniture store going out of business, campaign ads for the upcoming election in November, and a notice from the heating oil company reminding her it was time to fill up for winter. At the bottom was a white envelope with no return address.

Kathleen made her way back into the house and entered the small kitchen where she had made lunches and dinner for herself and Robert for thirty-seven years. She put a kettle on for tea and opened a tin of cat food for Mr. Smiley. The gray tabby raced down the hall at the sound of the can opener and skittered into the kitchen. She reached down and stroked him, bending from the waist because kneeling down was out of the question with the arthritis in her knees.

"You're a good kitty, aren't you?" she said as she petted him. He purred in agreement.

Drew Carey was helping a contestant on *The Price Is Right* negotiate a game of Plinko, and she watched from the kitchen doorway as a skinny woman dropped discs down through the peg board. The heating oil quote in the reminder was a bit high, she thought as she looked at it. She'd been a customer of Greely's for the last few years but she should probably give Terry over at Cloverfield's a call. Just check things out and make sure she wasn't paying more than she should.

The junk mail went into a shredder on the kitchen counter near the sink. Her daughter June had bought it for her last year, saying it wasn't good to just throw stuff out in the garbage anymore. People could go through it and find information they could use to steal your identity. Mr. Smiley looked up as the motor growled and reduced the junk mail to cross-cut bits of paper little bigger than snowflakes. When the can was full, the bits would be added to the compost pile out back.

The envelope with no return address was last. She looked at it, thinking it looked funny. Then she realized why. Her name and address were typed out, like with a typewriter, instead of printed out with a computer. The letters were indented in the paper.

She got a mug from the cupboard and dropped in a tea bag. A letter opener lay near the shredder and she used it to open the envelope. The kettle whistled and she turned off the burner. She unfolded the letter and read it as she poured water into the mug. Her face went rigid and she slammed the kettle back down on the burner.

"What is this?" Tears welled up in her eyes. "Who . . . ?" She turned the letter over, looking at the back, and then picked up the envelope again. There was no marking on it except for her name and address. The letter was typed as well, just like the address on the envelope. She read it again.

Your husband died fucking Nadine Harch because he hated
humping your ugly ass.

It was the only sentence on the paper. Kathleen was mad, as mad as
she could remember being. Hot tears rolled down her cheeks. She felt a
scream well up inside and she let it out. The cat looked up, shocked that
his gentle owner could make such a sound. The mug of tea went into the
sink, shattering against the stainless steel basin. She picked up the kettle
from the stovetop and hurled it into the dining room. It banged off the
large table and came to rest on the buffet, knocking papers to the floor.
Mr. Smiley ran from the room, tearing back down the hall to the safety
of the spare room, scooting under the guest bed instead of climbing up
on the windowsill where he usually spent hours lying in the sunlight.

She couldn't think of anyone who would write such a thing. Robert
had died of a heart attack in the backyard shed, which she could still see
from the kitchen window. One moment he had been working on the
lawn mower and the next he had rolled out of the open door into the
grass, clutching his chest. Kathleen had seen it happen as she walked
out carrying two glasses of lemonade. She had seen it! He was dead
before the ambulance arrived.

And he had never been unfaithful. She was sure of it. And especially
not with a waitress from down at the Peppermill.

She grabbed the envelope again, flipping it back and forth, looking
for a mark, something that would tell her why someone had mailed this
thing to her, but there was nothing, just her name and address. It was
typed neatly in the center of the envelope, just as she had been taught to
do in high school typing class. She made her way back to the living room
and slumped down into the wingback chair. Drew Carey had moved on
to the Showcase Showdown. Kathleen looked outside, still holding the
letter, and watched as the leaves danced in the wind.

One

The first time Tim Abernathy saw Amy Sashman, he knew exactly how her face would look with a smile. She had been waiting on a customer at Degman's Hardware, and after bagging his spackle and drywall sanding block, she told him to have a good day with a beaming grin. It had looked as good as Tim imagined. That had been eight months ago, on his first day at Degman's. Saying hello to her and seeing her face light up when she said "hi" back was still the best part of his day.

Tim drove the delivery truck for Tate Degman, delivering building supplies and furniture. It was one o'clock and he was coming back from his lunch break. The bell above the front door jingled when he entered, and he waved to Amy when she looked up.

"Busy this morning?" he asked.

"Not too bad," she said from behind the checkout counter. "You'll have a couple deliveries in the morning tomorrow."

"Oh, yeah? Furniture or building supplies?"

"Furniture. Marjorie sold two living room sets."

Tim looked at the addresses on the sales slips and wrote them down in the notebook he kept in his back pocket. He'd need them to plan his deliveries for tomorrow. Furniture meant the box truck, not the flatbed with the hydraulic crane. It also meant he'd need help, so Mac, one of the stock boys, would be riding along.

She leaned across the counter on her elbows and looked back at Tate's office, flipping her blonde ponytail as she did so. "Have you heard anything from those affiliates?"

Tim ran a hand through his short, wavy hair. "No, nothing yet. It's a long shot, you know."

"Come on, you did great at Channel 26."

"That was just an internship, and they didn't hire me when it was over. If I couldn't impress them with coverage of the county fair I may not have a future in TV news."

"Your butter cow story was cute," she said.

He flushed. "It wasn't supposed to be cute. It was supposed to be journalism."

"Well, you'll hear back."

"Tim, you out there?" The voice came from Tate Degman's office.

"Yes, sir." Tim waved to Amy and made his way to the office door. He was unwilling to commit to going inside unless he had to. Tate had moods.

"Sit down, and cut the 'sir' crap."

"Okay," he said, and sat in one of the two chairs in front of Tate's desk.

"Deliveries go well this morning?"

"Sure, no problems."

"Dieter called. You know why?"

Tim sighed. "Probably because I left ruts in his yard."

"Yeah, because you left ruts in his yard."

"You have to understand, I didn't want to park in his yard. He told me to pull around the side of the house, off the driveway. I told him the rain had made the ground soft but he insisted. He wanted that sectional sofa in the basement and didn't want to go down the steps inside the house."

Tate held up a hand. "I know. I've been out to Dieter's place before and I know he's a pain in the ass."

"So how come I'm in here being chewed out? I just did what he wanted."

"That's right, you did, and you almost got the truck stuck and that could have cost me a tow bill. I don't give a damn about Dieter's sectional sofa or his wife's living room carpet. When you go out on a delivery, you're in charge, not the customer. You decide the best way to do your job. You don't let them push you around."

"Okay, I just don't want someone calling in here telling you I'm giving them a hard time."

"There will always be unhappy people. Dealing with them is just something you have to do, especially if you are in business for yourself. What I need you to do is manage the customers when you get to their homes. I'm not saying you have to be difficult and argumentative, just size up the situation and do what you think is best. If guys like Dieter want to get pissy, it's their problem. Can you handle that?"

Tim nodded. "I can handle it." He stood up. "What about the ruts?"

"Dieter told you to drive around the side of his house?"

"That's right."

"Then Dieter can fill in his own damn ruts. Stage your deliveries for tomorrow and then knock off for the day."

"Okay, thanks."

Tim finished up at Degman's and by three was rolling across town to the *Hogan Weekly Shopper* in his wreck of a Chevy S-10 pickup. The faithful truck had gotten him through college but since his graduation last spring it had been acting up, sucking away more and more of his paycheck for repairs. He was going to have to do something soon to improve his transportation situation.

He parked in the rear and walked around to the front of the newspaper. Charlie Ingram was at his desk tapping away at his laptop. He looked up and pointed to the phone headset he wore, indicating he was on a call. Charlie was the publisher of the paper, and Tim was his sole employee. It was a freebie handed out at supermarkets and local businesses.

Tim worked part time helping with the advertising layout and collecting announcements from emails and the website. The paper served as advertising for local businesses and announced weddings, deaths, anniversaries, garage sales, and a couple local columns for which Charlie paid two cents a word. It wasn't the kind of journalism Tim wanted to use his political science degree for, but at least it was in his field. He sat down at the desk opposite Charlie and logged into his laptop.

It took ten seconds of overhearing Charlie's side of the call for Tim to realize the boss was speaking with Gary Shellmack, the owner of Creekside Motors, a local used-car dealership. He took out his cell phone, slipped in his ear buds, and cued up a playlist. Listening to Charlie trying to sweet talk Gary into a bigger ad buy was nothing he wanted to hear.

The submissions box was full with updated ad copy. When people submitted their ads online they filled out a form on the *Shopper* website and paid via credit card. Looking through the submissions, Tim could see that garage and yard sale ads had mostly died off after the end of August. Now there were more church bazaar ads, notices for potluck dinners, and a few engagement announcements. Part of Tim's job was to review the submissions, check them for spelling or date errors, and make sure the content was family friendly.

Tim spent a half hour scrolling through the web forms, double checking the submissions, and then got up to retrieve the stack of mail sitting in a basket on the counter. Charlie was still engaged in his phone call but Tim couldn't tell whether he was being successful or not.

He sat back down at his desk with the mail and started going through it. Utility bills went in one pile, invoice remittances in another, business invoices into yet another for Charlie's review, and then another pile for general correspondence. Tim liked this pile the most. People sent all sorts of things to newspapers, even a free weekly like the *Shopper*. They ran a letters to the editor section but tried to keep the level of discourse fairly friendly. The tone of some of these letters could be downright mean, especially when the writer was discussing the Trump administration and its policies. It went both ways, though. Hogan was a Democrat stronghold, so anti-Republicanism was well represented. Tim knew people took their politics seriously, but the vitriol in some of these missives was still surprising. No, Tim reconsidered; it wasn't so much the vitriol that was shocking but the ignorance behind the writing. People had either forgotten their civics classes from high school or they just didn't care. What they did care about, he saw as he read through the letters, was that they were right and everyone else was wrong. He dug out three that were reasonably well written and put the rest in the reject pile. Charlie stood up from his desk, stretched and yawned loudly enough for Tim to hear through his music. He took off his ear buds and handed him the letters to the editor.

"Good afternoon, boss," Tim said. "I think these letters will be good for this week's paper, and here are some invoices you need to look at. There's also a letter marked to your attention. I didn't open it."

"Thanks. That was Gary Shellmack."

"I figured."

"I got him to take out a full-page ad rather than the half he usually takes."

Tim nodded. "That's good. Anything else going on?"

Charlie got up and poured himself a cup of coffee. "I don't know. The paper's doing well, you know, but I'd like to do something different."

"Other than publishing?"

Charlie shook his head. "No, I mean something with the paper. I bought this thing almost twenty-five years ago, and if you look at one of those old issues and the one we're setting up for printing this week, they're almost identical."

"So? The *Shopper* is the kind of thing that should be consistent. People like that about it. They expect that familiarity. They want to open it up and see a recipe column from Sandy and news from around town summarized by Betty. They want to look in the classifieds and see a lawn mower for sale. The ad revenue is solid, too, right?"

"Yeah, I guess so," Charlie said. "Maybe I just need to think about it some more."

"Okay, let me know if I can help."

• • •

Gary Shellmack hung up the phone with Charlie at the *Shopper* and smiled. He'd gotten the full-page ad Charlie was selling but it only cost him twenty-five percent more than the half-page ad he normally bought. Gary liked getting a deal.

Creekside Motors was a large used-car lot. It covered two acres and he had a repair shop that could handle collision work. Built up from the corner lot his dad had started, Gary was now the largest used-car dealer between Cleveland and Pittsburgh.

He hefted his three-hundred-pound frame from behind his desk in the corner office and wandered to the showroom. Unlike most used-car lots, he treated his stock like it was new. The showroom held the best of the current inventory. Classic muscle cars were fast movers, so he worked hard to find them. New dads trading up to minivans were a good source. Gary would also drive around looking for yard finds, such as muscle cars someone had bought with the intention of restoring but had finally quit on. With a good yard find, he spoke to the husband but negotiated with the wife. Make a good enough offer, usually about sixty percent of what they wanted, and while the guy was haggling or thinking about all the hours and money he had dumped into the car, Gary asked the wife how many other offers they had turned down or how many cars pulled in the driveway with cash in hand. Most of the time it worked; other times he left with an empty trailer on the back of his Hummer.

He walked across the showroom to look at their latest acquisition, a 1974 fire-engine red Cadillac Eldorado with a white convertible top. He'd picked it up when one of his "finders" called in about it. He kept a few guys on the hook looking out for cars and paid a finder's fee if they found something good. This time it was a guy named Julio who had bought a Honda Accord off him last year. Julio had a neighbor who passed away, and the widow was cleaning house before moving to Florida to live with her daughter.

It was a one-owner car, and Gary could hardly believe it when the widow showed him the original bill of sale. A few stories and a couple cups of coffee later, he'd loaded it up on the car trailer behind the Hummer and pulled it back to the shop. He'd spent just over a thousand dollars getting the brakes, exhaust, shocks, and springs replaced and then detailed it inside and out. He had a sticker price of fifteen thousand bucks on the side window and was just waiting for the right buyer to come in. It was featured in the full-page ad he had just spoken with Charlie about. Charlotte at the reception desk motioned him over when she looked up and saw him on the sales floor.

"What's up?" he said. Charlotte could handle almost anything on her own but she looked a little shaken.

"We got another one," she said, holding up an envelope.

"Another what?"

"Another one of those letters. One of the nasty kind."

Gary's face dropped. He took the envelope from her and looked at it. It was type-written, addressed to his attention at the dealership, and didn't have any return address. He braced himself and pulled out the letter. It had one sentence typed in the center of the page:

You're going to bust the springs on that Hummer if you gain any more weight, fatass.

Gary's faced flushed. He folded the letter and placed it back in the envelope. He bit his lip and tapped a corner of the envelope on the receptionist's counter. His gaze was out onto the highway. Route 52 crossed under I-80 about a half mile from the lot. He watched as a Maxhaul Transport truck got off the exit and made its way to the truck stop across the highway. When he felt calm again, he looked at Charlotte.

"What is this, number five?" he asked.

"Six," she said. "I've been keeping them in a file."

"One a week?"

She nodded. "Every Tuesday now since early August. What kind of creep would do this?"

He shook his head. "I don't know, but I'm getting sick of it." He looked out again at the highway. "Keep them all together. I think it may be time to speak with someone."

"An attorney?"

"That might be a good place to start. Just keep documenting them." He turned to walk back to his office and then stopped. "Has there been anything else? Packages? Phone calls? Anything else that might be considered harassment?"

"Nothing that I know of. No one has said anything."

"Does anyone else know about the letters? It's okay if you talked about them, but I'd just like to know who."

She took a deep breath. "Can I ask why?"

"Yeah. Whoever is doing this wants a reaction. I mean, these are mean but they're really personal, you know? I don't want to feed him any information."

"I did tell Debbie in billing after the third one. I mean, that's when we figured we had a real nut on our hands, you know?" She looked down at her desk. "I'm sorry."

"No, don't worry about it. I'm just trying to figure this out. File that one, okay?"

"Sure."

"I'll be in my office."

• • •

Tim stayed late working on the layout, until just past six o'clock. He helped Charlie get the electronic file set and staged in the proper format for the printer and then emailed it. He logged out of his laptop and checked the back door, making sure it was locked, and returned to the front office.

"We all set, Charlie?"

The publisher was standing at his desk looking at a letter. Tim could see he was upset. He was red in the face and the color crept up to the top of his ears. Tim hesitated.

"Charlie?"

He looked up at Tim and held out an envelope. "Was this in the mail today?"

Tim looked at the envelope. "Yeah, that was the one marked attention with your name. I didn't open it."

"No, I know you didn't."

"Is there a problem?"

"Do you have a moment? Can you stay and talk?"

"Sure."

They sat down at their desks again, facing each other. Charlie sighed and flipped the letter to him. Tim picked it up and looked at it. There were two lines typed in the center of the page:

Why are you still publishing that fag rag?

Tim flipped it over and saw the back was blank. He looked back at Charlie. "Do you have any idea who sent it?"

He shook his head. "I don't know who has sent any of them."

Tim leaned forward. "There have been others?"

Charlie nodded. "Yeah, there have been others. Dozens of them. I started getting them last year, right before Thanksgiving."

"Are they all like . . . this?"

"Homophobic? Yeah, that's the gist of them."

"Why didn't you say anything?"

"I don't know. I thought whoever it was would get bored, but they've got some sticking power." He pinched his nose under his glasses. Tim could sense his frustration.

"Have you called anyone?"

He snorted. "Like who, the police? What are they going to do?"

"At the very least they can take a report. Get it on file."

"Look, I kind of expect this. Every newspaper, even a freebie like the *Shopper*, gets its share of crank letters. Being gay just adds to the ammunition these assholes can use."

"None of that excuses this kind of behavior, Charlie."

"I know. I mean, things aren't as bad as they used to be. Hell, I can even get married. I just kind of thought we were past the point where some nut job would sit in his little room and send out this kind of garbage."

They sat in silence for a few minutes. The sun was setting and from the front window Tim could see the shadows on the street growing long. He wanted Charlie to speak next without being rushed.

"Earlier today I told you that I wanted to do something different."

"I remember," Tim said.

"How about you? Do you want to do something different?"

"Like what?"

"You want to be a real reporter?"

Tim sat up. "Yes, I do."

"I can't pay you much more than I am already, and the hours may stack up."

"That's okay. Going home and watching Netflix is pretty much the bulk of my social life."

Charlie nodded. "Okay, yeah. Hold on a minute." The older man got up and went to a filing cabinet. He pulled out a green hanging folder and removed a manila folder. It landed on Tim's desk with a thud.

"That's all of them," Charlie said. "I keep the crank letters in that drawer by date but these seemed to rate their own file. Run them through the scanner, put them on a thumb drive and work on it in your off hours. Take your laptop home with you so you can work outside the office."

Tim was flipping through the letters in the folder. "This is everything you have?"

"Yeah, that's it."

"Okay. I'm on it."

Two

Tim rolled through the Dairy Queen drive-thru on his way home and grabbed some dinner: two chili dogs, fries, and a chocolate milkshake. He also asked for an M&M Blizzard. As he drove up Route 9 toward home, he considered the assignment from Charlie. The thumb drive with the scans hung from a lanyard around his neck. It had taken half an hour to scan them all and save them. The laptop was in a black nylon bag on the passenger side floor of the truck. His first thought was to approach the problem logically.

Who would send letters like this? What was their motivation? And why would they keep at it with such dedication? Was it personal? It almost had to be, Tim thought. The *Shopper* was about as non-controversial as was possible. Unless someone had read something in the gardening column that had ruined their petunias or had followed some bad advice in the car care column, it was hard to believe the *Shopper* was the target of the letters. Besides, the letter received today had been personal and a bit threatening. He hadn't read the others yet. He had only scanned them and decided to work at home.

A large painted sign lit up by floodlights announced that Tim had arrived home at the West Wind Mobile Home Park. Another, smaller sign in front of the main one alerted passersby that lots were available. He turned left into the park and drove up to the first intersection. He turned right, drove down three trailers and pulled into the driveway of his brown single wide. It was almost completely dark now, and he saw his elderly neighbor sitting on the glider she kept on the little bit of concrete pad that served as her patio.

He got out of the little Chevy pickup and waved. "Good evening, Tilly."

The woman with blonde hair going to gray waved back, a cigarette between her fingers. She was wearing a pink housecoat and slippers and had a stack of magazines beside her. Tim saw the *National Enquirer* on top. "Evening, Tim. You're home late."

"Work," he said. "Getting a little overtime at the paper." He reached into the white takeout bag and pulled out the M&M Blizzard. "I got you something."

"Oh, well, wasn't that nice of you. I was just about to head inside. The evenings are getting cool now." She took the long red spoon that he offered her.

"Well, you go on and stay warm," Tim said. "I'm going to eat some dinner and see if I can't catch the Indians game."

She looked at him and smiled. "Watch them now. They won't be playing in October."

"I know. Their pitching is awful."

She held out her hand, and Tim helped her off the glider. "Same excuse every year. I think they're just not meant to win. That's the way it is in this part of the state. We get by well enough, but we don't win."

Tim smiled and realized she was just putting words to what lots of people thought about northeast Ohio. Hogan lay equidistant between Cleveland and Pittsburgh, smack in the middle of the Rust Belt. The steel mills in nearby Youngstown, Ohio, and Sharon, Pennsylvania, had moved out almost three decades ago and nothing had really taken their place. Tim liked it here, thought of it as a place that may not be down for the count but rather taking an extended rest on the ropes. People like Tilly lived here because they had always lived here and felt too old to start over somewhere else.

"You go inside and get warm, Tilly." He gathered up her stack of magazines and handed them to her.

"You're a good boy, Tim," she said as she mounted the steps to her front door, "and your dad would be proud of you, but you should take your education and go someplace where you'll have a chance to succeed."

He held up his arms toward his old truck and his trailer. "What, and give all this up? Tilly, you must be crazy."

She waved her hand at him. "Good night."

"G'night."

He carried his dinner and the laptop bag into the trailer by way of the back door facing Tilly's place. He walked the length of the trailer, past two bedrooms and a bathroom, through the kitchen and into the living room in the front that faced the road. He thumbed the power button on the remote control and found the Indians game. The score graphic in the upper left corner told him they were hosting Detroit tonight and were up two runs in the third over the Tigers.

He plugged in the laptop, turned it on and inserted the thumb drive into the USB port. He double-clicked the file holding the scans of the letters and started reading them. Charlie had written the received date across the top of each, so he was able to arrange them in order. He unwrapped a chili dog and made it disappear in three quick bites.

Each of the letters written to Charlie were similar to the one received today. In each of them the writer made reference to Charlie's sexual orientation or demanded the *Shopper* be closed down. Tim took a pull on his shake and considered that particular demand for a moment. The messages were not specific as to why the *Shopper* shouldn't be published. The writer simply made the demand. It wasn't even clear if Charlie being gay was the reason.

Next, he increased the magnification of the scanned documents to 150 percent. Tim went through them one at a time, looking for anything that might not be seen easily at regular size. The pages were unremarkable, as far as he could tell. Aside from the typed messages in the center of the pages, the only other marks he could see were the folds made when the pages were stuffed into their envelopes.

The remains of dinner lay on the coffee table. Tim checked the score of the game. The Tribe was still holding their two-run lead in the top of the eighth. He yawned and realized he'd been at it for a couple hours. If he was going to be worth anything at work in the morning, he needed some sleep. He turned off the TV, shut down the laptop, and then, almost as an afterthought, made an entry in his notebook: "Research who sends anonymous letters and why."

•   •   •

Bob Ellstrom lay awake in the darkness smoking a cigarette. His head rolled left and he saw the red numbers of the digital clock—2:53 a.m. The bedroom was so dark the numbers seemed to float in space. He took a final puff and the tip of his cigarette glowed bright orange. He stubbed it out in an ashtray on the nightstand next to the bed. Smoking in bed was just one of the stupid things he did, thinking about what his wife, Kate, used to say. He grunted and coughed a bit as he adjusted himself in the bed. The longer they were married, the more things she complained about. Nine years ago, the complaints had stopped. Kate had found a lump in her right breast, a large one, and six months later he'd buried her. The doctors had been aggressive in their treatment, but it had been too little, too late.

Lying there in the darkness, arms crossed behind his head, Bob thought about work and felt the familiar pangs of stress hit his belly. His pulse jumped a bit. He had been driving a tow motor at Brinco, an automotive parts supplier in the city, for about a year.

His house was out in the township. Like most people who lived in the township, he drew a serious distinction between the City of Hogan and Hogan Township. The township was for folks who liked a little more freedom. Zoning rules were looser and there was no income tax. City people liked a little more structure. The last thing Bob wanted was zoning inspectors out here roaming around his three-acre spread telling him what he could and couldn't do.

His boss, a skinny little geek named Ricky, probably lived in the city. He liked rules and butting his nose into things. Yesterday the wiry little dumbass had jumped all over him because he wasn't using his horn in the warehouse at intersections. It was ridiculous. Bob had been the only one in the section, reorganizing plastic bins full of parts. The job had too much crap to put up with for what he was paid.

Tomorrow would be more of the same. He sighed, knowing sleep wasn't going to come for a while. The mattress groaned as his weight shifted, and he pulled on his slippers. He had never used slippers when he was younger, but now the hardwood floor was too cold to walk around barefoot. A little bit of orange juice would hit the spot. He opened the fridge to see if he'd remembered to buy any. He had. He poured a bit into a small glass. He sat down at the dining room table in front of his vintage Smith Corona Blue Galaxy manual typewriter, a flea market special; two packs of generic copy paper; and a pair of white cotton gloves. He pulled on the gloves, adjusting the fingers until comfortable, selected a piece of paper and rolled it into the typewriter, stopping in the center of the page. He touched nothing with his bare hands. Next, he took up a small spiral notebook and thumbed through it, reading his entries, looking for a target.

The notebook went with him most places, though not to work. It would be too easy to lose there, or someone might steal it from his locker. Everywhere else it was usually in a coat pocket, available for him to record his thoughts and what he overheard—his nuggets, as he thought of the information he learned. People in Hogan and the surrounding small towns loved to talk, and Bob loved to listen. On Saturday mornings he had coffee with a group of guys he used to work with, back when he'd had a real job operating a crane at Ohio Axle, before it closed. Those guys were just as bad as their wives at gossiping, only they had the added bonus of knowing lots of the business owners in town. Their conversations always started out with politics, shifted to local events, but before too long they were grinning and spilling everything they knew about everyone they knew. Bob took it all in, remembering what he heard and writing it down in his notebook later.

Information could be gathered from anywhere, though. Bob often read through the local papers and perused the letters to the editor sections. If you did it long enough and paid attention, you could see many of the same names pop up over and over. People liked to have their opinions heard and liked to see their names in the paper, so a lot of people wrote often. He liked to think he understood why. Additionally, he kept his ears open as he went about his daily routine. People talked everywhere: at the deli counter in the grocery store, at the gas pump, in line at the bakery, and in the doctor's waiting room. He knew what to look for in order to hear the good stuff. A sideways glance meant the speaker was about to let loose with something considered secret. That's when Bob made sure he looked like he was concentrating on something else, like an article in *Time* magazine or the list of ingredients on a box of something in his grocery cart. He'd discovered that if he didn't look like he was listening, people assumed he wasn't, no matter how much their voices carried.

Lots of what Bob heard was irrelevant to his hobby or lacked a proper context he could use. If the nugget was good enough, though, he would do a little research and could usually discover enough to do what he wanted.

He thumbed through the most recent entries in the notebook. At breakfast two weeks ago Mark Packer, an old buddy from Ohio Axle, had let slip that his nephew Max, who worked at the AA Tire and Wheel Superstore, had seen the owner, Jerry, behind the shop getting busy with a blonde who was probably ten years younger. Mark said that his nephew knew Jerry's wife, Anita, and this hot little number was definitely not Anita. They'd all snickered. Bob made a note. He didn't know Jerry and had only been in the shop a few times.

A little research into county property records revealed that Jerry Donovan and his wife, Anita, owned the property the tire shop occupied. Bob closed his eyes and slowed his breathing. He liked to think of the best way to use this information, the way to get the biggest reaction. Who should the recipient be, husband or wife? If it was Anita, she would confront Jerry and things would probably blow up spectacularly. The problem was, that was a one-shot deal. If the letter went to Jerry, though, he could keep him dangling for months. The nugget could pay out over and over again. It would be easy to see the results, too. After a few letters he could stop in for a quote or to get some work done and see what was going on. See if Jerry had dropped some weight or if he was irritable with his mechanics or customers. Maybe the other guys could help if they were in the shop getting some work done? Yes, that was the way to go. If he overheard them say they had been in the shop, he could ask if they had seen Jerry and the blonde and how things were going. He looked at the blank paper and decided to start things off slowly.

That yummy little blonde is a bit young for you, isn't she?

He examined it carefully. He didn't want to impart too much information to the recipient. There was no reason for the shop owner to know how much information he knew or didn't know. No reason for him to know they had been seen behind the shop, when they had been seen, or what they had been seen doing. The sentence was crafted to let Jerry know he had been seen doing something inappropriate with someone he shouldn't be with, and there was just enough description of the other woman to let him know he really had been seen.

Bob smiled, rolled out the sheet from the typewriter and carefully folded it so it would fit in the envelope. He rolled the envelope into the Smith Corona, and typed the address of the tire shop on it, attention Jerry Donovan. The letter went into the envelope and he placed a Forever stamp on it. He'd bought ten books of them from the vending machine at the post office about a year ago. A damp sponge in a small glass dish sat in front of the boxes of envelopes. He swiped the envelope closure across it and sealed the letter. He would drop it in the blue mailbox in front of the Dollar General store on his way to work in the morning. Grunting and stretching, he rose from the table and headed back to bed.

He was asleep two minutes after his head hit the pillow.

• • •

Tim swung the twenty-four-foot box truck into the parking lot at Degman's hardware. As he swung around the back of the lot to the loading dock, he spotted a black Cadillac CTS parked in front of the store. It was immaculate, waxed shiny and gleaming in the noon sun. Tim scowled and felt like dropping a forty-pound bag of fertilizer in the backseat. He turned his face away, but Mac saw it from the passenger seat in the cab.

"Come on, man. Are you still hung up on Amy?"

Tim swallowed. The younger guy had just graduated from high school in the spring and was working for Tate until he figured out what he wanted to do. "Leave it alone, Mac."

The younger man smiled. "Just ask her out. That guy Jeremy is a complete douche. I bet she'd go out with you."

"Well, he's a douche with a Cadillac and a sales job over at Brinco, which means he makes about ten times what I do. He dresses in suits and travels all over the place. How, exactly, am I supposed to compete with that?"

"That S-10 pickup of yours has a lot of charm."

Tim backed the box truck into the dock, checking his mirrors to make sure he didn't hit the blue dumpster outside of the second dock door. "Just for that, you get to clean out the back of the truck."

He walked into the store with the clipboard containing the signed paperwork for the morning's deliveries. The signed receipts went into a hanging plastic file folder. The clipboard went back to its nail, where it would hang until tomorrow. Tim went to the employee's restroom and washed up before he went to see Tate and let him know they were finished with deliveries for the day.

As he approached the front of the store, he could hear Amy laughing. It was charming, like wind chimes in a spring breeze. Unfortunately, she was laughing at something Jeremy Pintar had said. The Brinco Auto Parts salesman was about six feet tall, rail thin, and looked as made up as any woman Tim had ever seen. His hair was full of some kind of styling product, and his skin was so clean and flawless Tim suspected some sort of exfoliation was a daily ritual. Tim nodded to both of them on his way to Tate's office, but Amy stopped him.

"Hey, Tim. I've got a list of deliveries for tomorrow, if you want them."

He grimaced and turned back, taking them from her outstretched hand. "Thanks."

"Still driving that truck, Abernathy?" Jeremy said. "I thought you were on TV now."

Tim managed a half smile. "That was my internship and it's over, so yeah, I'm driving the truck."

"He has demo tapes out, though, right, Tim?" Amy said.

"Yeah, that's right. Just waiting to hear back."

Jeremy's eyebrows dipped. "Man, you can't wait for opportunity. You have to go out and seize it. If you wait for someone to call you back you'll be driving that truck forever."

"And what's wrong with driving my truck?" a voice said from near the back office. Tate Degman walked toward the counter. "You got something against honest work, Jeremy?"

The salesman smiled. "Of course not, Tate. I'm just trying to give the guy some career advice."

Tim smiled but thought, *Career advice? You're three years older than me.*

"Yeah, well, buy something or get away from my counter. Amy has work to do."

"Actually," Amy said, "Jeremy is taking me to lunch. Can you cover the register?"

"Sure," Tate said, and turned back to Tim. "Deliveries all done?"

"Yeah. Mac's cleaning out the truck." He held up the sales slips. "Amy gave me these for tomorrow. We'll get everything staged." The bell on the door tinkled as Amy and Jeremy walked out to his car.

Tate looked over at the door. "She better be careful with that guy. He's a snake."

"Yeah," Tim said. "She won't know it until she gets bitten, though."

"You're not doing yourself any favors, you know, pining after her."

"I'm not."

"Yeah, okay."

"I'm not."

Tate just looked at him. "Okay. Anyway, grab some lunch, stage tomorrow's deliveries and keep an eye out for a delivery. I'm expecting a shipment of salt."

"All right." He started to walk back to the warehouse.

"You know, Jeremy was right about one thing."

Tim stopped and turned back. "What's that?"

"You have to make your own opportunities. The world waits for no one."

"Hmm, maybe I'll open a hardware store across town."

Tate grunted. "Yeah, well, good luck with that."

Three

Every family has a member, or members, who are cringeworthy for their exploits, Amy Sashman knew. As she returned from the restroom and took her place behind the service counter, she saw her brother, Boyd, wandering down the hand tool aisle. As usual, he was wearing what she thought of as his stealing outfit. It was a rusty-orange oversized hoodie that would seem just fine on a burly guy heading to the gym. On her twenty-six year old brother, it was a tip-off to any loss prevention officer that this was a guy you wanted to keep an eye on.

Boyd was tall, kind of rangy, with short, spiked hair and three days' beard growth on his gaunt face. He was wearing jeans that needed a wash and Converse All-Stars that looked suspiciously new. She considered ducking behind the counter but he would just keep wandering the store until he saw her. With a deep sigh, she snapped her fingers to get his attention and waved him over. He smiled when he saw her and walked up to the counter.

"What's up, sis?"

"You shouldn't be in here," she said, "especially wearing that hoodie. You know it makes you look like a thief."

"It's almost October and forty degrees outside. What am I supposed to wear?"

"Is there something you need?" She knew there was, of course. Boyd was a nice guy, but he only made it into the hardware store in the middle of a week for one thing. The look on his face said as much.

"Why? Are you busy? I don't see a lot of customers in here. Can't I just drop in and say 'hi'?"

She smiled and shook her head. "You can, but you don't."

He smiled back. When he did, Amy could see the older brother that used to be, the one who played Scrabble with her on snowy days when school was canceled and who taught her how to drive when their high-strung mother couldn't. The sadness and pity to see what he was like now crushed her, but she tried to keep things light.

"Ah, you know me. I'm doing fine. I was just over at the drugstore and thought I'd stop in and see how you were doing."

"What were you doing over at Mulligan's?"

"Picking up my allergy medicine," he said.

"Anything else? Something for your back, maybe?"

He shook his head. "No, nothing stronger than Advil or Tylenol for that, according to Doctor Simmons."

"Does it still hurt?" Amy was genuinely concerned.

His face fell a bit thinking about it. "Yeah, you know, a little. I still can't walk too far without it getting pretty bad." He smiled. "So you know what I do?"

She shook her head.

"I ride my horse." He grabbed invisible reins, made a duck face and pretended to ride a horse. It was an old joke from when they were kids. This brought a smile to Amy's face. She looked over Boyd's head and saw Tate cross the top of the hand tool aisle at the other end of the store. He glanced down at them but didn't stop. She couldn't tell if he recognized Boyd or not.

"Okay, well, I have some work to get to here so you better hit the trail, cowboy."

"Yeah, okay." He looked around and leaned in close across the counter. "Hey, um, you know, if you do have a couple bucks, I'm a little behind in the rent." He shrugged.

Amy nodded and just like that, her old brother was gone and the one who had been around for the last couple years was there. She reached under the counter, grabbed her purse, and dug around inside. He took the money she offered, and it disappeared into the pocket of his hoodie.

"Thanks."

Amy looked away. "No problem. Just get it back to me when you can." She pulled a stack of paperwork over and started going through it.

"Yeah, okay. I'll get my check next week, so I'll see you then."

"Mmm-kay." She wouldn't even look up as he left. The bell over the door tinkled, and she used a tissue to wipe the tears from her eyes.

• • •

Tate walked past the counter and when he saw the tissue in her hand, he kept walking. Boyd Sashman had used up all the goodwill his accident had generated over the last two years. In Tate's opinion, the best thing Amy could do for him was cut him off until he got his act together. He'd expressed that opinion many times, so he just kept an eye on the guy when he was in the store and held his tongue.

• • •

Outside, the afternoon sun was already pretty far west. Summer was well and truly over and cold days and nights would be coming soon. Boyd looked around the parking lot for his ride but didn't see Frank and his beat-up Honda anywhere. With any luck, his roommate wouldn't forget him. The hike from here out to their place in the township would probably take him the better part of an hour, and he hadn't been lying to Amy when he told her he couldn't handle walking long distances. His back had been worse lately, and Tylenol wasn't doing a damn thing for it. He pulled out a box of Marlboros and fired one up as he leaned against the cold brick of the hardware store, making sure he was far away from the propane tank refill rack. The portico that ran the length of the front of the store blocked most of the bright sun, so he could see without squinting, but it also blocked the little bit of its warmth.

He reached into his pocket and pulled out the money Amy had handed him. It was three wrinkled twenties and a five. It wasn't much, but it would get him through the next few days. Rent wasn't a problem. The house he and Frank Utzler lived in was owned by Frank's mom and she wasn't about to kick him out. The Oxy he needed to get through most days was another story. His dealer, a guy named Skillet, was a cash-only kind of guy.

His watch said it was about ten after three, so Frank should be here. He was working the lunch shift at Rocco's Pizza, which only lasted from eleven to three. Boyd shifted his stance from one foot to another as the pain in his back made him more uncomfortable. When Frank got here they were driving straight to Skillet's place, and he was getting the hook up. No matter what the doctors said, he was not going to be managing his pain with anything over the counter. A delivery truck with the Degman's Hardware logo passed him and drove around the back of the store. Boyd noticed the driver looking at him.

A dirty gray Honda rolled into the parking lot behind the truck and Boyd flicked his cigarette toward a bucket of sand full of butts at the edge of the store's sidewalk. Frank pulled up close and got out as Boyd opened the door. The stubby little guy stepped up on the doorframe to reach for the pizza delivery sign suction cupped to his roof.

"Grab that side, would you?"

Boyd, much taller than Frank, stretched across the car's roof and grunted with pain as he worked the rubber cup loose. It popped free and Frank carried the sign around to the back of the hatchback and threw it in. Boyd got into the car and rested his head against the window.

"What's up? Is your back hurting?" Frank said.

Boyd's eyes were screwed up tight in pain. "Yeah. Could you run over to Skillet's?"

"Sure, but I think you probably need a doctor more than you need Skillet. Can't you go to the emergency room and get something?"

Boyd grimaced. "I'll have to sit there for three hours and go through a bunch of tests. If I go to Skillet's I'll be better in fifteen minutes."

"All right, man. Let's go."

Boyd looked in the back seat. "You got a pie for dinner?"

"Yeah, someone messed up an order so it's sausage and mushroom tonight." Boyd started to say something, but Frank held up a hand. "You can pick them off."

• • •

Tim backed the delivery truck up to the dock door and went into the store. He dropped off his paperwork in the office and started cleaning out the back of the truck. A few minutes later, Tate wandered into the warehouse.

"Thanks for working late today," Tate said. "That customer was being a pain about afternoon delivery, and it was a big order."

"No problem. I'm not working at the *Shopper* today. Charlie's out of town until tomorrow, so this is actually a short day for me."

"Okay. Hey, how's he doing? Everything good at the *Shopper*?"

"Charlie's got no complaints. If he did, I don't think he'd let on." That made him think about how long Charlie had received those terrible letters before sharing them. No, Charlie would not complain unless he absolutely had to. Tim dropped a wad of plastic wrap into the recycling dumpster. "Oh, Tate."

"Yeah?"

"There was some sketchy dude hanging around out front."

"Skinny guy with an orange sweatshirt?"

"That's him. Looked like a panhandler."

Tate grunted. "That's Amy's junkie brother. He didn't have any merchandise, did he?"

"No, he was just leaning against the building and smoking." He finished sweeping the back of the delivery truck and rolled down the back door. "I didn't know she had a brother, let alone one of the junkie variety."

Tate was over by the vending machine. He pushed a dollar bill into the slot. Since this was the employee area, he kept the prices low at fifty cents. He walked back over with a couple Cokes and handed one to Tim.

"His name's Boyd. If you see him in the store, watch him like a hawk." He sipped his pop. "He'd steal Christ off the cross if he had the chance."

"Why do you let him in?"

"Well, I haven't actually caught him stealing anything out of my store. I'm going by what I've heard from other owners and managers in town. Second, I don't want to embarrass Amy. It's not her fault he's the way he is."

"Gotcha."

Tate sighed. "He wasn't always a bad guy. I've known the family a long time, and Boyd used to be a good kid. He was even going to college."

"Yeah? Did something happen?"

"About three, three and a half years ago, Boyd had a summer job with the county doing roadwork. They were doing culvert replacement out on Hucker-Thomasville road when Boyd got hit with the bucket of a backhoe and knocked into the ditch they were digging. It screwed up his back."

"Ouch."

"You bet your ass 'ouch.'" He sipped his Coke. "He had a busted arm, a couple of broken ribs, and his back was messed up. Boyd ended up having to take a semester off school to heal up, and they couldn't get his pain management for his back under control. He ended up getting a disability settlement from the county, but he never went back to school. Last I heard he's living on those monthly settlement checks out in the township with some roommate who delivers pizza for Rocco's."

"So he takes drugs for the back pain?" Tim asked.

"That's what Amy says. She doesn't talk about him much, probably because there's not a lot to brag about when your brother snorts Oxy. I heard a couple of store owners talking about him about a year ago at the VFW during a community business meeting. They were comparing notes about shoplifters, and his name kept coming up."

"That's not surprising," Tim said. "Hogan isn't a big town, even if you combine the city and the township."

"Exactly. So what we figured is that he's stealing to support his drug habit because whatever the doctors have him on isn't doing the trick. He's taken to self-medicating, and the settlement checks aren't supporting his habit."

"So when he comes in the store you just watch him?"

"Yeah, that's the easiest thing to do. Amy needs a job and I need a good clerk."

Tim finished his Coke and threw it into the metal recycling bin Tate kept in the corner. He grabbed his jacket. "If you don't need anything else, I'm going to take off."

"That's fine." Tate pitched his own can into the bin and followed him toward the warehouse door. "Keep what we were talking about to yourself, okay? Boyd isn't exactly a secret in town but Amy doesn't need to know we're talking about him."

"Sure, no problem."

· · ·

Jerry Donovan, owner of the AA Tire and Wheel Superstore, looked at the Ford Bronco sitting up on the rack in bay one. It was visible from the waiting room, where free coffee and daytime TV helped customers pass the time. Beyond the waiting room was the showroom. This was the pride and joy of AA Tire and Wheel. The showroom was a forty-by-sixty room dressed with displays of rims and tires of every type. Spinners, Cragars, mag wheels of every description, and high-end tires hung from wall displays. That room was where Jerry made his good money.

One of his mechanics, Max, was pulling the wheels and installing a set of heavy-duty off-road tires for the twenty-something owner of the Bronco sitting in the waiting room playing a game on his phone and ignoring the women of *The View*. Jerry was burly, a tall, big guy beefy without carrying too much of a gut. Moving tires and rims around all day kept him in decent shape for his size. The door to the parking lot opened with an electric chime, and the mailman walked in with a stack of envelopes and ads in his hand.

Jerry looked up and nodded. "Morning, Denny. How are things today?"

"Just fine, Jerry. How about you?"

"It's all good here in the land of rubber and rims." He took the offered stack of mail. "Jeez, you'd think the junk mail would slow down now that we're all emailing and on Facebook, but it just keeps coming."

Denny smiled. "I sure hope so. Junk mail is keeping us in business."

"Yeah, I guess so. Take it easy, man."

"You too."

Jerry looked at the Bronco and saw Max wrestling a back wheel onto the axle. He'd wanted to sell the kid new rims as well as the tires but he didn't want the Bronco to look better; the kid just wanted to be able to play around on the trails out in the township.

He started sorting the mail. One stack was ads he would look at despite what he had said to Denny about junk mail. Sometimes gems were hidden in the stack of catalogues and fliers. Bills went into a basket on the desk behind the counter to be looked at later. After separating everything, he was left with one envelope. It was plain white and addressed to him personally, with no return address. He sliced it open with a letter opener and pulled out the single sheet of paper inside. His face grew red when he read it.

That yummy little blonde is a bit young for you, isn't she?

A quick look around the shop revealed nothing out of the ordinary. The Bronco kid was still dicking around with his phone, and Max was wrestling the other back wheel on the truck. Jerry felt horribly exposed, as if someone was watching him.

He read the letter again and his breathing quickened. One time, one stupid time he'd strayed from his wife, Anita, and now someone knew. He flipped the letter over, looking for some kind of marking, and then picked up the envelope. There was nothing out of the ordinary except that it was missing a return address.

"Goddamnit," he muttered, but not silently enough. The Bronco kid looked up from his phone and then his head dipped back down.

Anita had been unhappy for years, and if he admitted the truth, so was he. The blonde the letter referred to was Kim, a sales rep for one of the rim distributors he did business with. They had gone out a handful of times and if he was going to continue to be honest, it had been exciting. Like how it had been with Anita back when they were first seeing each other and starting the business. Now they just sniped at each other about how long he worked, his weight and high blood pressure, how the shop wasn't making quite as much as she thought it should, and lately she was asking him about cashing out, about selling the business while they could get a good price for it. Kim had just gone through a divorce and was around a lot. He looked at the letter again and saw that it mentioned her age, but that was wrong. Kim wasn't much younger than he was, certainly not more than seven or eight years, and once you got up above forty that kind of shit didn't really matter unless the person you were bedding was collecting Social Security. She looked good, that was for sure, but she was a sales rep, so her appearance was important. And he could attest to the hours she spent in the gym because those legs of hers were what had initially attracted him.

Now someone knew. What would come next? Were more letters going to come with requests for money? *Is that what this is?* he thought.

Is this a blackmail thing? Was someone going to come to him with his hand out? How the hell would he ever afford to pay it? Would he pay it? What would happen if they threatened to tell Anita? His pulse started to pound in his ears. His breath grew shorter, like he had just run up a flight of stairs.

Anita. Oh, good Christ, what if this wasn't the only letter? What if one was also sent home to her, typed out to her attention the way this one had been sent to his? Why had he been so damn stupid? Of all the women he had flirted with over the years and gotten a little friendly with, why had he allowed this one to get in close and why in the hell had he gone so far? Why hadn't he stopped it?

Now everyone might know. His kids would know the minute Anita decided to leave him, and she would definitely do that. Her temper and the way she felt about him lately were enough to guarantee that, if this ever got back to her, she'd walk out the door so fast she would leave smoke trailing behind her. Both of the kids, Gene and Pam, were in college and now they would have to see their dad as just another middle-aged businessman who dabbled with blondes on the side because work was tough and he was unhappy at home. Could he be more of a cliché? And how would he pay for a divorce and their tuition and keep the shop afloat? How would he do it all? He groaned and realized he couldn't catch his breath.

His throat pistoned up and down as he tried to draw breath, but no air would come. His jaw clenched shut with a click of his teeth, and a loud groan escaped his lips. The letter in his hand crumpled, and he fell against the counter, knocking a cardboard cutout for Goodyear tires to the waiting room floor. A pen clattered to the tile next as his arms swept the counter clear of the sign-in clipboard and a bronze ashtray. The only thing spared was the cash register. He collapsed with the letter gripped in his hand.

• • •

The Bronco kid looked up in amazement at the old guy behind the counter, watching his face turn beet red. Then a tremendous groan tore loose from the guy. He jumped up just as the guy spasmed and wiped the counter clear of everything on it. The kid boosted himself up on the counter to get a good look and saw the guy in the blue Dickie work shirt and pants lying silently on the floor.

"Mister? Hey, mister, are you okay?" The guy with the "Jerry" patch stitched on his shirt was definitely not okay. He was, in fact, turning blue. The Bronco kid slipped off the counter and ran to the window, where he could see a mechanic tightening down the lug nuts on his Bronco's back wheels. He hammered on the glass with both hands. At first the sound of the mechanic's impact wrench drowned out the sound of his fists. He hit the glass again, as hard as he dared without breaking it. The mechanic with "Max" stitched on his blue Dickie work shirt looked at him in puzzlement. The kid pointed at the counter and gestured wildly. The mechanic dropped his impact wrench, and the kid saw the socket come loose and roll away across the concrete floor. The mechanic went through a side door into the office and yelled when he saw Jerry lying on the floor.

"Jerry? Jerry, are you okay?" He looked at the kid. "What happened?"

"I don't know. He was standing there looking at the mail and then knocked all this shit to the floor and hit the ground."

Max bent over his boss and rolled him onto his back, checking for a pulse and to see if he was breathing. He wasn't. "Call 911!"

The kid looked at the phone in his hand like he had never seen it before and then snapped to when he heard the mechanic counting as he did chest compressions. He told the 911 operator what he knew and jumped back up on the counter. "They're coming. Do you know how to do that? CPR?"

Max grunted and pushed down with enough force that it looked like he was liable to crack ribs. "Yeah, I'm on the volunteer fire department."

"Can I help?"

"Do you know CPR?"

"No."

Max looked up for a moment but never stopped the compressions. "Then go get Nicky in the shop and tell him to get in here, then go out front and direct the ambulance in. The fire guys will be coming, too. Tell them where we are."

"Okay, got it."

Max watched him run through the waiting room into the bays. He kept pushing on Jerry's chest, but he had done this enough to know a lost cause when he saw one. Too many cheeseburgers and too much work stress had caught up with his boss. He'd keep going until the ambo got here with the EMTs. They'd keep the CPR going all the way to the hospital in Youngstown, but he knew Anita Donovan was now a widow.

Four

B y mid-October, the weather was still cooler than normal. Tim Abernathy made sure his regular hoodie was supplemented by a thermal shirt on delivery runs, especially if any of them involved being outside. He was still sporting the thermal this evening, sitting on his couch with his laptop balanced on one crossed leg. The jeans he wore to work had been traded out for a pair of sweatpants.

The investigation into who was sending Charlie the letters was still ongoing, but Tim felt like things could stall at any moment. The PDF files on his laptop were always open, and he felt like, if he just examined them enough times, he would stumble across something he had previously missed. It occurred to him this sort of thing was fine for the police procedurals he was fond of on TV, but in real life sometimes there just wasn't anything to find. This meant discovering another angle to keep the investigation moving along.

On the couch beside him a legal pad lay open, and he was scribbling notes as he scrolled through websites. He had read a book once on how the FBI worked up profiles of criminals and how they used those profiles. It had stuck in his mind that the profiles themselves didn't point a finger at any one particular individual, but they did help narrow the field of who to look for and helped filter the information collected in an investigation, sorting out what was likely connected to a crime versus what was not.

Unfortunately, Tim didn't have a lot of information to sift through at the moment. His notes contained what he knew about Charlie, including personal information and items related to the business of running the *Hogan Weekly Shopper*. There wasn't anything in those notes to suggest why someone would dislike him enough to send him a hateful letter, let alone a series of them over the course of a year. Several of the letters commented on Charlie being homosexual, but Tim thought that was almost an afterthought, like maybe it was just a way for the writer to twist the knife a little bit.

To keep things moving in a positive direction, Tim decided to create a profile of the letter writer. That's what he was doing tonight, researching what kind of person wrote anonymous letters. He set the laptop on the couch for a moment and got up. His knees popped as he made his way to the fridge to grab a Coke. He threw a bag of popcorn in the microwave and tapped the START button. Not exactly the best dinner, but he wasn't feeling hungry enough for anything more substantial.

A few moments later he was back at it, scribbling notes. Luckily, the Internet was proving to be extremely helpful in defining the type of person who wrote and sent anonymous letters. Inexplicably, some sites actually had instructions on how to write such letters and under what circumstances they should be written.

Tim turned a sheet on the legal pad and wrote "POWER" at the top in large block letters. According to several websites, this was what the writer was interested in. When creating these letters, the writer wished to exercise a form of power over the recipient that was lacking in their everyday life. They could work an inadequate job, be in a dysfunctional relationship, or generally feel like they were not being recognized for their contributions. The letters could be a way of lashing out and feeling power over the victim.

Tim tapped his pen on the pad for a moment. One of the things that puzzled him was that many of the sites said the writer was frequently a family member or close associate of the victim. He looked back through his notes about Charlie's personal life. His immediate family was pretty small. Both parents had died and he had a brother in Colorado and a sister in Florida. His relationships with both were friendly, as far as Tim knew. He had overheard conversations with both in the office of the *Shopper*. The brother in Colorado, Jim, was a high school English teacher and as liberal as possible. Given the frequency of the calls and the way the brothers carried on when they spoke, Tim had no reason to suspect Jim

of writing the letters. Charlie's calls with his sister, Cheryl, were less fre-
quent, but mainly because she still had kids at home who kept her busy.
Tim knew she emailed Charlie a lot, because he had shown Tim pictures
of the kids. Charlie had also taken a short vacation to see her last spring.
That led him to suspect former lovers, and this was an aspect of
Charlie's life about which Tim had little knowledge. Charlie was discreet about his relationships. Tim realized he didn't even know if Charlie had a current boyfriend. He had met one of his dates back in the
summer, when the guy showed up at the *Shopper* offices to pick up
Charlie so they could walk down to the annual street fair. Other than
that, though, Tim had no idea if someone from his boss's past could be
lurking back there writing letters. He made a note to ask him.

Tim pulled up the letters again. The motivation of the letter writer
was equally puzzling. There were the homophobic slurs, of course, but
the writer seemed to really hate the *Shopper* itself. The gist of each was
that it should be shut down, that the town would be better off without
it. Why would anyone want the paper closed down, though? It was just
a weekly freebie full of ads and announcements with a few advice
columns. Of course, the writer could be upset about something he'd
seen in the paper, but what could have disturbed them so much they
kept writing for a whole year?

Next, Tim wrote "Lives close by" on the tablet. It almost seemed
ridiculous to assume anything else. They were obviously seeing the
Shopper and knew Charlie was the publisher. A couple of the websites
stated that the writer usually lived nearby so they could observe the
recipient to gauge their reaction. This was troubling, though. Charlie
and Tim were the only employees, except for the few columnists Charlie
paid by the word, and he had shared the letters with no one besides Tim.

Making several more notes, Tim began to see a pattern form.
"Charlie," he said to himself, "it looks like someone close to you doesn't
like you very much."

• • •

Bob Ellstrom was grimy. Saturday afternoon had been spent clearing
leaves from the property and dumping them in the woods behind the

house. There was a small hollow nearby with a creek running through it where at least a dozen cartloads of leaves had been left to compost. After locking up the tractor in the barn, he walked through the back door and made straight for the shower.

After cleaning up, Bob mixed up a dinner of burgers on an electric grill and macaroni and cheese. Working in the yard had left him with a big appetite. He sat down at the dining room table opposite the end with the typewriter and pulled a stack of newspapers next to his plate.

These were regional papers, everything from the local county papers to the *Cleveland Plain-Dealer* and *Pittsburgh Post-Gazette*. He read the local stuff every day, but on the weekend he liked the bigger papers. A few stories caught his eye, but no nuggets for his notebook. Next he switched to the local papers.

A countywide sales tax increase was being debated for the November ballot, and he gave it some thought. This he jotted down in his notebook. The county commissioner championing the proposal had been the recipient of several past letters, and obviously it was time to address his shortcomings once again.

By the time he got to the *Hogan Shopper*, he was opening a package of Twinkies for dessert. In fact, he'd picked up the *Shopper* with the rest of his groceries at the Hogan Savefast that very morning. This was one of his special projects. Looking through it, he didn't see anything out of the ordinary, just the regular bland anniversary announcements and ads for car dealerships. Then he turned a page and saw an ad with a familiar logo, a grinning bumblebee driving a cartoon hot rod. An alarm went off in the back of his head and it finally occurred to him why. That logo was for the AA Tire and Wheel Superstore downtown. The shop was for sale.

It had been a couple weeks since he sent the letter to Jerry Donovan. He got up, walked around the table, and opened up a drawer in the buffet. He removed a college-ruled notebook and sat back down, thumbing through the pages as he did so. This notebook recorded when letters were sent to whom and how often. Bob had certain people on a schedule, like the guy who ran the *Shopper* or the lady at Red Fannie Florist. Currently, there were almost one hundred letter recipients on a schedule that ran from once a year to once a month. Jerry Donovan's letter was delivered almost two weeks prior. Why was the business suddenly up for sale? Had the letter found its way to his wife? Swallowing the last of his Twinkie, Bob wondered if the wife was the secretary for the shop and had come across the letter. He let the fantasy play out in his mind, enjoying it.

He could see her—well, some generic version of her as he had never actually seen Anita Donovan—sitting at a desk and opening the envelope. After reading the letter, she would have confronted Jerry. Had they fought in the office? He wondered if customers had heard. Maybe the mechanics in the bays had put down their tools to listen to the boss's wife chew him out over getting a little on the side. Had Jerry lied? he wondered. Had he tried to squirm out of the accusation by saying it was just some crank letter? Bob stared at the blank dining room wall, breathing hard as he imagined the impact his letter might have had on the Donovans.

He grabbed the *Shopper* again and saw there was a sizable amount of print under the logo and the headline. It looked like it was placed by a broker: "Due to the sudden passing of beloved owner Jerry Donovan, the Donovan family has decided to sell AA Tire and Wheel . . ."

Bob read on and saw that the specifics of the business were listed but there was nothing more about the death of Jerry Donovan. A stack of papers several weeks deep sat in the corner of the dining room. These were being saved for starting fires in the living room wood burner during the coming winter. Bob hurried to them and starting digging through for the local papers. It took almost fifteen minutes of searching, but he finally found an edition of the *Humboldt County Reporter* with Jerry Donovan's obituary. It had been a heart attack. Bob checked his schedule notebook again and saw the date of the death was two days after the letter had been mailed.

He stood up with the paper gripped in one hand. Had his letter been the cause of Jerry's heart attack? It seemed like a coincidence, but it was easy to believe that receiving the letter had triggered something like this. His mind went back to his fantasy about Anita Donovan opening the letter. The obituary had scant details about the death, of course. Just getting a cause in an obit nowadays was a rare thing; most of the time people just "passed away" or were "called home to God" if they were of the Christian faith. He shook his head and got back to the issue at hand. Had one of his letters actually killed someone? Had he instigated something as cataclysmic as a death with a typed sentence? He made a note to make sure he was at the Peppermill in the morning with the guys. Maybe one of them would have more details. He grabbed a pair of scissors and cut out the obituary for his scrapbook. Few of his letters ever produced a result so spectacular it made the paper.

• • •

Boyd Sashman and Frank Utzler rolled slowly through the night in one of Hogan's better neighborhoods, looking at houses. Frank flicked an ash from his cigarette out the window of the beat-up Honda. He shifted uncomfortably in his seat and looked at Boyd.

"You sure about this?"

Boyd nodded. "Do we still need some cash?"

Frank took a drag on his cigarette and the tip glowed cherry red in the darkness. "I guess we do."

"Then I guess I'm sure we're going to do this."

Frank maneuvered around a car parked on the street and slid his eyes sideways at Boyd again. "My mom wouldn't really throw us out. You know that, right? She's just talking out of her ass."

"You want to take that chance? What if she really does throw us out? We won't find another place for the rent she's asking. We should just pay up and keep her quiet."

Frank took another drag. They lived in a house out in the township his mother owned. It was a little two-bedroom Cape Cod her uncle had left her. "How about her, y'know? If she throws us out, the house is going to be empty. Who's gonna want to live in the dump? She throws us out, and tweakers will strip that joint of copper in no time."

"It's easier to pay up and keep her quiet is all," Boyd said. "Why buy trouble?"

"We wouldn't be in this predicament if you'd quit buying trouble, you know that, right? If you'd get off that Oxy we'd be fine."

Boyd took a deep breath and let it out slowly. "You going to start this again? You know my back hurts."

"I know the doc doesn't think it hurts enough to prescribe you anything."

"Yeah, well, what he knows and what I know are two different things. Besides, what about you? Are you living large delivering pizzas?" Frank shrugged. "What else am I going to do around here? It's not like there's a ton of jobs. Maybe I should go to school. Learn a trade or something."

"Maybe," Boyd said. "You live in a house your mom owns and make minimum wage plus tips. I was doing better than that before I got hurt. You need to put the pipe down and quit smoking so much grass."

"Yeah, well, you don't work anywhere now, do you? Oh wait, is sitting on the couch stoned watching Netflix a job? 'Cause if it is, I'm sorry, I didn't realize you were working so hard."

"Blow it out your ass." It wasn't much of a comeback but it was all he could manage. They had a job to do and he wanted to be straight enough to function so he was balancing his meds against what he needed to do, but he wasn't feeling too sharp.

The Honda rolled quietly up another block and stopped in front of a white two-story Colonial house that looked like it belonged in an '80s John Hughes movie. Frank looked over at him. "This is the place."

"You sure?"

"Of course."

"And no one is home?"

"I'm as sure about that as I can be," Frank said. "I made a delivery out here last Thursday and they were packing. I heard one of the kids mention they were going away to one of the indoor waterparks in Sandusky this weekend. This house looks quiet, too, just that one light on."

Boyd stared out his window at the house. It did look quiet, but all the houses on this block looked quiet. "I don't know. Maybe."

Frank smiled. "Don't be so worried. I got the kicker right here." He held up his phone. "I found the mom on Facebook. Her privacy setting is wide open. She posted pictures of the kids at the waterpark five hours ago, so they're probably all snug in bed at their room in the resort. No one leaves on a Saturday night to come back."

"Yeah?"

"Yep. As long as they don't have an alarm system, we should be able to get in and out."

Boyd looked around at the neighboring houses. This development had pretty large lots, so no one was right on top of them, but they could still be seen easily. He hesitated. After all, they hadn't really done anything yet. The rent was due, though, and he needed enough to score for the rest of the month.

"Okay," Boyd said, "In and out in five minutes. Cash and whatever little stuff we can carry. No phones or tablets, though. I don't want that GPS shit tracking them to us."

Frank reached up and pulled the interior bulb from the assembly. He handed Boyd a pair of plastic cooking gloves from the pizza shop. Frank didn't know if the police would dust for prints on a break in but there was no reason to take the chance. They opened the car doors, closed them quietly and walked up the driveway. Boyd looked again for alarm signs or stickers on the window and found none. They moved around the side of the house to the garage's side door. His heart was beating fast and his back twinged with stress. He reached out and tried the doorknob. It was locked. He handed the small crowbar to Frank. "You do it. My back hurts."

Frank took it. "Whatever." The door popped easily. It didn't even have a deadbolt on it, just the knob lock. After a quick look at the house next to them reassured them no one was watching, they slipped inside and closed the door. Boyd produced a small LED flashlight and played it around. It was big, easily a two-and-a-half-car garage, but there was only one in there at the moment, Mom's Chevy grocery-getter by the looks of it. The rest of the garage was neat. There were some decent hand and power tools, but they would only take those as a last resort. They wanted cash and jewelry. Boyd walked over to the interior door and tried the knob. This time the door opened right up.

Frank went in first and they found themselves in the kitchen. Boyd killed the flashlight lest someone outside see it through the windows facing the street. Frank turned to him. "The stairs are right over here by the front door. I saw them when I made the delivery."

They moved through the dining room and living room combo, and found the staircase. The house reminded Boyd of his parents' place. They climbed the steps, Boyd moving a little slowly due to his back, and went different directions at the top of the stairs. Boyd lucked out and drew the master bathroom. He raised an eyebrow. This one room was easily as big as the living room in the house he shared with Frank. He went to the bed and stripped a pillowcase off a thick pillow.

"Mom first," he whispered. He went to the wife's dresser and popped open the jewelry box on top. He dumped the contents in and replaced the box. Next, he went through the drawers of the dresser, carefully hiding the light from the window as he pawed through lingerie, sweaters, and jeans. Satisfied there was nothing else, he moved on.

"Dad's turn," he said. Across the room, the father's dresser stood tall. He yanked the top drawer open and looked inside. "Bingo," he said. A silver money clip held a wad of bills. He thumbed through it, seeing nothing smaller than a twenty. He dropped it in the bag. A few watches and rings went in, as well. The flashlight beam fell across a mug on the dresser. It was handpainted, obviously, by one of the kids. "WORLD'S BEST DAD," he read, in sloppy red letters. He left it alone.

Dad's closet was next. Lots of clothes, he noticed. Dad looked like a fairly large guy, considering most of his stuff was 3x. He saw a box on the top shelf and reached to get it. A low growl of pain escaped his lips as he pulled it down. It had some weight to it and he nearly dropped it instead of setting it down on the floor. He shined the light up again, this time on the inside wall above the closet door. Sure enough, he saw a shotgun in a mount. This was meant for home defense, he was sure. Dollars to donuts he could pull that bad boy down and find it loaded and ready. Boyd let it go, though. Stealing guns was trouble. You could get good money for them but if someone got caught, they'd roll on you in a moment.

The box was locked. He pulled a small hammer from his coat and placed the flat end of the crowbar against the lock. Hefting the hammer and bracing his back against the pain, he swung twice and the lockbox popped open, spilling its contents across the floor.

Boyd put the light close to the floor and sifted through the pile. Birth certificates, passports, and a small pistol, maybe a .380. He moved it all aside and found nothing worth keeping. He grabbed the pillowcase and went looking for Frank.

The pizza delivery man was in the daughter's room, emptying her jewelry box into a pillowcase decorated with race cars. "You've already been in the boy's room?"

Frank nodded. "Yeah, there's nothing else here. You ready to go?"

"Yeah, let's get out of here but take a look in the kitchen on the way out, okay?"

They descended the stairs and hurried into the kitchen. Boyd looked around and pointed to a cookie jar on the counter. "Check that before we go."

Frank went over to the smiley face cookie jar and pulled the top off. Boyd saw him smile as he reached in and pulled out a few folded bills. "This must be where they keep the pizza delivery money for the babysitters."

"That's just what my folks used to do. Let's get out of here before someone sees your car."

They made it back to the car and drove off toward their place. Boyd smiled as Frank turned onto two-lane blacktop and the city streetlights faded in the distance.

Five

A my knelt down to place flowers next to the double headstone of her parents' grave. They were bright yellow and cheerful, and she set a pot on each side of the large granite stone. Jeremy set a bucket full of gardening implements like gardening trowels, a small hand rake, and a rolled-up bag of fertilizer down beside her. He took out a pair of sunglasses and put them on. "Bright out today."

"Yeah, I like fall days like this," Amy said, "but they can fool you. Looking out the kitchen window at the bright sunlight, it seems like it should be seventy degrees. Then you take a step outside and go back inside for a sweatshirt."

"Mm-hmm," he said. Amy looked up and saw him scrolling through his phone.

"I'm not keeping you from anything, am I?"

"No, just some emails from work."

She stood up and adjusted her floppy gardening hat. "Hey, today is Sunday. No work on Sundays. This is 'us' time."

He smiled and put his phone back in his pocket. "Sorry, you're right. We just have a big deal coming up, and Rob wanted me to be prepared for the preliminary meeting we're having tomorrow morning."

"Isn't Rob still divorced?"

"Yes."

"Well, he's alone on Sunday afternoon so all he has is work. You have someone. Take advantage of that."

He smiled again, two rows of perfectly bleached white teeth. "You're right. I promised you no work today." He looked around. "Now, what do

I do? I'm not much of a gardener, so you'll have to walk me through this."

She smiled. "Go to that corner of the stone and take a trowel with you. We're going to plant the mums by digging a hole a little bigger than the pot and fertilizing them. You'll do fine."

He moved off and put the pot down. "Is this all right?"

She nodded. "That's fine. Now dig." He dropped a folded towel to the ground to kneel on. She smiled at his attempts to keep his "weekend jeans" grass stain free.

As she dug her own hole, she looked at the dates on the marker. It had been almost two years since the traffic accident that took her parents. She hoped living without them was going to get a little easier, because it had been tough so far.

"Why these, um," he picked up the pot and looked at the label, "mums?"

Amy pushed the trowel through the dirt at one corner of the stone. "Mom always liked mums. She said they were the one beautiful thing that happened in the fall. Yellow ones were her favorite."

"Did she grow them around the house?"

Amy considered. "Sometimes. Mom gardened sometimes and sometimes she didn't. When she did, she always planted them." Her eyes fell. "Too bad you never met them."

"Boyd said your dad probably wouldn't have liked me."

She turned. "He said that?"

"I don't think he meant anything by it. It was a couple months ago, the last time you made Sunday dinner. He said your dad didn't like salesmen."

She dug back into the ground. "I wouldn't put too much stock in anything Boyd says, and you should know better. Junkies aren't known for telling the truth."

Jeremy smiled. "He was, though, wasn't he? About your dad not liking salesmen? It's okay, you can tell me."

She smiled a little, the corners of her mouth turning up. "Well, he had to deal with them at work a lot, you know? He used to say they weren't good for much but scoring Indians and Browns tickets." Her face fell. "I miss them so much. I even miss my dad complaining." She wiped away a tear with the back of her glove.

Jeremy stood up and went to her, putting his arm around her shoulders. He even knelt down right in the grass. "Why don't you talk about them a little? It might make you feel better."

She sighed but snuggled in closer. "I don't understand why they're gone. I don't understand why one stupid decision has to mean so much."

"What do you mean?"

A big fat tear rolled down her cheek. He pulled a handkerchief from his back pocket and dabbed at it. "They were out shopping when they had the accident."

"Right, that's what you told me." He shifted and the sun finally gave them a little warmth.

"Mom was feeling cooped up from taking care of Boyd after his accident. He'd had a couple surgeries to fix his back, and he was still at home. Dad was working, and Mom was taking care of him."

"You'd think he'd have a home nurse with it being a disability case and not his fault."

"He did, but she was only there a couple of times a week. Mom was doing the majority of the care, and Dad was working insane hours. They just wanted to get out of the house, so I volunteered to help with Boyd."

"This was about a year after his accident, wasn't it? Did he still need this kind of care? Someone around all the time, I mean?"

She shook her head a little. "I didn't think so, but Mom was babying him. He was well into his rehab, but Mom didn't want him left alone for any length of time. Boyd could walk but it was slow and with a cane. I think Mom was afraid that if the house caught fire he wouldn't get out, or something equally unlikely. I think she'd seen one too many 'I've fallen and can't get up' commercials."

Jeremy smiled. "Well, I've never had kids, let alone an injured one, so it's tough to judge." He was good at this, he knew. Empathizing with customers was part of what made him good at his job. It also helped with women.

"Well, it was a Friday and Mom wanted to be out of the house. Dad said he would take her to dinner and a movie, maybe do some shopping. There was some serious snow on the ground because it had been coming down all day. It was one of those cold, miserable February nights. Dad said the truck had four-wheel drive and if Mom wanted to go out, then she was going out. I remember thinking how sweet he was, trying to make something special out of a dinner and movie date they'd probably had a thousand times."

"He sounds like a good guy, despite his incorrect assumptions about salesmen."

Amy gave him a poke in the ribs but stayed in his embrace. "You know how it is around here in the winter. If you stay inside because the weather's bad you don't go anywhere or do anything. You just go slow and take care."

"Sure."

"Well, they shopped, had dinner, and decided to see a movie. It was just after eleven. Boyd was asleep, already zonked out on his painkillers." She spat the word out, he noticed. "Anyway, Dad was taking the back way home. I don't know why. The highway was in better shape, but people get into habits. I've thought about it and figured Mom and Dad were probably talking about the movie or something else and he was probably on auto-pilot, just taking the most familiar route home."

He smiled. "How many times do we all do that? You leave work, mind on stuff that happened or things you want to do, and you just find yourself almost all the way home with no memory of traveling all those miles."

"Dad was absentminded as hell," she said with a touch of anger. "He was always losing track of time or things. If something wasn't in front of him, it might as well have been invisible."

Sensing Amy could get angry, he tried to shift the conversation back to the night of the accident. If she started getting mad about her dad, the whole day would be shot. "What road were they on?"

"Cover-Thompson. It's the back way to the mall, and that's where they had been. I woke up on the couch about two in the morning with a crick in my neck. Boyd was asleep and I went to check on them. I figured they'd come home and just let me sleep but when I went to use the bathroom, I saw they weren't in their room. I got worried. You have to understand, not only was it a full-on northeast Ohio winter night, but I'm pretty sure my folks hadn't been out past midnight since Bill Clinton was in office." She snuffled a bit. "I got scared right then. I mean, really scared. I called Mom's cell phone and didn't get an answer. I tried Dad's number and he didn't answer, either. A few moments later, a deputy called back. He said he was at the scene of an accident and asked me where I was. A while later, a sheriff's cruiser showed up with a deputy and took Boyd and me to the hospital and we identified them.

"The deputy said they'd slipped off the road on that sharp turn by the pond. Dad's truck had flipped and gone through the ice and into the water upside down. They drowned. They drowned in an upside-down truck in February."

Jeremy pulled her tight. He knew that she needed to talk, needed to get this out because it was bothering her, but he wondered if the whole day was going to be morose. He knew no words were going to help. One of the things being a good salesman had taught him was that you had to have patience. You shouldn't push by speaking too much or saying the wrong thing. That could make people shut down, and right now he wanted Amy to work through this. He held her tight and brushed a stray hair from her forehead.

After a few moments she rolled her head and looked over at his hole. "That's deep enough. You did a good job."

Amy stood up and stretched, brushing dirt and grass from her knees. As she leaned over the bucket, gathering a few things, Jeremy studied her from behind. She looked good in her worn weekend jeans and gloves. What was it about jeans and gardening gloves that made a woman look so good? Maybe things could get friendly after they left the cemetery and finished up her list of weekend errands.

"Here," she said, handing him a plastic bag of fertilizer. "Throw a couple scoops of this in the soil, mix it up, and then we'll plant."

"How are your classes going?" He worked the fertilizer and soil together. Changing the subject was tricky but it could move things in the right direction.

"The exciting world of accounting? It's a daily thrill. I get tingles just thinking about it."

"You should be a sales rep. With your looks, you'd do very well." She blushed a bit, which was just the reaction he wanted.

"That sounds even worse than accounting. Going around selling auto parts to a bunch of sweaty guys? No, thanks."

"No, not auto parts. I see you in pharmaceutical sales. You could get into those doctor's offices and clean up."

She looked at him. "You think? It wouldn't be so bad, going to see all those young, handsome doctors."

"Hey, hey! Easy there, baby."

She laughed, the tears gone now. "Don't worry, I don't want to sell anything. No, I want a nice nine-to-five job. I don't know how you handle all that traveling. It would drive me crazy."

"It's not bad," Jeremy said. "I couldn't stand being cooped up in an office. Just the thought of being planted in a cubical farm with no windows day after day is enough to drive me crazy. I like being out, doing my own thing and making my own hours."

She looked at him with knit brows. "You work more hours than anyone I know."

"It's what I like. How's this?"

She looked in the small hole. "That'll do. Let's get them in and see if we can figure out a way to do something more pleasant with this rest of the day." He helped her tip the flowers out of their pots and into the holes. After Amy was satisfied, he helped her pick up their tools and put the bucket in the trunk of his Cadillac. He tied it in with a bungee cord so it wouldn't spill and get dirt everywhere. The passenger's side door closed as Amy got in. His phone vibrated and he looked at it with the trunk lid still up so she couldn't see him. It was a text from Linda, a waitress in Wixom, Michigan, he saw sometimes when he made trips to visit auto manufacturers. The text had a picture attached. It was a selfie taken in a bathroom mirror, and she was sporting an emerald bra-and-panty set he'd bought her two weeks ago when he'd last been up there. He smiled and texted back a smiley face and saved the pic to her file on his phone. He shut the trunk and slipped into the driver's seat.

Amy looked over at him. "Why don't we skip the shopping and spend the afternoon in bed? I want you to make me feel good."

He smiled and nodded. "I can do that."

• • •

"Someone close to me? Like who?"

Tim set his lemonade down and looked at his boss. They were sitting in Charlie's house, a nice Colonial in the area known as Hogan

Estates. Charlie was sitting on a white leather sofa wearing a pair of tan chinos and a white sweater, while Tim was slowly sinking into the matching love seat. An end table sat between them holding their drinks. The living room was sunken, and the bright October sun lit up the room from windows facing the backyard. Tim knew Charlie was an investor in several other businesses, but he was surprised when he saw the house.

They should have both been off enjoying a nice Sunday, but Tim had questions and needed answers. It was so different seeing Charlie in his private home; their relationship was one of boss and employee and now they were sitting here as interviewer and subject.

It was awkward as hell.

"Charlie, I know it sounds ridiculous, but all of the research I've done indicates that someone close to you is sending the letters. A friend, a family member, or someone else who may be close to you."

The *Shopper*'s publisher sank back in the sofa. "I appreciate what you're saying, Tim, but I really can't think of anyone who would be capable of doing this." He took a sip of his drink, an iced tea in a tall glass. "You have to understand, after I got a few of these things I did a little research of my own. I probably looked at a lot of the same websites you did."

"Charlie, I have to start somewhere. I examined the letters as best I could, and there's no physical evidence to indicate where they came from or who wrote them. The messages themselves don't point to any particular direction except for you to stop publishing. There's no singular incident in any of the messages indicating why they are being sent." He took another sip of his lemonade. "It appears that the only avenue I have left to examine is the motive, and my research points to someone in your life who's upset with you."

Charlie stood up and walked around the back of the love seat to the windows and the French doors that led outside to the deck and backyard. He opened the doors and stepped onto the deck. Tim sat for another moment, unsure of what to do. Finally, he stood up and followed Charlie into the sunshine and crisp air. He looked around, taking in a lovely backyard with a flower garden and small gazebo. There were woods beyond the yard. Tim could see why Charlie liked it here.

"Nice backyard," Tim said.

Charlie nodded. "I did most of it myself. I've always been pretty good with building things, and when I bought this place about ten years ago, I wanted a nice backyard. One summer I did the deck and another I built the gazebo and benches in it."

"You do the flowers, as well? I have an aunt who loves to garden and she would love what you have out here."

"Yeah, I did the flowers, too. It's quite a stress reliever taking care of them. No matter how wired I get at work, I always feel better after a few hours back here." The older man hugged himself. It was cooler than it looked from inside.

They were silent for a moment, and Tim watched as a robin lit upon a birdfeeder. It pecked at the tray of seed while balanced on the edge. "Charlie, we don't talk much about our personal lives at work."

"No, we don't."

Tim swallowed, unsure of how to proceed, but he knew he had to move things forward. "You've told me that except for your brother and sister and their families, you really don't have any family. Is that correct?"

"Yes."

"Well, I've heard you speaking to both of them on the phone, and I never got the impression your relationship with them is anything but cordial. I mean, my family is pretty screwed up, so I know what it sounds like when you're on the phone and things are strained. I've never heard that in any of your conversations."

"No."

"So, how about romantic partners, Charlie? Is there anyone who you're not friendly with any longer? Have you ever had a relationship that ended badly?"

Charlie looked out over the yard. "Relationships end, Tim. I'm sixty-seven and single. I haven't had a long-term partner for some time. Do you think that's indicative of bad endings?"

"I don't know, boss. Not every relationship has to end on a bad note and not every ex has to be someone who hates you."

Charlie turned. "Are you speaking from experience? At your age, do you even have any exes?"

Tim nodded. "A few, I guess, although I get dumped more often than I do the dumping. I was thinking more about my dad. He divorced my mom before he died and went on a holy tear through any single women who slowed down near him. He kept it loose and fun. They all liked him, even after they stopped dating. You'd be surprised how many of them showed up at his funeral and told me what a great guy he was."

Charlie smiled and shook his head. "You don't seem to have inherited his talent with the ladies. As you say, we don't talk about our private lives at work, but if you were doing as well as he I'm sure you wouldn't be quiet about it."

"No, I suppose not. I tend to be too selective and too serious. Women don't like that. I do all right, though."

"Are you seeing anyone now?"

Tim inhaled and took a moment to answer. "There's someone I would like to, but she's seeing someone."

Charlie outright laughed this time. "Oh, Tim, don't sit around waiting. That's the worst thing you could do. You've been on TV and you're not bad looking. You should get out there and date. Go have a good time. You don't realize it now, but you only get one shot at your twenties. Have some fun."

"Thanks for the advice, but we're talking about your exes. Is there someone who fits the description of the person we're speaking about?" Tim took a step forward and stood next to Charlie as he looked at the woods beyond. "Did you have a particularly bad break-up? One that was really sour?"

"Not really."

Tim turned. "That wasn't a 'no,' Charlie."

"Look, Tim, here's the thing. I had one bad break-up, but it was a while ago. His name was Keith. I haven't heard from him or seen him since the last time we spoke, and there were some particularly ugly things said. I'm not so sure it would be a good idea for you to go digging into him. The last thing I need is for that whole mess to be stirred up. If you start asking questions it could just lead to trouble, and I don't want trouble."

"I'll be discreet."

Charlie shook his head. "No, I really don't believe he would do this. The anonymity of it isn't his style, and I believe the letters would be of a more personal nature."

Tim deflated a little. This was really the only avenue of investigation open to him. He wanted to solve the mystery but couldn't think of any other way to continue. Something was nagging at him, though, something from the research he'd done. Leaves swirled across the backyard.

"You must get your share of leaves and more from those woods."

Charlie's eyebrows rose up. "Oh, yeah, all those maple trees make a hell of a mess. It's a chore every weekend in the fall, but it's nice to have the woods to hike in during the summer. Cleaning them all up is the price I pay. One thing follows another, you know?"

Tim nodded. He stared at the leaves a bit more and it came to him. He turned to face Charlie. "You know, one of things my research turned up is that the person sending the letters wants to see a reaction."

"Really?"

"Yes. They want to know they're having an effect. They want to know their efforts aren't in vain. They basically want to know they are getting under your skin, driving you crazy. In the examples I read, some people were driving toward a specific goal."

"Like what? All this loon seems to want is the *Shopper* to stop publishing."

"Well, that's his stated goal. What if he just wants to aggravate you? That's one of the strongest motivations for writing anonymous letters. People get to say something without owning it. They get whatever is bothering them off their chest without repercussion. Maybe they don't like the decisions someone is making, or the way they dress, or the way they conduct their business, and they can't speak truthfully. That aggravation drives them to send the letters. Usually they get to see the reaction because they're so close to the situation. In many instances, the person receiving the letters will even confide in them. That's the payoff."

"That's cowardly," Charlie said. "If someone has something to say, they should either say it or shut the hell up."

Tim could see he was getting upset now, pissed about the letters. Maybe they had gotten to him more than he let on.

"You'll get no disagreement from me, Charlie. I sign my name on everything I write. So, maybe who we should be looking at isn't someone from your past but someone in your life right now, someone who can see your frustration when you receive one of these things. I know you told me I was the only who knew about the letters, but what if it's someone who just sees your reaction?"

"I see what you're saying, Tim, but who could that be? Do you have any idea how many people I come into contact with every week?"

"Yes, and I bet it's one of them."

•   •   •

Bob Ellstrom pointed to a flathead screwdriver lying on top of the engine's air cleaner. "Harvey, don't forget that one."

The young kid from work looked over and grabbed the screwdriver. "It goes with the others in the top drawer?"

"Yeah, you'll see it."

He watched the young man walk into the barn stall where the rolling toolboxes were kept and made sure he dropped it into the correct drawer. "Thanks," he said. "I like to keep all those in order. It makes them easier to find."

"No problem, Bob. I really appreciate you helping me out like this. I don't know too much about fixing cars, so you're saving me a lot of money."

Bob waved him off. "Don't worry about it. It was just a bad starter."

"Yeah, but if you hadn't helped me get it started in the parking lot I would have a tow and a bill at some repair shop."

"Well, now you know how to do it yourself," Bob said. "Just remember, it takes two people to pull that trick—one to tap on the starter while someone tries to start the car."

"Yeah, I'll remember that." The kid looked around the barn. "You've got a nice set-up here, Bob. Look at all these tools. You must be good at fixing things, huh?"

Bob looked sideways at him. He thought of Harvey as a good kid. He was another forklift driver at Brinco, and Ricky got on his case almost as much as he did Bob's. That alone was enough to put him in Bob's good graces. Today Ricky had been especially mean when Harvey had spent half an hour putting bins in the wrong location. When he'd seen Harvey struggling to get his car started after work, Bob had taken pity on him. "Yeah, well, the more stuff you can do on your own, the less you have to pay someone else."

"Yeah," Harvey said. "I get you. Those are good skills to have when you work at Brinco. Making what we do, you can't afford to pay anyone for anything."

"Why don't you start it up, see if she turns over?"

"Give it a test, huh?"

"That's right."

The kid grabbed his red hoodie from the nail it had been hanging on and pulled it on, zipping it up halfway. He got in the Ford and cranked the engine. It started immediately and he lowered the driver's side window.

"Hey, how about that?"

"Sounds good," Bob agreed. "Let me get the doors." He walked around the back of the car and pushed open the heavy barn doors. The chilly air hit him. Harvey backed the car out and Bob shut the doors, putting the padlock on them.

"You sure I can't pay you?" Harvey said from the car.

Bob shook his head. "Don't worry about it. Just bring me a case of Bud Light."

"You'll have it tomorrow so you can drink it after work. Okay, man, I'm going home."

Bob waved. "Take it easy." He watched as the car backed up, turned around in the gravel and made its way down the long driveway.

Six

Halloween rolled around. Gravel crunched as Tim pulled into his driveway. The mobile home park was large, almost three hundred homes, so there were always a lot of trick or treaters. If the kids didn't live in the park, their grandpa, grandma, or aunts and uncles did. He hefted four large plastic grocery bags from the front seat of his pickup and waved to Tilly, who occupied her glider and waved back to him.

"All set for the little ones, Tim?"

He walked over, and she gestured to a lawn chair. He took a seat. "I guess so. It seems like we get more every year."

The elderly woman nodded. "I know. This year I gave up and went for suckers. The chocolate bars got to be too expensive."

Tim laughed. "I got the economy-sized Nerds bags." He pulled one out and showed her.

They sat in silence for a moment. It was ten of six and the kids would be making their rounds soon. From where they sat, Tim could see the sun sinking into the woods that surrounded the park. A few Canadian geese milling around the water's edge bent their long necks to the grass below.

Tim saw curtains move in several trailers as children anticipated the start of the festivities. He remembered the feeling well. Everyone was reluctant to be the first one out of their house and everyone was watching everyone else, wondering who would be first. Finally, he saw Maria Mendez open her front door. Her six-year-old twins jumped giddily down the steps, excited but hesitant. She took their hands and walked them to the road. Then with the first trick-or-treaters starting their rounds, doors up and down the circular street opened up and kids spilled out into the growing darkness.

"You have a nice smile, Tim," Tilly said. "You should do it more."

Unaware he was even doing it, Tim grinned wider. "I was just thinking back to how much I used to like this. Halloween was spooky but you got to help decorate the yard and put your costume together. We didn't buy our costumes at the store very often, but my mom was pretty good at helping us come up with stuff right out of the house."

A group of kids came by and Tim and Tilly dropped treats into their plastic pumpkins and pillow cases. There was a chorus of thank yous, and the kids ran off. The night was cool and Tilly shrugged into her sweatshirt and zipped it up. "Winter's comin."

Tim nodded. "The forecast has snow next week. Can you believe it? Temps down in the twenties."

"I used to like the winters here," she said. "A lot of my friends went south to Florida or out west to Arizona and New Mexico, but Walt and I always stayed here. When my Walt was still alive, he used to say that anyone could make it where the sun shined all the time but you had to be tough to stay here in Ohio, where the four seasons beat you down. I told him he was full of shit, but he genuinely seemed to love the different seasons." She paused, poured some tea into a cup from the thermos at her side and sipped it. "Now, I'm just too old to go somewhere and start over. And let me tell you, I hate winter."

Tim smiled. "I know what you mean. It feels like it won't be warm for six months."

"Well, that's because it won't be." She took another sip. "So what are you going to do?"

"What do you mean?"

A streetlight popped on and bathed the area in the weak yellowish glow of a mercury lamp. "You're out of school now, right? Your internship at the TV news is over. You can't just keep working two jobs. You need a plan."

"I don't know. I have a story at work—you know, at the *Shopper*— that I'm working on."

"One story is not a plan, and, if you don't mind me saying, neither is working at the *Shopper*."

He smiled. Normally he might be upset with someone saying all this, but Tilly was right. He'd been thinking along these lines for a while, even before Jeremy had opened his big mouth at Degman's Hardware. What was he going to do?

"You're right," he said. "It took a lot to get through school. And then I had the internship that I thought would turn into something, but it didn't, and it doesn't look like it's going to. Now I need to come up with a new plan."

Tilly leaned over and took his hand. "You really do, Tim. I've seen a lot of boys around here get out of high school and make nothing of themselves. It's not like it used to be, where you graduated and just got a job in a steel mill or at the auto plant. The work just isn't here anymore. If you aren't careful, twenty years will slip by and you'll still be living in that trailer and working at the hardware store."

Tim grinned. Like that was ever going to happen.

"Don't you laugh at me, Tim. It happens. You see these kids out messing around with drugs and their excuse is that they can't find work or go to school or whatever. The simple fact is they're lazy asses who feed off other people's misery. I heard these dopers have been breaking into houses and stealing stuff. You're smarter than that. You have an education and some experience you can put to work. Make sure you don't waste it hanging around here doing nothing."

Tim sobered up a little. "I understand what you're saying, Tilly. I really do. I just need to get my feet under me a little and find a direction."

She patted his hand. "Just find it soon, Tim, and you'll do fine."

• • •

"I really don't care, Bob," Ricky said. "You're on Saturday. The plant is in production, so we're in production. They need our parts. That means you're here with the rest of us."

Bob was fuming and anyone who could see him right now would be able to tell. The older man was starting to go red at the tips of his ears. "Damn it, Ricky, I have things I have to do Saturday. When I took this job they said Saturdays were voluntary."

"You're working," Ricky said without looking up from his clipboard. "Saturdays are voluntary if enough people volunteer. We're short, so you're coming in."

"You'll have three lift drivers here. You don't need me."

Ricky put the clipboard back on its hook. "I need four."

"You need three: one to unload receiving, one to stage outbound, and one to load outbound to the plant. They aren't even running full production."

Ricky looked at him and rolled his eyes. Bob wanted to punch the twenty-seven-year-old manager in the face and turn those eyes black and blue. "I'll need someone to pick up the slack in case we get behind."

Bob was breathing heavily through his nose. "I can't be here. I have things I have to take care of at home."

Ricky shrugged his shoulders. "Today is Monday, Bob. I'm giving you as much notice as I can. Look, you know how this works. I offered the overtime to everyone. I got three takers and I need four. You're the low man in seniority so you're forced in."

"I'm not coming in."

Ricky looked at him. "Where do you think you are? This isn't whatever mill you used to work at where some union rep is going to file a grievance for you. You work just like everyone else. If we say you're working, you're working. Now get out of here. I have things to do."

"Well, I guess we'll see."

Ricky came out from around his desk, his face beginning to show some color of its own. "Go ahead and play games, Bob. If you aren't here Saturday, don't come in Monday. I don't need this shit. I've got a stack of applications a foot thick. I'll just hire someone else. Do you know how fast I can train someone to drive a goddamn forklift?"

Bob just looked at him, jaw clenched, breathing heavily. He hadn't been this upset in a long time. "Whatever," he said.

Ricky backed around the desk. "I don't want to have this discussion again, Bob. You're always whining and bitching and I've had enough of it. There are eighty guys on this shift and you're the only one who complains about every little thing. You run your mouth at me again and I'm going to start giving you points so fast you'll be out of here in a week. You understand me?"

Bob hated the points system. Workers earned points for rules infractions like being late, calling off, or being a discipline problem. Managers could be subjective in handing them out. As far as Bob was concerned, it was just one more way to fuck with people and keep guys like him under the thumbs of guys like Ricky

He nodded. "Yeah, I understand."

"Then get out of here. You're shift's over. Go home."

Bob collected his coat from his locker, slammed the locker door, slammed the door to the employee's entrance behind him and slammed the door on his Chevy Silverado as he got in. He was so angry his hand was shaking, and he fumbled the key as he tried to start the ten-year-old truck. He dropped it to the mat and pounded the steering wheel. "Damn it!"

Fifteen minutes later, he was rolling down Owl North Road toward his house. He passed a guy walking, the same guy he saw occasionally wearing a vintage leather eight-ball jacket. He knew the guy lived farther down the road, across the bridge over Hammer Creek in the old Jensen house. Sometimes there was another guy there, but he wasn't sure if they both lived there or just the guy in the eight-ball jacket. The house had been nice once, but those two had let it run down. They seemed like deadbeats because they couldn't be bothered to put the rain gutters up after the ice brought them down last winter. They had just laid in the side yard until the weeds grew high enough to cover them.

Bob drove another minute and turned into his long driveway. It was bordered by trees for about seventy-five yards, and Bob liked that just fine. It gave him the privacy he liked. The driveway was a bitch to keep clear, though. He had to grade the dirt and gravel a couple times a year and plow it when the snow got deep enough to give his four-wheel drive a challenge. That's why he was pissed about working Saturday. He had been planning to get the plow out of the barn and get it on the Chevy. Now Ricky had fucked that up.

Bob thumbed the remote for the garage door and nothing happened. He hit it a few more times and the door stubbornly refused to rise. Dead battery, had to be. It had worked this morning when he left for work.

"Great," he said. "That's just great. Fucking piece of shit." He threw the remote against the passenger's side window and it fell down below the seat. Bob got out of the truck, let himself into the garage through the side door with his key, punched the garage door button, climbed back into the truck, and pulled it in. He punched the button again to lower the door and made a mental note to stop at Degman's Hardware tomorrow after work to get a new battery.

Dinner was a Marie Callendar chicken pot pie and a couple buttered slices of white bread. He watched the CBS *Evening News* and saw the world wasn't getting any better. More assholes in the Middle East were blowing shit up and no one was doing much to stop them. As far as he was concerned, America didn't have balls anymore. He turned the TV off and stepped onto the small front porch.

It was cold now. He could almost smell the snow in the air. It had that edge to it that always came in November. The trees were pretty much bare of leaves, and he could just about make out the road through the woods fronting his property. Ricky deserved to be punched, and punched hard, but he knew he couldn't do it and maintain even this crappy lifestyle. Too young for retirement and not qualified for the good-paying jobs meant he had to work for stooges like Ricky if he wanted to keep a roof over his head.

Back inside, he grabbed the mail and looked through it. It was just circulars and coupons. No letters (haha) but there was one envelope from the county. He cursed and ripped it open, almost tearing it in half as he did so. The document inside informed him that he was now two years behind on his property taxes and reminded him of the penalties that could be incurred if he did not begin making payments. He dropped the envelope and notice onto a pile of bills at one end of the dining room table. Bob sat down at the other end, the end with the typewriter, and thumbed through his schedule notebook. He slipped on the pair of white cotton gloves and rolled a piece of paper into the Smith Corona typewriter. Four hours later, his eyes were watery from concentration, and his fingers were cramped. Seventeen letters were stacked neatly on the table, ready to be mailed in the morning. Bob slept like a rock.

• • •

Tim swung the delivery truck into the parking lot of Degman's Hardware at five o'clock on Friday. As he backed into the dock, Tate was waiting for him and Mac. The younger man started cleaning out the back of the truck. Tim walked over to Tate and handed him the signed delivery paperwork. "Here you go."

Tate accepted it. "Thanks. I appreciate you doing this. I normally wouldn't bend on the delivery hours or ask you to work late, but Mrs. Donovan is one of our best customers and since she's remodeling, she's been buying a ton of construction material and furniture."

"No problem," Tim said. "The overtime will come in handy, and I didn't have much to do at the paper tonight, anyway."

"All right. Why don't you go ahead and knock off? We'll pick it up again Monday morning."

"Okay, Tate. Thanks. Have a good weekend."

Tim walked up to the front of the store and saw Alice, one of the night clerks, behind the counter. She was ringing up a customer but threw a wave his way. He threw one back and walked out to the parking lot, heading for his pickup. He saw Amy sitting in her car staring at her phone. He hesitated, looking at her for a moment, and decided to walk over. She saw him and opened her door.

"Can you help me, Tim?" She said. "My car won't start."

He smiled. "Sure, what's wrong?"

"When I turn the key, nothing happens."

"Pop the hood and I'll take a look."

He heard the hood release and felt around for the latch, found it and fought with it for a moment before realizing he had to move it to the right to get the hood open. He looked at the little four-cylinder and didn't see any disconnected wires or hoses. He poked his head around the side of the hood.

"Go ahead and turn the key," he said.

She did and he could hear the steady rapid click of the starter. He checked the battery and looked at the punched-out date on the calendar sticker. It was seven years old. He walked around the side of the car.

"Your battery is dead," he said.

"Can you jump it?"

"I can, I've got cables in my truck, but not only is your battery dead, it's pretty old. Do you want me to try jumping it or do you just want to put a new one in?"

She got out of the car and leaned back against the driver's side door. Tim took notice of how well the pink sweater fit her under her denim jacket. "This was my mom's car. I inherited it after my folks passed away. It's run so well I haven't had it in the shop for anything in a while."

"Putting a new battery in is easy." He looked back into the engine compartment to make sure there weren't any braces or plastic crap in the way. The last thing he wanted to do was over-promise. Thankfully, the battery was in the clear. "I could do it right now if you want, or we could see if the jump will work. The only thing is, with winter coming, I don't think you want a seven-year-old battery in your car."

"I couldn't ask you to do that," she said.

"It's no big deal, really, it will take ten minutes."

"Don't you have to get to work at the paper? I wouldn't want you to be late."

He shook his head. "Not tonight. I'm off because we had that late delivery for Tate. I can do either, but let's do it before we freeze to death." With the sun dropping down, the air was turning early-November cool.

"Where can I get a new one?"

"Come on, I'll run you over to Jim's Auto Parts and we can grab one. I hope you don't mind riding in my old truck."

She walked toward the S-10. "I wouldn't be too hard on it," she said. "It starts."

They were back with the battery in fifteen minutes, and it took another twenty for Tim to wrestle it in. Amy got back in her car and turned the key. It started immediately. Tim closed the hood, dropping it slowly and pushing it shut.

"Looks like that worked," Tim said.

She smiled and Tim felt floored. It happened every time, but this time he was hungry and tired so he just let the feeling wash over him.

"Have you had dinner yet?" she asked.

He shook his head. "No, Mac and I didn't even really have lunch because we were so busy. I'll grab something at home."

"Jump in. I was feeling like being kind of bad tonight, so I was going to grab a burger and shake. You want to come? My treat."

"You don't have to do that."

"Come on," she said. "Get in the car. Let me buy you dinner. It's the least I can do."

Tim smiled. "Yeah, okay. I can't let you be bad alone. Where are we going?"

"To eat food that's no good for you? Jupiter Joe's, of course."

She drove them out toward the interstate at the edge of town, past Creekside Motors, and got on Route 52. Five minutes later they pulled into Jupiter Joe's Burgers and Shakes. Pink, red, and orange neon lit up the parking lot, and Tim knew from experience the burger drive-in could be seen from I-80 for a mile in each direction.

He laughed. "There's no way you eat here. You're always talking about the Zumba you do down at the community pool."

She pulled into one of the little slots with an electronic menu board and smiled back. "Of course I do. I like a good bacon cheeseburger. Now, what would you like?"

"I don't know. Cheeseburger and fries?"

"No, no, a hardworking man like you needs some serious fuel. Let me order."

She lowered her window and the chill night air rolled into the car. Amy reached over, tapped the orange order button on the menu board and waited a couple seconds for a voice to ask her what she wanted.

"We'll have two number three combos, make one of them a double, and chocolate shakes."

While the voice on the speaker repeated her order back to her, Tim leaned forward to see what a number three combo was. Amy held up a hand to block his view while she finished up.

"Oh, no, it's a surprise."

He leaned back. She was beautiful in the bright neon, and he smiled. "I usually get the number one," he said, "just a single with cheese."

"Well, you'll like this more," she said. "Thanks again for helping me."

"I saw you there looking at your phone and figured you were having some kind of problem."

"Yeah, I was trying to figure out who to call. Jeremy is somewhere in Iowa on a sales call, of course. It seems like he's always gone. With my dad gone I don't really have any family except Boyd, and he's worthless because . . . well, you know."

Tim didn't know what to say, so he just kept his mouth closed.

"You don't have to spare my feelings," she said. "I know what Boyd is and I know that everyone knows."

"I really don't know him," Tim said. "I've just heard rumors."

She nodded, not smiling at all now. "Well, he deserves what's being said about him. A lot of people are willing to give him a pass because he was hurt working for the county and that wasn't his fault. What came after the accident is all him, though. All the stealing and drugs and crap, that's all stuff he has to own."

"Maybe he'll get it together," Tim said. "I've heard he had a lot going for him before he got hurt."

Amy slouched down a little in her seat, getting more comfortable. "He was smart and going to college, so you're right, he's got potential. He just needs to stop downing pain killers like they're M&Ms." She shook her head and changed the subject. "What about you? What's going on with you?"

"You know, working for Tate, working at the *Shopper* for Charlie. That takes up a lot of my time."

There was a knock at the window and Amy looked up to see a waitress in a winter coat holding a tray of food. She lowered the window, paid and took the bags. Tim took one of the shakes and jabbed a straw through the top while Amy doled out the burgers onto the dashboard and set fries beside them. Then she picked up her own shake and took a long sip with pursed lips. Tim looked at her in the neon light.

She nodded toward his burger. "Open it up and take a look at that bad boy. You're going to love it."

He unwrapped the biggest burger he'd ever seen. It was a double covered with two slices of cheese, a couple big strips of bacon, chili, and jalapeño peppers. "Come on," he said. "You don't really eat this?" However, when he looked over she had the foil wrapper on hers rolled down halfway and was taking a bite.

"Yes, I do," she said around a mouthful of burger, "but only once a month or so. My dad used to say that as long as you did everything in moderation, you'd be fine. So, once a month I grab one of these and indulge. And stop dodging the question. What's going on with you?"

He shrugged. "I told you, I work. That's about all there is to tell."

"Who are you seeing now? Are you still going out with what's-her-face from the TV station?"

He blushed. In the months he'd worked at the TV station he'd dated one of the assistant producers. "No, she dumped me when I didn't get hired."

"No way."

"Yeah, when my internship was over and they made the decision not to hire me, she said she was afraid I would try using our relationship to get back in. It was the dumbest thing. I mean, she took her job so seriously and thought she was really something important. You know Steve Carmen, the six and eleven anchor?"

Amy nodded and ate some fries.

"On no less than three different occasions I heard him call her by the wrong name." Tim started laughing. "So, about two weeks after I didn't get the job she comes to me all serious and sits me down, looks me in the eyes and tells me that she's sorry, but she'll never be able to tell whether I want to be with her for who she is or for her job at the TV station."

Amy set her shake down. "I have to be honest, Tim, I think you dodged a bullet with that one."

He grinned. "Yeah, I think so. How about you and Jeremy? Everything good there?"

"Oh, I guess so," she said. "I like him, but he's gone all the time and even when he's here he's all about work." She considered Tim for a moment. "Can I tell you something?"

"Sure."

"Sometimes Jeremy has this way about him that makes it seem hard to tell if he's being sincere or not. I've noticed it in the vendor sales people who come to see Tate, and then I started to see it in Jeremy."

"What do you mean?" he asked as he took another bite of the burger. Amy was right; these things were fantastic.

"Well, these men and women come in and they smile and they're always in a good mood, and they always remember my name but you can tell the smile is just a mask. I've seen them in the parking lot looking at their phones before they come in. They're out there rehearsing, making sure they know Tate's name, what they talked about last time, what his family is up to, and the names of the folks working the counter. It's like they have to pretend to be sincere."

"So you get that from Jeremy sometimes?"

She considered. "See, that's the thing. I can't tell. I mean, I think he's being sincere. He remembers things and he's attentive, but I almost think he's treating me like one of his customers, you know? Like, his phone reminds him when it's my birthday or he takes away one little thing from our conversations to remember later so I'll think he's listening to me."

"There are worse things than taking the effort to remember things," Tim said. Then he felt like kicking himself. The last thing he needed to do was defend Jeremy.

"No, you're not understanding me. We can't even have a real conversation because he's afraid to put forth an opinion. Whether it's politics or something that happened overseas or here in town, Jeremy always takes the safe ground. He feels me out before he puts forth his own opinion because he doesn't want to offend. Well, I like a good discussion; I like to argue a little. All he likes to do is close deals and screw."

Tim almost choked on his shake and grabbed a napkin.

Amy laughed. "Well, it's true. Whenever he gets a contract signed he really likes to celebrate."

"I think we're entering the land of Too Much Information."

"Sorry," she said, but Tim didn't think she was. "Poor baby. Has it been too long for you?"

"Oh, we are definitely not talking about my love life."

"My friend Sarah thinks you're cute. You want to go out with her?"

"I don't think I know who that is."

Amy dug her phone out of her purse and scrolled through the photo gallery. "Here she is."

Tim took the phone and looked at a selfie of an attractive brunette with her arms wrapped around Amy. They were both smiling and had New Year's hats on with beads draped over them.

"You think she'd go out with me?"

"I could ask, if you want me to."

"Aw, the burger's enough for fixing your battery. You don't have to pimp out your friends."

She leaned over and smacked him on the arm. "Ass."

"I don't know, maybe. Let me think about it."

"Come on, she's cute. What is there to think about?"

"Well, work is kind of tough right now."

"Really?"

He sat up. "Well, not at the hardware store, obviously. I mean down at the paper. Charlie gave me an assignment. It's my first real story and I'm not doing well with it."

"Bombing out, huh?"

"Seriously."

"Can you talk about it? What's up?"

"Yeah, I mean, it's not a secret, but I'd appreciate it if you didn't say anything. It's not the kind of thing Charlie would want to get around."

"Is it a gay thing?"

Tim grimaced and nodded. "Kind of, yeah, maybe, I'm not sure. I mean, it's more like harassment, you know?"

"Okay," she said. "Tell me more."

"Well, someone's been sending Charlie these obscene letters. In them this person is harassing him for being gay, telling him the *Shopper* should be closed and what a rag it is. They're anonymous and they keep coming. It's really starting to piss Charlie off, so he has me trying to figure out who it is."

Amy slowly sat up straight in her seat and set her shake in the cup holder. She had a very serious look on her face.

Tim grew concerned. "What's wrong?"

She considered him for a moment. "What you just told me, about those letters, was that the truth?"

Tim nodded. "Yeah, I've been looking into it for a couple months now."

She swallowed hard, and Tim saw a bit of concern creep over her face. "Tim, Tate's been getting letters just like that for almost a year."

Seven

On Saturday, Kathleen Brimley walked into the Peppermill restaurant and stood next to a sign that read "PLEASE WAIT TO BE SEATED." During the morning, customers could seat themselves, but the lunch rush was sufficiently busy to require a hostess. A young blonde woman walked out of the back and threw her a smile.

"Just one?"

Kathleen nodded. "Is Nadine Harch working today?"

"She is," the young woman said. "Would you like to sit in her section?"

"I would, thank you."

They moved toward the rear of the diner, and Kathleen took a seat at a table. She looked around the restaurant and saw most of the tables were full. The crowd was a mix of people in professional dress, probably from the auto parts plant and some of the small offices on Main Street, and others in blue jeans, probably folks who worked second shift at places around town.

The Peppermill was one of a few restaurants in Hogan. It was old, because she could remember coming here with her folks when she was a small girl, and she was fifty-six now. The décor was a little dated, with dark wood paneling and wallpaper that should have been changed at least ten years ago. People in Hogan didn't seem to mind much, though. Change wasn't something the town embraced, so some yellowed wallpaper just made the customers feel at home.

She and Robert had enjoyed coming here before his heart attack. Her rail-thin husband had liked the breakfast menu, which they served all day. As she looked around and took in the familiar sights, she thought about all the times they'd sat here, looking out the windows at Main Street and talking about what they were going to do. She had some regrets, for sure. They hadn't traveled as much as they wanted to. Robert's work as a millwright at Ohio Axle had always kept him busy, and she had the house to look after.

Across from her booth hung a football schedule for the local high school team, the Hogan Hawks. Someone had penciled in the scores for the season and she could see they had finished up 7 and 3, which meant they wouldn't be going to the playoffs this year. Their division was tough, full of Catholic parochial schools, Kathleen knew, and that record wasn't going to let them advance.

She'd pretty much forgotten about the letter from September, the obscene one implying Robert had been having an affair with a waitress here. It still puzzled her, why anyone would send such a letter, why then, and what they hoped to accomplish. After praying on it for a few days, she'd put the letter away in a drawer and forgot about it. If someone wanted to be disrespectful, that was their business. She wasn't giving them any more of her time.

Then she had run into Gary Ornoski.

Robert and Gary had worked together for years at Ohio Axle, where they repaired industrial machinery. Kathleen had been pushing a cart through the Savefast Supermarket and bumped into him. Unlike a lot of Robert's friends, speaking with Gary wasn't awkward. So many of his friends treated Kathleen like a fragile glass statue that would break if they said the wrong thing. Gary was a boisterous man who never failed to have a smile and a kind word and usually a funny story about Robert. That day in the Savefast, Kathleen smiled when she saw him picking through dinners in the frozen foods aisle.

"You need to eat better than that," she'd said.

He looked up, smiled, and gave her a hug. "Hey, Kathy, how you doing?"

Few people called her Kathy; really it had only been Robert, but she figured that's how Gary knew her from work conversations.

"I'm good, Gary, just doing the weekly shopping," she'd said.

"Yeah, me too. I just get this stuff because it's easy to make. You can only eat so much pizza, you know?"

She did know. Hogan had five different pizzerias, if one counted the new Pizza Hut out by the interstate.

"I understand. How's work?" Gary was a widower, having lost his wife to cancer about seven years prior. She didn't want to get into a conversation about home cooking, finding a wife, or any other insensitive topic. Gary was handsome. If he wanted another wife, he could find one.

He smiled. "Oh, work's pretty good. We got a couple good orders in to keep us busy."

"You haven't retired yet?" she said.

"No," he said, shaking his head. "I still want something to do when I get out of bed in the morning. I like what I do, so it's not a chore. Plus, these younger guys fresh out of school don't know anything. If someone like me wasn't there to hold their hands, they wouldn't do anything right."

She laughed. He was like Robert in the way they looked after the kids at the shop. She'd lost track of how many stories Robert had told her about how he'd helped some young guy do something the right way. Then for no reason, she'd thought of the letter from back in September.

"Gary, you and Robert used to go out for lunch, right?"

"Oh, yeah. We usually went on Thursdays because that's when Robert didn't pack a lunch. I imagine we kept a lot of those places in business over the years."

"Did you ever go to the Peppermill?"

Gary's face faltered. It was only for a moment, but Kathleen saw it. His eyes glanced down, just the way her daughter's had when she was five and fibbing about cleaning her room or eating her peas. Then he smiled.

"Oh, yeah, we'd go over to the Peppermill. I liked the cheeseburgers. Robert always got the pierogis. You know how much he liked pierogis."

"Yes, he did," she said. "He liked them with butter and onions."

He looked at his watch. "Well, I have to get going. My son's coming over tonight."

"Right," she said. "I'll be seeing you, Gary."

He waved and walked away. She stared after him for a moment and finished her shopping.

• • •

"Can I get you something to drink, hon?" a voice asked from her right. Kathleen turned her head and saw Nadine Harch standing there, a book of guest checks in one hand and a pen in the other. Nadine was younger than Kathleen by at least a dozen years, which put her in her early forties. She was tall, slender and had blonde hair that hung halfway down her back (Kathleen was sure the color came out of a bottle). She recognized Kathleen and smiled.

"Oh, sorry, Kathleen, I didn't realize it was you with your head turned. How are you doing?"

She smiled politely. "Oh, I'm fine. How are you?"

The waitress shrugged her shoulders. "Still here, but I'm doing well, you know."

"That's good," Kathleen said. A question hung on the edge of her tongue, but she held it back. Gary's hesitant glance in the frozen foods aisle of the supermarket wasn't exactly a smoking gun.

"So what can I get you to drink?"

"Oh, some chamomile tea will be fine, thanks."

"Coming right up," Nadine said. Kathleen watched her walk away, her behind sashaying under a tight blue waitress uniform. She could imagine Robert and Gary sitting here doing the same thing, a couple old horndogs away from work and the wives, admiring the view.

Hogan wasn't a big town so you tended to see people a lot if you made it out and about. Kathleen was a regular at the community pool's over-fifty water aerobics class. She'd seen Nadine there many times taking a Zumba class taught by one of the college-aged lifeguards. The blonde didn't mind wandering into the pool area wearing tight workout clothes and seemed to appreciate the second glances she got as she made her way to the workout room in the back. Kathleen had heard stories about her but didn't really know anything for sure. Old hens liked to gossip, she knew, and in a town like Hogan, divorced single blondes who wore tight skirts and spandex could count on being the topic of discussion.

She looked back outside. The noon sun was hidden behind gray clouds that matched the concrete of the sidewalk. It occurred to her that at this time of year, Ohio would be mostly gray and white. Another bleak winter was rolling in and spring was months away.

"Here's your tea," Nadine said, pulling her attention back from the weather. "Are you ready to order?"

Kathleen looked at her and swallowed. "I'll need another moment."

"Sure, no problem," she said. "Hey, you know. I saw Gary in here last week. He used to come in with your Robert all the time. I really miss him, you know. He and Gary used to make me laugh myself silly."

Kathleen forced a smile. "Yes, Robert had a good sense of humor."

"He sure did. You were lucky to have him, Kathleen." She glanced at another table. "Enjoy your tea. I'll come back and check on you in a moment."

Rather than turning back to the weather outside, Kathleen watched Nadine walk around the restaurant. She smiled, touched shoulders and arms, laughed, and Kathleen noticed the men giving her second glances. Once, at the pool, she'd seen Nadine in the parking lot being dropped off for her Zumba class. The waitress had walked around the car and shared a lingering kiss with an older gentleman in a Mercedes before going into the building.

Kathleen closed her eyes as a pool of feelings welled up inside her. Jealousy, anger, and embarrassment all struck her at once. She sipped her tea without tasting it, and her hand shook a little. All those hours Robert had been at work, all the overtime. Had those hours really been spent putting machines together or had he spent some of that time out at the trailer park where Nadine lived?

Despite the over-fifty aerobics classes, Kathleen thought she still looked like a frumpy housewife in her middle fifties. The kind of woman her mother would have called "matronly." She certainly didn't possess the spark or vibrancy that radiated from Nadine. Was that something Robert would have found attractive? Was it something he would have yearned for? Did he want to climb into bed with that much energy and expend himself? Right up to the end he had been vital, energetic and in good shape. He had been strong, stronger than she was, and Kathleen had often wondered if she was keeping him satisfied.

Why the hell had Gary glanced away that day in the grocery?

She stood up from the booth. The mug of tea was still steaming but Kathleen couldn't finish it, couldn't even think of eating. Nadine walked over to her.

"Change your mind?" she asked.

Kathleen looked at her, looked hard and accusingly, but didn't say anything.

"Oh, hon, are you okay? You look like something is bothering . . ." Her words trailed off as the intensity of Kathleen's stare bore into her.

They stood there, looking at each other. Kathleen was full of doubt. Had Robert and this woman been with each other? Was she wrong for thinking such a thing? She didn't want to cause a scene, didn't want to embarrass herself or anyone else, but she held Nadine's gaze. Just when she was about to break away the waitress blinked and dropped her stare, looking down at the carpet. Nadine took a deep breath.

"I'm so sorry," Nadine said softly. She started to say something else but her lips drew tight. She continued staring at the carpet.

Kathleen dropped a few crumpled dollar bills from her hand onto the table and walked toward the exit. Before she got to the door she stole a glance back and saw Nadine standing at the table with her head down, wiping her eyes with a paper napkin. Kathleen stepped out into the cool November air.

• • •

Bob Ellstrom, a Peppermill regular, sat at the counter ignoring his usual BLT and bowl of wedding soup in favor of staring at the two women. His face was slackjawed with surprise, and he dropped his glass of Sprite onto the floor. That seemed to break the spell, and he bent down to clean it up with a napkin, but Nadine walked over.

"Don't worry about it, Bob," she said. "I can clean that up."

• • •

That afternoon, Gary Shellmack pulled onto the lot of Creekside Motors in a bright yellow Hummer H2. The big SUV was a bit dated, but it accommodated his big frame and was comfortable. Three hundred pounds didn't fit well in a Ford Focus or Chevy Cruze, so he kept the Hummer around. He parked in his usual spot, just off the side of the showroom building near the business office entrance.

He looked out toward the road and saw that traffic on Route 52 was light today, but his lot had the plum spot where it intersected with I-80. He stayed open Saturdays until four and hardly a weekend went by without his moving at least one car. He walked around the Hummer and got his lunch from the passenger seat and the accompanying shake from the cup holder. It was a number three combo from Jupiter Joe's Burgers and Shakes. Having the best burger and shake joint in the area only five minutes from his business was probably a major factor in maintaining his weight, but Saturdays were cheat days. He waved to Tony Escobaro, the only salesman on the lot right now, and walked past Charlotte's empty desk. The receptionist was off today but he saw a stack of mail sitting on his desk blotter.

Tony walked over as he sat down at his desk. "How was Reno?"

The chair creaked as Gary swiveled around. He saw Tony's eyes glance down at the Jupiter Joe's bag and the shake cup. "Not bad. We had a nice time."

"Win anything?"

Gary smiled. "Not really. I think we broke even."

Tony laughed out loud. "You know that's code for 'I lost my ass,' right? Everyone says they broke even. If it really happened as often as people said, the casinos would have to close."

Gary started looking through the stack of mail on his desk. "Okay, I lost some. Not enough to close the dealership, but too much to give you a raise. How was business around here?"

Tony looked over his shoulder at a young couple getting out of their car. They didn't have kids with them, but the wife was clearly pregnant. "We moved enough to keep you in blackjack money. You'll have to excuse me. I'm about to go sell a minivan."

As Tony left, Gary got up and shut the door. He didn't like eating in front of people, especially when he had junk food. The last thing he wanted was to feel self-conscious about enjoying cheat day. It was especially tough with a health freak like Tony around. The guy weighed about one-sixty and competed in 5k races on the weekends.

He pulled a foil-wrapped burger from the bag along with a small bag of onion rings. As he flipped through the mail, he unwrapped a straw and poked it through the hole of the large chocolate shake. This lunch made up his daily allotment of calories on the diet he was supposed to be following but he'd been good, even in Reno at all the buffets. Now it was time to live a little.

Tony was right. While he had been enjoying casinos and drives up to Lake Tahoe for the last five days, the dealership had moved eight cars. Two of them had been high-end classic muscle cars—a 1969 Camaro and a 1958 T-bird. Tony had moved the Camaro, so Gary would have to let the salesman know what a good job he'd been doing.

The first bite of the chili burger was like heaven. Jupiter Joe's would make a fortune if they ever franchised, and if the opportunity ever came up, Gary would be first in line to open a location. He knew the owner, Joe Juraspiznyk, and although they'd spoken about franchising a couple times, the old guy never wanted to make it happen. Maybe his kid would once he took over? Joe was fifty-eight and couldn't flip burgers forever. Little Joe, as he was known, might be more willing to expand.

Gary liked investing in different businesses. He hunched down over his lunch and selected an onion ring from the bag as he looked over a statement from his accountant. In addition to the dealership, Gary was invested in eight other local businesses. He had a finger in all kinds of things, from a miniature golf course to a pizzeria, to a wing joint, a towing company, and a video rental place. That one had been risky because of the cable video on demand and Netflix, but damned if people in Hogan didn't still rent DVDs.

The burger and onion rings disappeared quickly and Gary realized his cheat day was over. He leaned back in the chair, making it creak, and put his feet up on the desk. One of the nice things about being the boss was not worrying about people catching you slacking off in your office. He glanced out the window and saw Tony laying on the charm in the showroom. The wife was pretty and the husband looked like he might have graduated from college yesterday. Gary remembered with a smile when he and Ellen had been like that. The years had taken their toll on both of them, but he had to admit, life was pretty damn good. Ellen still looked like a million bucks, and he was damn lucky to have someone like her. He reached for the next letter on the stack and his feet came off the desk with a thump.

Gary sat straight up and stared at the envelope in his hand. It was plain white with just the dealership address on it, attention his name. His heartbeat quickened and the lunch in his stomach suddenly felt like a metal lump. A greasy taste filled his mouth, and his breath became heavy. For a moment he contemplated just throwing the damn thing away unopened. Why ruin a nice Saturday?

He grabbed a letter opener from a desk drawer and almost cut his hand slicing the envelope open. As expected, it contained a single sheet of plain white paper. The envelope tipped and the paper slipped to the blotter on his desk. Gary looked at the letter like it was a viper waiting to bite him. With a sense of dread, he picked it up and unfolded it.

Your wife is too pretty to let a sweaty tub of shit like you climb on her. Should I write her and ask why she does it?

"Motherfucker!" he said, running the words together in one vicious outburst. He stood up from his chair and slapped at his milkshake. The paper cup flew across the office and smashed into the back of his door, exploding. "Sonofabitch!" he shouted. "What the fuck is this?"

Footsteps thudded across the showroom floor, and the door to the office opened slowly, accompanied by a soft knock. Tony stuck his head in and looked around. "Gary?" he hissed in a whisper. "Are you all right? I've got customers out here." He looked down at the floor and saw ice cream and whipped cream gathering in a puddle on the floor. A red cherry was stuck to the window to the left of the door.

Gary held up a hand and rubbed his forehead with the other. "It's okay, Tony. I just, uh, got some bad news. Sorry. Please apologize to your customers for me."

"Are you sure?" Tony said. "Is it Ellen? Is something wrong with her?"

Gary shook his head. "No, it's nothing like that. I'm okay. Just go back to your customers." Tony just looked at him. "Really, I'm fine. I apologize. That wasn't very professional."

"Hey, don't worry about it."

Gary nodded. "Yeah, I'm good."

Tony nodded and closed the door. Gary watched him walk across the showroom to the customers, and though he couldn't hear what he said, he saw the young couple smile. He was sure Tony had just told them a joke to gloss things over.

Gary turned to the mess on the floor and walked to the small closet at the back of his office. He picked up a roll of paper towels and unspooled them as he walked across the office. This bullshit with the letters was getting out of control, he thought. It was bad enough having some asshole take potshots at him, but now he was threatening to bring Ellen into the loop. He'd had to put up with cracks about his weight for a long time and could usually laugh it off, but this guy was a cowardly little schmuck who didn't even have the decency to face him like a man.

His hands were shaking, he realized. The anger produced by the letter had his adrenaline pumping. Normally a cool and level-headed guy, Gary wanted nothing more than to strangle the bastard sending these letters. He went back to the closet and grabbed a bottle of cleaner and sprayed down the back of the door. It took another fifteen minutes to sop up the mess from the carpet, and he was probably still going to have to have the damn thing steam cleaned.

He lay down on the sofa that stood against one office wall. Someone was getting his rocks off at his expense, but how? He had thought about it for months now, ever since the letters started arriving, and he couldn't understand what anyone was getting from it. Only his receptionist, Charlotte, Debbie in accounting, and he knew about the letters. He was reasonably sure neither woman was involved or talking about his reactions to anyone. So, if the writer wanted to get a rise out of him, how would he know?

The reason for the letters was just as perplexing. What had he done to deserve such treatment?

"Well, I *am* a used car salesman," he said and laughed.

Was that it? Some disgruntled customer? Could someone be that mad over a bad deal? Not for the first time, he thought over the list of customers who had complained about getting screwed over. You had to have thick skin in this business, that much was for sure. People were always mad about something. If it wasn't the price, customers were upset if the cars they bought were coming back for mechanical problems.

The only customers he had that seemed truly happy were the ones buying the classic cars and hot rods. Those guys came into the showroom with money burning a hole in their pocket. They wanted to spend.

He stood up, looked through the side window on the door and saw that Tony had the customers back in the lot with the doors of a Ford Windstar open. Charlotte kept a file drawer of customer complaints at her desk. He walked to her desk and pulled open the drawer to retrieve the files. There were quite a few, he saw.

Back at his desk he started going through them all, sorting them by date. The letters had started in August, so it stood to reason that if the writer was a customer, they must have bought a car prior to that month. It also stood to reason that the customer had bought the car recently, say in the spring or summer. He dug into the files.

An hour later, Tony knocked on the door and poked his head in. "Hey, boss, you hanging out or going home?"

Gary looked up at the clock. It was almost four. "Yeah, let's lock up."

Tony pointed to his desk. "What's all this about?"

"Customer complaints," Gary said.

Tony's eyebrows shot up. "Oh, yeah? Nothing for me, I hope."

Gary tapped a thick pile of files. "You know something? All of these are yours. What the hell are you telling people to get them to buy cars?"

The salesman put his hands up. "Hey, Gary . . ."

The big man chuckled. "You're so easy to get, do you know that?"

Tony put a hand over his heart. "Man, what is with you today? You're scaring me, scaring the customers. I may have to find another place to work."

Gary grabbed his keys and walked around the desk. "As if anyone else would have you."

"Oh, I don't know. That Chevy dealership over in Newtonville was looking for sales people. Maybe I could go over there and show them how the pros do it. I bet I'd get a raise, too."

They walked around the showroom turning off lights and setting the alarm, then out to the lot and stood in the cold. The sun was already dipping low, and the traffic along the interstate was a sea of red taillights. Gary shrugged into his coat and buttoned up. Tony pulled on a knit cap.

"You sell that couple a minivan?" Gary said.

Tony pointed to an empty spot on in the first row. The nice, clean Ford Windstar was gone. "Sure did, even after you scared the crap out of us."

"Yeah," Gary said, "about that, I'm really sorry. I can't get into it, but I got pissed about some news. That doesn't explain it and it's certainly not a good excuse for that kind of behavior, but I really am sorry."

"I know it's none of my business, but if you want to go across the street and grab a beer we could talk about it. I've got nowhere to be."

Gary considered the offer. It would feel good to tell someone the whole story and unburden himself. Whoever this guy was—and he did think it was a guy, based on the content of the most recent letter—he obviously wanted to piss Gary off and get a rise out of him. The thing was, Gary didn't know who he could trust. What if it wasn't a disgruntled customer? What if it was someone in the dealership? There were almost thirty people working here. They couldn't all be happy. He looked at Tony.

"Thanks, but I think I'm going to head home. Maybe I'll take Ellen out to dinner."

Tony grinned and let out a little snort. "You married guys, always running home."

Gary shrugged. "Hey, she's worth running home to, you know?"

"Yeah, yeah," Tony said. "Go on. I'll see you Monday, boss."

"You have a good one, Tony."

He watched as the salesman walked over and got into his Camry, started it and pulled off the lot. It was quiet now, and dark. He walked over to the Hummer and hit the remote start. The big motor growled to life, and he stood looking at the traffic. A large sign at the edge of the property facing the interstate promised good deals and fair treatment. Whoever was sending these letters to him wasn't playing fair, though. No, this was some coward who got his jollies from afar.

Gary pulled the letter from the pocket of his coat and looked at it again under the big mercury lights that illuminated the lot at night. He was taken back by how personal it was, and now that his rage had subsided, he noticed two things. First, the letter referenced how attractive Ellen was, and the writer was at least correct about that. She might be over forty, but she still turned heads. Second, the letter writer had broken pattern and put two sentences in the letter. All of the other letters had been one short sentence. This one was still insulting but it had more context.

A cold wind blew across the lot, chilling his exposed ears and nose, but he hardly noticed. Cold winds in Ohio during November were something you just accepted or you moved to Florida or North Carolina. There would be snow soon, and he made a mental note to have the guys move the four-by-fours out to the front row that faced the highway. November, December, and January were the months to move SUVs and Jeeps.

There was no one else here, he finally decided. What he wanted desperately was for the letter writer to be here, to be right where he could confront him. He hadn't been in a fight since middle school, but now, as he stood in the gathering darkness, he would be happy to show the writer the reaction he apparently wanted.

After one last look around, he opened the door and got into the Hummer. It was warm now and he flipped on the headlights. He took one last spin around the lot, looking up and down the aisles of parked cars. He liked to do this before he left on the weekends. The township police would be through a few times during the night, as well. With the lot being this close to the interstate they knew it could be a target for thieves, so they kept an eye on it. Convinced he was the only one here, he pulled back up through the lot.

He really did need to speak with someone, and he decided it should be Ellen. She would be angry he had kept the letters secret as long as he had, but after she got over that, she would be angry at the writer. She was very protective of family and held a grudge longer than the Hatfields and McCoys. As he pulled out onto the highway, he smiled. If the prick writing these letters thought it would be fun to make him angry, he was going to be surprised at what Ellen would do if she found him.

Eight

E ven though it was Sunday and Degman's Hardware was closed, Tim was waiting eagerly at the entrance for Tate. After Amy's revelation that Tate had received letters similar to Charlie's, he had to see them. After a few minutes Tate's Ford F-150 pulled into the parking lot and right up to the door. Tate got out and walked up to Tim.

"You sure about this, Tim?" Tate said.

Tim blew in his hands to chase away the cold of the November morning. "Not really. I mean, I won't be until I see the letters."

Tate unlocked the doors and the alarm started beeping. He punched in the code and locked the door behind them. He waved Tim back to the office. The store was different with the lights off and no customers. Their footsteps echoed in the darkened space. The only light came from the big windows along the front of the store. Shadows of the painted letters on the plate glass windows played upon the tiled floor. They walked around endcap displays for insecticide and a box of snow shovels. Tate unlocked his office and turned on the light.

"I'm not crazy about this," Tate said. "These letters, they're kind of embarrassing."

"I appreciate that, Tate, but what if the same guy sending them to you is the one sending them to Charlie? I have to follow up this lead."

"Christ, Tim Abernathy, boy reporter," Tate said, teasing him. He unlocked a filing cabinet and riffled through the folders. After a moment he pulled out a manila folder and sat down at the desk.

"There's half dozen or so in here," Tate said. "The first couple I threw out because I thought it was just some crank. Then, when the guy seemed to be persistent, I started keeping them."

Tim took the folder and sat down on the opposite side of the desk.

He flipped through the folder and looked at the letters. He wasn't interested in the content so much as the formatting and style. He set the folder down on the desk and laid the letters out to get a better look at them. There were actually eight letters in the file folder, but Tim set two of them aside. They were long, at least several paragraphs, and appeared to be printed from a laser printer. The other six appeared to be the same format as the ones Charlie had received.

Tim leaned in close to examine the letters. All of them appeared to have been typed. None of them had any other marks.

All six were short, just a single line, except for one that had three sentences. He picked one at random.

Your wife's B.O. smells like the devil's asshole.

"Tate, I am so sorry about this. By any chance, do you have the envelopes?" Tim said.

"No, I don't think so."

"Do you remember what they looked like?" Tim asked.

"They were just plain white envelopes with the address of the store on them. There was no return address."

"Yeah," Tim said. "I expected that. I was hoping for the date from the postmarks to try and put a timeline together."

"Sorry, I guess I should have kept them."

"Don't worry about it," Tim said. "This is a huge lead."

"So you think these were written by the same guy who wrote the letters to Charlie?"

Tim kept looking at the letters. "Yeah, I do. The formatting is the same, and these appear to be typewritten, just like the others. Would you mind if I took these with me?"

Tate leaned back in his chair and folded his hands across his belly. "Tim, what's the point of your article or investigation or whatever?" He pointed at the letters. "Like I said, those are embarrassing to me. It's bad enough I'm getting the damn things. The last thing I want is to see them in print, even if it is only the *Shopper*."

Tim leaned forward in his chair. "Tate, we will not print copies of the letters without your permission. If you don't want them to be seen by the public, then they won't be seen. Besides, if any of them actually see print, I imagine it would be Charlie's. He's boiling mad."

Tate's eye's narrowed. "He's not the only one. These letters? This is some cowardly shit. This is the sort of thing some small-balled pissant does. He's got his panties in a twist over something, so he takes it out by writing these stupid letters rather than just facing me like a man. When you figure out who this is, you're going to find someone who's scared of everything."

Tim gathered up the letters and put them back in the folder. "You know anyone like that, Tate? Someone who would be afraid to come in here and complain to you in person about whatever has them all pissed off?"

"What do you mean?"

"Well, I've been looking into the kind of person who sends these kinds of letters. They feel slighted or angry but they're unable to directly confront the person who made them feel that way."

"So they write anonymous letters?"

"That's right," Tim said, "but you've already figured that out. The person wants to provoke a reaction. Whether it's a change in your behavior or just to make you angry, the payoff for them is seeing you react to the communication."

"What do you mean by 'change in behavior'?"

"Well, in the examples I read online, there were several where people would send someone letters where they criticized their appearance or hygiene and suggested changes. Generally the writer wanted something to change but was not confident enough to talk about the subject openly."

"What, like, they send someone a letter telling someone their breath is bad? Let me tell you, I wish these letters were that tame."

Tim nodded. "I understand and yeah, many times letters are like that. This is weird, though. If you and Charlie are both getting letters like this, I think it points to someone who is angry at more than the two of you."

Tate considered this. "You think it could be more widespread?"

Tim shrugged. "I don't know. Maybe you guys angered the same person, somehow, some way." He held up the file folder. "I'll know more once I get into these and compare them to the ones Charlie received."

"You know, it's difficult to believe anyone would hate me this much," Tate said. "I'm not trying to brag or anything, but I've been pretty successful here, and I've managed to not piss off too many folks. When I read these, I can almost feel the hatred coming off them in waves. I mean, who feels this lousy that they keep sending me letters like this?"

"I'm hoping we'll find that out," Tim said. He started to get up, and then stopped. "Hey, have you told anyone besides Amy about these? Your wife, maybe, or the police?"

Tate frowned and shrugged. "I didn't want Joan to worry. I just thought of them as the cost of doing business with the public."

"You didn't call the cops?"

"No, I really didn't think it was that serious. I get them down here enough for shoplifting, you know? That's more important." He looked at Tim for moment. "Let me ask you, do you think this guy is dangerous? Do you think I should talk to the police?"

"You know what I think?" Tim said.

Tate shrugged.

"I don't think the letters are anything to worry about. I think the persistence of the person writing them is. If someone was here in the store and had bad service and then they went home and wrote a letter like this, well, I guess on some level I could understand that. I wouldn't do it, but I can see the appeal. What I really don't get is why you would keep doing it. You'd think all that anger and venom would be used up when you write the first one. How does someone keep that up?"

A low sigh escaped Tate, and he looked at Tim across the desk and, it seemed, across the years. "Let me tell you something, Tim, something you may not know about this town or even about this county. This is important, now, and I want you to remember it. People around here are friendly and generous. Some of them do acts of kindness that'd put tears in your eyes." He got quiet for a moment. When he continued, his voice was softer, barely audible in the small office. "We also have some people who are just not right. People who are angry, very angry at the way their lives have turned out. There isn't a lot of crime here. The cops do a good job of keeping a lid on things, and for the most part folks around here like the quiet and do everything they can to maintain that. However, there are times when a person just snaps. Do you remember Johnny Turnbull?"

Tim shook his head. "No."

"This was probably almost twenty years ago. He was a young guy, probably twenty-five or so, had a wife and a little girl. Anyway, he's out with his buddies over at the Pine Grove Tavern. He leaves late and stops at the Quick Bag in the middle of town. You know where I mean?"

"Well, yeah, Tate. It's still there."

"Right. So, anyway, his wife said later that she asked him to bring home milk. He goes in, gets his milk, a couple lottery tickets, and goes out to his car in the parking lot to scratch them. While he's doing that, another car pulls in with two couples. The girls get out and run into the store. The guys had been out drinking, and they notice Johnny sitting in his car. Now, they say Johnny was looking at the girls and made some obscene gesture to them."

"Is that what happened?"

"Who knows? They ran camera footage from the parking lot, and it was almost impossible to see anything. So, the girls come out, Johnny drives away and these two guys chase him down. They caught him out in the township near Perry Road. Now, you have to understand, this was the mid-nineties and few people carried cell phones. It wasn't like today. Johnny Turnbull certainly didn't have one.

"The cops said the guys chased him down, forced him off the road and pulled him out of the car. Have you ever been on Perry Road?"

"Sure. It gets pretty dark at night."

"Yes, it does. Imagine how afraid that poor kid must have been when these two assholes pulled him from his car and proceeded to beat him to death."

"Holy shit," Tim said.

"Yeah, his wife called the cops in the morning when she woke up and he wasn't there and neither was his car. They found him in the afternoon. He was stripped and tied to a tree with his belt and clothes. These two assholes beat him with tree branches after he'd been tied up. They even poured the milk over him. And it was a cold October night, so even if he hadn't died from the beating he probably would have died of hypothermia. They pushed his car over a short embankment to hide it."

"Jesus," Tim said.

"Yeah, I don't think Jesus had much to do with it. As you can imagine, what seems like a good idea at night when you're on a bender is often revealed to be a terrible mistake in the morning. It took two more days for one of the girls to break her silence and go to the police. Those two assholes are sitting on death row even as we speak."

Tim sat in silence for a moment, not sure what to say.

"There are other examples, too, if you look. You work for a newspaper. Hell, ask Charlie. He's lived in Hogan his whole life, so he'll know all the dirt."

"I will," said Tim.

Tate leaned close to the desk. "What I'm trying to tell you is that while we don't have a lot of crime around here, what we do have can be pretty nasty. I mean, they could have just told Johnny Turnbull to keep his eyes to himself or even just given him a bloody nose. They were two big guys and Johnny wasn't all that big. Hell, I can remember him coming in here to buy stuff with his old man." Tate got quiet for a moment. Tim could tell he was trying to go on without his voice cracking, and he stayed quiet until the older man was finished.

"Those two animals decided they would rather beat that kid to death. It was just what they were going to do that night, and no one could stop them. So, as nice a place as Hogan is, you watch yourself, because you never know when some asshole is going to blow something out of proportion and decide that today is the day they're going to be as mean as possible."

"A disproportionate response, Tate. I get what you're saying, believe me. You got to grow up here when a small town was synonymous with safe. My generation grew up with the Internet. I could go on CNN's website and find a story like the one you described every day. Believe me, I keep my eyes open."

"Yeah," Tate said, "maybe this kind of stuff does happen a lot. I'm just saying, when it happens here it can be a whole lot meaner than it needs to be. What did you call it, a disproportionate response?"

"Yeah."

"Well, it sounds right." Tate got up and moved from around the desk. "Let's go home. I only get one day off and I have stuff to do."

Tim held up the file folder. "Me, too."

They walked back through the store toward the front door, their footsteps echoing across the empty darkness again. A shiver went through Tim. It was ridiculous, he knew. The store was familiar territory and Tate was with him, but the circumstances of their visit and their subsequent conversation had him unsettled.

Outside in the noon sun, things seemed better. They went to their respective pickup trucks and got in. Tim saw Tate looking over at him and he rolled his window down. "What's up?"

"It occurs to me that Charlie and I have something in common."

"Yeah? What's that?" Tim said.

"You." The older man smiled at Tim and pulled out of his parking spot.

• • •

Frank pulled the little Honda into his driveway and got out. He unplugged the pizza delivery sign, yanked it off the roof and walked around the back of the car with it in one hand and a pizza in the other. He pushed the trunk button on the key fob but nothing happened. No click and the hatchback didn't rise.

"Damn it," he said.

He looked at the lock but didn't see anything wrong so he dug in his pocket for his lighter and set the pizza on the roof. He ran the flame of the disposable Bic over the key. He inserted it into the hatchback lock and wriggled it back and forth. Finally, the lid popped and rose an inch.

"There we go," he said.

He stowed the sign and slammed the lid, careful not to knock the pizza to the ground. The key was stuck, though. He pulled on it and wriggled it back and forth, but it refused to budge.

"Sonofabitch," he said and reared back. He kicked the hatchback to the right of the key. The pizza shot off the roof, and he slipped in the mud of the driveway. His arms pinwheeled as he grabbed for the pizza, and then he went down in the muck and gravel. The water was freezing, and it seeped into the seat of his jeans as he lay still for a moment. A cold wind blew over him, and he could feel it on every wet section of his skin. He rolled to his left side and got to his feet slowly, waving his hands to shake the mud and gravel loose. The key was still in the lock. He grabbed it, shook it hard. It popped free. The pizza was lying upside down in the driveway and he picked up, brushing mud from his and Boyd's dinner.

Climbing the front porch steps to the front door, he could hear a sitcom playing loudly from the living room. He took a deep breath and went in. As expected, Boyd was lying on the couch with the remote on his belly. He was clearly stoned, with a bottle of Oxy sitting on the coffee table, and the tiny remains of a joint in an ashtray. He opened his eyes and looked at Frank.

"Hey, there's the guy," he said. "I'm glad you're home, man. I need you to run me out to Skillet's place."

Frank shot him a glare. "Hey, you know what, Boyd? Fuck Skillet and fuck you."

Boyd rose slowly and unsteadily to a sitting position, propping himself up with one arm. "What's up with you? I just need a ride."

"Well, for one thing, I just got home from work. Oh, and here's dinner, you fucking stoner." Frank hurled the pizza at him, which landed half on Boyd and half on the couch. Boyd looked at it.

"What did you do to it?"

Frank took off his jacket and looked at the mud-covered mess it had become. "I slipped and fell in the driveway. Not that you'd notice from the couch. I could be lying out their unconscious and freezing to death for all you'd know."

"Jesus, calm down," Boyd said.

"Why? So I can be like you? All you do is lie on that couch and get lit all day. No thanks, man. You want to go to Skillet's place? Drive yourself."

"You'll let me take your car?"

"What? Of course not."

"Well, I don't have one," Boyd said. "So how am I supposed to drive myself?"

"Walk, then. I don't give a shit. I'm going to get cleaned up."

Half an hour later, Frank came back showered and in clean clothes. The pizza was half gone and Boyd had moved on to watching *Jeopardy!*. Frank noticed he was wearing the same clothes he'd had on yesterday.

"Did you really get up and sit on the couch all day?" He looked around the house and saw it was a mess.

"Pretty much," Boyd said. "My back really hurt so I just stayed here. I didn't want to tweak it."

Frank grabbed a slice and collapsed into an old recliner. "Well, I think your back is the only thing *not* tweaked around here."

"Oh, you're funny. I got a condition, man. You could have some sympathy."

"I just worked all day and I walk in the door and you're jumping on me to drive you over to your dealer. Give me a break."

"You were driving pizzas around," Boyd said. "It's not like you put in a shift at a goddamn steel mill."

Frank leaned forward and grabbed a second slice. "And what, you're the CEO of Sitting-on-the-Fucking-Couch Enterprises?"

"Are you going to give me a lift or what?"

"You'd think Skillet would deliver, you're such a good customer."

"Come on . . ."

Frank threw a piece of crust back into the box. "Fine, let's go. You're going to sit here and whine all night if I don't. I need gas money, though. I've got less than a quarter tank."

Boyd reached in a pocket of his jeans and fumbled around for his cash. He counted the wrinkled bills out on the coffee table and moved ones and fives into piles. He separated three fives out from the rest and handed them to Frank. "Here you go."

"Is that all you have until the end of the month?"

Boyd nodded.

"How are you going to eat?"

Boyd stood up and shrugged into his eight-ball jacket. "I'll eat shitty pizza. Let's go."

Frank hated driving to Skillet's place. The house was located in the middle of town, near the old elementary school. He was careful to obey the speed limit, come to a complete stop and use his turn signals. Stupid people got caught driving to their dealer, and he didn't want to get pulled over. Christ alone knew what Boyd was holding at any time. They stopped for gas first so they could drive straight home. He knew that once Boyd had his Oxy he was going to want it as fast as possible.

They pulled into Skillet's place and drove as far back in the driveway as possible. It was a crappy two-story house with beat-up white aluminum siding and a matching detached garage. A Ford F-150 pickup, murdered out in matte black with a lift kit and smokestacks in the bed, was parked off to one side in front of the garage. Frank didn't understand how the police hadn't arrested Skillet yet. The neighbors had to know what he was doing just from the traffic in and out of the driveway, and the truck looked like a cop magnet. Boyd got out with surprising energy as soon as the car stopped. Frank followed him. He didn't really want to, but sitting in the car looked too suspicious. Boyd was already knocking on the back door.

A skinny redneck-looking guy opened the door. He was wearing a black tank top, a baseball cap with the Ford logo on it, and jeans. He looked like he hadn't shaved for three days. He made the pretense of looking over their shoulders and then opened the door wide to let them in.

"What's up, Boyd?" he said. "Yo, Frank."

Frank nodded, and Boyd said, "Hey, Skillet, what's up, man?"

The dealer pointed out the truck. "I just got that six-inch lift kit I wanted. What do you think?"

Boyd nodded in appreciation. "Oh, yeah, that looks great, man. Nice." His eyes were glazed over, and Frank had doubts about whether he had actually seen the truck before Skillet pointed it out.

"Come on in, fellas," Skillet said, and they followed him through the empty dining room and into the living room. It was small and had a couch, a pair of thrift-store upholstered chairs, and a scuffed coffee table for furniture. A sixty-inch flat screen TV dominated one wall.

"Sit down," he said, pointing to the chairs. They creaked as Frank and Boyd sat. "So, what can I do for you fine fellas?"

Boyd fumbled in his pockets and dropped a wad of bills on the coffee table. "I need ten Oxy and a dime bag."

Skillet picked up the money and licked his lips. "How do you do both at once?"

Boyd raised a hand and gently brought it down. "I wait until the Oxy peaks and then ride the downside with a joint. It straightens the pain right out."

Skillet nodded and counted the money. "This will get you eight, not ten."

Boyd grimaced. "Come on, man. That's the right amount."

Skillet shrugged. "What can I say? The cost is going up. I've got expenses."

"Like lift kits?" Frank said.

Skillet had a wounded look on his face. "No, Frank, it ain't like that. It's just getting harder for my supplier to, you know, supply me. It's the economy, you know? Plus the holidays are coming up so all kinds of people are in the mood to celebrate."

Frank just looked at him.

"All right," Boyd said. "Just give me the eight, and I'll see if I can't scare up some scratch."

Skillet leaned over and patted him on the knee. "There you go, man. I got faith in you." He got up from the couch and went into the kitchen.

Frank leaned over to Boyd. "He's ripping you off."

Boyd just waved him off. "What are you going to do? Let's just get our shit and go."

"I should really only give you six for this price," Skillet called from the kitchen, "but you're a good customer, Boyd, and I take care of my good customers." He walked back into the room and put a pair of baggies into Boyd's hand. They disappeared into his coat pocket without being checked. Skillet flopped back onto his place on the couch.

"So, what else is up with you guys?"

Boyd was getting antsy, Frank saw. He knew he wanted nothing more than to get back home and get started. "Not too much," Frank said.

"Well, hey, my man Toomey said you guys scored pretty good with that last house," Skillet said. "He was asking if you were going to do any more. He was able to move a lot of that stuff you got."

He was talking about the last house they had broken into. Toomey was the fence they had sold the stuff to. Skillet had introduced them, which meant Skillet was getting a cut.

"I don't think we're going to do another one," Frank said before Boyd could open his yap and get them into something.

Skillet just looked at them for a quiet moment. "All right, all right, I hear you. It's just that Toomey said you guys had a good eye, you know. Like you didn't bring him a bunch of junk. He was able to move everything quick."

"We could maybe do another place," Boyd said.

Frank stood up and grabbed Boyd by the shoulder. "Okay, dude, let's get you home. I know you have some important stuff to do."

Boyd nodded and stood up. "Yeah, okay."

Skillet got up and walked them to the back door. Before they stepped out into the darkness, Skillet handed Frank a slip of paper with an address written on it.

"What's this?"

Skillet licked his lips. "I know a guy who knows a guy. The guy lives at this address and has some nice shit. It's out of the way, quiet, and the guy works steady days. You guys could do well for yourselves."

Frank looked at him. "What kind of stuff?"

"Lotsa tools. Hand tools, power tools, that kind of stuff. With the holidays coming up, Toomey can move that kind of stuff. It's all in a barn in the back. You probably wouldn't even have to go into the house."

Frank considered it. "Maybe. We'll see."

"Can't ask for more than that, brother."

"Right."

Nine

The wind was howling good and hard outside Tim's trailer. He swiveled on the couch and pulled the curtains to the side. Snow was in the forecast, and it was starting to come down. He could see flakes starting to fly through the air in the twilight of the setting sun. That meant brushing the truck off in the morning because he was too cheap to spring for a carport.

Turning back to the TV, he muted it and picked up the file from Tate. He'd had it for a few days but hadn't said anything to Charlie yet. He wanted to examine the letters carefully and have some discussion points ready before he said anything to his editor.

He put his feet up on the coffee table and went through them again. The letters to Tate were just as mean spirited and obscene as the ones Charlie had received. His favorite so far, though, was one that criticized Tate's price on PVC pipe.

> If you are going to charge six dollars for five feet of
> inch-and-a-quarter PVC pipe, you can just shove it up your
> wrinkled old ass.

He smiled again reading it. It was just so specific and so stupid. How far down the list of things to complain about was this guy that he was bitching about the price of drain pipe? It could be a clue, though. Tim had looked through the old advertisements for Degman's Hardware and PVC pipe wasn't in any of them. That meant the writer had most likely been in the store shopping for pipe, so they probably had him on the security cameras. Unfortunately, most of the city and township shopped there, so that didn't help.

Gravel crunched out in the driveway. Tim peeked through the curtains and saw a familiar Chevy sitting there. A moment later there was a knock at the door. "It's open," Tim called.

A tall, heavyset guy walked in. "Hey, what's up, Tim?"

"Just catching up on a little work, Doug. What's going on with you?" The big guy moved over to a chair Tim scored at a garage sale two years earlier and flopped into it. "Haven't seen you in a while, just thought I'd see if you were still alive."

"Sorry, just working a lot lately."

"No sweat," Doug said. He looked at the stack of papers on the coffee table. "Are you almost done with that? I haven't eaten yet and was thinking of going to Barrusas and getting chicken parm. Want to come?"

Tim looked at him sideways and smiled. "You're thinking of going to Barrusas because Angie works Wednesday nights and you like how her ass looks in those tight black pants the waitresses wear."

Doug nodded. "Well, hell yeah, brother. Are you telling me you don't?"

Tim looked at the mess in front of him and suddenly, he wanted to be anywhere but here. "You know, chicken parm sounds good. Give me a minute to change my shirt."

He walked back to his room and got cleaned up. Five minutes later, he walked back into the living room to see Doug looking over the letters on the table. The big guy looked at him.

"What's all this?" Doug said.

"A story for work, at the paper."

"I thought you just did advertising and stuff. You have a real story now?"

Tim shrugged. "Sort of. Some nutjob is sending anonymous letters to people in town, and Charlie wants me to figure out who it is."

Doug pawed through the papers and held one up. "Nutjob? This guy is one sick fuck. Have you read these?"

Tim nodded and straightened the papers up. "I've read all of them. The guy obviously has a problem. He's writing businesses and bitching about stupid stuff."

"Has anyone called the police?"

"No one wanted to go to the trouble, but as persistent as this guy is, I think someone should probably make a report. The thing is, these guys just see it as the price of doing business. I also think they don't want to make a big deal out of it. They're older, you know, and I think they just feel like they should deal with it on their own. Hell, to tell you the truth, I don't even know what laws, if any, are being broken. There are no overt threats in any of the letters. They're mostly just complaints and lewd comments."

"If you want," Doug said, "I could ask Larry about it."

"Your brother? He still works for the police department?"

"Oh yeah, five years now. I could ask him about what laws may be broken, if you want. I'll see him next week at Thanksgiving dinner."

Tim considered for a moment. He should probably get a law enforcement interview as part of the story. He might want to speak with Charlie first, though. "Why don't you tell him I want to talk to him about something but don't tell him why? We want the story to break at a time of our choosing. If you bring it up at Thanksgiving dinner with your aunts and uncles, it'll be all over town in no time."

"Okay, not a problem. Let's get a move on, okay?"

Tim laughed. "Relax, man. She works until closing. Why don't you just ask her out?"

"I'm working on it. Besides, I don't see you going out with that little honey from Degman's."

"That's different. She has a boyfriend."

"You said he's a douchebag."

They climbed into Doug's Chevy, and he turned on the wipers to brush the snow off the windshield. "He is, but she doesn't see it yet."

"Well, she will," Doug said. "Girlfriends are always the last to see their boyfriends are assholes."

• • •

Jeremy rolled over in bed and looked at the clock. The red digital display seemed to float in the absolute darkness of the hotel room. He blinked and his vision cleared enough for him to see it was 3:16 a.m. He lay still for a moment and tilted his head. The red numbers seemed to have no grounding. They drifted free in the blackness, untethered to anything. Then the time changed to 3:17 and his eyes adjusted to the darkness. He could now see the outline of the clock display and the numbers anchored themselves to the clock. The shape in the blankets beside him rolled away and sighed softly.

This trip had him in Pontiac, Michigan, and he was sleeping in a Double Tree. It was a very nice room. Normally he left a light on in the bathroom so he could find his way in the night, but the woman sleeping beside him would only do it in the dark so he'd shut off all the lights.

She was a waitress from the Chili's that shared the large parking lot of the hotel. Her name was Brenda, and he had been working on her for about a month. Brinco had him making weekly calls to a customer in Pontiac, and he'd noticed her on his first trip up. She was a college girl, a pretty brunette majoring in business, and she was chatty when she brought him dinner. Last week he'd taken her out for drinks, and this week he'd closed the deal. He didn't know why, but he was lucky with Michigan waitresses.

He knew how to talk to women, that was part of it. He had the confidence that his job demanded but he wasn't an asshole about it. These women had to put up with middle-aged guys hitting on them, telling them how they were directors of this or that, vice-presidents in charge of whatever, or how they wanted to celebrate because they just won a big contract. Jeremy was more laid back about it. A smile, a compliment, no talking about himself; he let them come to him. If they wanted a date, he was available. If they didn't, he just moved on.

This time Brenda wanted a date. She had texted him, and they met for drinks at Lucille's, a nice bar on Crooks Road. After settling into a corner booth, they'd ordered drinks and talked for a while.

"Are you allowed out this late on a school night?" he teased her. There wasn't that much difference in their ages, not even ten years, but he wanted it out there in the open, get it out of the way and move past it.

"I've been allowed out past ten o'clock for a few years now, so don't worry about getting me home early," she said. "You're the one up here on business. You have a meeting tomorrow? Can you stay out late?"

He wrapped an arm around her, pulling in her in close. She smelled good, like honeysuckle, and her long hair was silky against his arm. He was relaxed and had his shirtsleeves rolled up. "Don't worry about me," he said. "These weekly meetings are just to keep the customer happy. A little account management, you know? Take them out to dinner and make them feel special. Tomorrow I'll just be looking their plant over and making sure they don't have any problems."

She picked up her martini and raised it to her full red lips. "Is that where you were earlier when I texted you? Out to dinner with the clients?"

"Mm-hmm." He sipped his scotch.

She reached over and loosened his tie. He sat still while she worked his collar open. Her soft hands felt good on his chest. "That's better," she said. "You look more relaxed like that."

He played with her hair and traced the curve of her ear. "Thanks, I feel more relaxed."

There was a band in the opposite corner, three guys playing soft rock standards. He pulled her close and they snuggled for a while, sipping drinks and enjoying the low lights.

"You okay with this place?" he asked. "You want to go to a club and dance a little?"

"Nuh-uh," she sighed. "This is fine. It's nice to slow things down. If we were at a club, I wouldn't be able to hear you. Besides, this week was all midterms, and I need to decompress."

"Okay, let's just chill here."

An hour later, after finishing a Chicago ballad, the band announced they were taking a break. Jeremy leaned down and whispered in Brenda's ear. "Why don't you follow me back to my room?"

She smiled. "Okay."

"You're good to drive? I don't want you getting pulled over."

"I'm good," she said.

Now he was awake in the dark staring at the ghostly outlines of the room. He felt a little guilty about cheating on Amy, but it was what it was. She was young, still in college, and he didn't want to be tied down. It was nice, having someone at home, someone who cared about him, but he wasn't there a whole lot, and it was stupid to be alone when he didn't have to be. Some of these girls were up for anything. His phone was full of pictures and videos, some of which he took and others they sent him. They wanted to feel desired, if only for one night or a short while. He rolled over a little and ran his hands over Brenda's smooth, naked skin. She purred a little and snuggled back against him.

Brenda had been good. She was relaxed, took her time, not rushing it. He could tell she'd gotten a lot of the wild child stuff out of her system and was a little more mature. Amy was fine in bed, certainly good looking enough and caring, but did he want to be tied down? He wasn't even thirty, had a good job and traveled and he liked it, all of it. The company was on its way up, and he was along for the ride. In a couple years he would have contacts at bigger companies, the ones that had more than a few customers. There could be trips to Europe or Asia. Having a wife back home waiting for him to come back, asking him to check in all the time just seemed like an anchor around his neck.

On the other hand, Amy was the complete package. She was pretty, and not just because she was young. You could look at her and tell she was going to be a good-looking woman as she aged. She would always be sharp, as his mother said about good-looking older women. She was smart, too, and close to getting her degree. There was a determination in her that he liked. After her parents died, she had just kept right on pushing, working hard and staying in school. She even tried to take care of her junkie brother, so he knew she would be good with kids.

The question was, did he want a wife? He felt like he had found her too early in life. He was still having fun and there she was, all perfect for him to settle down with. Settling down wasn't what he wanted, though. That was for sure.

The first meeting with the client wasn't until nine in the morning. He should get a few more hours sleep, but the agenda was running through his mind. The meet and greet, the bullshitting about the weather, the families, who was going where for Thanksgiving, and the Lions. He reminded himself to look at Detroit's standings later in the morning. The guys here were diehard fans, so he should at least know how they played last week and how they were doing in the conference. Then they would get down to it. He would roll through his PowerPoint slides, see if there were any questions, and then they would tour the shop floor. He would also have to stop at the Dunkin' Donuts up the road for a box of coffee and a couple dozen donuts.

Brenda purred again as he ran his hands over her smooth curves. He moved closer, kissing her neck, and in the dark he worked out his anxiety. Sleep came easy after they were through.

• • •

The Sunday before Thanksgiving, Bob Ellstrom had his Chevy Silverado in the barn out behind the house where he was rolling a snow plow over to the front of the truck. The weather forecast for the coming week was snow, and lots of it. He wanted the plow attached. With Ricky having him work Saturdays, he was late getting the plow on, so now he worked fast. The little rollers on the bottom of the plow dropped into a broken floorboard and the whole thing tipped. Bob stumbled and fell.

"Damn it!" He put a hand out and steadied himself on the top edge of the plow. He'd meant to replace that board and had even reminded himself to watch for it, but his mind had been wandering.

"That's going to look great on camera," he said. He looked up out of habit at one of the cameras in the barn as a security measure. He had them around the property, pointed at the driveway, the barn, the shed, and the house. He had two here inside the barn. The cameras were triggered by movement and tied in to an online service that let him view them remotely from his cell phone. There had been burglaries in the township, and he wanted to know if anyone came to his place when he wasn't home. He had no illusions about Hogan. It was a nice town but he knew there were criminals here, as well.

"All right, you motherfucker, get straight," he said to the plow. He rocked the big piece of equipment backward and forward, working the small wheel out of the hole. Luckily, a bit of the board was still there and it allowed him to pull the glorified rollerskate loose. Once out of the hole, he got the plow in front of the truck.

It took another half hour to mount the plow to the truck and hook up the lights. He got in the truck, tested the electric controls and watched as the plow moved. Next, he tested the lights mounted behind it. Everything was working as expected, which was good. With the weather coming, the quarter-mile driveway would be impassable without a truck and plow to keep it clear.

The truck was good and solid, despite being ten years old. He'd bought it a year earlier from that fat-ass Shellmack out at Creekside Motors. Looking at the plow, he was reminded of the argument they'd had last summer. The transmission had gone out and his warranty should have covered it, but Shellmack wouldn't stand behind it. He claimed using the plow the previous winter was the cause of the problem and the warranty didn't cover damage caused by plowing. Bob and the service manager had nearly come to blows over it. In the end he had paid for the repairs out of his pocket. Thinking about it made him angry.

He heard a rustling from one of the stalls in the back and turned. Something was scratching against the wooden wall. He found barn cats in here sometimes, but this sounded different. Bob grabbed a metal gardening rake and walked toward the sound. It was darker in this section of the barn, but the overhead fluorescents threw just enough light for him to make out a small raccoon. The animal froze and looked up at him with wide eyes. He could see where its pudgy belly had it stuck in a gap between a couple splintered boards in the stall wall.

"Well, look at you," Bob said. "It appears you've got yourself in a bit of a situation there." The raccoon looked up at him and then furiously started kicking its legs trying to free itself.

Bob twirled the rake around. "It's annoying, isn't it? Being stuck in a situation that you got yourself into? I mean, you think you're doing the right thing, making all the correct decisions, and then all of a sudden you're in a place with no way out."

Bob stared off for a moment and then looked down at the raccoon. "You look like a Ricky. Do you mind if I call you Ricky?"

He knelt down. "I just wanted you to know that no matter how sorry someone may feel for you, there's nobody to blame but yourself for being in this predicament. Sorry, but I'm a guy who likes to tell it like it is."

Bob stood and screamed as he brought the steel claws of the rake down on the trapped animal. "Do you hear me, Ricky?" He swung, over and over again, obliterating the raccoon's skull. Boards in the stall splintered under his horrific attack. After a full minute of hammering, he leaned the rake against a post. The carcass of the animal was barely recognizable. Blood coated the stall and the wall of the barn. His breaths came in great gulps, and he put a hand on the post to steady himself.

After a few minutes, he calmed enough to move again and walked back to the gardening tools. He selected a coal shovel with a wide, flat blade and went back to where the raccoon lay. He scooped it up and walked past his truck to the big barn doors. One of the doors opened with a kick and he walked to the edge of the driveway. He flung the raccoon's body toward the edge of the woods and walked back into the barn.

He killed the lights in the barn and backed the truck out, then shut and locked the big wooden doors. Snow was falling already, he noticed. Fat, wet flakes were all over the ground and the air was cold enough that they weren't melting. It wasn't deep enough yet to run the plow over the driveway, but he'd be sure to leave himself some extra time in the morning.

Bob got back in the truck, drove it up to the house and pressed the button on the remote control for the attached garage. It was late afternoon, and he was hungry. He looked at the clock.

"Five thirty? Good enough. Time for dinner," he said.

After dinner there were letters to write.

Ten

It was just after three on the Monday before Thanksgiving when Tim pulled into the parking lot of the *Hogan Shopper*. Snow was falling and thick clouds made the sky a flat slate color.

A large brown expandable file lay on the seat beside him. This held copies of the letters from Charlie and Tate and the notes he'd made on the types of people who wrote anonymous letters. He looked in the rearview mirror and readied himself. It had been a while since he'd sat down with an editor to review his progress on a story, and that had been at the TV station where he did his internship. That meeting had been for his coverage of a city council meeting. Hopefully this would be a bigger story. He closed his eyes and let his nerves have free rein for a count of ten, then he drew a deep breath through his nose and exhaled through his mouth. He hefted the file and walked in.

Charlie had shoveled the snow from the walk, and Tim managed to get inside the office without slipping on the wet concrete. Snow was still piling up. The grass around the *Shopper*'s sign was covered. The winter storm bearing down on their corner of northeast Ohio wasn't unheard of for this time of year, but it was unusual. Hogan normally saw a few snowstorms between Halloween and Christmas, but those only dropped a couple inches or made the roads slippery. The storm coming at them now was like those that brought things to a halt in late January or February, when winter had set in deep. People were already grumbling about canceling holiday travel plans and expecting delays if they were pressing on.

The office was warm, and the windows had a fog of condensation on them. The sun was already a little less bright for this time of day than it had been a few weeks earlier. The office was empty, so Charlie was either out back or in the bathroom. The sound of a flushing toilet answered that question. Tim set the file on his desk and shrugged off his winter coat. It went on the coat rack in the corner. Charlie came out of the bathroom and up the short hall to the main office. He waved.

"Hey, Tim. How you doing?" He was wearing jeans with a blue dress shirt tucked in.

"I'm good, Charlie. How you making out?"

The publisher shrugged his shoulders. "We're doing good, actually," he said, talking about the layout for the Thanksgiving edition. "We'll be in stores early this week, on Wednesday morning with all the Black Friday ads."

"Hey, that's great," Tim said.

"To tell you the truth, Tim, I won't need you here after today until next Monday. We really got things done faster than I expected." He poured himself a cup of coffee from the machine on top of one of the file cabinets and dropped into the chair at his desk. His eyes fell on the expandable folder in Tim's hands.

"What's that?"

Tim sat down at his desk and hefted the folder. "I've made some progress in the letters story."

Charlie sat up straight. "What kind of progress?"

Tim could see the concern in his eyes. "Charlie, you're not the only one in town getting letters like the ones you showed me."

Charlie's eyebrows furrowed and his forehead wrinkled with concern. "What do you mean? There are others?"

Tim nodded. "At least one other person, and I have every reason to believe there are more."

"Who?"

"Tate Degman over at Degman's Hardware," Tim said. "He's been getting them pretty regularly for a while. Not quite as long as you and not nearly as frequently, but he's received them."

"Are you certain they were written by the same person? The same sender?"

Tim was quiet for a moment, considering the question. It was something he'd asked himself, too. The answer he'd come up with wasn't something he liked. He dug in the file and extracted a manila file folder with Tate's letters. He pulled one out and handed it to Charlie.

"As you can see," Tim said, "the format is the same and the content of the message is similar to the letters you received. Tate didn't have the envelopes, but he confirmed they didn't have a return address and were sent to the store to his attention, his name. If it's not the same sender, then it's someone who is using the same style."

Charlie looked over the copy of the letter. Tim could see him reading the message over and over. He flipped it around and held it so Tim could see it. "This is the same guy."

"Yeah," Tim said. "I agree."

"How did you get this? Did you just ask Tate if he was getting obscene, anonymous letters complaining about the service in his store?"

"Ah, no. It just kind of came up one night when I was out with someone who works there with me. She opens the mail at the store and during the course of our conversation, it just came up. It was pretty easy to put one and one together."

"Huh," Charlie said. "Let me see the rest of them." Tim handed the file folder over. Charlie leaned back in his seat and flipped through them. It didn't take long. "You know, it's interesting. All of mine allude to my being gay. I just assumed the guy had some kind of hard-on for homosexuals."

Tim raised an eyebrow.

"Well, so to speak. Anyway, none of Tate's letters mention anything like that. The guy seems like he's just pissed about prices and service at the hardware store."

Tim took a big breath. "Charlie, I've been looking into the kind of people who send letters like this. You know, what drives them to do it, what gives them the desire to sustain such a long campaign, and, most importantly, what they hope to get from it."

Charlie nodded slowly, sipping his coffee, considering. "I've thought about that myself. I mean, it's one thing to read something in the paper that pisses you off and you feel so strongly you sit down, write a letter to the editor and mail it. I get that. I understand that. That's discourse.

That's a discussion of the issues and that kind of feedback is good. Communication like that is necessary. Hell, I even get the anonymous bit, you know? I really do." He took another sip of his coffee.

"Sure," Tim said. "Look at the comments under news stories on the Internet."

"That's sort of what I mean," Charlie said. "Those people have a username that gives them anonymity. Even then, though, they build up a personality around that username. After a while you know how those people will comment, and you can even build a relationship with them. Some are fine and enjoy the interaction. Then there are those who seem to have nothing else to do but argue about politics or something the president said or whatever. They create an account, get themselves a handle and leave comments on what happened with the benefit of 20/20 hindsight. Having that Internet handle allows you to vent. But even then, there's the knowledge that if you go too far, someone, somewhere, can figure out who you are, and I think that makes some people hold back. "

"Yeah, but, Charlie, you know this guy isn't doing that."

"I know, Tim. That's what I'm saying. This guy just seems to have some bottomless well of hate to draw from." Charlie grabbed the file and held it up. "Just look at the effort he goes to. Who would give up this much time to a project like this?"

Tim stood up and took the expandable file back from Charlie. He dug around and pulled out a bound report folder. He held it out for Charlie to take. "This is what I've been able to put together in answer to that question. You can read it later, but I'll give you the summary. Now, this is my layman's opinion, and I've never had more than one psychology class, so take it with a grain of salt and feel free to consult someone who actually knows what they're talking about."

Charlie waved him off. "And I probably will if this turns into as big a story as I think it might, but go ahead, give me your best guess."

"The person writing these letters is fundamentally unhappy. Their life has not turned out the way they wanted it to and they feel powerless to change it. These letters are their way of trying to have some control over something. Whether it's telling you to shut down the *Shopper* because they don't like it or the fact that it's published by a gay man or

Tate's prices on inch-and-a-quarter drain pipe, I think the person writing these letters wants his opinion to matter and he feels like it doesn't."

"Well, I'm not surprised," Charlie said. "He sounds like an asshole."

"Here's the thing, though, Charlie. In all the research I've done, the people writing these letters want to see the effect they're having on the recipients. That's why I was asking about people close to you that day at your house. I figured the writer had to be someone you knew or someone close to you so they could see you getting upset. Now, I'm not so sure about that."

"Because Tate has been receiving them as well?" Charlie said. "Is that what changed your mind?"

Tim nodded and went back to the small fridge near the hallway leading to the bathrooms. He pulled out a Red Bull and popped the top. After a quick sip, he said, "Exactly. Unless you and Tate have one guy in this whole town who hates you enough to grind out these letters, I think the scope of this is much larger."

Charlie sat back and let the implications of Tim's theory sink in. "You think he's sending letters to more people?"

"I do, or at least more business owners. I don't know about regular people"

Charlie grinned but looked puzzled. "What, you think this guy goes into a place and has a bad cup of coffee or feels overcharged and starts writing letters? That sounds insane."

Tim held up the manila folders containing the copies of letters to Tate and Charlie. "What about this situation makes you think this guy is playing with a full deck?"

Charlie sighed. "Oh, man."

Tim leaned forward and set the folders down. "Charlie, this guy could be dangerous. I think we need to pursue this. When they were just letters to you I could understand keeping things quiet. I get why you and Tate did that. These are just annoying, you know? No matter how squirrelly they are, they were just something that got your blood boiling. Now that it's more than just one person . . ."

Charlie looked at him, considering the possible scope of the problem. "Now that it's more than just one of us, the problem has a new breadth. It's bigger."

"People need to know, Charlie. If this guy is dedicated and putting this much effort into this project of his, yeah, I think he could be a little unhinged. Letting people know someone dangerous is in their midst is something newspapers are supposed to do."

"Oh, whoa, Tim, hold on," Charlie said. "I know you're excited about this. I get that. But you need a hell of a lot more than what you have to make that determination or publish a story."

"I agree, Charlie, and I want to go get more."

"How? What do you want to do?"

Tim licked his lips, clearly nervous at the challenge. "I want to canvas businesses in town, small businesses, you know? Those owned by local people."

"You want to ask them if they've received letters?"

"Yes," Tim said, standing up and pacing. "I think you and Tate are not the only people who have received these letters. I'd bet you real money that when I ask around, I'll find a few business owners who also have received letters."

Charlie leaned back in his chair and rubbed his eyes, considering Tim's proposal. "It does seem unlikely that Tate and I are the only people receiving these. Especially when you consider that whoever this guy is, he's writing letters about the content of the paper and prices at the hardware store. He must have gotten a cup of bad coffee somewhere or been unhappy with the price of green beans."

"Exactly," Tim said. "What if a bunch of you guys are getting these things and just tossing them in a file or throwing them out?"

"Okay," Charlie said, leaning forward and picking up a pen. He rolled it over his finger like a drumstick, back and forth. Tim had seen him do it a hundred times before. He'd once admitted to being a drummer in the Hogan High School Band. "Here's what we're going to do. You get a press credential to show people so they know you're serious and not some random guy. We'll decide which businesses you go to, together, so I know exactly what you're doing. We make a list, you hit them up, ask some questions, and we find out if we have a problem that's city-wide or if there's just some random guy walking around who doesn't like me and Tate."

Tim smiled, a good one stretching ear to ear. "Thanks, Charlie. You're not going to be disappointed."

"Don't get too excited," Charlie said. "You have a lot of work to do."

"Yeah, but it's work I want to do. I like Tate, but delivering furniture and building supplies isn't what I went to school for."

Charlie nodded in agreement and looked at Tim. He didn't say anything.

"What?" Tim asked. "Is something wrong?"

"Lucky break, you know," Charlie said. "You working for me and Tate and we're both getting these letters."

Tim felt his face get hot as he flushed. "Charlie, this isn't me. I would never—"

"I know, Tim, but it just sort of occurred to me. You're a link between me and Tate."

Tim shook his head and leaned back. "You know, Tate said the same thing. I thought he was joking. Now I'm not so sure."

"I'm not accusing you, Tim. I'm just pointing out that the connection is there. If you're going to investigate this, you need to see those kinds of things."

"Okay, I understand, Charlie. I just don't want you to think I'm capable of something like this. I want a better job but there are enough stories out there without me making one up."

"I know," Charlie said. "Okay, let's get started on the list."

• • •

Boyd was on the couch again, Frank saw. Sitting there stoned out of his gourd and watching the Cartoon Network. He could hear Modecai and Rigby's voices from *Regular Show* as he walked into the kitchen. At least he was wearing sweatpants this evening, even if they looked a little grungy. Too often, Frank found Boyd lying there in a dirty t-shirt and his boxers. It was time for dinner. He snapped on the kitchen light and started hunting around for something to eat.

Frank opened the fridge and took a look at what he thought of as the great white emptiness. There was literally nothing in it but a pizza box he'd brought home yesterday. He flipped the lid up and saw nothing but grease-stained cardboard. He let the door close on its own.

The cupboards were equally bare. He did a quick calculation in his head and realized they hadn't been shopping for at least two weeks.

Generally he could sneak something to eat at work and Rocco gave them a free meal on their break. If it wasn't for that, he'd probably starve to death. He finally found a jar of Jif peanut butter and half a loaf of Schwebel's white bread. He rinsed off a dirty butter knife from the sink and made two sandwiches.

There were days, like this one, where Frank considered why he stuck with Boyd. They'd been friends since junior high school, back when Boyd was the more popular of the two. Frank didn't make friends easily but something had clicked between the two of them. As smart as Boyd was and for all the athletics he played, Boyd liked to screw off and party. Frank had always been up for a party.

After his accident, though, people had dropped away from Boyd, one by one. He wasn't the fun guy anymore. There had been long hospital stays and rehab, and many of the people they hung out with had gone off to college. Then Boyd had gotten addicted and any friends left had scattered rather than put up with him. Now it was just the two of them, friendless except for one another.

Frank wandered into the living room. He slumped into a chair with his sandwich and tossed the other at his roommate. It landed in his lap.

"Dude, we're out of food," Frank said. "Do you have any money left from your disability check?"

Boyd's head rolled over and he looked in Frank's direction. "I'm busted, man. I told you last week when we were out at Skillet's place."

Frank chewed white bread and peanut butter. "You were serious? I mean, when you said your plan for the rest of the month was to eat pizza I brought home from work, that was really the plan?"

Boyd nodded and smiled.

"That's great, man. That's just great. You realize I can't just take pizza home every day? Rocco gives us a discount, but he doesn't just give food away. He's running a restaurant."

Boyd smiled again. "Come on, Frank. You bring pies home all the time."

"If they're a mistake, sure," Frank said. "If we burn one or someone stiffs us on an order, but we don't make that many mistakes."

"You worked today, right?"

"Yeah," Frank said.

"So you got tips, right? Between tips and your check Friday we'll be good."

Frank snorted. "I made ten bucks in tips today, Boyd. I worked the lunch shift, and people in this town hold on to nickels and dimes like they're gold when they're at work. Anyway, I need gas for tomorrow. So that means we're eating peanut butter for dinner. Fuck you, man."

Boyd held his hands up. "All right, all right, don't get so mad. What about your mom? Will she hook us up with some dinner?"

"You're lucky she lets you live here with me after you stole her back pills. It's not about dinner, Boyd. It's about always being broke. We don't have groceries because you gave all your damn money to Skillet. That's fucked up, man. You have to snap out of this. We can't afford for you to sit around here and get lit all the time. I cover the utilities and you cover the rent. We're supposed to split the groceries and you're out of money."

Boyd licked his lips and took a pull on the water bottle balanced between his legs. "If we're short, you know what we can do." He gave Frank a sideways glance.

Frank just looked at him. "What? Pull that job Skillet was talking about? Fuck that noise. That sonofabitch doesn't know anything. If he's setting up a job, then you know it'll end up being some sideways shit."

"Come on, it'll be easy, man. He said the guy's at work all day and he lives alone. We buzz in, grab what's there to grab, and we get out. Easy."

"Then why isn't Skillet doing it, huh? An easy score like that, why doesn't his worthless ass just go do it? You ever think of that?"

"Come on, he's running a business, you know? He's gotta be home. Besides, he gets a cut just for setting it up."

Frank just looked at him and took another bite of his sandwich. Boyd smiled. "Come on, dude. You work Wednesday, right? We'll go over Wednesday morning, grab whatever is there and go right to Skillet's. He pays us and you have plenty of money for Black Friday shopping. You can get a big flat screen."

Frank considered it. Skillet had paid decently for the stuff they boosted before. If he didn't, Frank wouldn't take the risk of breaking in anywhere. He knew the dealer kept some stuff in his garage. That was one of the reasons his ridiculous black pickup was always parked outside, no matter what the weather. He looked at the last bite of his sandwich and his stomach rumbled.

"All right," he sighed.

"There he is," Boyd said.

"Calm down," Frank said. "Let's call Skillet and see if Wednesday is a good day. I want to be sure about everything. I don't feel like spending Thanksgiving in jail."

Boyd nodded. "Okay, man. Let's give him a call."

• • •

Skillet hung up with Frank and Boyd and dialed another number. It rang twice and a guy named Harvey answered.

"Yo, Skillet," he said. "What's up?"

"Hey, Harv," Skillet said. "What are you doing this fine evening?"

"Just watching TV, man. What are you doing?"

"Little of the same. Hey, the reason I called, you remember that thing?"

There was silence for a moment. "Not sure what you're talking about, Skillet."

Skillet held his phone and stared at it. He counted to three before he spoke again. "How many things we talk about, Harv?"

"Last time I was over your place we were watching a Cavs game and you said LeBron was going to get them into the playoffs and you wanted to get tickets to see a game. You talking about that? You got tickets? I'm in, man, just let me know when."

Skillet grimaced and his voice rose. "No, Harv, I don't have Cavs tickets. Christ almighty, man, the other thing, remember?"

"Skillet, you got to calm down, man. I can't have you calling me and yelling at me about some shit when I don't even know what you're talking about. Just calm down and get yourself straight, okay?"

Skillet kicked the coffee table, and it threatened to tip over. The Hungry Man Salisbury Steak he had heated up for dinner skated to the edge and stopped before dropping off. Luckily, his Pepsi was on the end table next to the sofa. He took another deep breath, rubbed his hand over his shaved head and wondered why he had to deal with brain-dead assholes. "Harv, I need you to listen to me. This is important. You listening?"

"I'm all ears, man. Lay it on me."

"Okay, when you were over here last time—"

"Watching the Cavs, yeah, I remember, man."

"Harv!"

"Sorry, Skillet, I was trying to be clear."

"S'all good, man. Just listen." He waited a moment in case Harv wanted to mention the Cavs game again. He was silent, so Skillet continued. "Okay, we talked about seeing the Cavs, but we also spoke about something else. A business opportunity, right? You remember that?"

There was silence for a few seconds and Skillet worried the call had dropped. "You still there, Harv?"

"Oh, yeah, now I remember. That thing about how the guy from work helped me fix my car. I got you, man. I got you."

"Yeah," Skillet said. "Now you got it. Okay, let me ask you, is Wednesday morning good? Are you guys working?"

"Yeah, we're working. We're off Thursday and Friday for Thanksgiving, you know, but we work regular on Wednesday."

Skillet let out a deep breath. "Okay, well then, Wednesday it is."

"Really?"

"Yep, in the morning," Skillet said. "I'll call you Wednesday night, okay? Tell you all about it."

"Yeah, man, that'll work. Don't forget about me."

"Okay, take it easy, man. See you later."

"Hey, hey, before you go?"

"Yeah, Harv, what's up?"

"Were you serious about getting those tickets?"

Eleven

O n the Wednesday before Thanksgiving, Amy Sashman was sitting on a wooden folding chair in the breakroom at Degman's Hardware, staring at her phone. Missy came in and put a couple quarters into the pop machine and pulled out a Diet Coke when it dropped. She was a couple years older than Amy and worked the paint counter. She sat down at Amy's table. "What's up?"

Amy looked over at her. "Oh, nothing, it's always nice to be reminded men are jerks once in a while."

"Uh-oh, did Jeremy do something?"

Amy shrugged her shoulders. "I'm not sure. We were supposed to have dinner this evening, and he just texted me that he won't be back in town until later tonight. I don't know why, though. It's only a four-hour drive from Pontiac. He should get here in plenty of time to go out."

"He travels a lot, right?" Missy asked. "It's probably just work."

"He did say he got pulled into a meeting this afternoon so he has to stay longer."

"Well, there you go," Missy said. She sipped her Diet Coke. "You know, he seems like a decent guy. Good job, anyway."

Amy looked at her phone again. "You know, he normally calls. I don't mind a text, but if he's going to miss a date he could at least call me. He's been spending a lot of time away from home lately and instead of phone calls, now we're down to texts."

Missy looked at her and her brows knitted together. "You think he's screwing around? Like maybe he has someone up there? Would he do that?"

Amy sniffed a little. "I don't know, maybe? How can you tell? How would I know?"

"With men? It's like the old joke. If their lips are moving they're lying."

"You've had guys cheat on you?"

"Sure, you haven't?"

Amy shrugged again. "I don't know. I haven't had so many serious relationships that I've had the opportunity to be cheated on. Jeremy is a good guy. At least, he's never given me a reason to suspect it from him before."

"But?"

Amy turned and looked right at her. "But lately he's been getting texts at all hours. He says they're for work, but it's crazy to think work is sending him messages at nine and ten o'clock at night."

"He has customers, though, right? Could it be them?"

Amy's face tightened up. "I don't think so. Sometimes he reads them and smiles, especially when he thinks I don't see him. We've been sitting on the couch watching TV and I've told him to take the phone out of his pocket because the damn thing vibrates so much. I don't know, it just doesn't seem like work."

Missy nodded and pointed a finger at her. "Pay attention to those feelings. Back when I was dating this guy Kyle, before I got married, he had one of his old girlfriends sending him messages constantly."

"Yeah?"

"Oh, yeah," Missy said. "She wanted to get back together with him and she was such a slut. She'd send him all these dirty text messages, pictures of her tits and ass, it was so pathetic."

"How did you find out?"

"Well, I noticed he was getting all these messages, and Kyle didn't have a job where work was texting him. I mean, he worked at the chicken place out by the highway. Anyway, I noticed he was getting all these messages, phone buzzing all the time. Whoever it was wasn't trying to keep anything a secret. So one day when he was in the shower I grabbed his phone and looked through it."

"And you saw all the texts and pictures?"

"Oh, hell, yes," Missy said. "There were thousands of messages and a ton of pictures."

"What did you do?"

"I got dressed and took off. I thought, if he wants that skank he can have her. I knew I could find someone better. You have to be careful about that, you know?"

"What?" Amy said.

"Don't settle for those kinds of assholes. Get someone good. If they'll cheat once, they'll cheat again. You find out Jeremy is cheating on you, you drop his ass. That's my advice."

"I don't know."

"What about Tim?"

Amy looked up. "What about him?"

"Oh, are you pretending you don't know he's crushing on you?"

Amy felt her face get warm. "What do you mean?"

Missy laughed. "Come on, everyone knows. There's no way you don't."

"He's never said anything," Amy said.

"He wouldn't. Tim's a nice guy and he knows you and Jeremy are serious so he's doing this whole Jim and Pam from *The Office* thing. I think he's just waiting to see how things go with you guys."

"He does come up and talk to me a lot."

"No kidding. He doesn't do that with anyone else. Haven't you ever noticed he's not dating?"

Amy chewed on her yogurt spoon. "I tried to set him up, but he didn't take me up on it."

"You may not want to send him too far away, especially if Jeremy's screwing around."

"I don't know that he is. It's just a feeling. I'm probably overreacting."

Missy got up. "Well, I'm just saying you could do worse than Tim if you find out Jeremy's messing around. Either you trust him or you don't. That's what it all comes down to." She pitched her can into the recycling bin. "I have to get back to it. Tate will be looking for me."

"Yeah, me too," Amy said and she stood up. "Hey, have you seen Tim today?"

"He's off. Tate has Mac doing deliveries with one of the stock boys."

• • •

Tim parked his truck at the curb and walked up to Red Fannie Florist through the snow gathering on the sidewalk. It was already a few inches deep, and the forecast was for another four to six inches. The small shop was located in a dark brick building like many others along Main Street in Hogan. Yellow wood trim ran up the façade, around the door and the shop sign. The large picture window was full of colorful floral displays and wreaths for the upcoming holidays. Tim heard a bell tinkle over the glass when he walked in. A solid woman about fifty years old with fire-engine-red hair came out of the back carrying a vase of colorful flowers. She wore a cheerful yellow blouse, blue jeans, and a bright orange apron. Tim thought the flowers might be carnations, but he wasn't sure. He didn't know much about flowers. She smiled at Tim and he waved.

"Hey, Glenda, how are you doing?" he said.

"Just fine, Tim. How are you doing?" She set the bouquet down on the counter and grabbed a small card from a nearby display.

"Oh, I'm good." He looked around the shop. A couple was in the corner at a small table being helped by one of Glenda's assistants. He couldn't remember her name. They were looking through a book that held wedding designs. "You look busy."

"It's the holidays," Glenda said. "Everyone likes to send flowers this time of year." She wrote a short message on the card and slipped it into an envelope. Next she picked up a small plastic pitchfork, put the envelope into the tines and placed it in the floral arrangement. "Did Charlie send you over about ads? I was going to call him next week."

"No," Tim said, "nothing like that. I'm actually here about a story we're working on. Do you have a moment, or would you like me to come back? I don't want to keep you from anything." Tim started to rethink his plan to do this on the day before Thanksgiving.

"Oh, don't worry about it. Why don't you come back here, though? I'll keep going while we talk." Tim followed her into the back of the shop.

The room was bigger than Tim thought. A large cooler full of flow-ers ran along one wall. Glenda slid the door open and placed the vase inside. Tim saw one side was filled with completed arrangements for pickup or delivery. The other side held flowers waiting to be sold. A large table filled the middle of the room, the top littered with cuttings, tissue paper, and a small shears. Vases and boxes of various designs and uses were stacked underneath. A small office and restrooms were on the other side of the room.

Glenda pointed to a stool at the edge of the table. "Have a seat. I hope you don't mind if I keep working."

"No, that's fine," Tim said as he settled onto the stool and pulled out his notebook. "If this is a bad time I can come back."

Glenda already had a vase up on the table and was looking at an order form. "There won't be any good time between now and New Year's, so we might as well do it now. What's your story about? Small business and the holidays?"

"No, it's nothing like that." Tim hesitated. It had been months since he sat down to interview someone and that time had been with a politician, a city councilor. He took a deep breath. "Some of the small businesses in town have been receiving anonymous letters that are obscene or threatening in nature. I'm canvassing small businesses to see how widespread the problem is. Have you received anything like that?"

Glenda was holding a bunch of roses in one hand and a pair of shears in the other. Her face had changed, and when she looked at Tim, it was with a look that was sharper than the edge of her shears.

"Glenda? Can I assume you've received letters like that?"

She set the flowers down and put the shears beside them. Then she smoothed her orange apron with both hands, top to bottom. "These letters, other people have gotten them?"

Tim nodded slowly. "Yes. I've been able to find a couple businesses but I've just started looking into it. So you've received some?"

Glenda picked up the shears and played with them, standing them on their curved end twirling them into the thick wooden top of the table. "Yeah, Tim, we've received some letters like that."

"Do you have them?" Tim said. "I'd like to see them if you do."

"Why?"

"I would like to see if they match the others."

"Hmmph. There aren't likely to be too many people like whoever is writing these." Glenda stood still for a moment, twirling the shears. Tim was afraid she was going to tell him to leave. Clearly, she was uncomfortable speaking about the letters. "Wait here, okay?"

"Sure."

Glenda set down the shears and went into the small office. Tim heard a metal file cabinet open and then bang shut a few seconds later. Glenda reappeared with a manila file folder. She walked over to the table, took a seat on her stool and tossed the file on the table to Tim.

"They started almost a year ago," she said.

Tim picked up the folder and opened it. There was a small stack of now-familiar-looking letters inside. Each just had a sentence typed in the center of the page. Picking one at random, Tim read the message.

Being a florist is the kind of thing I would expect from a whore who couldn't hold a real job.

Tim noticed a couple envelopes in the file. He looked at them and saw they were the same as the ones Charlie and Tate had received. No return address, and the letter had been addressed to Glenda's attention. He closed the file.

"Yeah," he said with a quiet voice, "this appears to be the same guy."

She looked at him with unexpected steel in her gaze. "Do you know who he is? I'd like to meet the SOB." Glenda held the shears in her hand and Tim imagined what she could prune with them if properly motivated.

"No, I'm sorry, I don't know who he is yet. Like I said, we're just starting to look into this. I can tell you that you are not the only one receiving these. Other business owners in town have gotten letters like this."

"By 'like this,' you mean the letters are mean-spirited? Whoever this guy is, he seems to have a problem with women, I'll tell you that. I've never been called a whore before in my life, and I can sure as hell tell you I wouldn't put up with it if someone said it to my face."

"I can imagine," Tim said. He picked up his notebook and uncapped his pen. "Can I ask you a few questions?"

Glenda picked up the flowers again and began trimming the ends. "If it'll help put a name to this guy? Sure."

"When did you start receiving the letters?"

Glenda thought about it. "The beginning of the year, around Valentine's Day, I think. They just started showing up once a month or so."

Tim started making notes.

"Do you have any idea if there was a precipitating event?"

"Like what?" Glenda was now stripping thorns from the roses with some other tool that enclosed the stems. She pulled and thorns dropped to the table.

"Something like an angry customer? Here in the shop or out on a delivery? Maybe someone complained about their flowers or the price?"

Glenda shook her head. "I considered that when I got the first one, but we really haven't gotten many complaints. I'm not trying to brag, but we do a nice job here and we're not too expensive." She pulled down and stripped thorns from another rose. "Most people seem to like us."

"Is there anything in any of the letters that would lead you to believe you know the sender?"

She stopped and looked at him. "Are you talking to me in jail through thick glass?"

"No."

"Then I don't know who this guy is. If I did, I might be incarcerated."

"You think the writer is a man?" Tim said. "Why is that?"

She gestured at the folder with her stripping tool. "The letters are misogynistic. Almost every one of them calls me a whore or some derivative of it. Most of them say a woman shouldn't be running a business or some other nonsense." She pointed again with the stripper for emphasis. "Those are being written by a man."

Tim looked in the file again. He picked up the letter he had read earlier. "This one references you not holding down a 'real job.' Do you know what he's talking about?"

Glenda shrugged. "I'm not sure. I worked a few different places before I bought this place."

"You bought this shop? I thought you opened it originally. It's been here as long as I can remember."

"Oh, well, thanks a lot, Tim. You really know how to make a woman feel young."

"Sorry."

"No, don't worry about it. I'm just snapping because of those letters." She dropped the roses into a vase. "I bought this place about five years ago, when Fannie Heldinger wanted to retire. She's the one who opened it."

"Oh, so it's her name on the shop."

"Yeah, I didn't change it because she had a good reputation, and I wanted to keep her customers. She had red hair, too, used to keep it up in this big beehive 'do."

"I get it."

"People get all kinds of naughty ideas about the name, and me, I suppose. I just let them think what they want." She threw a wink at him. Tim felt himself flush. "Anyway, about your other jobs. Were you fired from any of them? If he's referencing you losing a job, maybe it's someone who knew you from there?"

Glenda added baby's breath to the roses in the vase. "I don't know, that was such a long time ago. I did a lot of things. After school I worked in a lamp factory making parking lot bulbs, I worked in a few stores, a liquor drive-thru, and I bartended. Some of those places I left on good terms, some I didn't. The longest job I ever had was with Ohio Axle. I took the buyout they offered and used the money to buy this place."

"So nothing that stands out as being particularly bad?"

Glenda thought again. "No, nothing I can think of. I'm sure I would remember if I made someone mad enough to write letters about it. Besides, think about how many years you're talking about."

Tim considered that. "You said you've owned the shop for five years?"

"That's right."

"That would be a long time to hold a grudge."

Glenda nodded as she finished up the arrangement of roses. "That's true, but some folks are like that. They never let go of some wrongs, no matter how much time goes by."

"Do you think there is anyone like that in your past, Glenda? Anyone holding a grudge?"

"Tim, I can honestly say I don't think I've ever made anyone that angry. Whoever this is, they've got a screw loose."

"One last question?"

"Go ahead." She turned to him.

"Have you ever called the police? Have you ever reported the letters to the authorities?"

She sighed. "You bet I have. After the fourth one I figured I had a real nut on my hands, so I took them down to the station and filed a report."

"Did the police do anything?"

"They filed the report, made copies of the letters and attached them to it. They told me to follow up if anything else happened, like strange people around the shop or anything else odd. Every couple months I get a call from one of the detectives. It didn't seem like there's much they can do." They heard the bell over the door tinkle.

He slipped off his stool. "Well, thanks for your time. I really do appreciate it. I may be back in touch before we write the story."

"Okay."

"Can I make copies of these?" He held up the file.

"Yeah, there's a copy machine right there," she said, pointing at a cream-colored machine in the corner. "Help yourself. Just leave the originals here on the prep table."

Tim made copies and stuffed them in his backpack before gathering up the originals and putting them back in their file folder. He walked out onto the sales floor and saw Glenda with a customer, smiling and talking politely. She waved and he waved back as he left.

Next up was Cello's Muffler, half a block down. He zipped up his jacket and pulled an orange Browns winter cap down over his ears. The sidewalk was mostly clear, shoveled by the shopkeepers along the main drag, but it would be covered soon the way the snow was falling. He got to Cello's shop and stomped his feet on the mat in front of the door. The shop was older and hadn't been painted or even cleaned in a while. It had a lime-green glass sign out front. He could hear air tools whining and saw a couple cars up on lifts inside, and more were parked outside. He walked in through a glass door. An older man stood behind the counter on the phone and gave him a quick look. Thin and rangy, Gordon Cello had been a fixture in Hogan for decades. He was balding, with a ring of gray hair around his head and wiry glasses. He wore dark-green Dickie work clothes with a Cello's Muffler patch over the left pocket. Tim knew him by sight only because he'd been up to the *Shopper* offices a few times, and every time he'd been wearing the same outfit. He removed his hat as warm air blew over him from a powerful duct in the ceiling. Tim stood at the counter and tried to look busy while Cello finished his call.

"Nope, closed Friday. Everybody's off. Most of my guys are travel-ing," he said. He rolled his eyes in Tim's direction as the person on the other end of the phone spoke.

"I understand, but no one is going to be here," he said again. "My wife wants to go shopping. Believe me, I'd rather be here bending pipe. How about Saturday? We're open until two." More talking and more eye rolling. "Well, I don't know what to tell you, then. How about next week? No? Well, figure out what you want to do and give me a call back." He hung up the phone.

"Sorry about all that," he said. "Everyone thinks a holiday is the time to get mufflers fixed and brake jobs. Well, too frigging bad. I've got plans. I'll tell you, it's been worse since Jerry Donovan died and AA closed down. We can't pick up all the slack. Now, what can I do for you?"

Tim hesitated. "Mr. Cello, I don't know if you remember me, but my name is Tim Abernathy and I work over at the *Hogan Shopper* with Charlie."

Cello squinted at him. "Yeah, I think I've seen you in there. What can I do for you?"

"Well, we're working on a story and if you have a moment, I'd like to speak with you." Tim could hear air tools whining again in the shop behind the counter. "I promise, it won't take long."

"Yeah, what's it about? Taxes? I have to tell you, mine are too damn high."

"No," Tim said. "Actually, it's about anonymous letters some business owners have been receiving."

"What kind of letters?" Cello said.

"Well, they're not signed and they're usually obscene, sometimes intimidating. Have you received anything like that?"

Cello stood up straight. "No, I haven't, and let me tell you, if I did, I'd kick somebody square in their ass."

Tim nodded. "Right, well, we're trying to figure out who's writing them."

"What do the letters say?"

"Well, usually they contain a complaint about something related to the business, and then there is usually an insult to the recipient."

Cello looked at him so long with such a hard stare, Tim actually took a step back. "What kind of bullshit is that? Writing letters and not signing your name. That's just someone with too much time on their hands, that's what that is."

Tim nodded again. "I agree, sir. I'm just happy you haven't received any." Cello kept staring at him, not saying anything. "Well, I'll just get going, then. I have quite a few more stops to make today."

"Charlie getting these letters over at the *Shopper*?"

Tim put his notebook away and pulled his hat back on. "He is one of the people getting them. A few other business owners have as well. I can't really tell you which ones."

"The one's he's getting, they making cracks at him because he's gay?"

"Well, I can't get into the specific content, but you can imagine what they say."

"Well, Charlie's a decent guy, even if he does swing in that direction. You don't know who's doing this?"

"Not yet, no. We just started looking into it. You know, if you hear anything, maybe you could give us a call." Tim produced a business card and laid it on the counter.

Cello waved it off. "I've got your number. I write you enough checks for ads, don't I?"

"Sure, but that one has my cell phone number, in case it's after hours or something, you'll be able to get in touch."

Cello took the card and put it in his breast pocket without looking at it. "All right, I hear anything about pervert letter writers I'll give you a call. I have to get back to work."

Time waved, happy to get away. "Okay, see you."

"Yeah," Cello said and disappeared into the shop. Tim stepped back into the cold. He flipped open the notebook and moved down the sidewalk to the next stop on the list.

Twelve

Frank rolled over and looked at the clock. It said WED 10:37 A.M. and he jumped up, almost tripping in the blankets. He stumbled from his room into the hall and headed for the bathroom.

"Boyd, get up," he said as he passed his roommate's bedroom. "We're late. Come on, man."

When he came out of the bathroom, Boyd was standing in the hall, bleary eyed and sporting a serious case of bed head. "It's snowing," Boyd said as he stumbled toward the bathroom.

Frank went back into his room and picked up a pair of jeans from the floor. He parted the curtains with one hand. Boyd was right, he saw. There was at least four inches of snow on the ground and it was still coming down.

"Shit."

The snow was going to make things harder. They'd driven by the place last night and could barely make out the house at the end of the longest damn driveway Frank had ever seen. Boyd knocked on his doorframe.

"You ready to go?"

Frank turned and nodded. "Yeah, just let me warm up the car."

"Is the snow going to be a problem?"

"Maybe," Frank said. "It all depends on whether the guy cleared his driveway this morning. If he didn't, we call it off. I'm not getting stuck at the house we're trying to rob."

Boyd sighed. "I know."

"Look, we do it smart, okay? There's no reason to get caught while we're trying to dig our car out."

"I said I know. You don't have to treat me like a kid."

"I'm not. I just don't want to be stuck and have your gimpy ass trying to push us free. With your back, you're next to useless in that situation."

"Whatever, man. Can we just get going? We should have been gone and back already."

They walked downstairs. "You're blaming me?" Frank said. "You found that bottle of vodka in the freezer."

"You were supposed to set the alarm."

"Let's just get this done. I don't want to argue about the damn alarm."

They pulled their jackets on, and Frank started the Honda while Boyd brushed it off. Frank looked through the hatchback. The tools they had put in the car last night were still there. Boyd limped around the passenger side and got in.

"Okay, you ready?" Frank said.

"Yeah, let's go."

"I don't like it being so close to our place," Frank said. "What if the cops come by and ask us if we saw anything?"

"It's almost a mile away," Boyd said. "We just say we didn't see anything. I don't think I knew the house was even there until we drove past last night. It's way back and it's got all those trees between it and the road."

"It's just close, is all. There's a reason you don't do this close to where you live. Those other houses we went into? All of them were in the city, far away from us."

"Yeah, but most of them were places where you delivered a pizza."

"Shut up and let me concentrate."

Frank navigated through the snow without too much trouble. The Honda was front-wheel drive and sure footed in the gathering snow. They crept along at twenty-five, which was safe for the conditions. It looked like the plows hadn't made it out this far yet. After a few minutes, he pulled up to the driveway and turned to Boyd.

"You ready?" he said. The driveway was clear. Neat drifts of snow lined the length of the long driveway and a single set of tire prints led out to the road. "It looks like he plowed."

Boyd looked around nervously. "Yeah, man, do it. I don't want anyone to see us sitting here."

Frank turned into the driveway.

• • •

At 11:15, Ricky flagged down Bob with his clipboard. He stopped his forklift, carrying a load of metal bins, in the aisle. "What's up?"

"The plant is calling it at half a day," Ricky said. "The weather is getting bad and tomorrow's Thanksgiving, so we get to go home at 11:45."

"Good," Bob said. "Do we still get paid for the whole day?"

"Not unless you want to stay here all day."

"That's bullshit."

Ricky shook his head and started walking away. "You're never happy, Ellstrom. Have a good turkey day."

Bob put the forklift in gear and whispered under his breath, "Blow it out your ass."

• • •

Frank made his way slowly up the driveway, careful not to slide off into the trees. He stopped in front of the house. They looked to see if there were any lights on or if anyone looked out the windows.

"I don't see anyone," Boyd said.

"You think we should knock?" Frank said. "Just to be sure?"

"Skillet said the guy is at work until after three."

Frank turned and looked at him with a raised eyebrow. "Since when do we trust Skillet?"

"We're here, aren't we? Let's just get into the barn and get what we came for."

Frank eased the Honda around the house toward the barn. It was old and although it could use a fresh coat of paint, it looked solid. The snow was deeper here and hadn't been plowed. He stopped in front of the doors and looked at Boyd.

"What?"

Frank pointed at the doors. "They're padlocked. Get the bolt cutters and cut that thing off."

Boyd sighed and squirmed in his seat. "You do it, man. My back hurts."

Frank looked at him for another moment. Boyd looked back toward the house.

"You're unbelievable, you know?" Frank said. "I'm not doing this all myself."

"My back hurts."

"Whatever. Do you think you can pull the car in or will that strain it too much?"

Boyd looked at him and held his eyes for a beat. "Yeah, I can do that."

Frank reached into the back and grabbed a pair of heavy red bolt cutters. He got out of the car and walked up to the barn doors. Boyd slipped behind the wheel and shut the door.

The barn doors were held closed by a heavy-duty hasp with an impressive-looking padlock. The whole works was covered by a piece of rubber nailed to the door to keep the weather off. Frank hefted the bolt cutters and got the blades over the rounded shackle. He gripped one handle of the cutters in each hand and pulled them toward each other. The lock held. He grunted and tried again and lost his grip on one side.

"Sonofabitch," he said and set the cutters down, leaning them against the doors. He pulled a pair of gloves from the pockets of his brown Carhartt knock-off jacket and picked up the cutters.

"Let's try this again."

He reset the bolt cutters and set his feet firmly. This time they bit right through the shackle. He grabbed the lock, turned it and popped it off the hasp. He drew back his arm and fired it off into the woods in a high arc. He looked around to make sure they were alone and, satisfied, pulled the doors open. It was difficult to drag them through the snow, but he managed to get them open wide enough to pull the car in. Boyd sat in the car watching him.

He walked into the barn and, seeing it was wide enough for the car, waved Boyd in. He thought about closing the doors but figured that anyone coming home would see their tracks in the snow anyway. Boyd got out of the car.

"That lock was tough, huh?"

Frank nodded. "Yeah, and the doors were heavy, too. Just as well you stayed in the car."

"My back really does hurt," Boyd said. "I must have slept funny."

"We can talk about your back later, man. Let's just get what we came for, okay?"

They looked around and Boyd pointed toward one of the stalls. "Over there. Skillet said to look for the cabinets."

Frank followed his line of sight. "Yeah, that's got to be them."

They walked over and saw a couple of red Craftsman rolling tool-boxes, along with a couple metal cabinets. Frank pulled one open and saw power tools. They were stacked in their cases on shelves.

"These look good," he said. "Nice and clean. We better get a good price from Skillet."

Boyd was next to the toolboxes with a drawer open. "Take a look at this. All lined up and clean. You ever see tools this clean? My dad was a maniac about keeping his garage straightened up, but even he never kept his tools this nice."

Frank looked over his shoulder. "Cool, let's get it loaded up. This is taking too long."

Boyd shut the drawer and grabbed a handle on the side. He pulled on it and the whole thing threatened to tip over. Frank grabbed it and braced it. He pointed to the casters.

"Wheel locks, dude."

Boyd nodded. "Oh, yeah." He kicked the lever on the casters with his foot and the toolbox rolled smoothly over the wooden floorboards. He pulled it around the back of the Honda and opened the hatchback.

"Pack it in there," Frank said. "I want to get as much as we can. With Christmas coming this stuff will move fast, so let's make the most of it."

Metal clanked as Boyd shoveled handfuls of wrenches, sockets, and screwdrivers into the open hatchback. Frank walked over and started packing in power tools.

"If we leave the cases here," Boyd said, "we'll fit more in the car."

Franks shook his head. "No, the cases are good. The tools move faster with them and we'll get more for them."

It took ten minutes to load the Honda. Frank looked at the back of the car sagging under the weight of the load.

"You know," he said. "You don't realize how much this kind of stuff weighs until you try to move a bunch of it at once."

"Maybe it will help with the snow," Boyd said.

"Yeah. Okay, let me just get this covered up and we can go." Frank pulled a dark blue blanket from the floor behind the driver's seat and spread it over the haul in the back.

Boyd smiled. "Yeah, we don't look suspicious at all. Couple of guys in an ass-dragging Honda with a blanket covering up the hatch. If a cop sees us he's going to think we've got a kidnapping victim back here."

Frank shrugged. "It's better than someone being behind us and seeing a mechanic's toolset. Back out and I'll get the doors."

Boyd climbed into the driver's seat and started the car, the noise echoing in the quiet barn. He backed out and Frank swung the doors shut. He closed the hasp and pulled the rubber cover down as much as he could. He heard wheels spin behind him and he turned around.

The front wheels spun again. Boyd had the car backed into the deep snow trying to turn it around. Frank held up his hands. "Hold on, stop. Don't dig in."

Boyd popped the door open. "Sorry. I was trying to get turned around here."

"Just get out of the way and I'll get it. I have to work this afternoon and I can't have you screwing up the car. I can get it out, just give me a minute." Boyd held up his hands and walked away from the car. Frank got behind the wheel.

● ● ●

Boyd looked at the house. It had to be empty. They'd made enough noise to wake anyone inside, and if anyone was home, the cops would have been here by now. He walked over to the side door and peered in. The kitchen was empty. Tidy enough, clean like someone took care of it. He tried the knob but it was locked. He looked over his shoulder. Frank was still messing around but he'd have the car free in a moment. Boyd slipped a small crescent wrench from his jacket pocket and smacked it against one of the windows in the nine-light door. It shattered and he looked inside. Nobody came to investigate, not even a dog. No alarm rang. He reached in, found the deadbolt and twisted it, then the lock on the door knob. He opened the door and went in.

• • •

Frank dropped the transmission into low and lightly gave the car some gas. The tires got a grip with the extra torque of the low gear and the car inched forward. He pulled up to the house and looked for Boyd. Then he saw the open side door.

"Oh, come on," he said. He got out of the car and left it running. He jumped over the two steps in front of the door and walked into the kitchen. Boyd was looking in canisters on the counter.

"What are you doing?" Frank said. "We agreed to hit the barn, get the tools and get out of here."

"Don't sweat it," Boyd said. "The guy's at work."

"We've got what we came for. Let's go."

"You know, we sell that stuff in the car to Skillet and we only get what he gives us. Take a couple minutes and make sure there's no cash in here, okay? Everybody keeps a little cash around, especially people out in the township. They like to have a little extra on hand." Striking out at the canisters, he pulled open a drawer and pawed through it.

"Pizza money?" Frank said.

"You know it. Why don't you go check upstairs? Hit the bedrooms."

"I don't know," Frank said.

"Two minutes. You don't find anything, we're gone."

Frank thought about it. "Okay, two minutes." He walked fast down the short hall through the living room and ran up the stairs. There was only one bedroom made up like someone was living in it. The others were bare of furniture. He pulled open the top dresser drawer and saw a small wooden box. He opened it and smiled. There was a wad of bills in there. He grabbed them and ran back downstairs.

"You know, Boyd? You're actually pretty good at this." He walked through the living room and into the dining room. Boyd was standing at the table holding a stack of papers and reading them.

Frank stopped in the doorway and flipped through the bills. "Hey, did you hear me? I found about a grand up there. Good thinking, man."

"Dude, check this out," Boyd said. "This is fucked up."

Frank came off the doorframe. "What?"

Boyd handed him some of the papers. "These letters. They're all obscene. Read them."

Frank looked at one.

When you're on the road in your truck your wife fucks Jimmy and Charlie at the same time in room twenty-seven at the Night Night Inn.

"Whoa, what is this?" Frank said. "Are they all like this?"

Boyd nodded. "Yeah, there's about a dozen of them, and they're all nasty."

Frank looked at the dining room table. A typewriter sat at one end with a stack of paper and envelopes. He picked them up. Some were filled out already with typewritten names and addresses. He held one up. "No return address."

"We should get out of here," Boyd said. "This is kind of creepy."

"You know, Rocco got a letter like this a few months ago down at the pizza shop. It said something about his wife and he was really pissed."

"You think this was the guy?"

Frank raised his eyebrows. "Maybe. Hell of a coincidence if it isn't."

"Come on, man," Boyd said. "Let's get out of here."

A clock in the living room struck twelve and they both jumped.

"Yeah," Frank said. "Let's go."

• • •

Bob Ellstrom pulled into the Green Barn Drive-Thru and waited patiently for the car ahead of him to finish. He had four and a half days off and wanted to enjoy them, so he figured he needed at least a case of Bud Light to get started. He wasn't especially looking forward to Thanksgiving, since he would be alone, so he figured a little brew therapy was just what he needed. Thankfully, the drive-thru was close to his house. It was only a little ways up Route 17 to Owl North Road, and then a few minutes until he was home.

• • •

Frank drove slowly down the driveway and the car bounced over ruts, riding low because of the heavy load in the back.

"He really needs to pave this thing or grade it," Frank said.

"What do you care?" Boyd said. "We ain't ever coming back."

"True, I just don't want to leave my muffler here." Frank looked at the clock. It was five after twelve. He did some math in his head.

"Hey, Boyd, I don't have time to take you home."

"Why not?"

"I have to be at work at one," Frank said. "That means I have to get over to Skillet's place, get this stuff out of the car and then get to work. Rocco has been on me about being late. He said if it happens again he might fire me. Taking you home is out of the way and the weather isn't getting any better."

"Aw, man, what am I supposed to do?"

Frank shrugged and pulled up to the end of the driveway. "Just hang at Skillet's house. I'll get you after work."

"How late are you working?"

"Tomorrow's Thanksgiving and the weather sucks, so we're going to be busy tonight. I'll probably be on until eleven. I hope so, anyway. I need the tips."

"I don't want to stay at Skillet's that long."

"Well, I don't think we have any choice," Frank said as he started to turn left onto Owl North.

"Wait, wait, I'll just walk home," Boyd said.

"You serious? There's five inches of snow out there and it's getting cold."

Boyd pulled a dirty Browns hat on and got gloves out of his pockets. "Don't sweat it. Just go to Skillet's and drop the stuff. It's only a mile or so home from there. I can handle it."

Frank looked at the clock. "You sure?"

"You really think I can't walk a mile? Get out of here." Boyd opened the door and got out. "Don't let Skillet screw us on the price."

"Okay. You got your phone?"

Boyd patted his back pocket. "Yeah, call me when you get to work. Let me know how we made out." He slammed the door and started walking.

Frank made his left and rolled toward Skillet's place.

• • •

Bob paid for his Bud Light and put it on the passenger seat of the truck. He pulled forward, turned onto State Route 17 and saw Owl North Road a hundred yards away. He didn't even have to plow the driveway when he got home. He'd done it that morning, so the afternoon and evening were free.

• • •

Boyd walked down the shoulder of the road, trying to stay out of the deep drifts. He didn't have to worry about dodging traffic. There was no one out today. The world was silent, the kind of quiet that comes when the snow is deep and sound gets absorbed as soon as it's made. He pulled his phone from his back pocket and plugged in a set of earbuds. He thumbed through his music and selected My Chemical Romance, *The Black Parade*.

• • •

Bob drove slowly up Owl North Road, careful to keep the truck toward the center of the road. There were open storm ditches on both sides and the last thing he needed was to slide into one of them and then wait for a tow. It was clear the township plows hadn't made a pass since this morning. There weren't even many tracks in the snow. He saw someone walking on the side of the road, the kid in the yellow, green, and red eight-ball jacket again, the one who lived in the old Jensen place. Bob passed him and drove another minute before he saw his driveway.

He was thinking about what to watch on Netflix when he pulled up to the garage door and thumbed the button. He had started watching *Lost* and thought he might be able to squeeze in seasons two and three this weekend. He pulled the truck inside and grabbed his case of Bud.

The door from the garage went directly into the kitchen. He closed it behind him and set the beer on the counter. The bottles clinked inside the case and he bent to untie his boots. That's when he noticed the glass on the floor by the side door.

He looked around the kitchen, suddenly aware that he might not be alone. His hand went to the knives in the wooden block on the counter and he drew the largest one.

"If someone's in here, you better announce yourself," he said. His voice echoed and he didn't hear anything. "I have a gun and I'm calling the police." The only reply was more silence.

He moved into the living room, looked it over and moved to the bottom of the staircase. "Is anyone up there?"

The steps creaked as he slowly climbed them. His heart beat so hard, so very fast, that he was suddenly aware of being an overweight fifty-eight-year-old man. He swallowed hard when he got to the top of the stairs and then looked in the bathroom and the bedrooms. They were empty, but he saw the top drawer of his dresser open. He crossed to it in a few steps and saw the open, empty wooden box that held his rainy day fund.

"Sonofabitch!"

He turned and ran back down the stairs. The knife was in a tight grip in his hand. He was ready to use it but he didn't think anyone was here, not anymore. Realization dawned on him and he found himself racing for the dining room. He remembered what he'd done that morning. He'd woken up early, too late to go back to sleep but too early to go to work. He'd spent time writing letters.

The dining room table was in disarray. Clearly, someone had been in here looking through his things. His breathing slowed and he gripped the knife harder. The letters he'd written that morning were spread across the table. Some of the addressed envelopes were scattered on the floor. He slammed the knife into the dining room table. It stood straight up with the tip embedded in the wood.

He moved to the bookcase in the corner and found his laptop standing on end between some books. Whoever had been here had missed it. He opened the cover and booted up the machine. After an agonizing minute, the login screen displayed. He typed in his password and clicked the browser icon. The homepage was the provider for his camera system. He logged in and the page with his dozen cameras displayed. He looked at all of them and saw nothing moving outside the barn or the house. Whoever had been here was gone. He clicked on the camera pane pointed at the barn entrance and saw fresh tire tracks in the snow.

"No," he said. "No, no, no."

He clicked on one of the cameras inside the barn. He rewound the video file and saw a car parked inside the barn. A little Honda, it looked like. The image was relatively clear, with light from outside streaming in through the open doors. He watched as two figures moved from the stall holding his tools to the back of their hatchback. He slammed his fist down on the table.

"Who the fuck are you?" he said loudly enough that the sound echoed through the house. Then one of the figures turned and he saw a giant number eight on the back of his jacket. A magic eight-ball jacket.

"Are you kidding me?" He rewound the feed again and got up close to the screen. It was the kid from down the road, no doubt about it.

He raced back to the garage and started the truck. He was in such a hurry he almost forgot to raise the garage door. He stabbed the remote hanging on the sunvisor with his thumb and the door started to rise.

"Come on," he said as the door crawled up.

When it finally rose high enough he gunned the engine and backed out of the garage, whipping the big truck around in a wide arc to face the road. He engaged the four-wheel drive and tore off down the driveway, bounding over ruts and almost sliding into a tree as he got to the end. He slammed on the brakes and put the truck in park. He walked around the front of it and saw a couple sets of tracks in the snow. Smaller tires than the ones on his truck pulled out to the left. A set of footprints walked off to the right and went down the shoulder of the road. There were no footprints leading to the driveway from the left.

"Got you, got you, got you," he said and jumped back in truck. He put it in drive and roared out of the driveway, disregarding the snow. The truck's weight and the four-wheel drive kept him from sliding as he went the same direction as the footprints.

"No one is supposed to know," he said under his breath. "No one is supposed to know, goddammit."

He was coming up on the figure now, the colorful jacket standing out clearly against a background of brilliant white snow and the bare, dark trees that lined the road. He looked in the rearview mirror and didn't see anyone. The road ahead was also clear. The houses on Owl North Road were spread out, and none were along this stretch.

The kid was coming up on a hollow, which the road passed over with banked earth on both sides. There was a small creek at the bottom, with a large drainage pipe running under the road. Bob reached up and pushed the lever that controlled the plow's electric motor. The big metal blade rose up and angled right. The truck slipped onto the shoulder of the road. He pressed down on the gas pedal and the needle on the speedometer nudged over forty.

The kid never looked up. Right before impact, Bob saw that he had those things in his ears that all the kids seemed to have now. The blade hit him high, and Bob saw his head snap back over the top of it and then his skinny body was launched forward through the air into a tree.

"Nobody is supposed to know," Bob screamed and slammed on the brakes. In his haste to leave, however, he hadn't put on his seatbelt, and his head was driven into the steering wheel. The truck slid in the gravel and snow of the soft shoulder. The back end whipped around and the truck came to a rest with the front end facing back the way he had come.

Bob sat back in his seat, just a little dazed, and looked around. There was no one on the road but him. He looked in the rearview mirror and saw blood trickling down from a cut near his hairline. He opened up the glove box and pulled out a stack of napkins. They were emblazoned with the logo of Jupiter Joe's Burgers and Shakes. He held them to the cut and put the truck in reverse. He straightened it out and backed onto the shoulder. He got out and walked around the front. A bright red spot was in the center of the hood. Brain matter and pieces of bone were spattered halfway to the windshield.

The kid was at the bottom of the hollow, bent in an unnatural position. The tree he had been thrown into was stripped of bark in several spots, and a large bloodstain showed where his head had impacted. He was half in the creek, with his head and upper torso in the water. His legs were on the bank. Bob noticed he was wearing only one shoe. He looked around again. Bad weather or not, someone was going to come down the road eventually. He licked his lips and slid down the graded back of the hollow.

He approached the kid slowly, reaching out to him with one hand. He grabbed a leg and shook him.

"You alive?"

The scene remained quiet, Bob noticed. The only sound was the rumbling of the truck up on the shoulder of the road and the trickling of the water in the creek.

"No, you ain't alive," he said.

He noticed bulges in the kid's back pockets. He licked his lips again and gingerly reached for the first pocket. Two fingers pulled the kid's wallet out. He flipped it open and saw there was no cash. A license was in a small plastic window.

"Boyd Sashman," Bob read. "Well, Boyd, looks like your life of crime has come to an end." Bob looked around, nervous as hell that some hunter was going to come stumbling up on him. "Looks like everything about you has come to an end." He set the wallet in the snow beside him.

The next pocket held a phone. The screen showed paused music, probably because the headphones had pulled out of the jack when the kid fell down the bank. The phone was bad news. He had watched enough crime shows to know someone could track the damn thing. He held down the power button and the screen winked off after a moment. He flipped it over and peeled the back off. He took the battery out and chucked it into the woods. He looked around and found a large rock half buried in the creek bed. The water was cold and stung his hands, but he managed to pry it up, leaving a large, muddy hole under it. The phone and wallet went into the hole, and he let the rock slip back. He pressed down on it for good measure.

He went back to the body and took a look at the kid's head. There was a hole in the back, and Bob could see whorls of gray brain tissue. He retched loudly in the cold air, and it seemed to echo in the hollow. Vomit rose up in his throat, and he put a hand over his mouth to keep himself from spewing. He rolled Boyd over and saw that half his face was stripped away. One eye, punctured by a splinter of wood, lay on his cheek. The other stared up into the cloudy sky.

Bob took a deep breath through his nose and willed himself to calm down. He needed to do something with the body. Boyd was too heavy to haul back up to the road, and even if he could manage that, where was he going to hide him? Besides, what if someone drove by and saw him trying to lift a body into the bed of his truck? He looked at the drainpipe. It was large, big enough for a man to crawl through.

Bob stepped down into the cold creek water and it immediately flowed over his ankles and rose a few inches up his calves. He adjusted his stance and pulled his gloves on. Hooking his hands under Boyd's armpits, he pulled on him. The loose eye rolled around on Boyd's bloody cheek, and Bob again fought the urge to vomit. He looked away and tugged. The body was heavier than he would have expected, and he was soon breathing hard. Great puffs of warm breath came from his mouth as he wrestled Boyd toward the drainpipe. His heart was beating fast again, too fast, he realized, the way it did when he overdid it out in the yard or barn. He dropped Boyd with a small splash. The last thing he needed was a heart attack. He forced himself to wait a moment until his breathing slowed.

He grabbed Boyd again and started pulling. Lifting the young man was out of the question, but he managed to get him over to the corrugated drainpipe. It was full of litter from the woods. Sticks and leaves lay in the bottom of it, but that was all. He adjusted his grip on Boyd and pushed him into the pipe. It was much harder than he would have thought because of the kid's broken legs. They stuck out at odd angles and the body was limp, so it wasn't like shoving a log in. Bob wrestled with his legs for a moment but got them inside. He stood up, breathing hard and sweating from struggling so hard, even as his feet were numb from the creek water. He couldn't see Boyd's feet sticking out from the side, but he realized anyone coming up the hollow from the direction of the pipe's opening would see him. There was nothing to be done about it, he realized. Looking around, there was nothing to use to cover him. He started shivering and realized just how cold it was.

"Okay," he said. "Okay, just get out of here."

He stepped down into the creek and dipped his gloves in the icy water, washing the blood from them as best he could. Satisfied, he climbed back up to the truck, using small trees as handholds, but his numb feet made it hard. The truck was still running in the silent afternoon and snow had gathered on the windshield, most of it sliding down to the wiperblades due to the heat from the defroster.

He stood on the side of the road, gulping air and looking up and down the road. There was no one else around. "There's one more," he said. "There's still one more guy."

Bob got in the truck and used the wipers to clean the windshield. Breathing hard through his mouth, he glanced in the side mirrors and the rearview. He didn't see any other cars. Dropping the transmission into drive, he started to pull back onto the road.

A turkey walked out of the woods onto the road and he braked. It was a big one, he saw, black and brown. It strutted across the snowy road arrogantly, looking at Bob through the windshield. They stared at each other for a moment as the snow fell. Then Bob tapped the horn and the bird defiantly strutted into the woods on the other side. Bob let his foot off the brake and rolled home.

Thirteen

Frank pulled into Skillet's driveway at 12:30 p.m. The obnoxious black Ford was still in its spot outside the garage. The snow was slowing things down, and he didn't think he was going to get to work on time. Rocco was going to fire him if he didn't get this wrapped up quickly. He got out of the car and knocked on Skillet's back door. He saw movement behind the curtains and the door opened.

"Why you bangin' on my door like that?" Skillet said. Today he was dressed in raggedy black jeans, a black tank top, and a reddish plaid work shirt. "I don't need the neighborhood busybodies looking over here."

Frank held his hands up. "Sorry, I didn't mean it."

Skillet looked past him. "No problem, man. Come on in."

Frank followed him in and Skillet shut the door behind him, throwing the heavy-duty deadbolt. "Where's Boyd?"

"I have to go to work, so he's home," Frank said.

"Oh, okay. You have time to sit down?"

"Actually, it would be great if we could just get this stuff out of my car. I really need to get going. I don't want to be late."

"See, that's why I don't have a regular-type job," Skillet said. "Clocking in, answering to a boss? That is no way to live, son, no way to live at all."

Frank just nodded. He didn't have too much to say about Skillet's career choices. He was afraid Skillet was going to draw this thing out with a bunch of small talk and make him late. However, the dealer sat down in a chair and pulled on a pair of black leather work boots and a brown Carhartt work jacket similar to one Frank was wearing. Skillet's was real, though, Frank noticed.

Skillet walked over to the door and thumbed a button screwed into the wall. He opened the door and Frank saw one of the garage doors opening.

"Back your car in," Skillet said. "We'll get it unloaded."

Once in the garage Skillet turned on a light and shut the door. "Colder than a witch's titty out there today, you know?"

Frank nodded. "Yeah, it's supposed to get colder and drop more snow on us, too." He popped open the hatchback and pulled the blanket aside.

Skillet let out a low whistle and put a hand on Frank's shoulder. "Well, good golly goddamn. This is an impressive haul, Frank. I wasn't sure you guys had it in you."

"Well, everything was exactly where it was supposed to be," Frank said. "We rolled right in and there it all was, just waiting for us."

Skillet ducked his head into the hatchback and pawed through the hand tools and power tool cases. "This is really great. We're not going to have any trouble moving this."

"Great," Frank said, looking around. "So where do you want it?"

Skillet pointed to an empty workbench behind the Honda. "Right there. Damn, you even got the cases for the power tools. You have no idea how much easier that makes moving these things."

Frank started hauling tools from the back of the car. "It's top-grade stuff, too. Makita, Milwaukee, just look at it. This guy didn't scrimp at all."

Fifteen minutes later all the tools were piled on the workbench and the power tools in their cases were stacked on the garage floor beside the bench. Skillet was sorting the hand tools into sets.

"You guys got whole sets here," he said. "This is good, you know? Very good. Some guys are going to have a very good Christmas."

Frank glanced at the time on his phone. It was about ten minutes to one. "Hey, Skillet, I have to go."

The dealer looked up at him. "So go, man. Just come back after work and we'll settle up."

"I'd rather do it now."

Skillet didn't look at him, he just kept sorting tools. "Money's in the house, man. I'll have to go get it."

"Okay."

Skillet looked at him with a six-inch crescent wrench in his hand. "You sure you wouldn't like to come back later? Maybe you could bring Boyd. I'm sure he needs to see me, you know what I mean?"

Frank just looked at him.

"Come on, man. It ain't like I'm going anywhere. Besides, I have to sort through all this, see what I can make. You guys did better than I thought, so the pay day here may be bigger than you think. You trust me, don't you?"

Frank considered the situation for a moment. If they hadn't spent the night getting hammered, he wouldn't have to rush like this. Skillet was generally trustworthy, and if he did come back, he could bring Boyd. He could score and they would both have a quiet holiday.

"Midnight, okay?" Frank said. "That will give me time to finish up at work and go home to grab Boyd."

Skillet shrugged. "You could wait until the morning if you want." He gestured outside with the wrench. "Like you said, the weather isn't supposed to get any better."

Frank turned and looked at the snow coming down. He had a whole shift of driving in that crap and didn't relish the idea of still being on the road at midnight.

"Yeah, all right, first thing in the morning."

Skillet nodded. "Sounds good, man. Bring Boyd with you. Maybe he'll take some of his cut in trade."

"Yeah, we'll be here," Frank said. He reached behind the passenger seat and pulled out the small light-up Rocco's Pizza sign. He put it on top of the car and pushed down on the suction cups. The wire to light it up went through the passenger side window. He looked over to see Skillet shaking his head and smiling. "Can you get the door? I have to bounce."

"No sweat." He pulled a remote from his back pocket and thumbed the button. Frank watched the door go up and dropped the car in gear.

"Oh, hey," Skillet said as the car started to move. Frank hit the brakes and looked back. "When you guys come over tomorrow?"

"Yeah?"

"Don't forget the turkey," Skillet said with a smile.

• • •

Tim walked back up the street toward the *Shopper's* offices at three that afternoon. He had canvased fifteen businesses and spoken to more people than he could remember. His notebook was almost full, so he had quite a bit of writing to do. He walked past his little pickup truck still parked at the curb by Red Fannie Florist and decided to walk one more block back to the office. The snow was still falling, and he was glad that his mom's place was only in the next town over so he wouldn't have far to drive tomorrow. The bell over the office door rang as he walked in to the *Shopper's* office. Charlie looked up and smiled.

"How did you make out?" The publisher said.

Tim smiled. "Jackpot, boss." He shrugged out of his coat and hung it up. He put a thick folder on his desk with his notebook. "Out of the fifteen businesses I hit, eleven of them have received these letters. You add those to yours and Tate's and that's a baker's dozen. Our guy has been prolific."

Charlie nodded his head. "Good work, Tim. I think you're on to something now."

Tim sat down at his desk across from Charlie and opened his notebook. "I went to all the businesses on the list we put together. As you know, they were all locally owned, all advertise with us, so they were more comfortable answering questions."

"The letters were all like the ones I received?" Charlie said.

"Yeah, the format and content were the same," Tim said, handing the file folder over the desks. "They were all nasty in their own way, although some were more personal than others. I got as many copies as I could. Not everyone hung on to them. Some just wrote them off as the work of a crank and tossed them."

Charlie flipped through the copies. "Yeah, this is the same guy. Very short messages, very nasty, and personal."

Tim gestured at the copies. "As you look through those, you'll see some are more personal. I think he knows more about some of the recipients than he does about others."

Charlie nodded. "Good catch. Make sure you follow up on that in your article."

Tim smiled. "So I'm writing this up? We're going to publish this?"

"Oh, yeah, this is our lead for the next issue," Charlie said. "Hogan is a small town, so all those people you spoke to today are going to be talking about it at Thanksgiving dinner tomorrow, during their Black Friday shopping, and over the weekend when they're polishing off leftovers and watching football. We need a nice, solid story with the facts as we have them."

Tim leaned back in his chair. "I can work on it over the weekend and have a draft for you Monday."

Charlie was still flipping through the file. "Monday is fine. Just email me what you have."

"Okay," Tim said. He stood up and packed his laptop into a shoulder bag. He dropped in his notebook and reached for the file folder with the copies of the letters. Charlie was still holding it, staring off into space.

"Hey, Charlie? I need that."

"Oh, yeah, here you go." He handed it across the desks.

"Everything okay?"

Charlie nodded and smiled. "Yeah, I'm good. You know, when I started receiving these things and when they kept coming and they were so personal and mean spirited, I wondered what I'd done to someone to get them so mad. Now, I'm just one of many. It's not just me. It's kind of a relief in a way."

"Sure," Tim said. "Of course, it just means there's someone out there who is very angry at the whole town."

Charlie shrugged. "Beats being alone." He stood up and held out his hand. Tim took it and they shook. "Have a happy Thanksgiving, Tim."

"You too, Charlie."

• • •

Frank was out on his sixth delivery since coming into work. He had just delivered a pizza and a couple salads to a party in the city, just four blocks from Rocco's. He dialed Boyd's cell phone again, as he had at least at once an hour since leaving Skillet's house. It rang a few times and went straight to voicemail.

He sighed and at the beep he said, "Boyd, I need to talk to you. Give me a call back. It's important. We need to talk about Skillet. I think he's going to try and screw us on this deal." He sent a text message as well.

The snow was still coming down and the dinner rush would be starting soon. As predicted, no one wanted to cook tonight, and the deliveries were piling up, so he pulled out of the customer's driveway and headed back to Rocco's.

Where the hell was Boyd?

• • •

Bob Ellstrom had a bucket full of hot water mixed with bleach, and he was wiping down every surface in his house the burglars may have touched. The broken glass had been swept up and thrown out, the floor had been mopped and a piece of cardboard was taped over the broken window.

The truck was already cleaned. He'd taken care of that first thing after arriving back home and putting it in the garage. The water in the bucket had turned into a slick pink mess with tissue floating in it. When he poured it down the garage drain, bits of bone got stuck in the floor grate. He'd forced them down with his finger.

He reached into the fridge and pulled a Bud Light out. He popped the top and drank half of it in one swig. The wood trim around all the doorframes in the kitchen, living room, and dining room had been wiped down. The counters and tables were also done. He would go upstairs next, he decided. Then he walked into the dining room and sat down in a chair, suddenly very tired. He also felt violated. Those two guys had been in his house and had gone through his things. They had stolen from him.

The second guy, the one in the car, what was his deal? Why had he abandoned his friend to walk home in the snow? The tire tracks had turned left and the footprints had gone right. Why had they split up? It just didn't make sense.

It was dinner time but he wasn't hungry. The image of the snow plow hitting that kid in the eight-ball jacket kept replaying in his mind in slow motion. There was something dreadful and mesmerizing about the way his head had snapped back and exploded on the truck's hood and the way he'd flown through the air into the tree. Bob shook his head to try and clear the images, but they were stubborn.

The letters he'd written earlier that morning were stacked up neatly on the table again. He'd gone through them and the addressed envelopes four times. They were all there. In fact, as near as he could tell, nothing but the cash from his dresser was missing from the house. The barn had been pretty well wiped out, though. Most of his power tools and a good portion of his hand tools were gone. The two of them had really packed that little Honda of theirs as full as they could.

The guy in the car had to have his stuff, but according to the tracks, he hadn't taken it back to their house. Bob chewed his lower lip. What if they didn't both live there? He'd seen the kid in the eight-ball jacket out walking a few times, always near the old Jensen place, and he was pretty sure he'd seen the car there a lot, too. He took another swig of beer. Maybe he needed to go ask the guy what he knew. Just be friendly, one neighbor to another. Hey, you see anyone bust into my place? Ask him like that. See what he did.

He stood up, grabbed his jacket, gloves, and hat and opened the back door with the busted window. He'd have to stop at Degman's Hardware and get a new piece of glass and the glazing to install it. Before closing the door, he looked at the knives in the wooden block on the counter. He reached over and selected the big butcher knife again.

The snow was still falling, but not nearly as fast or as thickly as it had been. He walked over to the barn. The doors were closed but not locked. He added a padlock to the list of things he needed from Degman's. The snow all around the driveway leading up to the barn had been cleared away, and with it any trace of the Honda's tire tracks. There was a long bolt through the hasp now, holding the doors closed and keeping them from rattling too much in the wind. He hadn't found the padlock.

He walked back through the snow to the garage and got into his truck. When he got to the end of the driveway, he realized the county plows had made a couple passes. The road was relatively clear and drifts were piled high on either side near the treeline. He pulled out and headed in the direction of the old Jensen place.

As he neared the hollow where it had happened, his breathing quickened and he slowed a little. Any evidence in the snow on the side of the road had been wiped clean. The county plows had thundered down through here and obliterated his tire tracks and footprints from the side of the road. He came to a stop on the section of pavement over the drainpipe. He could see a dark spot on the tree Boyd had collided with, but he was sure no one else would notice it. Below him, lying in frigid water, tree branches, and leaves, was that kid in the jacket. Bob gripped the steering wheel in one hand and the knife in the other, feeling a familiar stirring down below and suddenly wishing his wife was back home waiting for him. Right now he wanted to walk in, see her standing in front of the sink in those jeans she used to wear and just . . . Headlights approached from behind and he slowly started up again.

The Jensen place was another minute up the road and he pulled onto the side of the road just before the edge of the driveway. The car behind him passed by slowly and continued up the road. Snow fell through the beams of his headlights and he looked at the house. There was no car in the driveway nor any evidence anyone was home. All the lights were out, and there wasn't even the flicker of a TV screen.

He sat there for a moment considering what to do. There were no neighbors for at least a hundred yards in either direction, so the odds of being seen were small. Besides, he wasn't actually doing anything wrong. Should he leave a message of some sort? Could he be clever like all those villains in the police shows on TV? Should he go back home, type up a note saying he knew who they were and what they'd done and nail it to their door? Freak the guy out a little and get him nervous?

No, that was Hollywood shit. You started doing that stuff in real life and you eventually screwed up. In every one of those shows the bad guy left something behind and some lab somewhere would end up figuring out exactly where it had come from. Not that little Hogan, Ohio, had a crime lab, but the state did. Surprise was what he had now. He was pretty sure he knew where this guy lived, he knew what he looked like from the video, and knew what his car looked like. He also knew the guy was alone and no longer part of a partnership. There was no reason to give up his advantage for the sake of being clever.

He pulled back into his garage ten minutes later. The house had been cleaned as much it was possible for him to do. He started running it down again, what to do if the body was ever found and the remaining burglar ended up back here. There was no reason for anything like that to happen, but he wanted to be prepared. If some cop knocked on his door asking about a dead body and the other burglar was dumb enough to say this was the last place the kid in the eight-ball jacket had been seen, he wanted to be able to play dumb. Burglary, officer? Why, no, we haven't had any trouble like that out here at all. He would fix the window, take care of that with no problem. His gaze fell on the pile of letters and he sighed. They had been thrown all over the floor, so there was every chance the paper they were written on held fingerprints. The last thing he needed was the fingerprints from a dead body being found on his letters. He gathered them up, grabbed the open box of envelopes and the open package of typing paper and walked outside. There was a burn barrel halfway between the house and the barn. Bob dropped everything into it. He selected a few sheets of paper from the open package and balled them up like snowballs. He dug in his pocket for his Zippo and lit them. The letters, paper, and envelopes flared up, flames beating back the darkness and snow for a few brief moments.

Bob looked out across the yard toward the woods, feeling for the first time a little trepidation at how isolated he was out here. Anyone could be in those trees watching him, observing what he was doing. He felt uncomfortable and exposed.

When he was sure everything had been burned up, he walked back toward the house. He had more paper and more envelopes and a long holiday weekend ahead of him. He was hungry now and there was some hamburger thawed in the fridge. Burgers and beer sounded good.

• • •

Amy snuggled under a blanket on the couch in her apartment, half a glass of wine beside her. The TV was off because she didn't feel like being distracted right now. She was still pissed at Jeremy for bailing on her, and his excuses were wearing thin. Her phone was beside her on an end table. Thinking about her conversation with Missy earlier in the day, she picked it up and scrolled through the contacts until she found Tim Abernathy's name. The clock on the cable box said it was five after eight. She tapped the dial button. He answered on the third ring.

"Hey," she said. "You eat dinner yet?"

"No," Tim said. He sounded slightly distracted but she didn't care.

"I feel like Chinese. Do you want to meet me at the Singing Moon? We could get some General Tso's chicken."

"Right now?" he said.

"If we wait I'm just going to get hungrier."

"Okay," he said. "Twenty minutes?"

"Twenty it is," she said and hung up.

• • •

At eight thirty Tim walked into the Singing Moon and Amy waved to him from a booth. She looked so much better than he did, he realized. She was wearing a nice red sweater, and her hair and makeup looked like she'd gone to some trouble, considering she'd gotten off work a couple hours ago. He, on the other hand, was wearing a pair of blue jeans, a Fall Out Boy t-shirt, and a thermal hoodie under a denim jacket. He slipped into the booth and shook off his hoodie and jacket as one.

"Can you believe this weather?" he asked.

"In this part of Ohio?" she said. "I'm never surprised by the weather. If you told me it was going to be eighty degrees tomorrow I'd just plan on swimming."

He looked at the menu, gathering himself. Heart beating too quickly, he didn't know what was going on. "So what's good here?"

"I like the General Tso's chicken with rice and some egg rolls," she said. "You like chicken?"

"That sounds good," he said, "and crab rangoons. You ever eat those?"

"Yeah, those are good. They do it family style here, you know? Bring out everything in bowls."

"Cool," he said.

She looked out the window, and he followed her gaze. The window was fogging up around the edges, condensation creeping in from outside. The snow was finally tapering off.

"So what's up?" he said.

She shrugged. "I just didn't want to sit at home and didn't have plans. What were you up to today? You weren't at work."

A waitress came over and took their orders. Tim ordered dinner and they each ordered a beer.

"Charlie had me out working the letters story. Tate let me have the day off."

"You figure it out yet?"

He shook his head and smiled. "No, but I found out that our weirdo's been sending these things all over town. I found eleven more businesses who've been receiving them."

She raised her eyebrows. "Eleven? Really? Psycho boy really needs to find another hobby."

The waitress brought their drinks, and they both took a sip. Tim set his down on a coaster. "Yeah, maybe stamp collecting instead of threatening letters."

She looked good in the soft light of the restaurant. He took another sip and reminded himself not to have too many beers. He tended to get too honest when he drank, and he wasn't sure how honest he wanted to be tonight.

"So you're going to write a story about the mysterious letter writer?" She said. "That's going to get tongues wagging around here."

"You think so?"

She laughed a little. "Are you kidding? You know how things go around here. That story's going to come out and everyone will have an opinion. It's creepy, someone here in town sending letters around. Everybody is going to have a theory and they're all going to want to share it. There are Facebook groups about the goings on in Hogan, and this will be a big one."

He paused, beer bottle halfway to his mouth. "I hadn't thought of that."

She smiled again. Every time she did that, he melted a little. "You went out today and found eleven people who got these letters?"

"That's right."

"Well, when you publish the story, how many people do you think will call you and say they've gotten them? It may not even just be Hogan. You think this guy is containing himself to one little town?"

He slumped back a little in the booth. "Wow, you're right. He could have sent letters to hundreds of people."

"You betcha."

"Can I ask you a question?" he said.

"What's that?"

"What are we doing here? Shouldn't you be out with Jeremy?"

She shrugged and looked out the window again. "If he was around, maybe I would be. He bailed on me tonight. Again. For work."

The waitress appeared with their order and made a show of setting it up on the table. It smelled delicious. Tim gestured for Amy to start and she took some rice. He spooned chicken onto his plate and forked a piece into his mouth.

"Wow, that's good."

"Hungry?" she asked.

"Sort of," he said around a mouthful of chicken. "I haven't eaten since lunch and I think I walked Main Street twice today."

They ate in silence for a moment. "So Jeremy works a lot?"

"It's all he does," she said. "Drives all over the place selling his stupid parts, visiting customers."

"I didn't think that bothered you. I mean, he makes a decent salary, has a nice car."

"Oh, who gives a damn," she said. "I'm tired of waiting for him to show up and being available whenever he wants. Like my whole life is being on hold for him."

He just looked at her.

"What? It's true. He wants me to be available when he's around but I get blown off whenever that stupid phone of his rings." She jabbed a fork into the air. "Do you know he takes me to all these dinners with clients and instead of enjoying myself I sit there like a dressed-up doll he shows off? It's my job to keep the wives occupied so he can do his sales thing. He's exhausting."

"It doesn't sound good when you put it that way."

She took another pull on her bottle. "Hey, you're not a fill-in for him, okay?"

Tim smiled. "So, if he was in town you'd still be sitting here with me instead of him?"

She looked at him and he stared back into dreamy blue eyes. "I just needed to talk with someone. We're friends, right? Friends go out for dinner and they talk. That's what we're doing. Besides, you're smart and when I talk to you I feel like you're paying attention. I feel like you help."

He flushed, hard, and could feel the redness creeping into his face.

"Holy cow, you're blushing!" she said.

"Stop it," he said. "I'm not."

She giggled. "You totally are. Oh, man, I can't remember the last time I made a guy blush."

He smiled. "The chicken is spicy, that's all."

"Oh, Tim, you're one in a million."

They finished dinner, and Tim moved to pay but Amy snatched the check. "I invited you. I got this."

"At least let's go Dutch."

"Get the tip."

He tipped, generously, and they walked outside into the cold night air. They stood on the sidewalk under the dark, starless night. Tim knew thick clouds would be the norm until the temperature dropped, and then it would be too cold to stand outside stargazing.

Amy took his hand. "I'll see you at work Friday?"

"Black Friday at Degman's Hardware? I wouldn't miss it." He looked at her. "Are you okay driving? I could take you home."

"One beer? What kind of lightweight do you think I am? Besides, I live over Mimi's Bookstore," she said, pointing across the street and down two buildings. "You can walk me home if you want."

"Sure."

They walked across Main Street toward the bookstore. "Did she get one?" Amy said. "Mimi? Was she one of the business owners who got a letter?"

Tim shook his head. "No, I talked to her, and she said she hadn't received one. Maybe our guy doesn't read."

"Good, she's a nice lady. I'd hate to think this guy was bothering her."

They got to the dark brick building, and Amy walked around the side facing an alley. There was a wooden staircase leading up to an apartment over the bookstore. Almost every business on Main Street had at least one apartment over it.

"This is me," she said.

"Okay, see you Friday."

She moved quickly, pulling his head down and kissing him. Her lips were soft and firm and everything he had ever imagined. He slipped a hand around the back of her head into her silky hair and he stood there, not feeling the cold or snow, just the kiss as they moved back and forth, their bodies so close. Then it was over. She stepped back.

He exhaled heavily and a cloud of breath wafted up between them. "What was that?" he said.

She smiled. "It was nice."

He watched as she went up the stairs, not hiding the fact at all that he was enjoying the view of her climbing stairs in her jeans. She unlocked her door, waved again and slipped inside.

Tim turned back to the street and started walking back to his truck. "Damn."

• • •

At twelve thirty in the morning Frank let himself into the house he and Boyd shared. He slammed the door and moved into the living room.

"Hey, Boyd, you home? What the hell, man, I've been calling you all night."

He turned on the living room lamp, and the couch was empty, which was odd. If Boyd was home he was either watching TV on this couch or sleeping. He turned off the lamp and started up the stairs.

"Come on, Boyd, quit screwing around. I need your help with this Skillet thing. The sonofabitch is going to try and screw us. We have to meet him in the morning."

He switched on the upstairs hall light. "You here, Boyd? How goddamn high are you, man?"

Frank looked in Boyd's room. It was a mess, as always. The bed didn't even have sheets on it, just a pile of comforters they'd bought at the Goodwill. His jacket wasn't here, he noticed. Boyd always threw it on the thrift-store chair that occupied one corner of the room, and it was empty.

"Fuck it, man," he said from the doorway. "I'll take care of it myself."

Frank collapsed into his bed, exhausted, and fell asleep almost immediately.

Fourteen

Amy woke up early on Thanksgiving Day and lay in bed staring at the clock as the time approached seven. A few seconds after the digits changed to 6:59 she reached over and shut off the alarm. The last thing she wanted to hear was that buzzing. She had enough irritating things in her life already.

She walked into the kitchen and spent half an hour preparing a small turkey and setting out side dishes like potatoes, the makings for a green bean casserole, stuffing, and rolls. She was making an early dinner for herself, Jeremy, and Boyd. They would be at her apartment around one.

Once the turkey was in the oven she spent another half hour in the bathroom showering and getting ready. Fixing her hair, she stared at herself in the mirror and realized she had zero enthusiasm for any of this.

"Oh, Boyd, why do you have to make everything harder?" she said to herself. "First that stupid accident and then your stupid pills and now you can't keep it together. I mean, you can't even drive. I have to make dinner and then go pick you up? What is that all about? What would Mom and Dad say?"

Talking to herself was something she did a lot, she realized. Vocalizing her problems helped, and since Jeremy was never around, she ended up talking to herself most of the time. She curled her hair and looked at herself in the mirror.

"And what the hell was that kiss all about last night? Is that who you are? Jumping from guy to guy, making sure you have one ready in case one doesn't work out? And let's be honest, did you need Missy to tell you that Tim had feelings for you? Was that some big secret?"

She went through the rest of her routine and walked back into the bedroom to get dressed. There was a nice dress in her closet she'd bought especially for the holidays. She pulled it out and looked at it. It was tan with a splash of red, and when she'd bought it she'd wanted to look nice for the families. Now, she put it back in the closet. If Boyd and Jeremy couldn't put forth any more effort than they had been into considering her feelings, she wasn't wearing anything more complicated than sweatpants.

• • •

Frank woke up with pale sunlight in his face. He was stiff and realized he wasn't under any blankets and was still in the jeans and Rocco's Pizza t-shirt he'd worn to work the previous night. The clock said 8:37 a.m. He sat straight up and his feet hit the floor when he realized he had to meet Skillet.

"Boyd?" he said. "Boyd, you make it in last night, man? We have to go see Skillet this morning."

Boyd's room was still empty. Frank shook his head and wandered into the bathroom to get cleaned up for dinner at his mom's house. Twenty minutes later, he was showered and shaved. His mom insisted on him being cleaned up for holiday dinners. He pulled on the one pair of khakis he owned and a green sport shirt with a collar.

Where the hell was Boyd? Frank was getting a little concerned. The last time he'd seen him was walking home from the job they'd pulled. He could have caught a ride, but Frank couldn't imagine who would have picked him up all the way out there. Boyd had been invited to Amy's place for Thanksgiving. Could she have picked him up last night? He looked at the clock on the stove, which showed five after nine. Whatever was going on, he had to go. His mom would expect him to help with dinner, and he still had to swing by Skillet's place and get paid. He threw on his coat and headed outside.

The ever-reliable Honda started with one try, and he let it warm up while he brushed snow from the windows. Once he could see through the windshield, he pulled out onto the road.

After a couple minutes he neared the driveway of the house they'd hit yesterday. It was funny, but he'd never really noticed it before. Of course, he was aware it was there in general, but there were so many long driveways and access roads for natural gas wells and cell phone towers out this way it was impossible to keep track of them all.

He slowed a bit to get a look. The trees between the road and the house were bare, but he could still just barely make out the house. The barn was more visible simply because it was bigger. He didn't see any activity. No cars, no people, and most importantly, no police cruisers. That didn't mean they weren't around, though. He checked his rearview and kept moving. The last thing he needed was some township cop thinking he was taking too much of an interest in this particular house.

The roads were much clearer than they had been last night, and he made it into the city and to Skillet's place ten minutes later. He pulled into the driveway and parked near the back door to the house. He knocked on the door, softly this time so as not to attract undo attention. He had to knock again before he heard someone moving around.

The door opened, and he saw Skillet was sporting a black Metallica t-shirt this morning and dark-gray sweatpants. He held the door open for Frank without saying anything and waved him inside. He closed the door, and Frank followed him into the living room, where he gestured to a chair and flopped onto the couch. Skillet picked up a bowl of Count Chocula and spooned some into his mouth. A parade was on TV with the sound muted.

"I didn't figure you for a parade fan," Frank said.

"I like the big balloons," Skillet said. "My mom used to watch them every Thanksgiving."

"Mine, too," Frank said. They sat in silence for another moment. "Speaking of moms, Skillet, I have to go see mine. You get a chance to total everything up?"

The dealer tipped his bowl and slurped down milk from the cereal, then set it on the coffee table and wiped his mouth with the back of his arm. "Where's Boyd? I thought he was coming with you."

Frank held his hands up. "I don't know, man. He never came home last night. Maybe he went down to the Hoover and got lucky, you know?"

Skillet raised his eyebrows. "Frank, I'm not sure I've ever seen a woman in the Hoover you'd want to get lucky with."

"Boyd's not picky," Frank said.

"Yeah, I hear you. Hey, we can settle up, but I want it understood that I'm paying both of you. I don't want him rolling in here in a couple days saying I owe him or some shit, you understand? He's your partner, you take care of him."

"It's all good," Frank said. "I expect I'll see him later, after he's had dinner with his sister. There's no way he'll miss that, because she'd kill him."

"His sister from down at the hardware store? Dude, she's so fine."

"I hear you, man, but she's dating some sales douche who works over at Brinco."

"That's too bad."

"Yeah, so hey, what number did you come up with? You know, for the stuff."

Skillet got up, collected the bowl and spoon from the coffee table and walked into the kitchen. Him being out of sight made Frank nervous, but there wasn't much he could do except stand up.

"You guys knocked it out of the park, Frank, I have to be honest with you," Skillet said from the kitchen. Frank could hear him opening drawers. "You got whole sets of wrenches and screwdrivers, metric and standard, plus cases for all those power tools and tonnage. I mean, I couldn't believe how much you got in the back of that little Honda. That was outstanding."

He walked back into the living room with an envelope and held it out to Frank. He took it and opened it up, quickly counting it.

"There's two grand there, my man. My guy was suitably impressed."

"Just two grand?" Frank said. "I thought there was at least five there. That was top-notch stuff. I mean, there wasn't any Chinese crap. That was all American. I made sure we took the good stuff."

Skillet shrugged and held up his hands. "It's just business, Frank. My guy has to make a profit when he sells it, I get a cut, and the guy who turned us on to the job gets a cut. Believe me, you guys got the biggest slice of the pie."

"Just feels light is all."

Skillet grinned and started walking them toward the dining room. "It's always going to feel light, man. What you guys do has a lot of risk, you know? Sneaking in a place and rooting around when folks aren't home. That takes balls of steel, but you have to remember, you get to dump the stuff, and then I have to find a buyer."

They were by the door now and Skillet opened it. Cold air spilled in. "If I hear of anything else I'll let you know, okay? Have a good turkey day, Frank."

Then the door closed and locked, and Frank was standing outside in the winter air. He shoved the envelope in his pocket and got into his car.

• • •

At ten o'clock, Bob Ellstrom finally got out of bed and shuffled into the bathroom wearing a robe and slippers. He looked in the mirror and remembered what had happened yesterday. Staring at his reflection, he was surprised how little he cared about killing that guy. He was more upset that they'd been in his house, had seen his things and had stolen so many tools. That really pissed him off. Most of those tools had been collected over the years, bought back when he'd been making a good salary. With what he made at Brinco, he'd be lucky to replace half of them.

After he was cleaned up he went downstairs and looked at the dining room table. A stack of twenty-two letters were all ready to go: sealed up, addressed, and stamped. He decided to make a coffee run and put on his boots, coat, and gloves. He scooped up the letters and carried them with him to the truck in the garage.

He turned on the overhead light and examined the snow plow again. There was a small dent where it had struck Boyd, but it didn't look out of place. It had plenty of dings and scratches from being well used. Hitting some skinny little thief had made less of an impact than pushing tons of snow. He got in and started the truck up, backed it out into the driveway and worked the electric controls. The plow blade moved up and down, left and right without a hitch.

He got to the end of the driveway and turned right. This morning he passed over the hollow and the drainpipe that ran under the road and barely slowed down. Acknowledging the body lying in the freezing water, he whispered, "Fuck you," and went on to the kid's house.

He slowed down in front of the old Jensen place, now owned by one Martha Utzler, as he'd discovered last night by looking at county property records on the auditor's website. He'd never seen a woman there and the kid in the drainpipe was named Boyd Sashman, according to his wallet, so the other guy was probably a roommate. Maybe the two of them were renting the place. He hadn't been able to find anything out about who actually lived there.

The driveway was still empty, just like it had been last night. Maybe Sashman lived here alone. He'd seen cars there before but had never paid that much attention. Maybe people just visited him a lot. He picked up speed and headed toward town.

Last night he'd done a lot of thinking about his position, and he was still angry. He was out quite a bit of cash and tools and these two idiots had been inside his house, had seen his letters, but did it matter? That was the real question, and maybe he was asking it a bit too late—certainly too late for Boyd Sashman. It's not like they knew what he did or how often he did it. Hell, they may not have even read the letters lying on the table. They could have just thrown them around while they were looking for stuff to steal. They had missed his laptop on the bookcase, so maybe they didn't have time to be thorough enough to read the letters.

He picked up a coffee at the Dunkin' Donuts out by the interstate. Holiday or not, they were open. Route 5 went further out of town and he took it twenty-three miles north, up to Kishman Township. There was a small strip plaza there with a blue mailbox on the end near a tanning salon. The parking lot was empty this morning and no businesses were open. He pulled in and swung around so the mailbox was on the driver's side. He lowered his window and shoveled the letters into the box, letting the heavy door slam shut. He pulled it open again just to make sure the letters had all dropped down. They had.

He pulled out of the parking lot and threw a wave to the Kishman Township officer sitting in the parking lot of a convenience store across the road, sipping his own cup of coffee. The cop threw a wave back to him.

• • •

Jeremy was sitting on Amy's couch watching the football pre-game show. At twelve thirty, the network cut over to the kickoff. The Cowboys and the Bears lined up for the coin toss. His phone vibrated again, lightly, and he checked the message and smiled.

Amy came out of the kitchen stirring a bowl of potatoes. She was wearing a t-shirt with the word "Pink" emblazoned across it and tight black sweatpants. He had a shirt and tie on and a sport coat was thrown over a chair in the dining room.

"Who is that?" she asked, nodding at the phone.

"Just work stuff."

She looked at him. "Really? On Thanksgiving? I didn't know anyone built cars today."

He looked up at her. "It's just a report. They go out automatically every day on a schedule. Hey, where's your brother?"

"I don't know. He didn't answer his phone when I called, and when I went out to his house, no one was home."

"Wasn't he expecting you?"

"Yes, but like I said, no one was home when I got there."

"You think he was high? Maybe he just didn't hear you knocking."

Amy set the bowl down on the dining room table. "Okay, look, Boyd has a problem, we both know that, but you don't have to bring it up every chance you get."

"I'm just saying." He glanced back toward the TV.

"Oh, I know you're just saying. I get that and it doesn't make what you're just saying any better. Boyd's an addict. You think I don't know? Do you know how much of my parents' life insurance money I spent to put him through rehab?"

"And look how that turned out." He stood up. Like static electricity in the air on a still summer night predicted a coming thunderstorm, she could sense a fight coming on from the tone of his voice.

"Don't give me a hassle, Jeremy. I know my brother has a problem, and I know how you feel about it. That's why I have to cook a dinner here before we go to your folks' place. After all, we can't have Boyd around the good silver and china. He might clean the place out."

"Seriously?" he said. "That's why you're pissed? Because I won't let your painkiller-addicted brother into my parents' house? How many times has he been caught shoplifting from the drugstore in town? Hell no, I don't want him in my parents' house."

She looked at him, all fire and smoke now, arms crossed and weight on one hip thrust toward him. "Who are you seeing besides me?"

He actually took a step back because the question surprised him so much. "I'm not, what? Where is that coming from? I'm not seeing anyone else."

"Bullshit," she said. "You're always on the road and when you're here that goddamn phone never stops vibrating."

He held his hands up. "It's work. You know that. It's just emails and texts from customers and my boss."

She laughed and pointed at his phone. "Don't lie to me. I may be nothing but a clerk in a hardware store, but even I know your boss isn't texting you on Thanksgiving. You're a salesman, Jeremy. Why would they need to get ahold of you that often?"

He held his hands out and took a step toward her. "Customers need to have their hands held, baby. Every time something goes wrong they email or text me. They want to know we're on top of everything."

She shook her head. "I don't believe you. Not anymore. We had plans last night, and you blew me off." Her face got some color in it now, letting him know she was angry. "I have a life, you know. I'm not just at your beck and call whenever you blow into town or when you need someone pretty on your arm for those boring business dinners you're always hauling me to."

He moved over to the window and looked out at the street. "I told you, I had an afternoon meeting, and I didn't get back until late last night. I really couldn't help it."

She crossed the room behind him. "Then turn around and tell me all about it while you look me in the eyes."

He turned. "What do you mean?"

"What I mean is, when you lie you look away. You can't maintain eye contact." She bobbed her head and kept her gaze locked on his eyes even as he moved his head around. "See? You're doing it now. Come on, tell me all about the meeting. What was on the agenda? Who was there? How late did it go?"

He glanced away.

"Tell me," she said, this time with more force behind it.

He held up both hands, almost in a defensive posture. "You know what, just give me a minute."

He walked into the bathroom and closed the door hard. She heard the lock snap into position. She turned back toward the small dining room and moved to pick up the bowl of potatoes. Then his phone buzzed lightly.

It was laying on the end table next to the couch where he'd left it. She reached down and picked it up, staring silently at it, trying to make up her mind. She either trusted him or she didn't. The answer came with a swipe of her finger.

It was locked, of course, as always. She thumbed in his code the same way she'd seen him do a thousand times while they watched a movie or ate dinner. He probably didn't even realize she knew his code, she thought.

She tapped the text icon and there was a list of messages. There were a few work names she recognized, but some others were women's first names. The work names were all first and last names. She opened the first unread one, from someone named Brenda. It was a topless selfie, some woman with chestnut brown hair lying on a bed. She was attractive and young, probably college aged. Tears welled up in Amy's eyes.

She scrolled through the text conversation between the two of them and saw more pictures and suggestive texts, both from him and to him. Just fifteen minutes ago he had asked her to send him a picture. While he was sitting on her couch and she was cooking dinner, this was what he had been doing.

The bathroom door opened and Jeremy came out. He looked at her and his eyes fell to the phone in her hand. "What are you doing with that?" he asked.

She threw it at him and he caught it one-handed before it sailed into the bathroom.

"You're such a fucking liar," she said softly. "Get out of my house."

He looked at the phone. "What, this? I can explain this."

"Really? You can explain asking some slut for topless pictures while I'm in the kitchen making Thanksgiving dinner? How, exactly, would you do that?"

He threw his arms up and walked toward her. "It's nothing. She's just someone flirting with me. Nothing is going on. Come on, I'm sorry."

"No," she said. "That is, that is not okay. Don't you see how you're disrespecting me? Why would I allow you to do that?"

"Amy, please," he said stepping closer, trying to embrace her. "It's just a little harmless flirting. It's nothing. Lots of people do it."

"I don't," she said and brushed his hands away. "Just go. We're done."

He crossed his arms defiantly. "Oh, that's it? We're done? That's what you say?"

"I already told you to leave," she said. "I would appreciate it if you would just go. I don't want to do this today, okay? Just go."

He was angry. She could see it in his eyes. Suddenly he wasn't in charge anymore. She was calling the shots, and he didn't like it.

"You're being a little naïve about this," he said, his voice starting to rise. "This is nothing. It's just some stupid college girl flirting with me. She's a goddamn waitress. It's nothing."

"You keep saying that: it's nothing. Look at me, look at my face. Does it look like nothing to me?"

"Oh, and everything has to be about poor little Amy, doesn't it? Why don't you just run home crying to Mommy?"

As soon as it came out, his face fell. Amy stood there, mouth open in shock. "Oh, Amy, I'm sorry, I didn't mean . . . I shouldn't have said that. Please, I'm sorry . . ."

She looked at him, ice in her eyes and a white-knuckle grip on the bowl of potatoes in her hands. In a voice no louder than an angry whisper she said, "Get. The fuck. Out of. My house."

He walked past her into the dining room without saying another word and put on his sport coat, then his overcoat. "Call me when you calm down. We can straighten all this out."

Amy turned and threw the bowl of potatoes across the dining room and they exploded against the doorframe. Jeremy ducked. Amy saw potatoes and pink crockery all over the wall and floor. He looked down and brushed a lump of white mashed from his coat.

"Christ," he said. "You're so small town." Then he walked out.

Fifteen

Tim walked into his trailer and collapsed on the couch after Thanksgiving dinner with his mom and her new husband. It had been a tiring day, but it was over now. He sat there for a few minutes and picked up his phone. He thumbed through the contacts until he came to Amy's number. He stared at it, wondering if she would want to talk. It would be awkward if Jeremy was around, but that kiss last night, what had that been? He pressed the green phone icon.

"Hello?" she answered.

"Hi, can you talk?"

"Yes," she said. "What's up?"

He laughed a little. "Worst Thanksgiving ever."

"Me too," she said. There was something in her voice, like she had been crying.

"You okay? Because you don't sound okay."

"No, I'm not," she said, a sob catching in her throat. "I broke up with Jeremy today."

Tim swallowed. "Amy, I'm sorry about that." He stopped talking because he didn't know what else to say.

"He was such a jerk. I see that now."

"Did something happen?"

"Yeah, something happened," she said. "He's been seeing other women. I found texts and pictures on his phone. They were sending him all these photos of themselves and he was having a pretty good time. He was just playing me. I was his woman here. Apparently he had us all over the place."

"I'm so sorry," he said. "That's a dick move, and you deserve better. You know that, right? This kind of thing, it's not about you. It's about him. You're just collateral damage. It's like you were in a hurricane and just got knocked down by the wind."

"I thought you were good with words," she said, laughing a little. "That was terrible."

"You kissed me last night."

"Yeah."

"What was that about?"

She sighed a little. "Tim, I don't know. I think I've suspected Jeremy was cheating for a while, and I just didn't want to face it, and you've been so nice to me. You always are and there you were just walking me home and being so sweet. At that moment, it just felt right so I did it. I'm sorry."

He swallowed hard. There was a lump in his throat. "I have feelings for you."

"I know," she said, "and I don't want to complicate your life."

Neither of them said anything

"What happened with you?" she said finally, breaking the awkward silence. "What made your day so bad?"

"Well, let me tell you about that."

They talked until midnight.

Sixteen

Saturday morning, Bob walked into the Peppermill and looked around for Ted Handrew and Mark Packer. Both waved a hand at him from a corner booth near the window facing the street. Bob dropped onto the bench next to Mark. Both were fellow retirees from Ohio Axle. Mark was the eldest of the bunch, closing in on sixty-five. He was tall and lean, almost gaunt, and had been for as long as Bob had known him. Ted was the same age as Bob, fifty-eight, shorter than Mark and working on a serious belly. Neither looked happy.

Ted slid a newspaper across the table. "You see this yet?"

Bob picked it up and read the headline aloud. "Ohio Axle Retirees Lose Appeal in U.S. Circuit Court."

"Really?" Bob said. "We're just going to keep getting screwed, you know?" Mark and Ted nodded.

Ted pointed to the paper. "You know what this means? This basically says they can cut our pensions and there's nothing we can do about it."

A waitress came by and Bob ordered a cup of coffee and waffles. When she walked away, he picked up the article and read it more thoroughly. "So, retirees over sixty-two get their full pensions, and those of us younger lose our supplemental benefits and have our pension reduced. Is that right?"

Mark nodded. "Yep, that's right. Everyone younger than sixty-two who took the early buyout got their pension and the supplemental benefits that were supposed to carry them over until they reached sixty-two, because they would keep getting their pension and start getting their Social Security."

Bob sighed. "You know, they offered the early retirements as a cost-saving measure. Get the high earners out and get some younger guys in."

"More like get the high earners out and don't replace them with anyone," Ted said. "They just pushed more work off on anyone who couldn't take the buyout."

Bob blew on his coffee. "The point I'm trying to make is I put my thirty years in, I take the buyout for early retirement they offered, and then a year later they go bankrupt and we find out the pension is underfunded. Now they're taking our supplemental benefits and they're cutting our pensions. This is why I have to drive a tow motor for Brinco. I should be done working. I should be sitting at home enjoying my retirement."

Mark spoke up. "My boy explained that since Ohio Axle went belly up, the government takes over the pensions with that PBGC. He says they don't pay the supplemental benefits and they cut the pensions to make the funding last longer."

Bob slapped the table hard enough to rattle the silverware. "Whether it's Ohio Axle or the government, I'm the guy not getting what was promised," he hissed. A couple other people in the restaurant looked at their table. Bob nodded apologetically and turned back to Mark. "It's just one more way the working man gets screwed. Now I have to put in at least four more years at Brinco before I can retire with seventy percent of the pension I earned over thirty years. I'm supposed to be done."

Ted nodded. "I know, Bob. I'm in the same boat. You know my brother got me on part time down at the garage at Creekside Motors. You think I want to be turning wrenches at my age?"

Bob's waffles came, but he just looked at them. "I had a life planned out, you know? I was supposed to retire, and then Kate and I were going to travel. We were going to get to do all the things we put off. Now, she's gone, and I'm stuck making a third of what I used to working the same hours. It's not fair."

Mark and Ted looked down at their coffee and their plates, not knowing what to say.

• • •

The following Wednesday, Tim walked into the Savefast grocery store and saw a stack of *Hogan Shopper* newspapers. This was the new issue, and he picked one up off the top of the pile. He unfolded it and smiled at the headline, "Mysterious Letter Writer Plagues Hogan." Charlie was certainly laying it on thick.

He leaned up against the plateglass window near the buggy return and read through the article. It was exactly as it had been when he and Charlie had finished working on it, but it was still exciting to read it in its final form the way everyone else would. Charlie had added a map of Hogan with arrows indicating which businesses had received letters.

He got to the end and noticed one small change. Charlie had added a postscript in italics asking anyone with information about who the letter writer may be or anyone who had received a letter to contact the paper. The office phone number, email, and website were listed. Tim smiled again, grabbed three more copies of the paper and went inside for his Red Bull.

Ten minutes later he walked into the *Shopper*'s office and heard Charlie on the phone. He took off his coat and sat down. He looked at his desk phone and saw eleven missed calls. He leaned forward and scrolled through them. The calls weren't from the normal advertisers. They were all local numbers. A few of the last names he recognized. He looked over the desks at Charlie, who motioned for him. The editor covered up the phone receiver.

"This guy's been sending letters to a lot more than business owners," he said. "I've been getting calls all day from all kinds of people. Start returning the calls on your phone, get the bare minimum information, and a copy of the letter if you can." He dropped his hand and went back to his call.

Tim shook his head and pulled a clean notebook from a desk drawer and opened it. He scrolled back through the missed calls on his phone's display and wrote down the names and numbers, then started calling.

Four hours later, Charlie looked at his watch. "Okay, Tim, let's call it a night. No one's called in for an hour, and we're going to start waking people up if we keep returning calls."

Tim nodded and took off his headset. A few hours ago his neck had developed a serious cramp, so he'd dug the headset out of the closet where they kept extra equipment. "This is much bigger than we thought, Charlie. I talked to a dozen more people."

Charlie nodded and smiled like a maniac. "I got fifteen. That's twenty-seven today, added to the thirteen we wrote the story on, so that's forty all told. When you said he was prolific, you were correct."

"That was something," Tim said, stretching. "I don't think I've been on the phone that much since I was fifteen."

Charlie sat back in his chair and picked up a pen. He rolled it through his fingers like a drumstick, quickly and effortlessly like Tim had seen him do a hundred times before. He stared at Tim.

"What's up, Charlie? You look funny."

"I need you on full time here at the *Shopper*," he said. "Following up on all this will be impossible for me, and you can be more useful here than delivering building supplies and furniture."

Tim just looked at him. "Charlie, I appreciate that, but there's a reason I work two jobs. Student loans, rent, and food aren't cheap."

Charlie held up a hand. "I know you want to be a full-time reporter, and up until this point it hasn't made much sense to bring you on full time, but I can see now you have the chops for this. Plus, I've been thinking of cutting back my hours. If I bring you on full time, I can do that." He held up his arms wide with his hands splayed. "It's not local TV news, but it's not driving a delivery truck, either."

Tim leaned back in his chair. "What's it pay?"

"More than you make now working both jobs. You told me once what Tate pays you, and he's getting you cheap." Charlie leaned forward. "This is a real job, Tim, in the field you went to school for. You'll learn how journalism works, at least in a small town, and you'll learn the business side. You'll build a résumé."

Tim bit his lip and nodded. "Yeah, okay, Charlie, I'm in."

Charlie stood up and put his hand out across the desk. Tim stood and took it. "Congratulations, Tim."

Tim smiled, ear to ear and all teeth. "Thanks, Charlie."

"Your first assignment is to tell Tate Degman you quit. I need you in here tomorrow morning."

"That's kind of a crappy thing to do to him," Tim said.

Charlie sighed. "Yeah, but he'll find someone else to drive the truck. I know it's not nice, but we have to move quickly. Next assignment is to get all this information into a database. That's your job first thing tomorrow morning. After that we pound pavement and return more calls. We're going to be busy, so go get some sleep."

"Yeah, okay."

• • •

Bob Ellstrom was sitting at his dining room table with a copy of the *Hogan Shopper* spread wide. He had picked it up at the Savefast when he stopped after work for a case of beer and almost passed out when he saw the headline. There were four empty beer cans lying on the table and a fifth in his hand.

He had put away the typewriter in its case, along with the packages of copy paper, envelopes, and stamps. He wouldn't make the mistake of leaving things out again. It was almost inconceivable that another robbery would occur, but apparently the township wasn't as safe as he assumed. He still wasn't sure if anyone else lived at the old Jensen place. In the times he had driven past after work the last few days, no cars had been in the driveway. All the times he had seen a car parked there, had someone just been visiting that Boyd guy? It kind of made sense, after all. The guy had been walking away from the robbery. Whoever had been in the car that day had driven in the opposite direction.

He took another pull on his beer and wondered for the hundredth time why the story was in the paper now.

The story was fairly accurate. He had written all the letters listed to all the people mentioned in the article. Did they feel powerful? Talking to a reporter about the letters they'd gotten? Did they like airing their dirty laundry in public?

The byline listed the reporter as Tim Abernathy. Did this Tim Abernathy know the burglar who had been in his house? Did he somehow draw a connection between the letters they had seen here and the ones he had mailed to the *Shopper*?

Was the story a coincidence? If it was, would the other burglar go to the paper and tell this reporter what he had seen? It was too much to think about. He tipped the can back and drained the last of his beer.

"Relax," he said. "There was always a chance somebody was going to put it together, discover one person was doing this." His voice echoed around the empty house and reminded him of just how alone he was. There were acres of space between him and the next neighbor.

Was there something wrong with him? He had asked himself that question before and never really came up with a good answer. It just . . . it felt good to lash out. All these people with their perfect lives doing nasty things behind each other's back were just hypocrites. They needed someone like him to keep them honest. If someone didn't call them out, they would just keep getting away with it. And doing it, writing the letters, felt so good, so soothing, like all his pain was gone.

Now this reporter and the fag rag he worked for were going to go digging into things that didn't concern them and fuck it all up. Maybe he should do a little digging of his own.

He stood up and pulled his laptop down from the bookshelf. "Yeah, you little bastard, we'll see how you like people poking around in your business. I know where you work. Let's see where you live and what else we can find."

• • •

"Frank, honey, are you hungry?" Martha Utzler called from downstairs. Her voice jerked him awake. He had been snoozing, he realized, with the TV on in his old room at his mom's house. The clock beside his bed said 3:12 p.m.

"Do you want me to fix you something to eat before you go into work?"

He rubbed his eyes and turned off the TV with the remote. "Grilled cheese, Mom? Is that okay?"

"No problem," she said.

Frank changed into his work clothes, a red Rocco's Pizza t-shirt and a clean pair of jeans. He had the late shift tonight. It had been almost a week since he had been home. Boyd wasn't answering his phone, wasn't returning his messages, and he had stopped by the house a couple times in the middle of the day over the last week, and there was no sign of him. It was freaking him out.

He walked downstairs just as his mom was sliding two grilled cheese sandwiches onto a plate. Frank picked one up, grabbed a Coke from the fridge and went into the dining room.

"Thanks, Mom, for lunch. I appreciate it." He bit into the first sandwich.

She sat down at the table, still wearing the housecoat she had been wearing since this morning, and lit up a cigarette. "Frank, I wanted to ask you, how long do you think you'll be staying?"

Chewing, he looked at her. "You want me to go?"

She shook her head. "No, honey, you're always welcome here. It's just, if you aren't going to stay at the house out in the township I'd like to get another renter in there. I need the money."

Frank looked around the dining room. There was a curio cabinet in the corner full of ceramic figurines. It shook and they rattled dangerously anytime he walked into the room. A large wooden cross hung on the wall near the entryway. A framed montage of all his school pictures hung beside it. Lace doilies were spread on the back of the chairs and sofa in the living room. This might be the house he grew up in, but it was now the home of a single, sixty-year-old woman.

He smiled and took her hand. "No, Mom, I guess after you invited me to stay Thanksgiving night I just liked being here. It's silly, though. It's probably time to get back out there."

"Have you heard from your friend?"

"Boyd? No, he hasn't turned up."

She squeezed his hand. "Frank, honey, that boy is a loser. I don't mean to judge anyone . . ."

"Ah, Mom, come on . . ."

"No, I know he's your friend and I know you've tried to help him, but you just can't. When someone is addicted like that, sometimes it just gets the better of them. Like your father, you know? I tried to help him get sober more times than I can count but he just couldn't put the whiskey down. It killed him, Frank."

"I know, Mom."

"You just can't save everyone," she said. "Some people will beat their addictions and others will be beaten by them. Why don't you just move back in here? The township house needs some work and this way I can get a contractor in there."

"Mom, I'm a grown man. I like living on my own. If I move back here it's like admitting I can't make it on my own. Can you understand that?"

Now she gripped his hand with both of hers. "Oh, Frank, I've been out there and I've seen the way you two live. Believe me, you aren't making it on your own. Come back home."

He finished up the last bite of his sandwich and stood up, sliding his hand from his mother's. He picked up the dirty plate and dropped it in the sink. "Mom, I'm going home tonight after work. I appreciate what you're saying, I do, but whatever's going on with Boyd, he probably needs my help."

She nodded and stubbed out her cigarette in a milk-white glass ashtray on the dining room table. "Okay, Frank, if that's the way you feel."

He walked over and kissed her on the forehead. "Thanks."

When he pulled into a parking space at the pizza shop his phone rang. There was no name, just a number.

"Hello?" he said.

"Frank? This is Amy Sashman, Boyd's sister."

"Oh, hey, Amy. How's it going?"

"Pretty good, Frank. You?"

"I'm just going into work."

"Okay, well, I won't keep you, but I'm just calling to ask if you've seen Boyd. We were supposed to have Thanksgiving dinner, and he never showed up."

"Weren't you going to pick him up, Amy? You know Boyd can't drive, and he didn't ask me for a ride."

"I understand that, Frank, but I drove out Thanksgiving morning to get him, and he wasn't home. I knocked on the door hard enough to hurt my hand, but he never answered. Have you seen him?"

Frank held his breath and ran a hand through his hair. "Uh, you know, it's actually been a while since I've seen him."

"How long?"

"Last week?"

"I don't understand," Amy said. "Are you asking me or telling me?"

"No, it was, uh, last week. It was actually Wednesday, the day before Thanksgiving. I saw him right before I went to work." He gripped the steering wheel hard. Goddamn Boyd. Where was he?

"What was he doing?"

"He was, uh, actually feeling pretty good. His back was feeling good, I mean. He was taking a walk. The last thing I did was wave to him as I left for work." There was silence on the line.

"Didn't it snow really bad last Wednesday? Why would Boyd be out walking in a blizzard? If he slipped he could hurt his back."

Frank gripped the wheel tighter. "Amy, I just don't know. All I can tell you is what happened."

"Yeah, okay. It's just strange. He's not answering his phone and you say he hasn't been home for a week."

"Hey, I hate to cut you off, but I have to go into work. If I'm late Rocco will get pissed and I just started working a shift where I'm getting decent tips." He got out of the car and slammed the door. The parking lot was still wet from the misty rain that had been falling earlier in the day.

"Okay," she said. "Frank, I'm going to call the police and file a missing persons report."

He stopped and grimaced, leaning back against his car. "I don't know, Amy. Are you sure you want to get them involved? I mean, with Boyd's problem, it may lead to more trouble than help."

"Frank, do you have any idea how worried I am? It's been a week. I know he's disappeared before, but he could be lying in a ditch somewhere. I'm calling the police."

Frank's breathing was coming too fast now. The last thing he needed was police involved, looking around their house. "Amy, you know, Boyd uses."

"I don't care, Frank. I'd rather know he's safe."

"Yeah, I know, but he lives with me in my mom's house. The last thing I need is cops looking through there. If Boyd has some stuff in the house that shouldn't be there, it could cause trouble. I mean, she could lose the house if they find something that shouldn't be there, right? Isn't that how it works? I can't remember if that's how it works."

Amy's voice was very calm but firm when she spoke next. "Frank, I'm calling the police in an hour. If there is anything in that house you're worried about, you'd better get it out."

"That's not enough time. I just got to work."

"One hour, Frank."

The call cut off.

Frank looked at the back door entrance to the pizza shop. Jimmy Newmantowski, one of the day shift delivery guys, was smoking a cigarette, one boot cocked up on the side of the building. Frank jogged over to him.

"Hey, Jimmy, you want to earn a little extra money?"

• • •

Bob Ellstrom rolled down State Route 9 until the Magellan GPS unit on the windshield dinged, and he saw a painted sign announcing he had arrived at the West Wind Mobile Home Park. He turned left into the park and followed the long driveway back to where the trailers were set up. The GPS dinged again, and he turned right this time. Three trailers up on the right, he saw a brown single-wide with reflective address numbers matching the ones he had found online. He slowed down and stopped on the side of the road.

This was where the reporter lived, the one who was writing about him. He smiled. It was one more thing he knew about them that they didn't know about him. He already knew where the publisher, Charlie Ingram, lived. They were out there, spinning their wheels looking all over Hogan for him, asking people if they knew anything that could help them, and there wasn't. No one knew any answers except for him, and he certainly wasn't talking.

The problem now was what to do with this knowledge. Could it be used to his advantage? In order for any of this to be any use to him, he had to be very careful about how he used what he knew. He was woken out of his thoughts by a rapping at the passenger's side window. He looked over, heart beating quickly, and saw a woman standing beside his truck. She had a coat on and was holding a cane up. She tapped on the window with it again, and he clicked the button to lower the window.

"Can I help you with something, ma'am?" he said.

"My name is Tilly. I noticed you parked out here and wondered what you needed," she said. "You lost?"

"Maybe," he said. "I was looking for an old friend of mine, and I understand he lived here in the park, but I'm a bit turned around."

She looked at him suspiciously, trying to make up her mind about him. "What's your friend's name? I've lived here a long time, so I'll probably know him."

"Oh, yeah, well, that would be very helpful," Bob said. "His name is, uh, Ricky."

Her eyebrows knitted together. "Does Ricky have a last name?"

"Oh, yeah, of course. Sorry, ma'am. It's Rogers. Ricky Rogers. Like I said, he just moved back to the area and was just supposed to have moved in."

"You all right?" Tilly said. "You're sweating pretty hard. Maybe your heat's up too high."

"Oh, well, I haven't been feeling too well. Maybe I'll just go."

"Don't you want to see your friend?"

"Well, sure. Do you have any idea where he may be?"

Tilly looked at him again with an inscrutable look on her face. "I haven't seen any new trailers come in lately. I don't see everything, though."

"Well, I'll just keep looking," he said and dropped his truck into drive. "You have a good night, ma'am. Thanks for the help."

She stepped away. "Yep, all right. You have a good night, too."

Bob drove off and followed the road around in a large square. Eventually he came back out to the driveway he had followed in and turned right. Ten minutes later, he was back on Owl North Road. He was almost past the old Jensen place before he realized there was a car parked in the driveway.

He slowed down and took a good look. It was a Honda, just like the one in the surveillance video. Afraid he was going to be spotted but unwilling to give up the opportunity, he stopped and looked at the license plate. It was the same as the one he had seen in the video from the barn. This was the car used in the robbery. This was the other guy, the other one who had seen his letters and stolen his tools. This was the car he had seen here those other times. He knew it. There was no way this guy was just a visitor. Looking at it there in the driveway, he was confident he had seen it here before and often. Why hadn't he seen it over the past week, though? Maybe they just worked opposite shifts. Yeah, sure, that could be it. Maybe the kid just worked evenings.

He sat there on the gravel shoulder and wondered what he should do. The immensity of what he had done to the other burglar hit him square in the chest, and his breathing increased. Should he pull in and confront this guy? He wanted to. More than anything, he wanted to kick down the front door of this house and strangle the guy inside. What if he wasn't alone, though? Both of the burglars looked like they were in their early twenties. Was he really up to fighting someone thirty years younger? It was one thing to hit them with a pickup truck, but quite another to initiate a fight. Hell, the guy could have guns in there. In fact, given that he was a criminal, he probably did. He checked his rearview mirror and pulled back onto the road. This was another situation that needed a little consideration before he acted.

Seventeen

Thanks for coming down with me," Amy said to Tim. They were sitting in the small waiting room of the Hogan Police Department. She was balancing a clipboard on her crossed legs while filling out a form.

"Not a problem," Tim said. "I need a break from the office, anyway. The phones have been ringing off the hook."

"Are they all calls about your letter freak?"

Tim yawned and stretched. "Yeah, he really needs another hobby. We've gotten calls from almost seventy people. Charlie has me following up with everyone and writing a follow-up to the story that came out this week." He looked over her shoulder at the clock on the wall. Seven ten and he hadn't eaten since lunch.

Amy got to the bottom of the form and signed it, then starting looking things over to make sure everything was complete. Satisfied, she stood up and returned the clipboard and form to the officer sitting at the desk. He took it, checked it and pulled it off the clipboard. Tim got up and walked to the window.

"So what happens now?" he heard Amy ask.

"We'll start keeping an eye out for him. Tomorrow morning, the detective will see the report. They'll start their investigation. Is this a cell phone number right here?" he asked, pointing to a box on the form.

"Yes," Amy said.

"Okay, well, they'll call you and get started. I see here that your brother is an adult and a drug user?"

"Yes, but he's still missing."

The officer held up a hand. "I understand, miss, and I'm not casting any aspersions. It just affects the investigation. There are some places in town where we would take an extra good look."

"Oh, sorry."

"Okay, if we find him or hear anything we'll be in touch. Have a good night."

Tim walked Amy out of the police station and to her car in the lot. "I'm really sorry about all this," he said.

She moved forward a step and hugged him. After a moment he put his arms around her and gathered her into himself. She was sobbing. He held her and didn't say anything. After a moment she turned her head but stayed in his arms.

"I've always been afraid of this," she said. "Ever since he got hooked on the painkillers, I've been afraid he was going to start using heroin and overdose or cross the wrong person and get hurt."

He stroked her hair. "I don't know what to say, Amy. I think you're doing the right thing getting the police involved. I mean, if they come across him they'll know someone's looking for him."

She pulled away, wiped her eyes and looked at the stars in the cold clear sky above. "It's late. Have you eaten yet?"

"No, you want to get something?"

"Actually, why don't we go back to my place? I'll cook."

He laughed. "Absolutely not. The last thing you need to do right now is cook dinner. We'll grab something. My treat."

"I can't let you do that," she said.

"Aw, it's okay. I just got a new job and a raise. Let me splurge a little."

Half an hour later they were sitting on opposite ends of the couch in Amy's apartment eating salads and chicken wings from Barrusas. *Modern Family* reruns were on TV, but they weren't paying attention.

"Tate was pissed at you for quitting, you know," she said.

He sipped his Coke. "I know, but I needed to get started on this story. It's getting big, and Charlie wants to make sure we stay in front of it. He's gotten a couple calls from the bigger papers and news stations, so he doesn't want them taking over."

She poked him with a stockinged foot. "Oh, Charlie doesn't want them to get ahead of you, huh? Just Charlie?"

Tim smiled and flushed a little. "Well, maybe Charlie and me."

She laughed again. "Yeah, that's more like it."

He looked at her and felt overwhelmed. It was nice being with her, but the situation with her brother and her breakup with Jeremy had him feeling like he couldn't fully express himself. Would opening up to her now just overwhelm her? The safest thing, it seemed, was to just be there for her and see how things progressed. Besides, having dinner with her in her apartment was a hell of a lot better than sitting at home eating alone and watching Netflix.

"I really am sorry about leaving Tate with no notice. Did Mac take the truck out today?"

She nodded and set the foam container from her salad on the coffee table. "Yeah, Tate had him go out with one of the stock guys." She moved closer to him and laid her head in his lap and yawned. "I wouldn't worry too much about Tate. Finding delivery guys isn't really that hard. I mean, I know you were like the king delivery man of Hogan, but I bet he'll make do."

Tim caught her yawn and stifled his own as much as he could. "I'll have you know I was three-time county champion delivery man. I thought you'd be more proud." He sipped his Coke and set the can back on her end table. He looked around her apartment.

"I'm jealous, you know, of your furniture. It all matches. Nothing at my place does. It's all second hand and looks like it came from a frat house after an exceptionally long party."

She didn't say anything, and he looked down. She was asleep. Tim adjusted his position, sinking deeper into the couch, and softly raised his feet up to the coffee table. He stroked her hair, and she started breathing deeply. He didn't mind at all if she took a nap. In fact, he was fairly certain he could sit like this all night.

• • •

At eleven thirty, Bob Ellstrom walked out to his truck and threw a small gym bag in. He made his way down the long driveway and turned right, headed for the old Jensen place. The night was dark and quiet as he drove. There was no moon tonight, so there wasn't any light reflecting off the snow that still covered everything. As usual, there was no traffic on Owl North Road this late. He approached the old Jensen place slowly and saw the Honda still sitting in the driveway, though not in the same spot. It appeared to have moved since he'd seen it this afternoon, like someone had left and returned.

There was one light on in the front of the house, probably the living room. He took a deep breath and pulled into the driveway as slowly as he could to reduce any noise the pickup might make. He kept an eye on the windows but didn't see anyone looking out. No curtains moved and no faces appeared.

Bob took a deep breath, pulled on a pair of thin leather gloves, picked up the small gym bag and got out of the pickup, closing the door softly until the latch clicked. He took a look around and didn't see anyone on the road, so he crossed to the front porch. He mounted the two steps and peered inside through the small window of the front door.

There was a couch inside with a blanket strewn across it. An old easy chair was against another wall. No one was in the living room, but he could hear the TV playing loudly. Bob reached down and pulled the screen door open. It squeaked, and the slower he went, the louder it became. He looked back through the window in the door but no one moved inside. He tried the knob for the wooden door but it wouldn't turn. He unzipped his bag and took out a small pry bar. A quick look through the window confirmed no one was inside, so he inserted it between the jamb and the door and leaned his weight on it. The door popped open with a dry crack. He pushed the door open and stepped inside the living room.

Bob reached into the gym bag and pulled out a small semi-automatic, a Ruger nine millimeter he used for plinking cans in the back field. He set the gym bag down on the beat-up coffee table and moved a few steps to the left so he could look up the staircase. No lights on. He bit his lip and moved to the kitchen. A light glowed over the sink. Bob gripped the gun with both hands, starting to sweat now. It wasn't particularly hot in the house but his heart was beating quickly, and he was breathing hard. He took a moment and inhaled deeply to calm down. There was a wallet, keys, and a cell phone on the small round kitchen table. A landline phone hung on the wall. He picked up the receiver and put it to his ear. If he heard someone talking to a 911 operator, he was going to haul ass out the front door. There was nothing on the line, though—no voices. Not even a dial tone. It probably wasn't even hooked up. He laid the receiver on the table instead of hanging it up.

He looked around and still didn't hear anything. Was it possible no one was home after all? The keys seemed to indicate whoever drove the car was still home. He grabbed the wallet and flipped it open with one hand. There, in a little plastic window, he saw a driver's license. The name on the license was Frank Utzler, and the address was for the house he was standing in.

If he was a betting man, he'd say Frank was somewhere in the house. He took a deep breath.

"Frank Utzler!" he said to the house. "I need to talk with you. Why don't you come into the kitchen and save me the trouble of finding you?"

No one answered.

•   •   •

Frank was in the basement making sure their stash was hidden as well as it could be. The basement was damp and chilly, even with the furnace and water heater occupying one corner. It was dark, too. A single forty-watt bulb with a pull chain lit up the whole thing. After speaking with Amy that afternoon he'd convinced Jimmy Nemantowski to cover him for an hour at work and ran home. He had swept through the house, gathering up all of their paraphernalia and hauling it down here. There were several glass bongs, baggies of weed, and the money from Skillet in a box marked "Christmas Decorations." Now that his shift was over, he was trying to do a better job of hiding everything. He was nervous as hell. A joint would have calmed him down but he had no idea when the police would be coming to talk with him. He had seen enough crime shows on TV to know that any missing persons case was going to start with the last person who had seen them.

He held the small cardboard box and looked around the basement. It was as square as the rest of the house and just as small. Then he saw the door to the root cellar and smiled. The root cellar ran under the porch, and if you weren't looking for it in the dark basement, you could miss it.

Frank set the box down on a workbench and walked over to the root cellar door. Boxes of his mom's junk were stacked up around it. He pushed them aside and crouched down. The door was only half the size of a regular door. It was more of a crawlspace used to store items that needed to stay cool when the house was built in the early twentieth century. Frank turned the latch on the door and tugged on it. It was stuck in the frame, so he braced one hand and pulled harder. This time the door came loose and scraped across the floor because it wasn't square in the frame anymore. Frank looked inside and noticed it was much cooler than the basement, but not as cold as the air outside. It was dark, too, like a mineshaft at midnight. The basement light didn't penetrate the small space. He couldn't remember if there was a light in here or not so he reached in, groping in the dark for a pull chain. Sure enough, he found one. He tugged it, and the space was illuminated for a brief moment before the bulb went out. Frank tugged the chain again but nothing happened. He sighed and pulled away from the space. He looked around for a spare bulb on one of the shelves along the wall where the washer and dryer sat.

Then he heard someone yelling his name from the kitchen.

● ● ●

Bob listened intently to the empty house. No one answered him. He sighed and picked up the cell phone from the table and slipped it into his jacket pocket. He didn't want anyone calling for help. Given how small the house was and the fact that he hadn't seen anyone in the living room, kitchen, or small dining room, he made his way back to the bottom of the staircase.

"Frank," he said again, like he was calling a misbehaving boy to come down from his bedroom. "Come downstairs. I want to talk with you about you and Boyd breaking into my house. That's all we're going to do," he said, gripping the pistol and hiding it down near his thigh. "We're just going to talk."

● ● ●

Frank froze for moment. Was that the police calling his name? Were they actually here and inside the house? Would they just walk in like that? Didn't they need to knock or have a warrant or something? He grabbed the cardboard box and set it inside the root cellar, then he pushed some cardboard boxes in front of it. He took a deep breath and moved back to the bottom of the staircase. Just as he was about to put his foot on the bottom step, he heard the second announcement from the guy upstairs. His foot froze in mid-step. It was the guy from the job last week. He started to shake.

• • •

"I'm not playing games, Frank," Bob said. "I just want to talk about my tools and where they are. As long as I get those back we're going to be fine, okay? Just come down here and we'll talk about it like men."

Bob listened again, the gun in his hand. He figured he'd let the guy come down about three steps and then do it. He wouldn't have anywhere to go. The problem was, no one was answering him.

"Frank, if I have to come up these stairs I'm going to be really pissed off. Just get down here. Let's talk, just you and me."

There was no answer.

"Okay, Frank, I'm coming up and if you jump out at me I'm going to be very unhappy."

Bob raised the pistol and started up the stairs.

• • •

Frank was frozen to the spot. This really was the guy from the burglary. What he said about the tools proved that. He didn't know what to do. He looked at the rickety basement stairs and thought about how loudly they creaked. He might be able to get up them and out the back door in the kitchen, but where would he go? If the guy was parked behind his Honda he would be stuck in the driveway. The backyard was covered in snow, so running would be difficult, and how long would he survive wearing nothing more than jeans and a Rocco's Pizza t-shirt? He didn't even have his hoodie.

He looked back at the root cellar.

• • •

Bob got to the top of the stairs and felt around the wall for a light switch.
He was almost gasping for air now his heart was beating so fast. If some
twenty-year-old kid jumped him he honestly didn't know it he could
fight him off. Well, that's why he had the gun, wasn't it?

He found a light switch and flicked it. There were four doors, three
bedrooms, and a bathroom, he guessed. He stood at the top of the stairs
and tried to calm himself. He raised the gun.

"Enough of this cat-and-mouse stuff, Frank," he said. "Just come on
out and we'll talk like men." Nothing. "We're practically neighbors,
right? Let's just talk about things." There was more silence.

"I saw your keys and phone downstairs," Bob said. "I know you're
here. Just come on out."

• • •

Frank pulled the door to the crawlspace open and peered inside again.
He grabbed the pull chain for the light and yanked. Nothing happened.
He felt cobwebs caress his hand. The floor appeared to be dirt, not
cement like the basement floor. The guy upstairs was yelling again.
Frank moved back to the center of the basement and pulled the chain
for the light. It went out, and he started to move back toward the root
cellar. Then he stopped, turned back, yanked the beaded chain and the
light came back on. He grabbed the bulb to twist it out of the socket and
burned his fingers. He shook his hand and blew on his fingertips.
Looking around, he spotted a pile of laundry on the floor and grabbed a
dirty white tube sock. He pulled the chain and turned off the light, then
put his hand in the sock, hoping to hell it was one of his and not one of
Boyd's. He twisted the bulb and it came free of the socket.

Holding his hands out in front of him, he moved slowly back toward
the root cellar until he felt the wall. He ran his hands down the wall to the
rough opening and pulled the door open. His heart was slamming in his
chest like he was back in high school gym class running laps around the
basketball court. He took a deep breath and crawled into the root cellar.

It seemed filled with spiderwebs. Thick curtains of them settled softly over him as he turned himself around to face the door. He held a hand out and found a shelf and set the bulb on it. Something ran across his hand and skittered up his arm. He didn't know what it was but it felt like it had lots of legs. He brushed at his arm with his other hand.

He reached out through the small doorway and tried to slide boxes in front of the door. Then he pulled it shut and locked himself in with whatever called the root cellar home.

• • •

Bob moved through the bedrooms slowly, looking in closets and under beds. When he got to the bathroom, he started to consider that no one was home. He may have been wandering around talking to an empty house.

He went back to the top of the stairs and looked down at the light in the living room. He didn't hear anything except the TV. Maybe the guy had gone out with someone else. Would he leave his keys, phone, and wallet behind, though? No, no one would do that. Bob moved down the stairs and back into the living room.

The door was still shut and he was fairly certain he would have heard someone going out, the way that screen door squeaked. There were no closets to look through on this level. He went back into the kitchen. The landline phone was still on the table where he had left it. His heart was still beating too fast, and he was breathing too hard. It was exhilarating and frightening to be standing in someone's house uninvited, being somewhere he shouldn't be, maybe doing them harm. There was a back door leading out to the backyard. Bob flicked the light switch and a light came on outside. He looked over the little bit of backyard the light illuminated and didn't see any footprints in the snow. It was pretty clear no one had run out this door.

Then he saw the door in the corner. He opened it and saw steps leading down into a basement.

"Hey, Frank, you down there?"

• • •

Things were crawling over Frank. He brushed them away as quietly as he could but it felt like the whole root cellar was alive. He couldn't tell what was a cobweb brushing against him, what were insects, or what was his imagination. What he did know was that the more he moved, the more things touched him in the dark. He considered changing the light bulb in here with the one he had snagged from the basement light, but if he did, the light might shine around the edges of the root cellar door. Then he heard someone calling his name from the top of the stairs.

• • •

Bob reached out and slid his hand over the walls on either side of the steps looking for a light switch. There wasn't one. He looked down the stairs as far as he could with the light from the kitchen. There was some laundry piled up on the floor at the bottom of the stairs, but that was all he could see. He moved down the stairs slowly and quietly, but they squeaked with every step.

"Frank, you down here? Hey, if you are, don't jump out and hit me, okay? I just want to talk about you and Boyd robbing my place. I just want to talk about getting my stuff back. Don't hit me with a baseball bat or anything."

He got to the bottom of the stairs, and now the little bit of light shining down the stairs from the kitchen wasn't helping at all. He felt along the wall for a switch but didn't find one. The pistol was down behind his leg. He groped around in front of him and found a beaded chain hanging from the ceiling joists. He gave it a yank but nothing happened.

"You got a light bulb out here, Frank, so if you're at the store you may want to pick some up."

He stood there in the dark, listening.

• • •

Frank drew his knees up and hugged them. He could still hear things skittering in the dark space. He became aware of how small the little root cellar really was but couldn't do anything, could barely breathe. How had this guy found them?

• • •

Bob reached into his jacket pocket and pulled out Frank's cell phone. He pushed the power button and it woke up, casting a weak light around the cellar. Bob brought the pistol up, pointing it around as he slowly turned in a circle. The basement was small, he saw. There weren't a lot of places for anyone to hide. He moved past the washer and dryer, toward the furnace and hot water tank. Both had spiderwebs and dust on them and it didn't look like anyone had been near them for ages. Bob moved back under the steps and saw boxes stacked up. There was no room for anyone to hide.

Listening carefully, Bob couldn't hear anything except his own labored breathing and his rapid heartbeat. He took one last look around and walked back up the stairs to the kitchen. He threw Frank's cell phone onto the table and moved back into the living room. He snatched his gym bag from the coffee table and put the pistol into it. Then he moved to the front door and left.

"I'll be back," Bob said. "I'll make sure you're home next time."

• • •

Frank woke up later when something stung or bit him. He barely remembered the danger that had forced him into the confined space, but he knew he couldn't stay inside one more second. He didn't know how he managed to fall asleep in the dismal root cellar but now he kicked the door open and spilled out onto the basement floor. He lay silently, listening for movement from upstairs. He was cold and stiff and could barely move without his muscles rebelling. Something crawled across his scalp, and he jumped up, running his hands through his hair, brushing things out of it. It was still dark in the basement so he moved to the stairs and listened for sounds from upstairs. The house was quiet.

He moved up the stairs as quietly as he was able, but they still squeaked. The kitchen light was still on and he peeked around the corner. The clock on the stove said 4:05. He had been in that cellar for hours. His wallet, keys, and cell phone were still on the small round table. Something moved down his back and he slapped at it. His nerve broke and he raced through the living room, stripping off his t-shirt. He went up the stairs two at a time, shucking his jeans by the time he got to the top. He went into the bathroom and spun the shower spigot handles and jumped into the tub without bothering to pull the curtain closed. He ran his hands all over his body and saw bugs fall to the enamel. A couple of them were centipedes or earwigs or some other bug that had a million legs. He was covered in red welts from bug bites.

Ten minutes later, Frank was stuffing clothes and other items into a large black duffle bag he had picked up at a flea market. Looking around his room, he didn't see anything else he might need and went downstairs. He put on his winter coat and grabbed his stuff from the kitchen table. He turned off the lights and looked outside. The driveway was empty except for his car. He opened the door and ran for the Honda. It started, and he gunned the little four-cylinder engine, making it scream as he got out onto Owl North Road. He made sure he went the opposite direction of the house he and Boyd had robbed. He decided his mom could rent their place out if she wanted. He was never going back.

Eighteen

Tim woke up stiff, with his neck bent across the back of the couch. He moved it slowly and saw that he was still in Amy's apartment. The sun was coming up outside, and she was curled into him. He blinked and the clock on the cable box said 6:17. He rubbed his eyes and Amy stirred, looking up at him with confused eyes.

"Did we sleep out here all night?" she said.

He rubbed his neck. "I think so. I can barely move my head. You okay?"

She sat up and nodded. "Sorry. I didn't mean to do that."

Tim stood up and stretched his hands over his head. His back popped as he twisted from side to side. "Don't worry about it. Spending the night with you isn't the worst thing that's ever happened to me."

She laughed and shook her head. Her hair was matted to one side and sticking up on the other. "Well, I hope it was everything you thought it would be."

"Bathroom?"

She pointed. "Right there."

"Thanks."

A few minutes later, he came out. She was in the kitchen making coffee. It was one of those Keurig single-serve things that used the little plastic cups. She slipped past him and went to use the bathroom. Walking back into the kitchen, he saw she had her phone in her hand and she was scrolling through it.

"Anything yet?" he asked, putting a steaming mug in front of her.

She shook her head. "No." She blew on the coffee and took a sip. "There's nothing yet. I expect I'll be hearing from the police later this morning." She moved past him to the machine. "Let me make you a cup."

"I really can't," he said, looking at his phone. "I have to get home, grab a shower, change, and get to work. I get the feeling today is going to be a busy day."

"Yeah? Something up?"

He held up his phone. "I have thirty-seven new friend requests on Facebook and one of them is from a new group called 'Hogan Letters.'"

She raised an eyebrow. "Really? Let me see."

Amy leaned over his shoulder, and he could feel her pressing into him as she put a hand on his shoulder. He was very aware of how good she smelled. "Scroll down," she said.

There were posts from people who had received letters and users wondering what was going on. Tim scrolled down and saw that some people had posted pictures of letters they had received.

"Wow," he said. "This is great."

"Yeah?"

He nodded and kept scrolling. "I recognize some of these names, but not others. I need to get into the office and start following up on all this." He got up and grabbed his jacket.

"Will you be okay?" he asked.

Amy nodded. "I think so. I'm just worried."

He moved to her and drew her into a hug. "Hey, they'll find him. Hogan's a small town. There are just so many places he could be. We could try calling his roommate again."

"Frank isn't much use," she said. "He can barely hold down a job."

"You're doing everything you can. You know that, right? I mean, you've called around and talked to the police. I'm sure the detectives will be in touch. They've got experience finding people."

"Yeah. I just wish Boyd wasn't like this, you know? I mean, him disappearing isn't exactly abnormal. When we were at the police station, did you catch that the cop at the desk knew Boyd's name?"

"No," Tim said.

"Well, he did. He knew who my brother was because he's been picked up for shoplifting and for possession, and now he's the kind of guy cops just know. When his name comes up in connection with any-thing, they aren't surprised. That's who my brother is."

"I'm sorry, Amy. I know a little about having a screwed-up family, and I really am sorry you have to go through this."

She smiled and a tear ran down her cheek. "I just want him to be okay, you know? I just want him to be safe. He's all the family I have left."

Tim hugged her again. "I know."

She put a hand on his chest. "Okay, get out of here. Go do your reporter thing. Figure out which degenerate is sending these creepy letters."

"You sure?"

"Yeah, I have to get to work anyway, and I have to catch up on my homework. Believe it or not, working for Tate isn't my lifelong ambi-tion, either."

"Okay," he said. "I'll call you later. Text me if the cops get in touch or find anything out."

"I will. Now go. I need to get cleaned up for work."

He leaned in and kissed her goodbye. It was nice, he thought, to do that.

• • •

Tim was in the office before eight o'clock, scrolling through the Face-book group page. There was a treasure trove of data, he saw. A lot of the posts were copies of letters from people he and Charlie hadn't spoken with. He was busy grabbing names and copying the images into a data-base he'd set up so they could keep track of who they spoke with and what the letters said. Another browser tab was open to Twitter. There were a few tweets about the letters and the letter writer. Tim noted the relevant hashtags on his yellow legal pad. The bigger papers didn't have anything up on their websites yet, but he expected that to change.

A couple of the posters mentioned they had called the police. Tim made a note to go to the police station and request copies of the reports. There were probably names on the reports he didn't have yet.

The phone on his desk rang and he picked it up. "*Hogan Shopper,* Tim speaking."

"Tim, this is Gary Shellmack over at Creekside Motors. Is Charlie in?"

"No, Mr. Shellmack, I'm sorry. He isn't in yet. Can I take a message?"

"I don't know, maybe you're the guy I want to talk to. You wrote the story about the letters, right?"

"Yes, I did. Have you received a letter?"

Tim heard a heavy sigh on the other end of the phone. "Yeah, you could say that. It's more like a dozen. All since August."

Tim leaned forward in his chair. "Yeah? That's quite a few, Mr. Shellmack."

"Call me Gary, please. Anyway, you bet your ass it's a lot, and I'm tired of getting them," he said. "I don't suppose you guys know who's doing this, do you? Some hint?"

Tim chewed on a pen. "Everything we know was in the story we printed, Mr. Shellmack. Let me ask you, do you have copies of the letters you received? Is it possible I could get copies?"

There was silence on the other end of the line for a moment. "Yeah, I think that would be okay."

"I can be out there later this morning. Would that be all right?"

"Sure. Look, Tim, I've done some research, and I may have more for you than the letters."

"Yeah?"

"Well, the way I see it, I must have done something to make this guy mad because of how many letters I've gotten, so I've put together a list of people who may be angry with me. Is that something you would be interested in?"

"Sure, I'd be happy to take a look at your list. Is ten o'clock okay?"

"See you then."

"Right." Gary hung up the phone, and Tim leaned back in his chair. The door to the office opened, and Charlie walked in, clearly surprised to see Tim in before him. Tim looked up and waved.

"Coffee's on in the back," he said. "Why don't you get settled and I'll fill you in on what we've learned overnight."

Befuddled, Charlie nodded. "Okay."

· · ·

Bob Ellstrom glided through the Brinco warehouse with a load of plastic bins full of brake rotors on his forklift. He was happy this morning and he drove through the warehouse stacks with a smile on his face. What he had done the previous night, going into that house, had been exhilarating. It may not have been successful, but he felt alive, more so than he had for years. He had been in control. It was still a mystery as to whether Frank Utzler had been in the house. The car was there, and his keys and phone, but he had gone from top to bottom and hadn't seen anyone. He could try again. He would try again.

The walkie-talkie sitting in the plastic holster on the roll cage of his forklift squawked his name. He stopped in an aisle and picked it up.

"Go for Bob."

"Need you in the office," Ricky said.

Bob rolled his eyes but felt like even Ricky couldn't spoil his mood. "I'll be right there after I make a drop at the dock."

"Thanks."

Bob dropped the bins of rotors at the dock in the staging area and parked his forklift. He walked down to the little line of offices that ran perpendicular to the wall with the shipping dock doors. He found Ricky in one of them sitting at a desk. He knocked on the doorframe.

Ricky looked up. "Come on in. Have a seat."

Bob entered the office and sat down facing the desk in one of the black plastic chairs with chrome legs. "What's up?"

"It's time for annual performance reviews," Ricky said, sliding a piece of paper across the desk to him. "I just need to go over yours and have you sign off on it."

Bob picked it up and looked it over. "What do they use these for?"

Ricky leaned back in the desk chair. "They're used to give you an idea of how you're doing and what needs improvement. You work on any items listed and maybe your increase is bigger next year."

Bob looked at him, concerned. "Wait a minute. You use these to help determine wage increases?"

Ricky smiled. "That's right."

"I thought the union contract specified the amount of raises."

Ricky kept right on smiling like the little prick Bob thought he was. "The contract provides for the minimum increases, which this year are two and a half percent. However, supervisors can bump that up to four percent if they're so inclined, with an excellent performance review."

Bob looked down at the review. In a text box titled "Needs Improvement," he saw a number of bullet points. "Poor attitude in general, unwilling to work extra shifts to meet production requirements without arguing, two incidents of unsafe practices."

Bob shook his head and smiled as he threw the paper back on Ricky's desk. "Let me guess, I'm only getting two and a half percent?"

Ricky nodded with a smug look on his face. "It's in line with the contract. If you work on these items," he twirled the paper around and pointed at the text box, "I'm sure you'll do better next year."

Bob stared at him and then leaned forward. He picked up a pen from the desk and pulled the form back toward him. He saw the line for his signature and scribbled his name.

"Hold on one second," Ricky said. "You get a copy." He picked up the form and walked out of the office to use the copier. He walked back in and laid the copy on his desk. Bob stood up with it.

"Ricky, do you like being a bully? Being the big man?"

The younger man put his hands up. "Okay, we're done here. That's your copy to keep." He moved to the door and waited for Bob to leave.

Bob stood up with a smile on his face and moved toward the doorway, but then he grabbed the edge of the door and shut it softly. Ricky took a step back, and his ass bumped into the office wall.

"Do you like being a bully? Does it make you feel powerful?"

Ricky held his hands up in front of himself in a protective manner. "Okay, Bob, just go back to work, okay?"

Bob stepped back. "Is this your first job, Ricky? Like, your first real job?"

"I don't see how that's relevant to our conversation here, Bob. Just go back to work."

Bob spoke in a very calm and even voice and took a step toward him. "The way I see it, Ricky, is you haven't really worked all that much. Not like a man works. I see you more as the kind of guy who goes to college, learns a bunch of shit that makes him think he knows how the world works, and then you land a job like the one you got here. You get to jerk us around with the little bit of authority the company gives you, but you don't know what it's like to build something with your own hands." He crumpled the review in his hand.

"When I was at Ohio Axle we did that, we built things with our hands. We were men who forged steel and operated machines that could kill someone if we did it wrong. We didn't. We did it good. Then some college-educated assholes higher up the food chain started screwing around with the money, started playing games and forgot that they were stewards of something greater than themselves." Ricky stood, transfixed, staring at Bob.

"You see, we worked hard for our pay and our pay was fair. That was the deal and those fellas up the line, the ones managing things, they screwed all that up. They played games with the money we earned. Instead of sitting at home enjoying my retirement, I'm here driving a fork-lift for pennies. And once again, some guy who never really worked a day in his life, who doesn't understand how it feels to take a lump of metal in his hands and turn it into something useful, is smiling at me and dicking around with my money. I have to tell you, Ricky, there are only so many times I'm going to allow that to happen. Like I said, you are using the authority this place grants you to mess with working men. Have you ever considered what you would do if one of those men decided to seize authority for themselves? What would you do if they just decided to push back?"

Bob took another step forward. "I have to be honest, Ricky, I don't think you'd fare so well."

He stepped back, opened the office door and held up the crumpled review form. "Thanks for this. I'm going to give the items on it quite a bit of thought."

Ricky looked at him from the office, unsure of what to do.

• • •

Frank pulled into Skillet's driveway and saw the black Ford F-150 sitting in its usual spot, indicating the dealer was home. Frank pulled his Honda around the back of the house as far as he could and got out. He knocked on the back door of the house, hard, and heard heavy footsteps hurrying to the door. It opened and Skillet looked at him with fire in his eyes.

"What did I tell you about banging on my door like that?"

Frank held his hands up, fingers spread wide. "Hey, I'm sorry, really, but we have to talk." He started to enter, but Skillet put a hand on his chest.

"We don't have to do anything, Frank," he said. "Take a step back." Frank leaned in close. "We have to talk, and we can't do it on your back stoop."

Skillet looked past Frank, into the driveway and backyard. Satisfied they were alone, he stepped aside and said, "Get in here."

Frank squeezed past him, and Skillet shut the door, turning the knob lock and two deadbolts as he did so. He gestured to the living room. Frank went ahead of him and dropped into the same chair he'd sat in on his last visit.

Skillet went to the mantle over the small fireplace, pulled a cigarette out of a Marlboro box and tamped it down before lighting it. He inhaled and looked at Frank. "You're getting on my nerves, Frank."

"This is important."

"Okay, so what's up?"

"That last job we pulled? The one with the tools?"

Skillet exhaled smoke from his nostrils. Frank was suddenly aware of his neck tattoos and the menacing look on Skillet's face. "Yeah, what about it? I'm not paying you anything else."

Frank shook his head. "It's not like that, it's not. The guy we ripped off? He came to our house."

Skillet's eye's narrowed. "What are you talking about? He came to your house? How does he know where you live?"

"I don't know, but he was there and he knew who we were. I mean, he used our names, okay? He told us what we did and he wants his stuff back."

Skillet walked into the kitchen and Frank became uneasy. He hated when he couldn't see Skillet. "You want a beer?"

"Hell, yeah, I want a beer."

Skillet walked back into the living room and flipped a can of Budweiser in Frank's direction. "Okay, so this guy comes to your door and confronts you, right? What did you tell him?"

"I didn't talk to him," Frank said, and he took a pull on his beer.

"Okay, so Boyd talked to him. Did he just play dumb and act like he didn't know what he was talking about?"

"No, Boyd didn't talk to him, either. You see, neither of us actually spoke with him, as such, you know? He came in while I was in the cellar, and I was able to hide while he went through the house."

Skillet looked at him with a raised eyebrow. "Hold on, this dude just walks into your house and you let him? There were two of you. Why didn't you just bounce him out of there?"

"Well, I haven't seen Boyd for a while," Frank said. "In fact, I haven't seen him since the day we robbed that guy's house. I had to get into the city so he volunteered to walk home. He got out of the car, and I haven't seen him since. I'm not even sure he made it home."

Skillet stared at him for a minute, evaluating him. "Let me get this right. You guys rob a place, and your idea of a successful getaway is to walk home?"

Frank leaned back in his chair. "I had to get to work. I wanted to make sure I had an alibi in case anyone asked around."

Skillet chuckled. "Man, I don't think I've ever heard anything that stupid. You rob a house, and let Boyd walk home so you're not late for work. And now you can't find Boyd."

"You think he killed him?"

Skillet got up and walked around the living room to the front door and looked outside, turning his head left and right. Then he came back to the couch. "Anybody talk to you?"

Frank shook his head. "Not yet, but they will. Boyd was supposed to go to his sister's for Thanksgiving, but he never showed up. Now she's calling me asking where he is. I can't exactly tell her the last time I saw him we were breaking into some guy's house, can I?"

"No," Skillet said. "You most definitely cannot do that. You understand? As far as you're concerned, you went to work and Boyd was sitting on the couch watching cartoons."

"Yeah, yeah, I know. The thing is, she's going to the police so they're going to talk to me and it's going to happen soon."

"She told you that?"

Frank nodded. "Yeah, she did."

Skillet bit his lower lip and looked out the window living room window behind him. "Did he threaten you? This guy, when he was in your house?"

"I took his walking in uninvited as a threat. And the stuff he said, yeah, he was threatening me."

"He must be pissed."

"Very," Frank said. "His house was kind of weird, you know."

Skillet turned to him and set his beer can down on the coffee table. "What do you mean his 'house' was weird? You guys were only supposed to be in the barn. Get in, grab the tools and take off. Why were you in the house?"

Frank sighed. "It was Boyd, man, not me. I was closing the barn doors and pulling the car up and Boyd broke into the house."

"That dumbass. What did you guys find in there?" Skillet said. "This was supposed to be an even split."

"There was nothing in there, okay?" One lie about a little cash couldn't hurt. "No cash, no jewelry, nothing like that. What was in there was kind of old. I mean, he had a typewriter on the dining room table and all these letters he was writing."

"He was typing letters on a typewriter?"

"Yeah, and those were weird, too. I read one and it was to someone about their old lady cheating on them when the guy wasn't home. Kind of bizarre."

"So you got no Boyd, and this guy is breaking into your house now, right? And now the cops are going to talk to you about Boyd vanishing. That's where you are?"

Frank nodded. "Yeah. I moved out, too. I'm not staying in that house. I moved back in with my mom."

Skillet laughed. "Frank, you have to toughen up, man. You can't let some guy chase you out of your home. You should have just told him to get the hell out of your house before you called the cops on him. What's he got on you?"

"He knows we did it. How do you think that happened?"

Skillet leaned forward. "You accusing me of something, Frank? You find your balls now?"

"Four people knew we were doing that job, Skillet: me and Boyd and you and your guy who told you about the tools. Well, I can't find Boyd and the guy is breaking into my house threatening me, so how solid is your guy? Did he open his mouth?"

Skillet went back to chewing his lower lip and thought about Harvey. He wasn't too bright. It was possible this guy went to work and started complaining about his place being broken into and maybe Harvey said the wrong thing. Yeah, that was a possibility. He looked at Frank. "I think my man is solid, but I'll talk to him. In the meantime, you just stay with your mom. If the cops come by and ask about Boyd, you don't know anything. Just tell them you don't know where he went. You understand?"

Frank nodded.

"You got a good thing going, Frank. As far as they're concerned you work and you let your friend stay with you because of that accident he had, right? You're a good guy. You just stick to that story, okay?"

Frank nodded again. "Okay, I can do that."

"Sure you can. Now, you have to get out of here." They stood up and walked to the back door. When they got there Skillet unlocked the door and turned the knob but held it shut.

"One more thing, Frank."

"Yeah?"

Skillet took a step toward him. "You don't mention me. You don't know me at all. You have never heard of me. You don't know where Boyd gets his stuff. All you know is he tokes up once in a while but you don't know where he gets it. You don't even know my name."

"Oh, hey, yeah, of course not. No problem," Frank said, a little hitch in his voice. "I have no problem with that."

"That's good, because making the situation more complicated won't do anyone any good, right?"

"No."

"Okay then, man, go have a good one." Skillet pulled the door wide.

Frank started to go and then stopped. "You'll let me know if you hear anything about Boyd or your guy?"

"Of course."

"Okay."

Frank walked to his car and saw Skillet watching him until he pulled out of the driveway.

Nineteen

Tim and Charlie walked into the Hogan Police Department at nine thirty to put in a public records request for any police reports regarding the letters. The officer at the desk asked them to sit for a moment.

"You didn't have to come, you know," Tim said.

"If you're going to meet one of our biggest advertisers in relation to a story after this, I'm coming," Charlie said.

"I've done this before, you know."

"Yes, I know. You had that months-long TV internship career," Charlie said, smiling. "Don't sweat it. I should probably see Gary anyway."

At quarter to ten the side door to the waiting room buzzed and a lock clicked. A portly, small man in a blue suit with a badge clipped to his belt came into the waiting room with manila folder in his hand. "Tim Abernathy?"

Tim and Charlie both stood up and Tim held his hand out. "I'm Tim Abernathy."

The man shook his hand. "Hi, Tim, I'm Larry Coogan. You know my brother Doug, right?"

Tim looked a little puzzled. "Yeah, I do, but you know we've met before, right? I've been to your parents' house a couple times when you were there."

Larry looked him over. "That's right, you're right. Sorry, it's just been a while."

"Sure, uh, this is my boss, Charlie Ingram."

Charlie shook his hand. "Nice to meet you. I'm the publisher of the *Hogan Shopper.*"

"Oh, right, okay. Well, do you guys have a moment to talk?"

"About what?" Charlie asked.

The detective held up the file folder. "About all these reports I have regarding the story you wrote."

"I'm not sure how we could help you," Charlie said. Tim noticed the publisher was standing up straight now, assuming a more aggressive posture than he normally held.

Larry Coogan looked over the waiting room and didn't see anyone there. "Well, to tell you the truth, I drew the short straw and have to look into these. Since you're here I thought I could just ask you a couple questions. See if maybe you guys have some information I don't have."

"We have a meeting in fifteen minutes," Charlie said. "We can give you ten."

Detective Coogan nodded. "Thanks, I appreciate it."

He led them through a suite of offices to a conference room and opened the door for them. Larry motioned to seats on the far side of the table and Tim and Charlie sat down. The door closed and Larry sat across from them.

"Do you guys need a coffee or anything?" Detective Coogan asked.

"There's really no time," Charlie said.

"Right, right. Anyway here's a copy of the police reports we have for the letters."

Tim picked up the file. It was almost an inch thick. "That was very fast. Don't records requests usually take longer?"

Coogan nodded. "Yes, they do, but I was actually putting that one together for myself this morning, so you can have it, and I'll print up another."

"Thanks," Tim said as he flipped it open. There were dozens of reports in the file. He slipped it into the messenger bag he carried.

"So, what can we do for you?" Charlie asked.

The detective put his hands together and leaned forward. "Do you guys have anything that wasn't in the story you printed? Something you may be holding back until you can confirm it?"

Tim and Charlie looked at each other. Tim shook his head. "No, everything was in the story."

"Everything?"

"Detective, where are you going with this?" Charlie said.

Coogan leaned back in his chair and rubbed his eyes. He was obviously tired. "Well, Mr. Ingram, I've got a serial wacko writing anonymous letters to half the town. The problem is, I have real problems in addition to this guy. There have been a rise in burglaries, and we're pretty sure they're drug related. That's what I'd like to spend my time on. Instead I've got a disgruntled yo-yo writing letters about who's screwing who and insulting a bunch of people. I'd like to clear this off my desk and get to some of the real problems stacking up."

"You don't see this as a real problem?" Tim said. "The people I've spoken to are pretty shook up. They're scared and feel pretty intimidated."

"As well they should," Coogan said. "The problem is that while these letters are a nuisance, I can't charge the guy with much."

"What about harassment?" Charlie said.

Coogan smiled. "What do you think the penalty is for harassing someone with anonymous letters, Mr. Ingram? I can charge him with menacing or maybe something under harassment. That'll get him anywhere from thirty days to six months, depending on whether the judge is in a particularly bad mood the day we end up in court."

"That's it?" Tim asked.

Coogan shrugged. "The letters I've seen so far are vile, there's no doubt about it. They're the kind of thing that would get you punched out in a bar for saying them to someone, but they aren't threatening harm. They aren't extortion. They're just the work of some asshole who's pissed at the world."

"Have you spoken to the post office?" Charlie said.

"Yes."

"What do they have to say?"

Coogan looked them over. "Are we sharing information?"

"I'm interviewing a police officer in connection with a crime," Charlie said.

"I'm afraid I can't comment on an ongoing investigation," Coogan said.

"Then we're probably done here," Charlie said.

"Hold on," Tim said. "You know something, right? About the post office?"

Coogan just looked at him.

"Okay, we can share one thing," Tim said. "Your timeline is about one year. No one I've spoken with has had a letter older than that."

Coogan nodded. "Okay. Thank you for that." He pulled out a small pocket notebook and made a note. Then he flipped forward a few pages. "I spoke with the post office and showed them some of the envelopes. Looking at the postmarks, all of the letters have been mailed from communities all around Hogan, but none from within Hogan itself."

"So he likes to go outside and mail his letters."

"Yep," Coogan said. "Unfortunately, that's all they could tell me."

"Tim, we have to go," Charlie said.

They rose from their chairs, and Coogan extended a hand, shaking both of theirs. "Thanks for your help, gentlemen."

"No problem," Charlie said.

Coogan walked them back to the waiting room. He swiped a plastic badge and the door buzzed, the lock clicked, and they found themselves back in the waiting room. Before the door closed, Tim turned back. "Detective Coogan?"

He turned. "Yeah?"

"A friend of mine filled out a missing persons report about her brother, Boyd Sashman. Do you know anything about that?"

"Yes, but we only just started looking into it."

"So he's still missing?"

"As far as we know," Coogan said. "We'll let his sister know if we find anything."

"Right," Tim said. "Well, thank you."

Coogan nodded and let the thick door shut with a heavy click of the lock.

They walked out to the parking lot and got in Charlie's car. The Cadillac was still warm. Charlie took a side street exit from the public administration building and then a left on Main Street. Tim looked out the window at the snow until they passed by Red Fannie Florist. Then he turned to Charlie.

"I got the feeling in there that you were less than pleased Detective Coogan wanted to speak with us."

Charlie shrugged and kept staring straight ahead at the road. "It's nothing specific, Tim. I just think they should do their thing and we should do ours. If you get too friendly with the local cops, they start asking favors. Besides, they're grownups. They can do their own jobs."

The snow was blowing around in the air now, trying to make up its mind whether it was going to ruin the day or just be annoying for a little while. "You're afraid of compromising your objectivity?"

Charlie laughed and threw a glance at Tim. "You really did just get out of school, didn't you? No, I'm not so worried about our objectivity. I just like the relationship we have with the police. We print the weekly blotter, we print their annual warnings about scam artists pulling driveway blacktop cons, and when a real crime happens we can ask them questions without feeling like we owe them anything. Being too friendly with them is a double-edged sword. Things are good the way they are."

They rolled over a set of railroad tracks that marked the edge of the city and followed the road toward the interstate. Charlie cracked his window and let some fresh air into the car. "Who's missing?"

"I have a friend from Tate's store. It's her brother. He was supposed to show up for Thanksgiving dinner and he hasn't been seen."

Charlie nodded. "How old is he?"

"In his twenties. I'm not sure exactly."

"Drug user?"

Tim turned and looked at Charlie. "What makes you say that?"

"They've had the report for almost twenty-four hours and it's not on the local news, and I haven't gotten a request to put it in the *Shopper*. That means they'll keep an eye out for him and ask some questions, but they aren't getting the public all riled up just yet and won't unless they think he's missing because a crime was committed against him."

"Oh."

Charlie flicked the turn signal and made a right into Creekside Motors. "Don't worry, they'll find him. Coogan is actually a pretty good detective. That means he works hard and doesn't just push the reports around his desk. He knows who to talk to and where to look. He'll find your friend's brother."

"I hope so."

They pulled up in front of the big glass showroom and Tim followed Charlie inside the warm building. The publisher walked up to the receptionist's desk with a big smile and his arms stretched out.

"Charlotte, my dear," he said. "How are you doing on this fine morning?"

She stood and smiled. "I'm good, Charlie. How are you?"

Charlie leaned on the raised shelf that ran around her desk and helped himself to one of the mints in the candy dish next to the sales staff business card holders. "I'm fine, just fine. What could be better than weather like this and being awake early?"

She laughed. "Who is this with you?"

Charlie held his hand out at Tim. "This young man is Tim, and we're here to see Gary on newspaper business. Is he around?"

Tim extended his hand and Charlotte shook it. "Nice to meet you," she said. "Let me buzz him and see."

She picked up the phone. Tim found himself staring at a 1969 seafoam green Chevelle Super Sport. It was clean, like it had rolled off the assembly line and been trucked into the dealership just last week. He was bent down and looking into the passenger's side window when a large man walked up behind him.

"I can make you a deal on that, son, if you're interested."

Tim turned to see a tall, round man in a nice suit looking at him. Charlie walked up behind him and spoke before Tim could answer.

"He works for me, Gary. He can't afford it no matter how good the deal is."

The big man laughed. "Sorry, son, if I'd known you worked for this cheapskate, I would've suggested you go look at our budget specials in the back of the lot. I'm Gary Shellmack." A card appeared in his hand as if by magic.

Tim took it and slipped it into his pocket. "Tim Abernathy."

"Oh, okay, we spoke on the phone. So, you guys are here about the letters, right?"

Charlie nodded. "That's right. Seems like our little city has a real head case running loose, and you've caught his fancy."

Gary looked out at the snow. It was falling a bit heavier now, Tim noticed. Apparently it was going to ruin the day. "Yeah, Charlie, I seem to have caught his attention," Gary said. He looked at his shoes for a moment. "Why don't you guys come back to my office, and I'll show you what I've got."

They followed Gary back to his office. Tim noticed Charlotte looking at them as they went. She wasn't smiling any longer. Gary sat behind his desk and Tim and Charlie took the chairs in front of him. The big man opened a side drawer of his desk and took out a thick green file folder. Tim had seen so many file folders recently he was actually pleased to see one that wasn't manila.

Gary laid the file on the desk and opened it. "You guys want some coffee or something?"

They both shook their heads.

"I got the first one in August," he said, and handed a copy of the letter to Charlie. Tim looked over and read it.

Do the world a favor and eat another double cheeseburger from Jupiter Joe's so you can get that heart attack out of the way.

Tim nodded and sighed. "Yeah, that's our boy," he said. "The format, the way the message is in the center and middle of the page? All the ones I've seen look like that. The message is just about as nasty, too."

Charlie handed the letter back to Gary. "You've gotten more than this one?"

"Oh, yeah," Gary said. "One a week or thereabouts. I've got about a dozen here."

"That's more frequently than anyone else," Tim said. "The others are about one a month."

Gary looked at him. "How many people are getting these?"

Tim inhaled and thought for a moment. "I've spoken to dozens of people. It may even be close to a hundred."

Gary shook his head. "This guy, he seems to be very angry, you know? Somebody who's that mad worries me."

"If it's any consolation, he hasn't threatened anyone directly in any of the letters," Tim said. "He seems to go right up to the line of being insulting but not threatening."

"Do you eat at Jupiter Joe's?" Charlie asked.

"Yeah, probably more than I should."

"He does that," Tim said. "He finds out these little personal details. A couple of the others I've seen all reference something that make the recipient think the guy knows something about them. I think he does it to get under their skin."

Gary laughed. "Well, hell, guys, I do all my own commercials on TV, so I'm pretty recognizable. He could have just seen me down at the drivethru. Mentioning where I eat my lunch doesn't mean I know the guy."

"No, no, of course not," Tim said. "It's just part of his process."

"Now that you mention it, though . . ." Gary's voice trailed off. He flipped through the file folder and came up with the most recent letter. "This letter mentions Ellen, my wife. None of the others do."

Tim and Charlie read it. Tim let out a low whistle. "I'm sorry, Gary. No one should have to put up with this."

"Yeah, no kidding. Anyway, Ellen isn't really involved with the business. She doesn't hang around here very often, and she isn't in any of the commercials, so I don't know how he knows about her."

"I've met her," Charlie said, "at that party you threw last Christmas. She is a looker. That's what makes you think this guy has seen her? The fact that he mentions how pretty she is in the letter?" Tim looked at the pictures hanging on Gary's office wall. In several of them, Gary was standing next to an attractive blonde. She had a little Uma Thurman thing going on.

"Yeah," Gary said. "He wouldn't be the first guy to look at the two of us and wonder why she's with me. Hell, I still do that sometimes, but yeah, mentioning her makes me think the guy knows us or has seen us together." He reached for the water bottle on his desk and took a sip. "To tell you the truth, I got angry when he did that. It's one thing to insult me, but I don't want her brought into this. I don't want letters going to her."

Tim nodded. "I can certainly understand that. When we spoke on the phone, you mentioned you had some kind of list?"

Gary nodded. "Yeah, I started thinking about why I would be getting these, you know? I mean, we sell used cars here, so not every customer is happy, but we've never had anyone react like this. I started digging through all the complaints we've had since last spring, you know, because the letters started in August. I figure we made someone angry prior to that." He flipped to the back of the file and pulled a sheet of paper loose and handed it to Tim. "This is a list of everyone who registered some kind of complaint with us."

"What kind of complaints?" Tim asked.

"The usual stuff, mechanical problems and warranty issues. Everyone wants everything fixed for free. No one wants to hear their car is going to cost them money. Lots of people think once they give you a check it entitles them to free engine rebuilds and maintenance for life. It doesn't work like that."

"Used-car salesmen are the most maligned people on earth," Charlie said.

Tim smiled and kept looking at the list. There were a couple dozen names on it. Apparently Gary did make a lot of people angry. "What are these names with asterisks next to them?"

Gary let a deep breath out. "Those are customers who were memorably angry. The real hard cases." He chewed his lower lip before continuing. "A couple of them are taking us to court, and the others were especially upset about their issues."

"Well, I get the court cases, but what makes the others stand out?" Tim said.

"Those would be the customers we had loud arguments with or almost came to blows about their issues."

"Really?" Tim said. "You've had people get mad enough to throw punches?"

Gary smiled, but it was thin and kind of grim. "Young man, nowadays people will throw punches over getting nine chicken nuggets in their order instead of ten. You better believe they get upset when you tell them a thousand-dollar repair isn't covered under their warranty."

"I see your point," Tim said.

Gary leaned forward and pushed the file folder toward them. "You guys can take this. Normally I wouldn't air my dirty laundry, but I'm tired of this guy. I'm tired of his goddamn letters and this cowardly anonymous bullshit. If he has something to say, he can just walk in here and say it like everyone else who's ticked off at me. That's what a man's supposed to do. You say something and you put your name on it."

Tim started gathering up the papers and putting them back in the file. "Our research indicates the people who write letters like this are kind of maladjusted and don't do well in confrontational situations. They prefer the anonymity of letters because they don't have to deal with the fallout of what they say. In some cases, they enjoy getting a rise out of the recipient and seeing that without the recipient knowing they were the cause of their frustration."

"Well, hell, that just means it may be someone here in the dealership. Who else is going to see me getting upset? The letters come here, and this is where I lose my cool. Christ, this could be one of my own people."

Tim shook his head. "I don't know about that, Gary. If you were the only one getting the letters, I'd definitely agree with you, but this guy is prolific. He's writing to lots of people, more than he could possibly know or interact with."

"Well, if it could be anyone, it could still be someone who works here. You said it yourself—no one has gotten more letters than me."

"I actually said that no one has gotten them as frequently as you," Tim said.

Charlie stood up, indicating it was time for them to go. Tim rose out of his chair with the green file folder in his hand. Gary stood up as well. Charlie put his hand out. "Gary, good to see you as always. Thank you for the information. Rest assured we'll be in touch."

Gary shook their hands. "I'm glad I could help. It was driving me crazy not to do anything. I even entertained the thought of putting a reward out there, see if anyone knows this guy and wants to turn him in." He walked around the desk and opened the door. They all walked out into the showroom.

Charlie smiled. "Maybe we'll try that later if Tim here can't figure out who our guy is."

"I'll figure it out," Tim said.

"Thanks, guys. Good luck," Gary said. They started to walk toward the door. Then they heard him call out. "Oh, guys? One more thing. The contents of that file are private, okay? I don't want to see any of that in print unless I say so."

Charlie nodded. "Absolutely. We'll just use it to develop leads."

"Yeah, okay. Have a good one."

They got back in the car and started back toward the office. Tim flipped through the folder as Charlie drove.

"You want some advice, Tim?"

"Sure."

"When you're interviewing people, take a nicer manner with them. Don't correct them quite so often; it just derails the line of inquiry you're trying to develop. It didn't really matter whether Gary was getting the most letters or getting them more frequently than other people. Just concentrate on getting the information you need."

Tim closed the file. "Yeah, you're right. I should have let that go. I don't know why I didn't."

"You like to be right," Charlie said. "Everyone does. Just don't let that get in the way of collecting information for your story. Remember, that's what you need to be right about."

"Got it." The driveway dumped them out onto the highway.

"Want to get some lunch?" Charlie said.

Tim looked to his right and saw the bright orange and purple neon of Jupiter Joe's. "I could eat a burger."

• • •

Kathleen Brimley walked out to the mailbox through the snow after the little mail truck pulled away. She shuffled back up the driveway, taking note to call the Clarkson boy to see if he could come over after school and clear it before she fell on her can. She smiled. That was a Robert saying, "falling on your can." She didn't hear it much anymore because someone would just say "ass" instead, but Robert had always had a way with turning a phrase.

She had his old denim work shirt on again. After her confrontation with Nadine Harch down at the Peppermill, she had stopped wearing it for a while, but now she wanted to feel close to him again. Whatever may have happened between Robert and Nadine, it was irrelevant. She didn't forgive him, but how could you hate someone who wasn't even there to argue with? If he was still alive, if he was still there for her to shout at or accuse, it would be different. No matter how angry she was, at the end of the day she still missed him.

She made her way through the garage to the door into the mudroom, where she kicked off her boots and hung up the denim work shirt. A cup of tea waited for her next to her chair, and it was cool enough to sip now. She flipped through the mail, dropping the ads in the basket where all the items to be shredded went and put the bills in a small plastic tub on the end table. The last envelope was missing a return address and her breath hitched up in her throat.

The address on the envelope was typed, not printed. She could see the indentations in the paper, could feel them when she ran her hands over the letters and numbers. Tears welled up in her eyes and she slowly pulled open the flap of the envelope. There was a single sheet of paper inside and she carefully unfolded it.

You should have punched Nadine Harch instead of walking out.
A big girl like you could have knocked her on her skinny ass.

She crumpled the letter in one hand and took several deep breaths as tears rolled over her cheeks. He had been there. Whoever was writing these letters had been in the Peppermill that day when she had gone in to see Nadine. Was he someone who worked there? Was he a customer? She remembered the restaurant being full the day she was there. She picked up her tea cup to take a sip, then put it back down. Instead, she got up from the chair, and the letter fell to the floor.

Another basket sat on the floor in the kitchen near the back door. It held all her paper recycling. She picked it up and dug through the copies of the *Humboldt Inquisitor* and the *Hogan Shopper*. The former was still delivered to her house every day, and the latter she picked up on her trips to the Savefast grocery store. The most recent edition was on top. She picked it up, unfolded it and saw the story she was looking for, the one about the letters. She read it again, standing at the counter in the kitchen, letting her tea grow cold. At the end of the article was a request for anyone who had received a letter to call the *Shopper*. She bit her lip and moved to the kitchen phone, a dark-green landline still hanging on the wall where Ma Bell had put it thirty years ago. She dialed the number from the article. There was no reason for her to feel like a victim, she realized, when she could help catch the SOB who was doing this to her.

Twenty

"I t's been almost a week since we filed the police report," Amy said.
"Don't you think we should have heard something by now? It's going
to be Christmas soon."

They were at Tim's trailer on Wednesday night, curled up on the
couch under a blanket watching a DVD. Tim sat on the end, propped up
by the arm of the couch, and Amy leaned against him. It was clear she
wasn't paying attention to the movie, so he picked up the remote and
stopped it.

"I would have thought so, yeah," Tim said. "Have you heard anything from them?"

She snuggled in a bit closer. "I've talked to that Detective Coogan
twice. Once when he called me about the report and then earlier today
when I called him. He said he hadn't heard anything."

"Did he talk to Boyd's roommate? What's his name? Frank?" Tim
absentmindedly played with a lock of Amy's hair.

"Yeah, or he said he did, anyway. Apparently Frank told him the
same thing he told me. That he had seen him the day before Thanksgiving and not since."

Tim looked outside. It was dark and cold, but it wasn't snowing and
the roads were mostly clear.

"Let's go out to Boyd's place," he said. "Come on, we'll go look for
ourselves."

"At his house? The police already did that."

Tim pulled the blanket off them and squirmed free. "So? We'll go
look for ourselves. Plus, we'll be doing something. Sitting here isn't
going to help Boyd, right?"

She looked at him and smiled. "Okay, let's go."

Fifteen minutes later they were on Owl North Road in his pickup. The headlights cut through the darkness and showed snow and bare trees lining the road. "You know where it is?" Tim said.

"A little ways up on the right," she said.

"Boyd and Frank must have really liked their privacy. There's not much out here."

Amy grunted. "No, it's more like they were cheap. Frank's mom owns the place and was having trouble getting tenants, so they moved in. Boyd had a little money from my folks, and he gets disability from his accident. Of course, I think he's snorted most of it."

Tim reached out in the darkness and took her hand. "Hey, don't think about that now. Let's concentrate on finding him."

They passed over a hollow with a creek under the road, and a couple minutes later Amy pointed. "That's it."

Tim pulled into the empty driveway and stopped, leaving the truck running and the headlights pointed at the house. The driveway was still snow-covered, like it hadn't been cleared after the last snowfall.

"It doesn't look like anyone's home," Tim said. "The house is dark."

Amy opened her door and got out. Tim followed her but reached behind the seat for a flashlight first. He flicked it on as he walked up to the front door. Amy pulled open the screen door. It squealed loudly. She knocked on the wooden front door, and it opened on its own.

"That's not a good sign," she said.

"No, it's not. Look here." Tim shined the light over the doorjamb. The door casing was splintered.

Tim put a hand on her shoulder and squeezed past. He entered the house first and shined the light around. It was messy, he saw, but it hardly looked ransacked. The overhead light came on and Tim turned to see Amy standing next to the switch.

"Frank?" she said loudly enough to be heard anywhere in the house. "Are you here? It's Amy Sashman, Boyd's sister. Are you home?" They stood silently, listening for an answer, but none came.

"He may be at work," Tim said. "Didn't you say he delivered pizzas?"

"Yeah," she said. "Will you look at this mess? How do people live like this?"

Tim looked around. The place was clearly home to a couple of young guys. It didn't look like a vacuum had ever been run or any of the furniture had been dusted. He chuckled. Amy turned.

"What's so funny?"

"It's not really funny, it's just that this place looks exactly like I thought it would. Young, single guys aren't great housekeepers. Nothing here shocks me."

She walked over and looked in the kitchen. "Your place doesn't look like this."

He shrugged. "I picked up before you came over."

They made their way upstairs and looked through all the bedrooms and the bathroom. Tim led them back downstairs. "Doesn't look like anyone is here," he said.

Amy walked back into the kitchen and to the back door. She opened it and the cold night air spilled in, but they were still wearing their coats. She hit the switch beside the door and a low, yellow light lit up some of the backyard.

"What if Frank did something to him, Tim? What if he's out there lying in the snow?"

Tim didn't know what to say. The guy was a drug user who had been missing for a week. There were so many possibilities, and he didn't want to raise them with Amy. Someone could have killed him for the money or drugs he had on him. He could have made some dealer angry. Hell, he could have overdosed, and someone just hid him away somewhere. There were a lot of woods around Hogan and a lot of empty fields. *Hell,* he thought, *the ground probably isn't even frozen yet.*

He put his hands on her shoulders. "We'll find him. Come back inside."

They closed the door, and then Amy saw the second door. "What's that?"

Tim opened it and saw stairs but no light switch. He shined the flashlight into the darkness. "It looks like a basement."

Amy took a deep breath. "Well, let's go take a look."

"I'll do it," Tim said.

She shook her head. "No, it's okay. I'll go."

They went down the steps with Tim leading the way. Amy spotted a chain hanging from a ceiling light and pulled it. Nothing happened. Tim shined the light up at the bare socket.

"That's not going to help," he said.

"Can you shine that over here?" Amy asked from a corner.

He played the light in her direction and saw her standing near a washer and dryer. There was a pile of dirty laundry on the floor in front of the machines. Amy walked around the edge of the basement, looking behind boxes and the water heater.

"There's nothing here but junk," she said.

"I don't see anything else, do you?" Tim said.

Amy shook her head. "No. Let's go."

They made their way back upstairs to the kitchen. Amy pulled out a chair at the small table and sat down. Tim looked in the fridge and saw a few Cokes on the door. He grabbed two of them and wiped off the tops on the tail of his t-shirt. He sat down at the table with Amy and opened them, handing her one.

"He doesn't drive, Tim. Boyd doesn't drive, so where is he?" She took a sip of her pop and set the can down.

"He got rides from Frank? That's how he got around? I noticed that one time I saw him at the store he was waiting for a ride."

She nodded. "Yes, Frank always gave him rides."

"Then we should ask Frank."

She looked at him. "Yeah, let's do that. Do you know where Rocco's Pizza is?"

• • •

Twenty minutes later they pulled into the parking lot at the pizza shop and Amy pointed to a beat-up Honda near the side door. "That's him," she said. "That's Frank's car."

Tim pulled into a space and Amy was out before he shut the key off. He followed as best he could, catching the door to the restaurant as it closed. Amy was at the counter, stretching to look into the back. A teenage girl wearing jeans and a pink Rocco's Pizza t-shirt came up to the counter. "Can I help you?"

Amy looked at her. "I need to speak with Frank Utzler. Is he here?"

"Sure, let me get him." The girl went into the back.

A moment later, Frank came out from around the counter. As soon as he saw Amy, his face fell. Tim raised an eyebrow. It certainly looked like Frank was guilty of something.

"Amy?" Frank said.

"We need to talk. Do you have a minute?"

Frank looked into the back of the kitchen for a moment. "Well, I'm working, but sure. Come over here." He led them back outside and leaned up against the side of the building. He took a cigarette from a pack and lit up, blowing smoke up into the sodium parking lot lights.

"What can I do for you?" he asked.

Tim hung back as Amy paced in front of him. "Where's Boyd?"

He blew more smoke. "Amy, I told that detective everything I know. He was at home when I went to work and he was gone when I came home after my shift. That's all I know."

"He doesn't drive, Frank. How would he go anywhere?"

Frank shrugged. "I don't know. Maybe he called someone else for a ride."

Amy got right up in his face. "There is no one else, Frank. You're his only friend. If he needs a ride and you aren't around he calls me, and he didn't call me."

Frank shrugged. "Amy, your brother hung around people who were not his friends, you know what I mean? You and I both know he had a problem. He was getting stuff, Oxy, weed, and whatever else he used, and he wasn't always getting it from people I knew."

"Dealers gave him a ride?" Tim said. "Is that what you're saying?"

Frank looked him over. "Who are you?"

Amy kept staring at Frank. "He's with me, Frank. He's a reporter and he's looking into Boyd's disappearance. So, who are these dealers?"

"What?" Frank was getting nervous now, looking from Amy to Tim and taking hits off his smoke.

Tim moved up, crowding him a little. "You said Tim would get rides from dealers, so who were they?"

"I don't know if he got rides, man. I just meant that there were people in his life other than me and Amy."

Amy poked him with a finger. "Stop lying to me, Frank. We were just at your house and it's clear something bad happened. The front door was broke open and that place was a wreck."

"You went in my house?"

"Frank," Tim said, "someone broke into your house and now Boyd is missing. Tell us what you know or we're going to the police and they'll come back and ask you."

Frank shrugged and looked away from them. "I really don't know anything."

"Did you guys owe money to someone?" Tim said. "Did someone come looking for you guys and they found Boyd? This is starting to look like you guys got into something you shouldn't have and now someone is pissed off."

Frank looked away again. "I didn't know the house had been broken into. Ever since Boyd disappeared I've been staying with my mom, here, in town. Maybe someone broke in after I left."

"Maybe you're lying, Frank," Amy said. "I can see it in your eyes, you know. You keep looking away from me. You know more than what you're saying."

The door to the shop opened and a tall guy with dark hair and a mustache looked around the lot until he found them. "Your break is over, Frank. Delivery up. Let's go."

The man stared at them and Frank stubbed out his cigarette on the ground with his foot. "Be right there, Rocco." The man went back inside.

"Look, I'll see if I can find anything else out and call you, okay?"

Amy glared at him and pointed her finger. "Tell me the truth, Frank."

He walked along the side of the building to the door. "I will, I promise." Then he disappeared inside.

"He knows more than he's telling," Tim said.

She nodded. "I know."

"Come on, I'll get you home," he said, looking at his phone for the time. It was almost nine. "I have to prep for tomorrow. I have a lot of people to see."

They got back into his truck. "Why so many?" she said.

"We ran a follow-up story today and it looks like a fresh batch of letters went out, so we got a ton of calls. Charlie wants me following up on all of them."

"Are any of them helpful?"

Tim pulled out onto Main Street and went in the direction of Amy's apartment over the bookstore. "Yeah, one lady said she thinks she may have been in the same place as this guy because the letter she received referenced an incident that happened there."

"Where?"

"At the Peppermill. You know, the diner."

"Yeah."

"Well, I'm going to go out to her house and see her about it and return a couple dozen calls from other people."

Tim pulled to the curb in front of her building and they got out. He walked her up the wooden stairs leading to her second-floor apartment and she unlocked the door. She turned, and he kissed her goodnight, but she surprised him by pulling him close, and they tumbled through the open door.

The emotions of the night caught up to them: the danger of the empty house, the exhilaration of confronting Frank, the feeling of doing something, of taking control. Tim reached out and closed the door without breaking away from her.

Amy pushed him down onto a dining room chair and straddled him. His hands explored her body as they kissed, and he tugged on her sweater. She responded by pulling it and her bra over her head and grinning at him. He buried his head in her breasts and sucked one into his mouth, biting down lightly on one of her nipples. She moaned and arched her back, grinding hard into him.

Her hands dropped down and grasped him through his jeans. She rubbed him furiously until he couldn't stand it. He stood up, carrying her into the living room, and she wrapped her legs around his waist. They broke apart just long enough to strip each other's clothes off. She pushed him down on the couch and straddled him again, letting him slide into her. He put his hands on her hips and she leaned forward, breathing heavily in his ear, as she rode hard. He was overwhelmed by it all and struggled to control himself. Finally, she began screaming, and he allowed himself the sweet mercy of release. They held each other and he felt the tension of the day evaporate. He rolled to one side, and she slipped between him and the back of the couch. Tim wrapped his arms around her as Amy pulled an afghan from the back of the couch, and they lay under it.

He smiled at her. "Now, that's what I thought spending the night with you would be like."

She threw a smile right back at him. "Yeah, we should have done that a while ago."

His hands moved over her sweat-slick skin. "I think we can make up for lost time."

• • •

Frank got home that night and walked inside. His mom was sitting in her favorite chair watching TV. She smiled at him, and he handed her a small pizza box. "Pepperoni calzone, Mom, with green peppers, just how you like it."

"Oh, thanks, honey." She opened the lid and smiled. "Could you get me a Pepsi from the fridge before you sit down?"

Frank wandered out to the kitchen and snagged her a can. "You really shouldn't drink pop this late," he said as he returned. "The caffeine will keep you up."

She shrugged. "I don't sleep well, anyway. I keep getting up at odd hours. A little Pepsi isn't going to hurt."

The news came on and Frank leaned back on the couch and closed his eyes. He was thinking about Amy, about Boyd, and what he was going to do about the guy who had been in his house. He couldn't stay with his mom forever.

"That's just terrible," his mom said.

Frank opened an eye. "What is?"

"Haven't you heard? Someone is writing harassing letters and mailing them to people all over town." She took another small bite of her calzone. "It's been going on for a while. He sends these obscene letters just full of filth to people. I just don't understand it. It was in the paper."

Frank was sitting forward on the couch, listening to the report. Sure enough, it said people had reported receiving more letters. The report referenced the *Hogan Shopper* and a Facebook group.

"Do you have a copy of that paper, Ma?"

She gestured into the kitchen with her pop can. "I don't think I've thrown it out yet. It should be on the counter."

Frank got up and looked for the paper. It was lying under some junk mail. He unfolded the front page and read the article. There were pictures of a couple of the actual letters on an inside page. Frank looked at them and felt sick to his stomach. The letters in the grainy black-and-white images looked exactly like the ones he and Boyd had seen in that house they had robbed—a message typed out in the middle of a sheet of paper—and they had had been just as nasty.

He took the paper and walked back into the living room and sat on the couch. The guy doing this was the guy who had been in their house. Frank shuddered at the thought of hiding in the root cellar with the bugs crawling over him. He read the article again and noticed the name on the byline. This must have been the guy with Amy tonight.

"Isn't that just horrible?" his mom said. "It's like there always has to be some kook causing trouble for folks. I hope they put him in jail when they find him and don't let him have anything to write with."

"Yeah, Mom," Frank said. "I hope so, too."

How had he found them, though? How had he known he and Boyd had been the ones to rip him off? It just didn't make any sense, because they had been careful.

And what had he done to Boyd?

•   •   •

Bob Ellstrom drove by Tim's trailer again. It was dark and the driveway was empty. He looked around at the other mobile homes and saw they were similarly dark. He took a deep breath and noticed how hard his heart was beating. He had a plan. He wanted to show the reporter that there were consequences for getting involved in something that didn't concern him. He hesitated long enough to look at the trailer of the old biddy who lived next door, the one who had approached him last time. All the lights were out, and he didn't even see the glow of a TV. Taking another deep breath, he got out of his truck and grabbed a burlap feed sack from the bed of his truck.

You should have stayed out of it, he thought as he approached the reporter's trailer. A quick look around showed him the surrounding homes were still dark. His heart was beating so hard his hands started to shake a little. This wasn't what he was used to, and he questioned again why he was taking such a risk. The letters were one thing, but this kind of action was something that could get you caught. He crossed the gravel driveway and decided it was worth the risk.

He knelt down beside the trailer, under the kitchen window, and looked at the aluminum panels hiding the space between the bottom of the trailer and the concrete pad it sat on. He selected one and gripped it with both hands. It was snug, but he applied steady pressure and it moved up. The aluminum squealed as he slid it loose, and he looked around. No lights turned on, and he didn't see any curtains move. He laid the panel on the gravel and picked up the sack. He reached in, grimacing at the touch of what was inside, and pulled it out. A small rope was attached to the object. He felt around the bottom of the trailer for a brace or a strut, but it was covered with a sturdy fabric that formed a moisture barrier. That was okay, he'd thought of that.

He reached into a pocket and pulled out a box cutter. A quick slice with the razorblade created a hole in the fabric. The rope had a hook on the end. He inserted the hook into the vapor barrier and left the object hanging.

Now time was of the essence.

He hurried back to where his truck was parked and pulled a small digital camera from his pocket. He snapped a few pictures and put it away. The flash was brighter than he expected, but it didn't appear to have alerted anyone. He jogged back to the trailer and put the panel back in place as quickly as he could. It scraped again, making noise, but it snapped home.

The burlap sack went back in the bed of the truck, and he drove away as quickly as he could. He needed to get home. There was writing to be done.

Twenty-One

Tim spent the next few days returning calls and meeting with people who had received letters. Charlie knew they were onto something big and wanted to make sure the story didn't go away. Circulation had picked up over the weeks since the first story had been published, and he was using those numbers to get more advertising at more favorable rates.

Charlie was in the small conference room with a few of the writers who contributed to the *Shopper*. There were half dozen of them in there, going over assignments for the regular columns that ran in the small paper: gardening, do-it-yourself, car care, child care, computer maintenance, and local government coverage. Tim smiled as he heard Charlie's voice handing out assignments.

The web browser on Tim's computer was open to Facebook and he scrolled the group set up to discuss the letters. There were pictures posted of a few letters and lots of speculation in the comments under them, but nothing concrete. Some of the comments contained serious vitriol, and Tim hoped no one did anything stupid based on Internet rumors. His desk phone rang, and he picked it up.

"*Hogan Shopper*, Tim speaking."

"Hello. Are you the person we should speak with if we've received a letter?"

"That's right, sir. Have you received a letter?" Tim said.

"Yes, I have."

"Okay," Tim said and grabbed a pen as he reached for the legal pad where he was recording calls. "I'd like to ask you a few questions, if that would be all right?"

"Yes."

"What's your name?"

"Bob Ellstrom."

"Thank you Mr. Ellstrom. Now, do you live in Hogan, and if so, can you give me your address and phone number?"

Bob gave him both.

"This letter you received, is there a return address on the envelope?"

"No."

"Can you describe the letter?"

"It's on, uh, white paper, and has one sentence typed in the middle of the paper."

"Very good, sir. You don't have to tell what it says if you don't want to, but can you tell me if the message is disturbing or obscene?"

"Yes," Bob said. "Yes, it is. It says,

You'll die alone.

Tim shook his head and wrote the message down. It certainly sounded like one of the letters from their anonymous author. "Thank you, sir. I'm sorry you received that. Obviously we're working to discover who the person is writing these."

"Your article said a lot of people were receiving these? I mean, this sounds like one of those?"

"Yes, sir," Tim said. "The content of your message is similar to the others."

"All right, I just wanted to make sure it wasn't someone just singling me out."

"It doesn't sound like it, Mr. Ellstrom. One more thing, can you tell me if there are any marks on the letter or envelope? Anything out of the ordinary?"

Paper rustled on the other end of the phone. "No, I don't think so. There are no marks or anything."

"Mr. Ellstrom, could I get that letter from you? I'd like to look at it closely."

"Oh, I don't want it published in the paper."

"No, it wouldn't be, sir. It's just that we're trying to collect as many of the letters as possible."

"Well, I work quite a bit," Bob said. "Why don't I just come by and drop it off? Your office is in Hogan, right?"

"Yes, it is," Tim said, and gave him the address. "You can drop it off as late as seven most days, if that helps."

"Okay, I'll see if I can swing by after work one afternoon."

Tim smiled. "I'd really appreciate that, sir. Thank you."

"Thank you," Bob said, and hung up.

Tim sat back in his chair and considered the conversation. It was pretty routine. He turned to his laptop and pulled up the ACCESS DATA-BASE he'd built to house all their data on the letter writer. He started entering it and noticed the conference room emptying out. He waved to a few people as they headed out into the cold December evening.

Charlie sat down at his desk across from Tim and said, "Anything new?"

"I just got a call about another letter."

"Yeah?"

"I asked him if we could have it, and he said he would drop it off one night this week after work."

Charlie nodded and started looking at some papers on his desk.

"How did the staff meeting go?" Tim asked.

"Nothing too exciting," Charlie said. "Ned's getting a lot of letters about cold weather car problems, so I'm doubling up his space next week."

Tim nodded and looked at the database on his screen. "Huh, would you look at that?"

Charlie raised his head. "What's up?"

"The letter I just entered into the database, I got a hit on it."

Charlie set his paper down. "Yeah? What is it?"

Tim looked at the screen. "The guy who just called, the one who received the letter, is named Bob Ellstrom. He's on Gary Shellmack's list of disgruntled customers. Gary says he was angry about some transmission work on his truck not being covered under the warranty."

"I like Gary," Charlie said, "but I've heard stories like that before."

Tim grunted. "No one's ever happy with used-car salesmen.

"You about ready to knock off for the night?"

"Yeah, let's get out of here."

They turned off the lights and packed up their laptops. Charlie locked up, and they walked through the back door to the small lot behind the building. Tim got his keys out and walked toward his little pickup, parked next to Charlie's Cadillac.

"Maybe you shouldn't park so close to me," Charlie said.

"Why's that?"

"I don't want my car to catch anything."

Tim laughed and looked down at his truck. It was quite a rust bucket, more flaky orange than white. "I'd get something better if I got a raise."

"You should work on earning one, then," Charlie said. "See you tomorrow."

"Yeah, have a good night."

Tim pulled out of the lot and hit Jupiter Joe's on the way home for dinner. Twenty minutes later he pulled into the entrance of the West Wind Mobile Home Park. He swung by the cluster of mailboxes and picked up his mail.

He went into his trailer and flopped down on the couch. He turned on ESPN, decided he didn't want to hear about basketball, and flipped around until he found a *Big Bang Theory* rerun. He unwrapped his burger and leaned back on the couch. The mail lay on the coffee table, and he leaned forward to grab it. There were only a few pieces, mostly junk mail and the water bill. Then he saw a plain white envelope with his name and address typed on it with no return address.

Tim stopped chewing and swallowed.

"Well, now," he said. "I've been expecting you."

Tim picked up the envelope and examined it. There were no marks on it, just the typed name and address. He pulled his Swiss Army knife from his pocket and slit the envelope open with a small, sharp blade. He put the knife down on the table and pulled out the letter. He saw there were two pieces of paper folded together. He examined them carefully but didn't see any markings on them.

Tim unfolded the letter and read it carefully.

Thanks for playing, but you're too goddamn stupid to figure out the puzzle. Enjoy your parting gift.

Tim set the letter aside and picked up the second sheet of paper. It was folded and secured with Scotch tape. He picked up his knife and slit the tape open. Unfolding the paper, he saw it was a black-and-white picture of his trailer. Whoever had taken it had been standing on the road in front of Tilly's trailer.

"So you know where I live, huh, you crazy fuck?"

It was a clue, though—an actual printed picture from a computer, not just a typed document. It was a change in the pattern, something different in the process. Tim dropped the paper on the coffee table and stood up. He walked around the couch and looked outside. It was irrational, he knew, to expect anyone to be out there. It would have been some crazy coincidence for the writer to know Tim was opening the letter at this very moment and be parked outside, but he still pulled the curtain aside and looked.

The street outside was empty except for slush and snow.

This was how all those people felt, Tim realized as he sat back down. What he was feeling right now, the violation of something ugly coming into his life, this was what the letter writer wanted.

Tim looked at the picture again and noticed something. There was a dark spot in the metal skirting that ran around the bottom of the trailer. Tim realized the dark space was actually a hole created by a missing panel. He was suddenly, eerily, aware of that space.

He put his coat on and walked down the back steps with the picture in his hand. In it, the missing panel was lined up with the kitchen window. Tim saw that none were missing. That meant one had been moved, the picture had been taken, and then the panel had been replaced. Referencing the picture again, he found the correct panel.

It looked ordinary. It was brown, just like the others, and didn't look out of place at all. Tim never gave the skirting a second thought unless the wind was blowing hard enough to dislodge them and spread them around the field behind his lot. He grabbed the panel and pulled it loose.

The smell hit him right away. Something was obviously dead inside. He was surprised he hadn't smelled it before. Another day and he probably would have. It was too dark to see, though. He stood up, went to his truck and retrieved a flashlight from behind the seat. He clicked the button and played the light into the space under the trailer. As soon as he did, he fell back on his ass and scrambled away from the hole.

It took him a few seconds to catch his breath. He picked up the flashlight from where he'd dropped it and shined it into the hole again. Inside, hanging from a short rope, was the body of a kitten. It was gray and white and very small. A cardboard sign was tied around its neck with twisted wire. It read, "Curiosity."

"What the fuck is wrong with you?" Tim said to himself. "And what have I gotten myself into?"

• • •

The next morning, Tim rolled into work and opened the office. The sun was up and bright, reflecting off fresh December snow. He hadn't slept well the night before because of the discovery under his trailer, but he had been making it a habit to get there earlier than Charlie for a couple reasons. First, he wanted Charlie to know he was taking the job seriously, and second, the letter story demanded a lot of time, but it wasn't the only thing he had to do. He was helping Charlie with layouts and sales calls, and he wanted the extra time to spend on the story, especially now that the guy was mailing him letters personally.

He booted up his laptop and put the letter he had received on the desk. Half an hour later, the coffee had been made, and he had added a copy of his letter to the database they were maintaining. A knock at the locked front door startled him. He turned and saw a young man about his age standing there wearing blue Dickie work clothes. Tim got up and opened the door.

"Hi, can I help you?"

The name "Max" was stitched over the guy's pocket. "Yes, I read your story about the letters and I think I have one."

Tim nodded. "Oh, yeah? Well, come on in." Tim swung the door wide and the young man entered the office. Tim closed and locked the door and pointed to a chair near his desk. "Sorry about the door, but we're really not open yet. So, you have a letter?"

"Yeah, my name is Max, and I work over at the AA Tire and Wheel Superstore."

"The place with all the rims?"

Max nodded. "Right, we have the big showroom where they all hang on the wall."

"I've been there," Tim said. "So what's up?"

"My boss, Jerry Donovan died a little while ago."

Tim nodded. "I remember hearing about that. You have my condolences."

"Thanks. Well, anyway, he had a heart attack right there in the shop, you know? So, after everyone left, the paramedics and the firefighters, I was cleaning up the office. When Jerry had his heart attack he knocked a bunch of stuff off the counter and, well, I found this." Max pulled a folded-up envelope from his breast pocket and handed it to Tim. He seemed relieved to unburden himself.

Tim unfolded the envelope. It was crumpled and he had to smooth it out before he could read it.

"I'm sorry about that," Max said. "I guess Jerry had it in his hand when he had the heart attack, so it got all wrinkled up."

"Don't worry about it," Tim said. He pulled the letter from the envelope and unfolded it.

That yummy little blonde is a bit young for you, isn't she?

Tim re-folded the letter and put it back in the envelope. "So, you think he was reading this when he had his heart attack? You think this caused it?"

Max hung his head. "Yeah, I do. I think he read that and . . ."

"Hey, man, this guy, the one writing the letters, he's twisted."

Max looked up and slumped back in his chair. "Yeah, but I think I did this. I think I'm responsible for this."

Tim's eyes narrowed. "Why? What would make you think you're responsible?"

"I caught Jerry and this blonde sales rep out back of the shop, being pretty close. They were making out like a couple of sixteen-year-olds, you know? Well, I was the only one who saw it."

"No one else?" Tim said. "None of the guys in the shop?"

Max shook his head. "No, if anyone else had seen it, the guys would have been all over Jerry. She was really cute. I mean, when she would come in for sales calls all the guys would find some reason to go by the office for a look. If anyone would have caught them hooking up, they would have told everyone."

Tim nodded. "But you didn't do that?"

"No, man. Jerry was a pretty good guy to work for, you know? I need this job because I just got married last year. Whatever he was doing, it wasn't my business. I didn't want to screw things up."

"So, if you didn't say anything," Tim said, "why do you think you're at fault?"

Max scratched at an ear and shrugged. "I did tell one person."

"Who?"

Max chewed his lower lip. "My uncle Mark. I don't know why. He was just over to the house one night and while we had a couple beers it just came out in conversation."

Tim's first instinct was to reassure the young man that this wasn't his fault. He ignored that. "Max, do you think your uncle wrote this letter?" He held up the envelope.

"Who? Mark?" The young man laughed a little. "No, I don't think Mark wrote the letter or any of the letters. He's a retired pipefitter. I don't think he even knows how to type."

"Yeah? Where did he retire from?"

"Over at Ohio Axle."

"So, what, you're thinking he told someone else, and that person may have written the letter?"

Max went back to scratching his ear. "Someone wrote it, right? If I was the only one who knew about Jerry and Kim, how else would they have known?"

"Kim is the sales rep?" Max nodded. "You know her last name?"

"No, I was only introduced to her once when she brought donuts for us guys in the shop. I never knew her last name."

"That's okay," Tim said. "Can I get your uncle's number?"

"You're going to call him?"

"Well, yeah, probably. I'm just going to ask him who he may have told."

"Man, I don't know."

Tim leaned forward. "Hey, Max, you came here for a reason, right? You feel a little guilty because you think this letter gave your boss a heart attack, right?"

He nodded.

"Well, I'm trying to figure out who this guy is, okay? You're being a good guy here. You're stepping up and saying something when you could have just thrown that letter away. Let's give your uncle the same opportunity."

Max chewed his lip some more, and after a moment, he nodded. "Okay, yeah, you can talk to him." He gave Tim his uncle's phone number. "I just don't want him to be in trouble."

"Gossip isn't against the law, Max."

"Yeah," he said. The mechanic took out his cell phone and looked at the time. "I have to get going to work. Are we good?"

Tim rose up and put out his hand. "Yeah, thanks for coming in, Max. This is a big help."

Max shook his hand. "Yeah, okay. Thanks." Tim unlocked the door and let him out. Tim sat back down and entered his lead into the database, one more thing to follow up.

• • •

Bob was sitting in the breakroom at Brinco, sipping a cup of coffee during the morning break. He was calm and felt more in control of things than he had been in a long time. The only loose end was that Frank was still running around. He hadn't been back to his house for a week from what Bob could tell. That night he had been at Frank and Boyd's house, he should have been able to end this. Frank had been there, he was sure of it. It just didn't make sense that he wasn't home.

He finished off his coffee and started peeling the paper cup apart. The problem was that Boyd was going to be found eventually. Killing him had been a huge mistake, he knew now. He should have kept a lid on his temper. He should have planned things out better, hit both of them when they were home and gotten his tools back. If he had done that he could have controlled things more, maybe kill them and burn down that house, make it look like they had been getting high and torched the place by accident. Now the kid in the drainpipe was like a time bomb just waiting to go off.

If Boyd was discovered, Frank was going to go to the police. It didn't matter that he'd be confessing to a burglary. Hell, the cops would make him a deal to ignore that if it led to them capturing a murderer. Until Boyd was found, though, Frank would probably keep his mouth shut.

Last night he had driven past Frank's mom's house twice. The first had been around nine o'clock, and he had seen a light and TV on in the living room and the driveway had been empty. But the second time, just after eleven, Frank's little Honda, the one he recognized from the old Jensen place, had been parked in the driveway. It seemed like that was his quitting time. Frank had run home to Mommy.

"Bob?"

He looked up from the table to see Ricky standing in the doorway to the breakroom.

"Yeah?"

"Buzzer sounded, man. Break's over."

Bob stared at him. Ever since their talk in his office, Ricky had done his best to steer clear of him. Bob stood up, swept the remains of the shredded cup into his hand and threw them away. When he turned around, Ricky was gone.

Things had changed, he realized. He was more in control of his life. It was a good feeling. He thought some more about Frank and made up his mind about what to do.

• • •

Amy was curled up on Tim's couch with him, both of them under a blanket. It was only six o'clock but they were both exhausted. He had an arm around her. The local news was on. The remains of grilled chicken salads lay on the coffee table.

"This is the station you used to work for?" she asked.

"Where I did my internship, yeah."

They watched four minutes of lead stories and then Boyd's picture flashed on the screen with a number for the Hogan police department. The anchor gave a short mention that Boyd had been missing since Thanksgiving and that his family was concerned, then they went to commercial.

Amy played with his fingers. "Thank you for calling them. It's getting pretty clear Coogan's not doing anything."

"No problem," Tim said. "I still talk to Alan Darling over there from time to time. He was always a decent guy, and he didn't mind running the story."

"The cops should have done it," she said. "We shouldn't have had to rely on your having worked there."

"Well, I just hope it helps. It'll air at eleven, too. Someone'll see it and call in."

"I hope so," she said.

"Hey, stay positive."

She sat up. "I'm trying, Tim, I really am, but he's never done this before. He's gone off for a while but he always calls, he always lets me know he's okay. This time just feels different. I can't believe he'd miss Thanksgiving dinner."

Tim didn't know what to say so he just put his arms around her and held her. His experience was with a drunk mother who was either yelling at him or passed out. She had never disappeared for days or weeks on end.

"I'm sorry, Tim. This is a lot to lay on you."

"Don't worry about it."

They sat like that a while longer, Amy curled into him. "Are you scared?"

"Why? Because of that letter and the cat?"

"Yeah," she said. "That would've freaked me the fuck out. I mean, it still does, but if it happened where I lived? I'd have to move."

"I feel like it, believe me, but I'm not letting someone chase me out of my house. When I leave here it'll be because I want to, not because I'm scared off."

"What did the police say?"

He sighed. "I didn't call them."

She looked at him with a shocked expression. "Why not?"

"Charlie and I spoke about it. He thought I should call but I want to wait. The story's about the letters, not me. If I file a report and the other papers pick up on it, then the story could become about the letter writer harassing me. It's also a huge break in his pattern. As far as we know he's never done anything like this before. The last thing I need is someone speculating that I did this myself."

She considered that. "I guess. But did you at least take pictures? It may be important later."

He nodded. "I sure did, and I kept the sign. I can always file a police report later."

"Did you ever ask your neighbors if they'd seen anyone? My landlord, Mimi, keeps track of everything and anyone who comes around. She used to warn me about Jeremy, actually. I suppose I should have listened to her."

Tim sat up. "Oh, man. How could I have been so stupid?"

"What?"

He got up and started putting on his shoes. "Tilly, next door. She watches everything, I mean, usually it's TV, but she does keep an eye on the neighborhood. I should have thought of this before." He walked over to the couch and kissed her. "You're a genius."

"You're going over there now?"

"Yep, you coming?"

"Yes." She got up and slipped into her shoes and coat.

They walked across the snow-covered yard to Tilly's trailer. Tim mounted the aluminum steps to her door and rang the doorbell. Tim looked at Amy. "Don't tell her about the cat, okay? I don't want to scare her."

"Okay."

"Who's there?" a voice called from inside. Tim heard the sound from the TV go quiet.

"It's Tim, from next door."

He heard her moving around slowly inside and then the door opened a crack. She had the security chain on, and she peeked through the gap. "Tim? Is everything all right?" She looked past him and saw Amy standing on the concrete patio. "Hold on, let me get this thing." She closed the door, and Tim heard the chain rattle. Then she swung the door open.

"It's freezing. You two come in here." Tilly was dressed in a blue floral housecoat and had slippers on.

Tim motioned and Amy followed him in. Tilly shut the door. "Is something wrong?"

"No, I just wanted to ask you a question."

"Well, sit down first. Go on."

Tim and Amy sat down on the sofa and Tilly collapsed into a recliner. Her trailer was neat and clean, with no dust on any of the knick-knacks, which were arranged in an orderly fashion along a bookshelf unit next to the TV.

"Now, first things first, who is this?" Tilly said, pointing at Amy.

Tim flushed a bit. "Oh, Tilly, this is my . . . friend, Amy."

Amy got up and shook her hand. "I'm Tim's girlfriend."

Tilly clapped her hands together. "Oh, good, he's needed one. You know, he's a good catch, what we used to a call a keeper." Tim flushed harder. "Oh, and he blushes so easily. Isn't that cute?"

Amy smiled. "It is. He does it quite a bit."

"Okay . . ." Tim said.

Tilly waved a hand at him. "Can I get you something to drink? Some tea or Diet Coke?"

"No, thank you," Amy said.

"Nothing for me either, Tilly."

"Okay, so what did you want to ask me?"

Tim rubbed an eye. "I'm not sure I remember." Amy elbowed him. "Oh, okay, yeah. Tilly, have you seen anyone around lately who doesn't belong? Maybe someone who was out front taking pictures of my place?"

She leaned back in the recliner and thought about it. "It's funny you should ask that. I've seen a man in a pickup truck a few times. I even spoke to him once and he seemed very odd."

Tim raised an eyebrow. "Oh, yeah? What did he say?"

"Well, it seemed like he was lost. This was a couple weeks ago, you see. I was sitting in here watching *Hawaii Five-O* and I could hear this truck out front. It was just sitting there with its motor rumbling, making a racket. So I put my boots and coat on and went out to see what they were doing. I was afraid we were having trouble with the waterlines again."

Tim nodded and turned to Amy. "We have a lot of trouble with waterlines breaking in the trailer park, especially when the weather gets cold." Amy nodded.

"Anyway," Tilly said, "it was someone I didn't know, and he was staring at your trailer. I tapped on his window to see if he needed something."

"Really?" Tim said. "What did he say?"

"He said he was looking for a friend, so I asked him who, to try and help him." She looked at Amy. "I know everyone in here."

"It's true," Tim said. "She really does."

"So he gave me the name but I didn't recognize it. After that, he left."

"What was the name?" Tim said.

"Now let me see, it had a kind of rhyme to it, you know? Sort of like the first name and last name rhymed together, but not really."

They sat there for a moment while Tilly concentrated. Tim looked down and saw that he was holding Amy's hand tightly. The only sound was the ticking of the anniversary clock on an end table near Tilly's chair. The muted TV played a rerun episode of *NCIS*, and Tim watched as Mark Harmon talked to someone on a phone.

"Ricky," Tilly said. She clapped her hands together. "It was Ricky Rogers. You see how the names go together? They don't rhyme but they fit, you see?"

Tim smiled. "They're alliterative. The first consonants are the same."

Tilly laughed and looked at Amy. "See? He's a smart one."

Tim got off the couch. "Thank you, Tilly. That helps quite a bit."

The ladies stood up. "Is this about that person writing the letters?" Tilly said.

"Yes, it is. Have you been keeping up with that?"

"Yes. I've read your stories about it in the *Shopper*. I pick it up when my daughter takes me to the store. I also saw it on the news a few nights ago." Her face fell. "Was that him, Tim? Was that the man doing this?"

Tim put a reassuring hand on her shoulder. "It may have been, but I don't know that for sure. Can you tell me anything about him?"

She nodded. "He was white, he looked like he was in his fifties, and he drove a pickup truck. A big one, not small like yours. It had a plow on it, too."

"Anything else?"

"He wore a red ski cap. Does that help?"

"It may. Is there anything else you can tell me?"

She thought about it for a moment and shook her head. "I've seen him back since then, at least twice."

"Did you speak to him again?"

"No, he just stopped for a moment each time. Just pulled up or passed by. I remember the truck, though. Does that help?"

"Yes, quite a bit. Thank you so much, Tilly." He looked over at the TV and saw a car chase taking place. "We'll get out of your hair."

"All right, now be careful, okay?" Tilly said. "Anyone who would write those letters is someone who could be dangerous. Men like that are full of anger, and it can get the better of them."

Tim nodded. "You be careful, too. If you see him again, just make a note. Don't approach him."

She waved him off. "I do what I want, young man. Always have, and I'm not going to stop now."

"I don't imagine you are."

They went back to Tim's trailer and took off their coats and shoes. "What do you think?" Amy said.

"I don't know," he said. "She may have seen him, may have spoken to him."

"Or it may just be some guy looking for another guy," Amy said. "What are you going to do?"

He looked up at her from the couch. "I'm going to see if I can find Ricky Rogers."

Twenty-Two

There were two weeks until Christmas, Bob realized, looking at the decorated houses. He was sitting down the street from Frank's mom's house but close enough to see it. Frank's Honda was not in the driveway yet. The houses were close together in this part of town, so there was a lot of street parking. No one had looked at him in the fifteen minutes he had been sitting here. Of course, it was a little after ten o'clock, and the streets in Hogan rolled up early.

This time of the year bothered him. He really had no family left since his Kate had passed away. There was a brother in Florida, but they didn't talk much and certainly didn't buy presents for each other. Kate hadn't wanted children, and he had wanted to be with Kate, so there were no kids or grandkids. The driver's side window was cracked open an inch, and Bob tapped the ash from his cigarette onto the street.

The night was silent and cold. It would have been nice if it had been snowing. In fact, a great big blizzard like the one that had pounded the city Thanksgiving would have been perfect. The weather in northeast Ohio rarely cooperated, though, he knew. The only constant was that no matter what you wanted it to do, it wouldn't do it. The clock said 10:17, and he figured that was good enough. He opened the truck door and flicked his cigarette into the street. The orange tip bounced and sparked as it dropped hot ash on the plowed street before finally fading.

He pulled on his thin leather gloves and grabbed the small gym bag from the front seat of his truck. He took a quick look around to see if anyone was watching him, but the porches were empty, and the curtains still. His steps echoed softly on the shoveled sidewalk as he walked the half block to Martha Utzler's house. The boots he was wearing were old and would be going into a burn barrel, along with all his clothes, when he got home. Criminals got caught because they were stupid, and Bob wasn't about to make any mistakes. He was careful, and he stuck to the plans he made. That was how you stayed successful. You made a good plan, and then you executed it.

The living room light and the TV were on when he got to the house. He stood on the street for a moment, taking another look around. The letter he had mailed to the reporter, the one that had a picture of his trailer, had been a break from process. The picture was already gone. The SD card from the digital camera was burned up and the printer was in a box in his attic buried in a pile with dozens of other boxes. It may have been overkill but if he was going to break process, he needed to plan for it. He wondered about the reporter's reaction. There had been no stories in the local paper and no mention in the police blotter. Had he been too clever? What if Abernathy hadn't found the surprise he'd left him? Well, it didn't matter. There were always more barn cats running around.

He walked up the steps to the front porch. The house was small with white aluminum siding, pockmarked from years of things banging into it, like hailstones from spring storms. The front porch was covered with green indoor-outdoor carpet that had been swept clean of snow. The house was well maintained, but he figured the next owners might put on vinyl siding and install new windows. He stood before the front door and stole a look inside.

Martha Utzler was sitting in a recliner watching TV. He didn't recognize the show, but one of the actors looked familiar. He pressed the doorbell, and her head jerked up. She clearly wasn't expecting anyone. After a moment she got up, and the curtain parted as she looked out. Bob smiled and waved at her.

The porch light came on, and the wooden door opened with a heavy sigh. She leaned on the screen door and opened it a few inches. "Yes?"

Bob smiled. "Hi, I'm looking for Frank. Is he home? He gave me this address and said he was staying here for a while rather than his house out on Owl North. Is this the right place?"

Martha nodded. "Yes, he's staying here, but he isn't home right now. He's at work and won't be home until eleven. Would you like me to take a message?"

"Oh, I'm terribly sorry for bothering you at this time of night," Bob said. "I work with Frank at Rocco's. I'm a cook but I usually work days. Anyway, Frank asked if he could borrow some DVDs and I just live a couple blocks over so I said I'd bring them by when he got off work tonight." He held up the small gym bag and Martha looked at it, seeing it for the first time. "I thought he quit at ten and would be home by now. I'm very sorry. I didn't mean to disturb you." He turned to go, glancing around as he did so. It didn't appear that anyone was looking at them.

"Well, you could just leave them with me," Martha said. "I'll make sure he gets them when he comes home."

Bob turned back. "Okay, that'd be fine. Thank you so much."

Martha pushed the screen door open a bit more and reached for the bag. Bob grabbed the door and opened it wider with his left hand. He punched Martha in the face with his right. It was a hard punch, meant to stun her. He followed it up with another and something in her face broke with a crack, either her nose or cheekbone, he wasn't sure. She took a deep breath to scream, and he slammed his fist into her face again, and then he was inside the house. Martha fell to the floor behind her recliner. He shut the heavy wooden door behind him and turned the deadbolt.

She curled into a ball with her arms over her head, anticipating another blow. She was whimpering and crying, but not loud enough to be heard outside the house. Bob reached down and put his glove-covered hand over her mouth and jerked her head around until she was looking at him. Her eyes were filled with fear. He hadn't understood how scared someone could look, how so much emotion could be conveyed just with a glance, but now he understood. Martha Utzler was clearly afraid for her life.

Bob jabbed a finger at her as he held her mouth closed. "Martha, do as I say and you won't be hurt anymore. Nod if you understand me."

She nodded. Tears streamed from her eyes, and she gasped for breath under his hand. Blood streamed from her broken nose, flowing down her cheeks and puddling on the carpet under her head.

"I'm going to move my hand, and you are going to be quiet. If you yell, scream, or make any noise, I will hit you again. Do you want that to happen?"

She shook her head.

"Good." He took his hand away and she gulped air, whimpering.

"Who are you?" she asked. "What do you want?"

Bob was kneeling. "Is there anyone else in the house? Anyone I need to worry about?"

"No," she said softly. "What do you want?" She rolled over and put her hands to her face and smeared blood away from her nose. Her hand started to shake at the sight of it.

Bob stood up and walked over to the living room window. He pulled the curtains closed. "Your son's a moron, Martha. Him and that idiot roommate of his broke into my house and stole from me." He stepped back to her and reached down, grabbing her with both hands. "Let's get you off the floor."

He struggled to get her up, but eventually he did and walked her to the dining room. "Sit in a chair and, remember, Martha, not a sound." She sat down in a chair at the head of the table, trembling. Bob saw blood trails all the way back into the living room. The next owners were going to need new carpet.

There was a napkin holder on the table, and he grabbed a few and held them out to her. "Use these, Kate."

She took them and held them up to her nose. "My name is Martha."

"What?"

"You called me Kate. My name is Martha. Are you sure you have the right house?"

"Oh, yeah, I'm sure. You have an idiot son named Frank, don't you?" He pulled out a chair and sat down. The wooden chair creaked under his weight, and he wondered if the spindly legs were up to the task.

"Please don't hurt him," she said. "Whatever he's done, I can make it right. You don't have to hurt him. Please."

Bob shook his head. "No, I'm sorry, Martha, but we're too far down the road for you to do anything for Frank. You see, it's not just what he took, it's what he learned."

A puzzled expression crossed her face. "What did he learn?"

"Too much, Martha." He set the gym bag on the table and unzipped it. He pulled out a roll of gray tape, brand new and still shrink wrapped in plastic. "Your idiot son learned too much."

. . .

Frank pulled into Skillet's driveway at ten thirty. The truck was there, so the dealer was probably home. Frank had gotten off work a little early because it was a slow night, and he wanted to come here and not be late getting home. The door opened before he even knocked. Skillet looked exasperated.

"Frank, what are you doing here? I know meth heads that don't come around as often as you."

Frank looked worried. "I have to talk to you."

Skillet nodded. "Okay, then get in here."

Frank went directly to the living room without waiting for Skillet to direct him and sat down in a chair. "I think I know what happened to Boyd."

Skillet sat down and lit a cigarette. A Cavs game played on the TV, and he muted it with a click of the remote. "What are you talking about?"

"I think Boyd's dead, and I think that guy we robbed killed him," Frank said. "I think we saw something in that house we weren't supposed to."

Skillet checked the game and saw LeBron sink a three pointer. He pumped his fist and looked back to Frank. "What?"

"Listen to me, I think Boyd's dead."

"Why? Because he hasn't been around?"

Frank leaned forward in the chair. "No, because he hasn't been seen since we pulled that stupid job."

"So? Maybe he found some cash in there and bugged out." Skillet turned back to the game.

"Will you concentrate?" Frank said, a little louder than he meant to. "This is serious. I think Boyd's dead, and I think this guy killed him."

Skillet glared at him. "Why, Frank? Why do you think that?"

"When we were in the house—"

"Where you weren't supposed to be," Skillet said.

"Yeah, Skillet, I know, but Boyd went in and I had to get him." He didn't need a dealer chewing him out about how to pull burglaries.

"Anyway, when we were in there, we saw the guy's dining room table and all this stuff was laid out on it."

"Yeah, Frank, a typewriter and letters and shit. You told me all this, remember?"

"So I think this guy is the freak writing letters to people in town. He's the guy, and I think he killed Boyd to keep him quiet." Frank chewed his lower lip.

"What letters?" Skillet said. "What are you talking about?"

Frank stood up and waved his arms around. "You haven't heard about the guy writing letters? It's been all over the news, man. He's writing all these obscene letters to people in town and no one knows who he is but I do because me and Boyd saw a bunch of them sitting on his dining room table when we were in there. They looked just like the ones I saw in the newspaper."

Skillet looked at him and took a drag on his cigarette. "They looked the same?"

"Exactly the same. The message was right in the center of the paper, and the ones we saw in the house were just like the ones we saw in his house. Just mean stuff. There's no way there are two people like that around."

Skillet looked back at the game but Frank didn't say anything. "The guy was at work, Frank. You guys were in and out of there hours before he got home. How could it be him?"

"I don't know, but who else would it be? I'm telling you, he saw us somehow."

"Hand me that phone."

Frank turned and saw a phone sitting on the end table next to him. He picked it up and tossed it.

Skillet scrolled through the contacts and tapped the call button. "Harvey?" he said when someone answered. "Hey, how you doing, man? Yeah, I'm watching it. Don't worry, they'll pull it out. Hey, I need to ask you a question. You alone? Okay, look, do you remember Thanksgiving, that thing we did the day before?"

Frank chewed on a thumbnail and listened.

"Harvey, concentrate, okay? Remember that thing we set up and afterward you bought a new Xbox?" Skillet shook his head. "Right,

right, well, hey, you guys worked that day, right? It wasn't a day off or anything was it? No? Good, okay."

Frank leaned forward. "Did they work the whole day? With the holiday, did they work the whole day?"

Skillet shrugged. "Hey, Harvey, did you work the whole day or half a day?" Skillet's face fell. "Half day? They sent you home before lunch?" He stared at Frank and Frank leaned back in the chair deflated.

"Damn it," Frank said.

"Okay, Harvey, this is important, you only worked half a day? Okay, why didn't you tell me that? Why didn't you give me a head's up that day? What if our boys got caught? All right, man, no, don't worry about it. I'll call you later." He thumbed a button and dropped the phone on the couch. "That guy's a moron."

Frank was leaned back with his hands on his head. "He came home early, didn't he?"

Skillet nodded.

"Damn it. He came home early and saw Boyd walking down the road and then he saw his house was broken into and he killed him."

"You don't know that," Skillet said.

"I know Boyd hasn't been seen since that day when I let him out of the car. What do you think happened to him, Skillet? Do you really think he's anywhere but in a shallow grave somewhere?"

"There's no proof of that, Frank. You can't just jump to conclusions."

Frank shook his head. "This guy was in my house. He knows who I am. I don't know his name or what he looks like. I'm screwed. What am I going to do?"

"Nothing," Skillet said. "We do nothing."

Frank jumped up. "That's easy for you to say. You get to sit here in your house. I have to live with my mom and hide. He's looking for me, Skillet."

Skillet got up and walked around the coffee table. "Look, Frank, do not panic. Give me a day to think about this, and I'll come up with a plan. We can fix this."

"Boyd's dead, Skillet. How are you going to fix that?"

"First, we don't know if that's true or not, but if it is, there's nothing we can do about it. It is what it is. We have to worry about us, now. We have to make sure our names do not come up. Do you understand me, Frank?"

Frank looked at him and saw that Skillet was really talking about himself. It was crystal clear that whatever happened, Skillet's name was not to be mentioned. Frank suddenly realized where he was and got scared. There were guns here, he knew, and he was alone.

"Yeah, Skillet, I get you, but what are you going to do?"

He put an arm around Frank. "I don't know, but I'll figure something out. Whatever this guy is up to, he's fucking with the wrong guys. No way does he get to just bust into your house and threaten you. Give me until tomorrow night and I'll have a plan."

Frank nodded. "Okay. I can do that."

Skillet walked him to the back door. "Just hang tough, Frank. Go home, see your mom and relax. We'll get this sorted out."

"See you tomorrow," Frank said and walked out into the cold night.

Skillet nodded and locked the door behind him.

● ● ●

Frank was home less than ten minutes later. He got his keys out and opened the side door, the one he used when he parked in the driveway. After hanging up his coat on one of the hooks near the entryway, he walked into the kitchen. The TV was on in the living room, and the local news was just starting.

"Hey, Mom, I'm home. You need anything from the kitchen?" He opened the fridge, yawned and pulled out a gallon of milk to take a drink.

"We're in the dining room, Frank," a man's voice said. "Why don't you come in here?"

An icy lightning bolt of fear shot through Frank. Every muscle in his body went rigid, and he gripped the milk jug, unable to move. That voice was familiar. Without a doubt, he knew it was the man from the house on Owl North Road. Why was he here in his mom's house?

"Come in here and do it with your hands up. No games, Frank. You understand me?"

Frank put the milk back in the fridge and walked through the kitchen into the dining room. His mom was sitting in the chair at the head of the table. She was duct taped to it, Frank saw. Her hands were taped down to the arms and her feet to the legs. Her cheeks were streaked with tears and blood and she was having trouble breathing. Frank saw her nose was swollen. A middle-aged, heavy-set man stood behind her with a gun pointed at her head.

"Sit down, Frank." He motioned to a chair on the opposite side of the table.

"Who are you?" Frank said. "Why are you here?"

The big man gestured with the gun. "Sit down."

Frank looked at his mom and saw fear in her eyes. There was no tape on her mouth, but she didn't say a word. She just sobbed quietly, swallowing hard. He pulled the chair out and sat down.

The man with the gun sat down on the other side of the table and pointed his weapon at Frank. It was a small semi-automatic with some kind of half-assed silencer fitted over it, Frank saw. It was a length of pipe with steel wool in it. It looked homemade, like something a person would make after watching a video on the Internet.

"You know why I'm here?" the man said.

Frank shook his head and tried to speak but his throat was dry. He managed to croak out, "No."

The man sat there for a moment. "So, you're just going to play stupid with me? How many guys have you made mad enough to come into your mom's house with a gun, Frank?"

"Not too many," Frank said in a whisper.

"Yeah, probably just me lately. Tell me something, you and your buddy break into a lot of houses?"

Frank looked at his mom. The guy snapped his fingers. "Frank, do you and your buddy Boyd break into a lot of houses?"

Frank nodded. "Yeah, sometimes."

Martha hung her head.

"I read the paper a lot and watch the news, so I know someone has been doing it. Did you know the cops are looking into your little burglary ring? Too bad they didn't find you instead of me."

Frank looked at him. "I know who you are. Is this is about your tools? We can get those back for you."

Bob sighed. "Yeah? Where are they?"

Frank cleared his throat. "We sold them to a guy here in town. He sells them to other guys. I think he still has them. I can take you there."

"What's his name?"

Frank bit his lower lip and looked down at the green tablecloth.

"What's his name, Frank?"

Still looking down at the table, Frank said, "Skillet. His name is Skillet, and he lives over on Leslie Street."

Bob nodded. "His name is Skillet? Does he have a real name?"

"I'm sure he does, but I don't know it. I just know him by Skillet."

"He's a fence? He moves the stuff you steal?"

"Yeah," Frank said. "He does that and he deals."

Bob nodded. "I guess I'll have to go see Skillet, then."

"I could take you there. I know he's home. I just came from there."

"Seriously? Did you rob someone else, Frank?"

Frank shook his head. He caught sight of the photo montage his mom had hanging on the wall. It was made up of all his school pictures, kindergarten through high school. Most of his life was captured there. From gapped-toothed sandy-haired little guy to moody teenager with longer hair, year after year was recorded there and displayed proudly. He looked at his mom.

"I'm so sorry, Mom. I'm so sorry for letting you down." He reached out and held one of her duct-taped hands.

"It was the cameras that did you in, you know," Bob said. "I put them in a couple years ago. You didn't see them, did you?"

Frank shook his head a little. "No, we didn't see any cameras."

Bob shifted in his chair, comfortable and in charge of the situation. "I passed your buddy in his eight-ball jacket on my way home. He was walking through the snow and when I went in and saw that someone had broken in I checked the video, and there you two were. I recognized his coat and your car." He paused a moment and Frank let it sink in. "I was so mad," he continued. "Do you understand, Frank, how angry it makes someone when you break into their house?"

Bob leaned forward and slammed a hand on the table. Frank and Martha both jumped, startled by the noise. "There's a violation. You no longer feel safe in your home, because now you know just how easily someone can come in and take whatever they want. That's what you do to people, Frank, you and your buddy Boyd."

Frank looked up at this. "Where is Boyd? I haven't seen him since that day."

"Well, like I said, Frank, I came home and saw that you two had been in my house and I have to tell you, I was pretty upset. I wasn't thinking straight. In fact, I may have acted somewhat rashly." He paused for a moment, and Frank thought he looked unsure of himself. "I took my truck and just ran his ass over."

Frank's head fell. "No, please. Come on. You didn't do that, did you?" His mom just looked at him and gripped his hand.

Bob nodded. "I was mad, Frank. You guys had my tools and you'd been in my house. You saw what was on the dining room table, and I just, well, I don't know if 'panicked' is the right word, but events certainly did spiral out of control. Boyd is in a drainpipe under the road between our houses. Hell, you've probably driven over him a few times.

"I saw him on the news, Frank. People are looking for him and you were the last person to see him. The police will talk to you, you'll tell them what you know, and then they'll start talking to me. Eventually they'll find him, and then I'll go to jail for running down some thieving junkie, and I'm not going to let that happen."

"It's not the tools you're mad about, is it?" Frank said. "You're mad about the letters. We saw them, so we know it's you sending them to people."

Martha looked at Bob, her eyes large. "You're doing that?"

Bob grimaced. "You had no right. You came in and you saw things no one was supposed to see." He waved his gun around. "This is all your fault."

"Do you really think anyone cares about your letters this much?" Frank said. "Can you even go to jail for sending them? I don't think it's serious enough to kill over. It can't be."

"What would you know about it?" Bob said. Frank noticed he was shaking now, clearly upset. "You don't get to just come into someone's life and screw with them. You don't get to do that."

"That's what you do with your letters," Frank said.

"You don't get to judge me when you're the thief," Bob said. "I worked hard all my life for what I have, and now it's almost all gone because of people like you. Do you have any idea how tired I am of people making decisions about me and my life and I just have to live with the consequences? Well, no more. I'm making the decisions now. You and your pal are just a couple junkies who messed with the wrong guy."

"I told you nothing good would come from being Boyd's friend," Martha said. "After his accident, he was never the same." Frank just looked at her as she spoke.

"What is Skillet's address?" Bob said. He stood up and picked up a pen and a pad of Post-Its from the wooden bill holder in the middle of the table. Frank had made it for his mom in ninth-grade wood shop.

Frank gave him the address, and he wrote it down, peeling the sticky note from the rest of the pad.

"He knows everything," Frank said.

Bob looked at him and his eyes narrowed. "What do you mean, 'everything'?"

"When I took him the tools I told him about those letters we saw on your dining room table," Frank said. "We talked a couple of times about it. Who knows who he's told? Don't you see, too many people know for you to keep it secret."

Frank watched as he licked his lips. He thought Bob looked confused.

"Maybe we can come to an arrangement with Skillet," Frank said. "Just untie my mom and I can take you there."

"No, you can't," Bob said, and Frank watched as he raised the gun and shot his mother in the head. Blood spattered all over the dining room walls behind her and beside her. Frank inhaled sharply to scream, and the last thing he saw was a flash of light before something hard and fast exploded against his left eye.

Twenty-Three

Tim had two stops scheduled this morning, and he had just arrived at the first one. He pulled his rusty pickup truck into the driveway of a neat little house in the city on Elm Street. It was painted a cheery robin's-egg blue and stood out against the dreary white of the snow covering the surrounding yard. He got out of the truck and knocked on the storm door. After a moment, the inner door opened and an older man greeted him.

"Mark? I'm Tim Abernathy from the *Hogan Shopper*. We spoke on the phone."

The older man nodded. He was smaller, bald, and wearing a Cleveland Browns sweatshirt and dark-brown sweatpants. The door opened wide. "Come on in, Mr. Abernathy."

Tim walked in and stomped his feet on the rubber mat inside the door. "Please, call me Tim."

"Okay, well, have a seat." Mark motioned to a couch in the living room. "Would you like some coffee?"

"No, thanks," Tim said. "I've already had a couple this morning."

Mark settled into a recliner and threw up the footrest. "So, what can I do for you?"

"Well, I'm working on a story for the *Hogan Shopper* about someone sending anonymous letters to residents here in town, and I think you may be able to help."

Mark looked puzzled. "That's what you said on the phone, but I don't see how. I'm certainly not doing it."

Tim smiled, trying to keep the mood light. "No, sir, I certainly don't think it's you, but your nephew Max spoke to me, and I think you may know something that will help."

"Max talked to you? He's a good kid. He works over at the tire and wheel store."

"Well, he told me that he caught his boss, Jerry Donovan, in a compromising position and passed that information on to you."

Mark smiled. "Yeah, he said Jerry was banging a sales rep for one of his rim suppliers. You know, Max caught them going at it right in the shop. If you're going to do dumb shit like that where people can see you, they're going to talk."

Tim bit his lower lip to hold back a smile. "No doubt, sir. What I wanted to ask you about was who you told that story to. You see, Max said he only told you. When Jerry died, he had just received one of these anonymous letters, and the letter referenced the affair Mr. Donovan was having. So, what I'd like to know from you is, who did you tell?"

Mark took a sip of his coffee and set it down on a coaster on the end table. "You think someone I know is the guy writing these letters?"

"Well, I don't know about that," Tim said. "You see, when you work a story like this you tug on a thread and see what it's connected to. Maybe it's something, maybe it's nothing. Right now I'm just tugging on the thread from Max to you and seeing if anything comes of it."

Mark nodded and took another sip of his coffee. He looked like he was trying to make up his mind about whether saying anything more made him a snitch or not and what the consequences of that might be. "I only told the guys down at the Peppermill."

"Downtown?"

"Yeah," Mark said. "There's a group of us who get together for breakfast on Saturday mornings. We're all retirees from Ohio Axle. Anyway, I told the guys what Max had said." He stopped for a moment, looking embarrassed. "We just get together and bullshit a little, you know?"

"Okay, well, could you tell me their names?"

"Are you going to go ask them questions, too?"

"Probably. Will that cause problems for you? I can be discreet."

Mark waved a hand at him. "Hell, I don't care about that. It's just a little gossip. Now, if I'm remembering correctly, these are the guys who were there."

Tim wrote down all the names in his notebook.

• • •

The second stop was at Brinco, the auto parts supplier. He pulled into the parking lot and drove to the northwest entrance. He walked in through double glass doors and a receptionist behind a circular desk smiled at him. Tim smiled back and looked around. The décor was outdated. It was all chrome and glass that had probably last been fashionable in the 1980s. In one corner of the room, product samples were set up on display. Tim saw strut assemblies, shocks, and brake components.

"Can I help you?" the receptionist asked.

"Hi, I'm here to see Ricky Rogers. My name is Tim Abernathy, and he should be expecting me."

"Okay, have a seat over there, and I'll give him a call," she said.

Tim sat down on a small black vinyl sofa that sank too low. He took out his spiral notebook and started a new page. After a few moments, the door to the reception area opened and a man walked out. When the door opened, Tim could hear all kinds of noises from the plant floor. The man zeroed in on Tim and walked over to him.

"Abernathy?"

Tim stood up, struggling a bit because of the deep seat on the sofa. "That's me. Please call me Tim. You're Ricky Rogers?"

"Yes." They shook hands.

"Thanks for meeting with me," Tim said. "I only need a moment of your time."

"Good. We're busy this morning. Can we just talk right here?" He motioned to the black vinyl furniture, and they sat down. Ricky took a chair. "On the phone last night you said something about this guy writing the anonymous letters in the paper and that my name had come up. You know I'm not the guy, right? I mean, I don't write letters of any kind. I have email."

"No, Mr. Rogers, I don't think you're writing the letters. What happened is, I think the letter writer has been by my place, and my neighbor spoke with him. She asked him what he was doing there and he said he was looking for a friend. When she pressed him for a name, he gave her yours."

"Okay," Ricky said. "What did he look like?"

"White guy, mid-fifties, on the heavy side. He drove a Chevy pickup with a snow plow."

Ricky smiled. "Sorry, Tim, but you just described half the plant."

"He was wearing a red hat, if that helps."

Ricky paused for a moment, eyes looking away, then shook his head. "No, sorry."

Tim nodded and made a note on his pad. "Let me ask you something, Mr. Rogers. Do you know anyone who's a little odd? Someone who might fit that physical description who seems upset with the way life has treated him? Maybe someone who has some anger issues?"

Ricky's eyes shifted to the door leading back to the plant floor for a moment, then he shook his head. "Sorry, Tim. I don't think I can help you."

"Are you sure, Mr. Rogers?"

He nodded. "Yeah. First, that doesn't sound like anyone I know. Second, even if it did, I can't just give you an employee's name."

Tim's eyes narrowed. "Mr. Rogers, why do you assume I'm looking for an employee's name? It could be someone you know outside of work."

Ricky stood up. "To be honest, it doesn't sound like anyone I know at all. I'm sorry, Tim. I have to get back to work."

Tim stood up and shook his outstretched hand. "Of course."

"How did you get my name and number, anyway?"

Tim smiled. "Google and the county auditor's website. You were the only Richard Rogers in Hogan."

Ricky nodded. "Well, good luck." Then he went back through the door and it closed behind him. Tim made a note on his pad and said goodbye to the receptionist.

He got into his truck and started it. He got the feeling Ricky was lying to him, but he didn't know why. It was getting on noon, he saw, and the temperature was still in the thirties. The heat was just coming up in the truck when his phone rang. He checked the display and saw it was Charlie.

"Hello, boss."

"I need you to meet me out on Owl North Road in the township," Charlie said. "You know where that is?"

"Sure. What's up?"

"The cops just pulled a body out of a drainpipe."

•   •   •

Tim pulled to the side of the road behind Charlie's Cadillac fifteen minutes later. The road was blocked with yellow sawhorses and a Hogan police officer. About a hundred yards away Tim could see red and blue lights from police cruisers, an ambulance, and a couple fire trucks. A dark-blue county coroner's van was parked off to one side. He got out, pulled on a stocking cap and walked up to his boss. "What's going on?"

"I'm not sure exactly. I had the police scanner on in the office and heard them talking about a body out here. I called you and got out here as fast as I could."

Tim squinted in the winter sunshine at the scene. Officers in heavy coats stood off the road, down an embankment. The ambulance drivers were leaning against their rig, one of them smoking. Two firefighters were looping rope and pulling a metal litter from the back of their truck.

"So what do we do now?" Tim said.

"Find a way to talk with someone," Charlie said. "Until then, get good notes about the scene."

For an hour they spoke and collected notes. Then Tim saw a face he recognized. He waved his hand but there was no response. He dug his cell phone out his back pocket and scrolled through his contacts before pressing the green call button.

"You see something?" Charlie said.

"Someone I know. That detective from the police station we spoke to." The phone rang and then it clicked as the other person picked up.

"Coogan."

"Detective Coogan, it's Tim Abernathy and Charlie Ingram from the *Hogan Shopper*. We're over at the barricade and were hoping you could give us a statement."

Tim waved a hand in his direction. The detective didn't wave back. "No comment." The line went dead and Tim put the phone in his jacket pocket.

"No comment?" Charlie said.

"Yeah."

"Good try."

The phone rang and Tim answered it. "Hello?"

"Abernathy?" Detective Coogan said. "Is your girlfriend the one with the missing brother?"

Tim felt his stomach drop and his voice caught in his throat, making it hoarse. "Yes."

"I need you and your boss to come here. The officer at the barricade will let you through."

"Is it him? Is it Boyd?"

"Just come here." The line went dead again.

Tim heard a squawk from the officer's radio, then the officer waved at Tim and Charlie. He pointed at the cluster of vehicles. "Detective Coogan wants to speak with you."

"Come on, Charlie."

They walked down the empty road and Tim could feel the gloomy press of the woods on either side. The stark trees were ominous in their lack of life. Tim's mouth was dry when he approached the detective.

Coogan was dressed in a long, heavy overcoat with a dark-blue knit cap, black gloves, and rubber boots that clashed with his gray suit pants. He stared directly at Tim and held out his hand.

"Hello, Abernathy. Thanks for coming over. Sir," he said, nodding in Charlie's direction by way of greeting.

"Is it Boyd?"

Coogan shrugged. "Probably. The description fits but we don't have a positive ID yet. It's a young adult male wearing an eight-ball jacket. That's what his sister reported him as wearing in the missing person's report. I think it's probably him. We haven't found a wallet yet, but we're still looking."

"Oh, God," Tim said. "This is going to kill her. He was the only family she had left."

"Could you take a look at him? Identify him?"

Tim shook his head. "I only saw him in person once, and that was across a parking lot. I wouldn't recognize him. Was he murdered or run over or what?"

"Oh, it's foul play for sure," Coogan said, pointing down into the hollow. "Dead bodies do not pull themselves into drainpipes. Someone put him there."

"How did you find him?" Charlie said.

"Turkey hunter." Coogan pointed into the woods. "He came down over that ridge of the hollow and saw the body lying in the pipe. Looks like some animals have been at it. We're working the scene now but we'll take the body down to the county morgue for an autopsy in a little while."

"We have to let Amy know," Tim said.

Coogan nodded. "Yeah, that's why I called you over here. Do you know where she is?"

"At work, over at the hardware store."

"I'll do the notification," Coogan said. "Do you want to come with me? It might be easier."

"Go ahead, Tim," Charlie said. "I've got this."

"Okay."

"My car is over there," Coogan said, nodding at a four-door silver Dodge Charger parked on the side of the road. "Mr. Ingram, I'll need you back behind the barricade for now. We'll do a press conference in a bit. It won't be long before the TV stations get here."

Charlie nodded. "Okay. One more thing, can you tell us how Mr. Sashman died?"

"The coroner did a preliminary examination, and right now it looks like blunt force trauma consistent with being struck by a vehicle. He's got bruises on his back and broken bones. He'll know more after the autopsy."

Tim looked at the detective. "So someone hit him, knocked him down the embankment and shoved him in the drainpipe?"

"That's what it looks like," Coogan said. "Let's go."

They rode into town slowly, and Coogan waited until they were almost at the store to speak. "When we get there, I'll do the talking. You're just there to support her. Understand?"

"Yes," Tim said. "There's a breakroom in the back. We should take her there."

"Good idea."

They pulled into the parking lot, and Tim was struck by how surreal the situation was. He had entered this store a thousand times to work, and now he was on his way to give Amy the worst news possible. She was inside, going about her day, through her usual routine. Very shortly, she would look back on this moment and realize it was the dividing line between the time she thought Boyd was alive and the time she knew he wasn't.

• • •

Hours later, Tim and Amy were in her apartment on the couch. After Coogan had broken the news to her in the breakroom at Degman's Hardware, Tim had driven her home in her car. Charlie and a police officer had dropped his truck off at her apartment building a little while later.

Amy was curled into him under a crocheted afghan. The coffee table was littered with the remains of a half-eaten meal of General Tso's chicken and too many tissues to count.

Amy poked her finger through a space in the afghan. "My mom made this and gave it to me the last Christmas we were all together. That was probably the last good year I had. My folks were alive and the future was still wide open." She was quiet for a moment before continuing. "Oh, Tim, you should have known him when he was younger. He was smart and energetic. He ran track in high school and worked down at the Dairy Queen. Before his accident and the pills, he was somebody completely different." She sighed. "Now he's gone. My whole family is gone."

Tim pulled her tight and kissed the top of her head. "You know, when you think of Boyd and your parents, there's no reason you have to think about the events of their deaths."

She sat up, blew her nose in another Kleenex and looked at him with swollen red eyes. "I know, Tim. A grief counselor Boyd and I saw after our parents' death gave us similar advice, but what's devastating is realizing what they're missing. Christmas is coming again, and I won't get to taste my mother's cooking." She gripped his hand. "I won't get to introduce you to them and tell them I found a great guy. You won't ever get to know a Boyd who is sober. All that potential is just lost, and that's what I'm mourning. All that lost opportunity."

"Yeah," Tim said. "I understand. I'd love to introduce you to my dad, but instead it's going to be my mom and step-dad, and believe me when I say how sorry I am for that."

Amy smiled, just a little. "They can't be that bad."

"You just keep thinking that."

She was quiet for a moment and then the weight of the day seemed to descend on them again. "Why do you think someone killed him, Tim? It was probably the drugs, but why? What did he do to make someone so angry they killed him? I don't understand.

"When my parents died, it was an accident. It was horrible, but I can understand icy roads and winter driving. This thing with Boyd is so senseless. Someone had to make the decision to kill him and hide him, and I don't understand why. What sin did he commit that demanded that kind of penance?"

Tim shook his head. "I don't know, Amy. I can tell you one thing, though: we're going to find out. You're right. Someone did this, and that means they can be found. No matter how careful someone thinks they are, they always leave clues behind. We're going to find them. We're going to ask questions until we get answers."

Amy nodded and Tim noticed her jaw set. "Yeah, and I know just who to ask."

"You're thinking of Frank? He wasn't very helpful last time we spoke to him."

"Yeah, well, this time he's going to tell me what I want to know. If anyone knows what Boyd was up to, it's him. He can make all the excuses he wants but nothing is going to keep me from getting the answers I want."

Twenty-Four

Friday morning, Larry Coogan and Darren Lewis rolled down Owl North Road in the silver Dodge Charger. It was early and still dark outside. Coogan watched as Lewis pulled out a pack of Marlboros and opened them.

"If you have to do that in here, roll down your window," Coogan said. "I hate the smell of those things."

Darren pushed the window switch and cracked it a few inches. "Yeah, I know."

Coogan was senior detective, but that didn't mean a whole lot in a department that only had two. He noticed Lewis was dressed nicely today, wearing a dark-gray suit with a peach shirt. He looked an awful lot like Wesley Snipes in *Rising Sun*. Coogan lamented that he himself looked more like Kevin James than Sean Connery.

"What are you all dressed up for?" Coogan said.

Lewis blew smoke out the window. "Did you see yourself on the news last night? I want to make sure if we run into cameras today I look good."

"I didn't look good?"

Lewis shrugged his shoulders. "You looked fine. I want to look good."

"Yeah, well, we aren't likely to run into too many cameras canvassing neighbors about the late and lamented Mr. Boyd Sashman." The Dodge slowed in front of a driveway up the street from the crime scene. "I think this is our place."

"This guy wasn't home yesterday?" Lewis asked.

"No, he was still at work when we were working the scene. I made a note to hit him up early this morning." The car turned onto the gravel driveway with a crunch and moved slowly toward the house.

"Can you imagine having to keep this thing clear?" Lewis asked.

"That's why I live in town. I have no desire to maintain property like this."

"Yeah," Coogan said. "You'd need a plow for sure." Switching subjects, he asked, "Did you talk to the roommate?" Lewis had done some of the canvassing yesterday.

"No, when we checked the house no one was home. There were signs of forced entry, though. We have a BOLO out on him. I'll look into his employment records later this morning and see where he works."

Lewis keyed the radio and reported their location, then flipped down the passenger's side sunshade. A set of red and blue LED lights were strapped to it, and he turned them on. "That should get their attention."

Coogan pulled to a stop in front of the garage and looked at the house. There was a front door to the right of the garage and a barn farther down the driveway to the left of the house. An outside light blinked on and the garage door rolled up. He and Lewis got out of their car.

A heavyset man wearing black sweatpants and a blue t-shirt stood inside the garage, looking at them from a doorway that led into the house. "Can I help you?"

Coogan waved a badge at him. "We're police officers, sir, and we need to speak with you. May we come in?"

The man looked at them for a long moment, and suddenly Coogan wasn't sure he was going to let them in. He stopped short of entering the garage. Lewis stopped a step behind him.

"I guess so," the man said, and held the door open wider. "Come on in."

The detectives moved around a pickup truck parked in the garage and stepped up into the house. "Thank you," Coogan said. "Are you Bob Ellstrom?"

The man shut the door and the three of them stood in the kitchen. "Yeah, that's me. What can I do for you?"

They introduced themselves and took out their notebooks. "Sorry to bother you so early in the morning, but we wanted to catch you

before you went to work. We're here about your neighbor, Boyd Sashman. Did you know him?"

After a second, Bob shook his head. "No, I don't know too many of
my neighbors. Most of the older ones have moved away and I haven't
gotten to know the new folks."

Coogan knew that "new folks" out in the township could live here
for a decade before they got on a first-name basis with those who had
lived here longer.

"He was a young guy, lived up the road in that white house," Coogan
said.

Bob licked his lips. "The old Jensen place? I knew someone had
moved in but, I don't know who they are. Couple of young guys, from
what I've seen."

Coogan watched as Lewis moved around the kitchen, keeping a
lookout and seeing what there was to see. It was his job to hold the
attention of the person being questioned and keep them off balance. "So
you have seen them?"

"I guess."

"This guy had a distinctive coat. It was kind of retro, you know? It
was green and red and had a big eight ball on the back of it. You remember
seeing that coat?"

Bob looked at Lewis, and Coogan could see he was uncomfortable
with him roaming around the kitchen and looking into other rooms
through the doorways. "Mr. Ellstrom, do you remember that coat?"

Bob looked back at him. "Uh, I guess so. I think I've seen him out
walking on the road. Did something happen to him?"

"Yes, sir, he was found dead yesterday."

Bob's eyes slid left, in the direction of the road and the drainpipe,
then he looked back at Coogan. "That's too bad. What happened?"

"Well, we're still looking into that, but we were wondering if you'd
seen anything suspicious in the area lately. Anyone around who doesn't
belong or anything going on out here that shouldn't be."

Bob shook his head. "No, things have been quiet. That's why I live
out here, you know? I like the quiet."

Lewis walked around behind Bob, and Coogan saw him make a
motion with his eyes toward the side door leading out into the yard. He

turned and saw cardboard duct taped into place in one of the small window panes. He gestured toward it with his notebook. "What happened there? Someone break in?"

Bob's eyebrows rose up in surprise. "Oh, that? No, I just came home one day and it was cracked. Might have been the cold, I guess."

Coogan looked at him. "Mr. Ellstrom, are you sure you don't have anything to tell us? You never had any trouble with those boys, did you? They weren't loud or anything like that?"

Bob coughed and crossed his arms over his chest. "No. Like I said, I didn't know them, and I never had any dealings with them. Sorry."

"Yeah, that's what you said." Coogan stared at him, something nagging him in the back of his head, but he wasn't sure what. An uncomfortable silence dropped over the kitchen.

"Well, I have to get to work, unless you have any more questions," Bob said.

Coogan took out a business card and handed it to him. "If you think of anything else, let me know. My cell number is on there."

Bob took it and nodded. "I don't know what else I'd think of, but if I do I'll be sure to give you a ring." He moved back to the garage door and opened it. Coogan and Lewis moved through it and Coogan stopped at the pickup truck, remembering what had nagged at him.

"You plow the driveway yourself?"

Bob got a perplexed look on his face. "Yeah, that's what the plow's for."

Coogan looked at it with the light of the kitchen streaming into the garage. "HTX, twenty-seven inches," he read from the label painted on the corner of the blade face. "This does the trick? I've been thinking of getting one myself."

Bob nodded. "Yeah, it doesn't give me any problems."

Coogan pointed to a dent on the driver's side door. "What happened there?"

Bob shrugged his shoulders. "I don't know. I bought it used. It was there when I got it."

Coogan smiled. "Okay then, Mr. Ellstrom. You have a good day."

"You too," Bob said, and he closed the door.

The detectives got back in the Dodge. Coogan started the motor and pulled a wide turn around in the gravel and snow. Lewis shut off the red and blue lights and they started down the driveway.

"Did you catch how he looked right at the crime scene when I told him Boyd was dead, even though I didn't say how or where we found him?" Coogan said.

"Yeah, it was almost like he knew more than he was saying."

"You get a chance to read the coroner's preliminary report?" Coogan asked.

"Skimmed it a little last night," Lewis said. "What's bothering you?"

"Boyd Sashman was killed by blunt force trauma consistent with being struck by a vehicle. The coroner noted two horizontal marks, one on his back and one on the backs of his legs, twenty-seven inches apart."

Lewis turned back and looked at the house they had just left. "How about that?"

Coogan nodded in the weak sunlight just starting to spill over the horizon. "Yeah, how about that? I think we're going to take a harder look at Mr. Ellstrom today."

• • •

Bob watched from the living room window as the cops drove down the driveway, then collapsed to his knees. He leaned forward and rested his head on a recliner, and then he started shaking uncontrollably. His chest tightened, and he was having trouble getting a full breath. He started breathing more rapidly. He looked at the cordless phone on the end table and wondered if he would be able to reach it if he was having a heart attack.

He closed his eyes and clamped his mouth shut to force his breathing through his nose in an effort to get it under control. He saw Frank and Martha Utzler, their brains decorating the walls of their dining room. That made it harder to breathe. He opened his eyes and looked at the light from the rising sun. He couldn't see the sun itself because of the trees, but things were brighter outside than they had been a few moments ago.

When the red and blue lights from the police car had come on, he had been sure they were here to arrest him. He had been watching the TV news obsessively and checking the local news websites, but no one had reported finding their bodies. Eventually his breathing calmed and he was able to pull his bulk from the floor and fall into the recliner.

Last night's eleven o'clock news had covered the discovery of Boyd's body extensively, but there hadn't been much substance in the story. They just talked about how the young man had been found and speculated about how he had been killed. That would change, Bob knew. The authorities would find more evidence. Hell, they might even come back to talk to him again. After all, he lived near the crime scene.

Things are spinning out of control, he thought. *And there's still that dealer to take care of. Tonight, maybe.*

Then he finally got a deep breath, and his heartbeat slowed. Maybe things weren't all that bad. The cop's questions had been non-specific. If they had anything tying him to Boyd's murder, they would have brought more than two detectives. There would have been flashing lights all around the house and he would be in the back of a squad car. The most important thing he could do was keep to his normal routine.

He stood up and looked at the clock. There was still enough time to get to work if he moved quickly.

• • •

A few hours later, Tim was in the offices of the *Shopper* going through the collected data on the letter writer. His article on the discovery of Boyd's body was completed and sitting in Charlie's email inbox waiting to be edited. Now, he wanted to be distracted, to think of anything else. Charlie was busy in the conference room, holding another meeting with the weekly columnists.

A spreadsheet of letter recipients who had answered his call to contact the *Shopper* for interviews was up on his screen. He sorted the list by those he hadn't spoken with yet and saw he had about half a dozen entries. Over the course of the next hour, he called each and either spoke with them over the phone about the letters they had received or set up appointments to do so. He left voicemail messages for a few of them.

His cell phone rang at eleven thirty, and he saw it was Amy. He stood up and walked out the back door into the parking lot before answering.

"Hey," he said, "how are you doing?"

"I'm good, I guess," she said with a voice that sounded like she had been crying not too long ago. "I'm just working through the arrangements for Boyd."

"How's that going? Do you need any help?"

She sighed. "There's not much else to do right now, but thanks. Hey, I've been calling Frank's cell phone, but he isn't answering. I've left him about four messages this morning."

"He probably heard about Boyd being found and is lying low," Tim said.

"Maybe," she said. "Do you think he did it?"

"What, killed Boyd?"

"Yes."

"Anything is possible, Amy. He seemed genuinely concerned about Boyd missing the night we spoke to him, but maybe it was an act."

"Maybe," she said.

There was a silence over the line. Tim realized he had come outside without his coat and was starting to feel the cold in the December air.

"Why don't you take it easy today?" he said. "Just take some time for yourself?"

"Because I'm mad, Tim," she said with a hint of anger in her voice. "Keeping busy helps me."

"Okay, sorry. I shouldn't have said that."

"It's all right," she said. "I'm just upset, and I don't know what to do. Detective Coogan called again today, asking more questions about what Boyd did and who some of his friends were. That wasn't a long list."

"Hey, you want to meet for lunch? We could go down to the Peppermill or out to Jupiter Joe's."

"Thanks, but I think I'm going to be busy. I'll see you tonight though, okay?"

"Sure."

"See you later," she said.

"Yeah, you too," he said. "Bye."

He knew it was too soon to start ending phone calls with "love you," but he had felt like saying it. He wondered what she would have done if he had.

• • •

Two hours later, Tim walked into the Peppermill and stopped at the wooden podium. A sign beside it said "Please wait to be seated." A plump woman in a waitress uniform came over to him. "Welcome to the Peppermill. Do you need a seat?"

"Actually, I'm here to speak with Nadine Harch," Tim said.

The woman turned and pointed. "Oh, there she is, over at the counter." Tim followed her gesture and saw an attractive fortyish red-head with good legs refilling ketchup bottles.

"Thank you."

He walked over to the end of the lunch counter, and the woman the hostess had pointed out came over to him. "Hi, can I get you something to drink?"

"You're Nadine, right? My name's Tim Abernathy. I called you earlier this morning."

"I remember," Nadine said.

"You said this would be a good time to speak with you. Is it?"

She looked around. "Sure. The lunch rush is over, and I could use a break. Why don't we go out back?"

"Okay." Tim got off the stool and followed her toward the side exit.

"Julie," she called to the hostess who had greeted Tim. "Can you watch the counter? I'm going on break."

"No problem," she said.

Nadine grabbed a sweater from a coat rack near the door, and they went out in the winter afternoon. She pulled a pack of cigarettes and a lighter from her sweater pocket. She lit one with practiced ease and blew smoke from the corner of her mouth.

"So what can I do for you, Tim? You said something about the anonymous letters on the phone."

Tim noticed she spoke casually about the letters, as if they were now something everyone was familiar with. Maybe they were now just one more thing in the news cycle.

"Yes. First, thanks for taking the time to meet with me. I'll try to keep this short."

She nodded. "No problem. I have to tell you, though, I only know about the letters from the news. I haven't received any."

Tim took out his spiral notebook and made a mark in it. "I'm happy to hear that. The letters are disturbing to most folks, so I'm glad you haven't had to put up with receiving one."

"So why are you here?"

Tim consulted the notebook again. "A woman named Kathleen Brimley has received two letters."

Time noticed Nadine's face change at the mention of Kathleen's name.

"You know her?" he said.

She took another drag on her cigarette and squeezed one eye shut against the afternoon sun. "Yes, I know who Kathleen is. Does she know you're here?"

"Yes."

"Really?" She regarded him with a wary eye.

"Yes, she does."

She paused a moment looking at him. "Okay."

"The first letter Kathleen received contained your name. The second letter mentioned you by inference, but not by name. It's this letter that is most important. The content of it leads us to believe the person writing the anonymous letters was in the Peppermill and witnessed an encounter between yourself and Mrs. Brimley."

Nadine leaned back against the brick building and sighed. "Yeah, I remember that day. What has Kathleen told you?"

Tim cleared his throat. "She mentioned that you may have had an affair with her deceased husband and that she confronted you about it."

"Yeah, that's about what happened," she said. "It wasn't loud or violent or anything like that. She just knew and I couldn't find it in myself to lie to her. I always thought I'd be able to, but the way she looked at me was so intense, like she already knew. I guess your letter writer must have convinced her."

"Ms. Harch, I want to be very clear. I don't care about any of that. None of that is my business. What I'd like to know is if anyone stands out in your memory as being in the restaurant that day. In order for the letter writer to reference what happened, he had to be here."

Nadine blew smoke into the cold air. "It was lunchtime. The place was packed."

Tim's heart sank. He'd known this was a long shot. "Is there anyone who stands out? Was there any regular who may have taken an interest in you and Kathleen? Both of you said your confrontation was low key, so it probably wouldn't have attracted a lot of attention. Was anyone taking notice of you that day?"

Nadine inhaled again and finished off her cigarette. She crushed it out on the side of the building and flicked it into a pile of snow. "Look, what happened with Kathleen kind of shook me up. I mean, I'm not proud of what I did, and to see her in here like that really threw me for a loop."

"This person would have recognized you both and may have been anticipating a confrontation. Did anyone pay special attention?"

She shrugged. "Well, Bob was in here. He always pays close attention to me."

"Bob?"

"Yeah, he's one of the regulars. He's always in here with the retired guys who sit in the corner booth. He was here eating lunch by himself that day."

"What makes you remember Bob?"

"Oh, he's got a little thing for me. He always says hello, asked me out once but he's not my type."

"Anything stand out about Bob that day? Did he do anything unusual?"

"Not really unusual, but I do remember he dropped his glass and broke it as Kathleen was leaving. I cleaned it up."

"Do you know Bob's last name?"

She shook her head. "No idea. Like I said, he comes in with the retirees and they drink coffee while they whine and complain. I don't pay too much attention to them." She looked at her watch. "I should probably get back to work."

Tim made a note in his book then pulled a card from his pocket. "Okay, thanks. If you think of anything else, please give me a call at that number, day or night."

"Okay." She took his card and went back in through the side door. Tim walked back up the street to the *Shopper* with something he couldn't quite pinpoint nagging at him.

• • •

"Who called it in?" Coogan asked. He was standing outside the Utzler house later that afternoon. He checked his cell phone and saw it was two thirty. The street was cordoned off and there was yellow crime scene tape around the house. Curious neighbors were out on their porches taking a break from game shows and talk shows to see what was going on. Lewis opened his notebook.

"Rocco Griselli over at Rocco's Pizza," Lewis said. "He's Frank Utzler's boss, and the guy didn't show up for work. He missed two shifts two days in a row, and this morning Rocco called to see if he quit or was just blowing off work. Apparently he's got a habit of doing that. When he didn't get an answer he called us for a welfare check. The responding officer saw the bodies through the window."

"You've been inside?" Coogan said.

"I peeked in. I thought we could do the initial walk-through together."

"How about the EMTs? Have they been inside?"

Lewis shook his head. "We held them back. It was pretty clear no one was alive. The patrol officers searched and cleared the house. It looks like all the action took place in the dining room."

Coogan nodded. "Okay, let's go take a look."

They mounted the steps to the front porch and pulled on booties and latex gloves to protect the scene. Coogan entered the house and saw that it looked like most homes in town. It was small but well-kept and clean. The living room looked undisturbed. He crossed to the dining room and saw that Lewis was correct. As clean as the living room was, the dining room was the exact opposite. It had suffered an explosion of violence. There were two bodies: one a woman, probably the aforementioned Martha Utzler, duct taped to a chair, and a younger man lying on the floor. Blood and brain matter were all over the floor, walls, and ceiling. Coogan's breath caught at the back of his throat and he cleared it noisily.

"Murder-suicide?" he asked.

Lewis shook his head. "I don't think so. I don't see a gun, so I'm thinking they were executed." He pointed at the bodies. "It looks like one head shot each."

Coogan knelt near the young man's body. He was lying on his side, facedown in the brown carpet. The young man's left hip jutted up and Coogan saw a bulge in the back pocket of his jeans. He reached over and pulled out a wallet.

"Shouldn't you wait until the state patrol guys get here?" Lewis said.

"Their forensic team is on the way."

Coogan nodded at the dead woman. "You said her name is Utzler, right? Well, we're looking for Frank Utzler in connection with Boyd Sashman's murder." He flipped the wallet open and pulled out a driver's license. "And this appears to be Frank Utzler."

Lewis clapped him on the shoulder. "Good catch."

Coogan stood up with the wallet. "So, we have Boyd Sashman stuffed in a drainpipe out near his house in the township, and we have his roommate, Frank Utzler, and Frank's mother, Martha Utzler, dead at her house in town. That's three bodies in two days, Darren. We haven't had a murder in Hogan for eight years. What the hell's going on?"

• • •

Tim and Charlie stood outside the Utzler house behind the yellow tape. Once again, Charlie had heard the call on his police scanner and they'd driven over. Tim had sent Amy a text and told her it was going to be a late night. The police officers watching the perimeter weren't talking.

"Any idea who the house belongs to?" Tim asked.

Charlie shook his head. "No, this one isn't familiar. Let's go ask the neighbors."

"Hold on," Tim said, pulling his phone out. "Let me check something." After a couple minutes of tapping, he held the phone up to Charlie. "County auditor website says the house belongs to Martha Utzler." He stopped for a moment and looked up. "Charlie, we've been trying to get in touch with Frank Utzler. He's Boyd Sashman's roommate. How many bodies did they mention on the scanner?"

"Two, a man and a woman."

Tim's mind whirled. "So Boyd is dead and now his roommate and his mother are. Charlie, something is going on here. These have to be connected."

"How?" Charlie said. "Is it drugs? From what you told me about Boyd, I don't see any other reason for him to be dead."

"Probably, but I just don't know yet. Excuse me a minute. I have to make a call."

"Okay, well, I'm going to start talking to the neighbors. I'll need your help, so don't be too long."

Tim nodded and walked back to their car. He leaned on the trunk and dialed Amy. She picked up on the second ring.

"Amy, were you able to get ahold of Frank?"

"No, the calls just go to voicemail."

Tim nodded. "I think I may know why. I'm over at Frank's mom's house and the police are here. There are two bodies inside. I'm guessing it's Frank and his mom."

"Holy shit," Amy said. "What's going on, Tim? Who's doing this?"

"I don't know, Amy. Charlie and I are down here now. We'll see what we can find out. I'll drop by later."

"Make sure you do. This is crazy."

"Yeah," he said. "I think that's a good word for it. Take care of yourself, okay?"

"You too, Tim. Be careful."

The connection broke, and Tim went back to help Charlie ask the neighbors questions.

Twenty-Five

Bob sat in his truck with the engine idling in the parking lot of the old elementary school on the corner of Cranston and Leslie. From this vantage point he could see the two-story house at the address Frank had given him—the dealer's house. Skillet's house. He couldn't imagine how anyone would come by such a stupid nickname.

He took a bite of the burrito he was having for dinner. He had gone through the drive-thru at Dos Loco Tacos in town. The sun was down, but he could see the house well enough under the street lights. No one had come or gone since he'd pulled in half an hour ago. The neighborhood looked quiet.

The local talk radio station was on, and the topic was the recent murders in Hogan. Callers to the radio show were all twisted up wondering if some serial killer were stalking the town. The calls had been non-stop worried small-town folks crying about locking their doors and wondering what the police were doing about it. Bob wondered that himself and burped with indigestion that had been haunting him since the police visit this morning.

This thing was out of control now. He should have never killed Boyd, but what other choice had there been? Those two idiots had broken into his home. They had seen his private things, and they had stolen from him. There had to be a penalty for that, and it had to be more than probation or whatever some wuss judge would hand down as punishment. Hell, if a judge let Ohio Axle steal his pension with no repercussions, there was no way one would punish a couple drug-addled little shits for stealing his tools. No, this was the way to handle things. Take care of it himself, no more relying on anyone for anything. Just take care of this Skillet guy and be done with it. That's all there was left to do.

Just kill one more guy, he thought, and everything goes back to the way it was.

• • •

Tim and Amy sat on her couch watching the six o'clock news. The lead story was the double homicide in Hogan. A reporter Tim recognized from his internship gave the run down and confirmed the two bodies found inside the house were Frank and his mother. The story wrapped, and Amy clicked the mute button on the remote and looked at Tim.

"So, Boyd and Frank are dead. Why?"

Tim shrugged. "I don't know, Amy. I've been asking myself that all afternoon. I suppose Frank's mom was unintentional. Maybe she was there when someone caught up with Frank. As for why anyone would want your brother and his roommate dead, I have to assume they either knew something they shouldn't or they owed someone money."

"Do the police think the murders are connected?" she asked. "I mean, Boyd was killed around Thanksgiving, and these two were a day or two ago. What if it's just a coincidence?"

Tim chewed the last of the grilled cheese sandwich Amy had made for dinner. "I think that would be one hell of a coincidence, don't you?"

She nodded. "Yeah, probably. I just don't understand what they were into that would make someone mad enough to kill three people." She picked up the pile of mail from the coffee table. "If these killings are all connected, it has to have been something serious. The last time I spoke with Boyd, he didn't say anything was up."

"Would he tell you if something dangerous was happening?" Tim said.

She flipped through the mail. "He would if he could buy his way out of trouble. Boyd was never shy about asking for money if it would get him out of a jam." She stopped sorting the mail and held up an envelope.

"What's that?" Tim asked. His heart dropped as he thought about her receiving a letter. After all, if the guy knew where he lived, he might know he was seeing Amy.

"Cell phone bill," she said.

Tim relaxed. "So?"

"Boyd is on my cell phone plan. I have access to his voicemail." She got up and retrieved her phone from the dining room table. "I can't believe I didn't think to check this before." Tim watched as she tapped numbers into the phone.

"Put it on speaker," he said.

The display said there were thirty-four messages. Amy started playing them. The first few were from Frank and didn't seem important. Then one came up with the date of the Wednesday before Thanksgiving, in the afternoon.

"Boyd, I need to talk to you. Give me a call back. It's important. We need to talk about Skillet. I think he's going to try and screw us on this deal."

"That was Frank," Amy said. "Did you hear that?"

"Yeah," Tim said. "I wonder what deal he was talking about. Play it back."

They listened to it again and then listened to the rest. The remaining messages were Frank and Amy calling Boyd looking for him, asking him to return their calls.

"Who is Skillet?" Tim said.

Amy sat back and an angry look crossed her face. "Skillet is Boyd's dealer." She got up and crossed the room to a small bookcase, grabbed a yearbook and brought it to Tim. She sat down on the couch beside him and flipped through the pages, landing on the graduating seniors. "Jimmy Stumpmeyer."

Tim looked at the picture. The guy was skinny with a shaved head. "This is Boyd's dealer?"

Amy nodded. "Yeah, back in high school he used to sell weed for his dad. The whole family is a bunch of dope-dealing white trash who live out in the township in a double wide set down on a couple acres."

"Hey, don't knock them for living in a trailer," Tim said with a smile. "We should tell Coogan. With that message, this guy is someone the police should be talking to."

Amy stood up. "We will, but we're going to talk to him first."

Tim looked at her. "We are? I don't think going out to some trailer in the township in the dark to ask a drug dealer questions about multiple homicides is a good idea."

Amy pulled her coat on. "He lives here in the city now. Boyd told me where once. Don't worry about him. He was a little shit in high school, and I don't think much has changed."

Tim stood up and put his coat on. "Are you sure we shouldn't just call Coogan?"

Amy shook her head. "I think he'll talk to us. If the cops approach him, he'll just claim he doesn't know what that message was about. They won't get anything out of him. I'm sure his dad has taught him not to talk to police."

Tim nodded. "Okay, but if things get weird, I'm calling the cops."

•   •   •

Detective Coogan knocked on the door of a very nice two-story brick home up the street from Martha Utzler's house. He and Darren Lewis had been up and down the block a couple times since the bodies had been found, but no one had answered at this one. A porch light came on and a dog barked. He saw a shadow move toward the door. A man with a silver mustache and thin hair peered out through one of the small windows set into the door.

Coogan held up his badge. "Hogan police, sir," he said. The door opened.

In addition to the thin hair and mustache, the man at the door was stout, wearing a red plaid shirt and blue jeans. "Can I help you?"

"I hope so, sir. I'm Detective Larry Coogan," he said as he handed over a business card. "I was wondering if I could speak with you about the incident a few nights ago?"

"The murders? Martha Utzler and her son? That what you mean?"

"Yes, sir."

"Okay."

"Thank you. We think Mrs. Utzler and her son were killed a few nights ago around eleven. Do you remember anything about that night? Anything out of the ordinary, perhaps? Was anyone around who didn't belong?"

The dog barked again, and the man pushed lightly at it with a slipper. "Jocko, be quiet, would you? I'm trying to think here. A few nights ago, you said?"

"That's right. Wednesday night."

"I watch *Hawaii Five-O* and *Blue Bloods* on Wednesday," he said, nodding slowly, as if remembering was as difficult as digging through an old tool box. "I like my mysteries."

"Sure," Coogan said, looking at the dark street.

"I usually take Jocko out for a walk sometime after ten," the man said. "He does his business while the commercials are on, and then we watch TV until eleven, when we go to bed." He paused for moment. "You know, I do remember someone being around."

Coogan's eyebrow twitched up. "Yeah? What did you see?"

The man pointed to the curb across the street. "A truck was parked over there. I don't remember seeing it around before, but it was there when I came out with Jocko. It was kind of loud when it started up later on."

"How much later?"

The man shrugged. "I don't know, before midnight. I was reading a little and heard it start up."

Coogan looked at the spot the man had pointed to and saw a streetlight lit up a few car lengths away. He took out his notebook. "Can you describe the truck?"

"It was a blue Chevy, not too old."

Coogan made a note. "Anything else?" he said. "Was there anything unusual about it?"

The man chewed his lower lip. "Well, it had a plow. That's not too unusual for around here, though, you know."

"Sure," Coogan said as he wrote. "Anything else?"

"It had a dent in the driver's side door. Looked like it had been banged into a pole or something."

Coogan looked up at him carefully, narrowing his eyes. "I don't suppose you got the license plate number?"

The man laughed. "Son, I like to watch *Hawaii Five-O*, but that doesn't make me McGarret."

"I'll need to get your name, sir, for the report."

"Sure."

• • •

Coogan got into his Dodge Charger and dug his cell phone out of his coat pocket. He dialed Darren Lewis's number.

"Darren," he said when the line picked up. "Are you still at the station?"

"Yes, just getting ready to go home."

"Hold up. Do you remember Bob Ellstrom?"

"The guy out in the township? The one you had a feeling about?"

Coogan put the car in drive and pulled away from the curb with enough speed that the tires slipped in the ice and snow. "Yeah, that's him. I just talked to one of Martha Utzler's neighbors, who saw a blue Chevy pickup with a snow plow and a dented door on the street the night and time of the murders."

"No shit?"

"No shit."

"We should go talk to Mr. Ellstrom," Darren said.

Coogan smiled. "I'll pick you up in five minutes."

• • •

Bob checked the clock in the dash radio and saw that it was a little past six. The neighborhood was still quiet. A few cars had come down the street, mostly people coming home from work. No one had gone into or out of Skillet's house, though. He pulled his gun from the gym bag on the seat next to him. The length of pipe attached to the barrel of the Ruger nine millimeter was stuffed with fresh steel wool. Hopefully it would work as well as it had a couple nights ago at the Utzler house. It was pretty good for something he'd made after seeing a video on the Internet. He ejected the magazine, checked to make sure it was loaded and reinserted it with a satisfying click. He pulled the slide and jacked a round into the chamber. The gun went back into the gym bag.

The plan to get into Skillet's was simple. He was just going to knock on the front door. It had worked with Martha Utzler, so he decided to do it again. He gripped the gearshift and dropped the truck into drive.

Just then a rusty little S-10 pickup truck rolled up the street and pulled into Skillet's driveway. Bob's head tipped to one side, and he watched as Tim Abernathy and a cute blonde got out of the truck and walked up onto the front porch. Blondie banged on the front door. Bob put the truck back in park and thought, *what the hell is he doing here?*

•   •   •

Tim hurried around the side of the truck to catch Amy as she mounted the steps to the porch. She was angry, he knew, that her brother was dead and that this Skillet guy might have something to do with it. He wanted to make sure she didn't do something stupid.

"Amy, wait," he said.

She just looked at him and banged on the front door. The sound of the aluminum storm door rattling in its frame echoed in the quiet darkness. "If he knows something, he needs to tell us," she said.

"Hey, I know," he said. "Just don't count on knowing this guy to mean he's not dangerous. And do not go into the house. We speak out here on the porch."

She nodded. "Okay." Tim saw her raise her hand to bang on the door again, and the porch light snapped on. A moment later the front door opened quickly.

Tim saw a skinny guy wearing a black t-shirt with a rebel flag on it and black jeans. He had a cigarette hanging out of his mouth. He took one look at them and pushed the storm door open with his left hand. His right stayed behind the doorjamb.

"Why you banging on my door like that?"

Amy took a step back, and Tim noticed an angry look on the guy's face. "Are you Skillet?" Tim asked.

"Who's asking?"

"That's him," Amy said. "That's Jimmy."

He took a look at Amy and recognition crossed his face. "Amy? Amy Sashman? What are you doing here?"

"Boyd's dead, Jimmy, and I want to know what you know about it."

Tim saw him take a drag on his cigarette and eyeball him. "Who's this guy?"

"Answer my question."

Skillet looked at her. "Look, I heard about Boyd, but I don't know anything about it."

"You were his dealer, weren't you?"

Skillet looked around. "Hey, knock that off. I don't need the neighbors hearing that. Come on inside."

Tim shook his head. "We talk out here. Answer her questions."

"And just who the hell are you?"

Tim took a card from his coat pocket. "My name's Tim Abernathy, and I'm a reporter. I'm working on the story of Boyd's murder and the murders of Frank and Martha Utzler. Your name came up in a voicemail between Frank and Boyd. Some deal you three were working together. Frank was worried you were going to screw him over."

Skillet looked at the card. "This says you work for the *Hogan Shopper*. Isn't that the freebie paper at the grocery store? Why should I talk to you?"

"Because your name's on a voicemail from one murder victim to another on the day Boyd was killed. You can talk to us or you can talk to the police."

"Fuck you, man."

"Just tell her what she wants to know, Jimmy."

Skillet's eyes looked past them to the other houses in the neighborhood. "Let's step inside."

"No, we're not doing that," Tim said. "If you want us off your porch you have to tell us what you know. If you don't want to talk to us, I have a detective's number in my phone. You can talk to him."

Skillet eyed them and dropped his cigarette butt to the porch and crushed it below one black engineer's boot. "I only know one thing, and I don't know if it's going to help you."

"What is it?" Tim said.

"This doesn't go to the police, understand? You two aren't the only ones who can show up at someone's house in the dark, and this one," he said pointing at Amy, "knows I have family who'll be more than happy to make a visit."

Tim nodded. "Okay."

Skillet sighed heavily. "Boyd and Frank pulled a robbery out in the township the day Boyd disappeared. They split up for some reason—I think Frank had to go to work or something—so Boyd walked home. That was the last time Frank saw Boyd. He thought the guy they ripped off found Boyd and did him."

"How would he know Boyd and Frank ripped him off?"

Skillet shrugged. "I don't know and Frank didn't know, but he was scared. That's why he was staying with his mom."

"That's all?"

"Well, Frank mentioned they saw some weird stuff in the guy's house."

"Like what?" Tim said.

"You know those letters on the news? The anonymous ones?"

Tim nodded, and he and Amy looked at each other. "What about them?"

"They saw a bunch of them at this guy's house, all typed out and stacked up, ready to mail. Frank started to get freaked out, came over here talking about how maybe the guy killed Boyd because they saw the letters."

"Holy shit," Tim said. He looked at Amy. "Did you hear that?"

She nodded. "Could he have killed Boyd over those letters? Would someone do that?"

"They're dead, ain't they?" Skillet said.

"Who is it?" Tim said. "What's the guy's name?"

Skillet shrugged again. "No idea, man. I got the tip from someone that the guy had a bunch of tools in a barn. Easy score for high profit. Boyd and Frank were just supposed to go in the barn and grab the tools. They weren't even supposed to be in the house."

Amy slapped Skillet across the face, and he took a step back. "You set him up! He's dead because of you."

Skillet pushed the storm door toward her to make her back up. Tim noticed his right hand was still behind the jamb. He grabbed her. "Come on, Amy, this isn't helping." She folded into his arms and sobbed.

"Okay, if you don't have a name, what about an address? You have to have that if you sent them there."

Skillet nodded. "Yeah, I got that. Hold on." He disappeared into the house. Tim turned to Amy. "Hey, keep it together. I know it's hard, but we're getting what we need. Please don't hit him again."

She nodded and walked to the edge of the porch. Skillet came back to the door with a scrap of paper.

"This is the address," he said. Tim reached for it and Skillet pulled it back with a quick motion. "I give you this and we're done, understand? You and her never come back here, and I better never have cops at my door. I'm dead serious, brother. You get me?"

"Not a problem," Tim said.

Skillet handed him the paper with the address. Tim took it and followed Amy down the stairs to the truck. They got in, and Tim handed her the paper. The door to the house closed and the porch light went out.

"What do we do now, Tim?" Amy said. "Where are we going?"

"First, let's get the hell away from this guy," he said as he backed the pickup out of the driveway. "I think we should go to *Shopper*. Charlie will still be there, and we can look up this address and call Coogan."

"Okay, that sounds good," she said. She broke down again, sobbing in the darkness as Tim drove to the newspaper.

• • •

Bob watched them on the porch, all three of them. Whatever they were talking about had the dealer all twisted up. He was angry, Bob could see. It was too much of a coincidence for Abernathy to be standing on his front porch. Somehow, he knew, the reporter had found out what was going on. Chest pain hit him again and he started to have trouble breathing, just like this morning. He grabbed his Coke and sucked it until the straw delivered nothing but gurgling noises. He was finally able to take a deep breath and calm down. *I'm in control,* he thought. *I can do this.*

After a few minutes, the dealer handed something to Abernathy and he and the girl walked down off the porch to the rusty little pickup. Bob reconsidered his plan. The dealer was aware now, unlikely to be taken by surprise by a knock on the door. He could follow Abernathy, though. See what they were up to.

After a few moments, he dropped the truck into drive and followed Tim's pickup.

• • •

Tim pulled into the parking lot of the *Shopper* and sure enough, Charlie's Cadillac was in its normal spot. He and Amy hurried into the office, and Tim sat down at his desk.

Charlie looked up with confusion. "Hey, Tim, what's going on?" Tim booted his laptop. "Hi, Charlie. This is Amy, and we've had quite an evening."

Amy extended a hand, and Charlie took it. "Your brother was that poor boy found out in the township?"

Amy nodded, "Yes, he was."

"Well you have my condolences, dear. I'm very sorry for your loss."

"Thank you. We have some news, but I think Tim should fill you in." Charlie looked across the desks to Tim. "What have you found?"

"We may know who's writing the letters, Charlie," Tim said with excitement in his voice. "Let me check something."

• • •

Bob saw Tim's rusty pickup pull into the *Shopper*'s parking lot and watched as they ran inside. He drove past the newspaper's office, pulled to the side of the road and took the first open spot he found. He got out with his gym bag, walked back to the little building and peered inside through the front window. He saw Tim Abernathy, the blonde girl, and Charlie Ingram. They appeared to be the only ones in the office.

He slipped into the parking lot of the paper's office and walked to the rear. There was a back door next to the dumpster. It was a steel door with a knob and a deadbolt. Bob put his hand on it and turned the knob very slowly. He was breathing hard, much too hard for the short walk to here from his truck. He closed his mouth and forced himself to breathe through his nose. The last thing he needed was another panic attack. After a moment, his breathing slowed. He looked down and saw his hand was still on the door. He turned it slowly, expecting it to stop. To his genuine surprise the knob went all the way around and the door opened slightly on a darkened hallway. He listened closely, hearing voices from the front of the office. He hesitated a moment, then made up his mind and quickly slipped inside, silently pulling the door closed behind him.

• • •

The county auditor's database was opening when Tim saw a stack of envelopes lying on his desk. "What are these?"

"A couple people brought letters in this afternoon after I got back here," Charlie said with a wave of his hand. "Some of it's just mail."

Tim flipped through the letters and saw a number which were now familiar in content and format. The others were letters addressed to him at the *Shopper*. Thankfully, they looked normal. He pulled out his Swiss Army knife and slit one of the envelopes. He snorted as he read it. "This one is a rejection letter from a TV station in Missouri." He lay it down on his desk.

Amy put a hand on his shoulder. "Sorry."

Tim saw the database sitting open on his screen and typed in a search query. "I've got it," he said. Amy leaned over his shoulder to look at his screen. Charlie was still seated at his desk. Tim looked at the screen and his brow furrowed.

"Who is Bob Ellstrom?" Amy asked. "Does that name mean anything to you guys?"

"Yeah," Tim said. "It sure does." He pulled up the database he had built with all the data from the letters and quickly performed a search.

"What is it, Tim?" Charlie asked. "Who is he?"

"Look," Tim said to Amy. "See how many hits I get off his name?" He looked up. "Charlie, Boyd and his roommate, Frank Utzler, broke into this guy's house on the day before Thanksgiving. We found that out tonight from Boyd's dealer, who brokered the job. Bob also claims to have received a letter, although he never brought it in. And look, he's on Gary Shellmack's list of disgruntled customers."

Charlie leaned forward across the desks, standing up from his chair. "Are you kidding me?"

Tim shook his head. "No. It says here they had a dispute about the transmission in a truck he bought and that it got pretty loud." Tim clicked on another entry. "He was also in the group of retirees who knew about Jerry Donovan having an affair. I haven't had a chance to speak with them all yet, but he was definitely on the list I got from Mark Packer. Charlie, I think this guy found out Boyd and Frank robbed him and saw some of his letters in the process. I think he killed them to keep his secret."

"Would anyone really do that?" Amy said. "Would he have killed my brother just to keep him quiet about these letters?"

Charlie looked at her. "People have killed for much less, my dear. I'm very sorry your brother was caught up in this." He turned to Tim. "Do you still have the number for that police detective we spoke to at Boyd's crime scene? I think it's time to call him."

Tim dug his cell phone from his back pocket. "Yeah, I think you're right."

A man stepped from the dark hallway with a gun in his hand. "Put the phone down or I'll kill every single one of you."

Twenty-Six

Coogan pulled up to Bob Ellstrom's house, and Darren hit the red and blue lights, illuminating the house and snow-covered yard. Coogan smiled. He wanted Bob Ellstrom to know they meant business this time. They walked around the front of the car, and Lewis looked at him.

"The pickup truck thing is a bit thin," he said.

"I know," Coogan said, "but let's rattle his cage and see what shakes loose. Are you telling me you didn't get a hinky feeling from him when we spoke last time?"

"Yeah, I got a feeling," Lewis said. "I'm just saying it's thin."

They mounted the small concrete porch and Coogan hammered on the door. His grandfather had been a letter carrier and he'd taught him that. No one came to the door.

"No one home?" Lewis said.

"Let's take a look around," Coogan said. "Do a little welfare check. Make sure nothing has happened to Mr. Ellstrom."

Lewis smiled and pulled out his radio and called in what they were doing. They walked around the side of the house via the driveway. Both of them took out flashlights and played them around.

Coogan looked up at the barn. "Is that a camera?"

Lewis looked up, the beam of his flashlight following Coogan's. "It sure is. That's kind of odd, isn't it? Putting cameras on an old barn out in the middle of nowhere?"

"No," Coogan said. "I think that's exactly why you'd do it. I've seen these setups before on other garages, especially if there are tools or expensive cars inside." He looked around, his flashlight shining over the house. The windows all looked dark. "I don't think anyone is home."

"You still want to talk with him, though, right?"

"Yeah."

"Let's see if we can find him." He radioed dispatch and asked them to see if they could locate a cell phone number for Bob Ellstrom.

• • •

Charlie and Tim stood at the same time when the man with the gun stepped into the light of the office. Tim moved in front of Amy, the cell phone still in his hand.

The gun swung toward him. "Put the phone down now," the man said, "or I'll shoot you. I mean it."

Tim looked at the phone and realized he would never be able to dial before the man pulled the trigger. He stretched out his left hand and set it on his desk.

"Good, now sit down," the man said. He waved the gun at their chairs. "Come on, everyone down right now."

Amy pulled up one of the spare chairs and sat down. Tim and Charlie sat at their respective desks.

The man moved closer. "You all think you're so goddamn smart, don't you, sitting in here figuring things out." He walked around toward Charlie. "You just couldn't leave things well enough alone, could you?"

Tim didn't like the way he was moving near Charlie. "You're Bob Ellstrom?"

"Yeah, I'm Bob Ellstrom. Proud of yourself for figuring that out? You should have left well enough alone, Abernathy. You had no right digging around in my business."

Tim swallowed hard. "You're the man who's been sending the letters? You left that cat for me? You killed Boyd and Frank?"

"Killed Frank's mom, too," Bob said. "I didn't want to, but I had to because of what Boyd and Frank did. Oh, and don't get too worked up over the cat. The damn things are a dime a dozen out at my place." He walked around Charlie's side of the office, staying wide of the publisher, and found the light switch near the front door. He flicked one of them and some of the lights went out, darkening the office. Anyone passing by outside would have a hard time seeing inside.

"You killed my brother, Boyd?" Amy asked. "Why? He never hurt anyone."

"Boyd was your brother? Well, let me tell you something, honey. Your brother was a thief. He'd be alive today if he and his buddy hadn't broken into my place." Bob became more agitated, Tim saw, as he advanced on him and Amy. "He wasn't harmless. I work for a living. I came home and found out they'd been in my place. They took my tools, my money, and they rooted through all my stuff. You know what that feels like?" Bob's voice was rising. "They were in my home! Don't tell me your brother never hurt anyone. He started all this." Bob walked around them, toward the back hallway of the office where he had come in.

He's working his nerve up, Tim thought. *We don't have much time.*

"How did you know it was them?" Tim asked. "How did you know Boyd and Frank broke into your place?"

Bob looked in the conference room. "I've got cameras set up all over the place. I came home from work early and saw that someone had been there." He walked back to the main office. "Those two idiots never saw the cameras. See, I'm smarter than your average junkie. I protect my place. They'd left just a few minutes before I got there. I just ran her brother over. Finding Frank took more time, but I got them both."

"You're a monster," Amy said through tears.

Bob shrugged. "Maybe, but I take care of my own. That's more than you can say. Maybe your brother would be alive today if you'd gotten him some help."

Amy broke down in sobs. "I did, I sent him to rehab. It didn't work. You didn't have to kill him." She slumped in her chair and put her head on Tim's shoulder. He held her hand.

"Why the letters, Bob?" Charlie said from his desk. "Why did you send all those letters?"

Bob turned to him. "Because someone needed to let the people of this town know they weren't getting away with it, that's why."

Charlie looked puzzled. "Getting away with what?"

Bob spread his arms wide. "All the nasty things everyone in this town gets up to when they think no one's looking. All the cheating, stealing, and underhanded shit they think they're pulling that no one knows about. Why shouldn't they be made to look over their shoulder? They'll probably be better for it."

"So you're the conscience of the town?" Charlie asked, slipping into a philosophical bent. "You get to terrorize people and threaten to expose their secrets?"

"Oh, boo hoo," Bob said. "Do you know what kind of shenanigans the good people of Hogan get up to behind closed doors? They cheat on each other, they steal from each other, and they don't care until they get caught. Well, tough. I've lived a good life, and I've got nothing to show for it. Why should the cheaters win?" He wiped his forehead with the back of his hand. Tim could see he was starting to sweat under his winter coat.

"What do you mean?" Charlie said. "When you say you lived a good life, what happened?"

"You ever hear of Ohio Axle?"

"Sure. They went bankrupt."

Bob nodded and got more agitated. "Yeah, they went bankrupt. They went bankrupt after they underfunded the pension." He held up the fingers on the hand not holding the gun as he counted off their sins. "I took a buyout and were supposed to give me supplemental pay, which stopped because of the bankruptcy. I had to go to work driving a forklift for a third of what I had been making and ended up working for some little asshole when I used to be a crane operator." He held up another finger. "My pension got reduced because they didn't fund it properly and now the government has to take it over." Another finger. "That's the same government who's going to seize my property because I can't afford to pay my property taxes." Another finger. "My wife died of cancer so now I get to live alone." His voice grew louder. "That's what happened to me. I did everything right and I've got nothing to show for it. If all those bastards think they're going to lie, cheat, and steal and get away with it, they have another thing coming."

"Well, Charlie didn't have anything to do with Ohio Axle," Tim said. "Why did you send him so many letters?"

Bob turned to face him. "You want to know why Charlie got letters? Ask him who Keith Fenton is."

Tim turned to Charlie. "I don't understand."

Charlie sighed. "Remember when you were at my house asking if there could be a personal component to the letters?"

"Yeah."

"I guess there was after all," Charlie said. "Keith was the man I considered may have been behind them."

"He's my cousin," Bob said. "You dated him and you cheated on him. It broke his heart."

"It wasn't exactly like that," Charlie said. "We just drifted apart. I'll admit it ended badly."

"He got so depressed afterward that he lost his job and ended up living with my aunt again. Can you imagine? Being my age and having to move back in with your mother? It damn near killed him. You cheated on him because you didn't have the decency to end it, and now he's living in his mom's basement and working in a grocery store. You deserved every letter you got."

"Your letter killed Jerry Donovan," Tim said.

"Who?"

"The owner of AA Tire and Wheel," Tim said. "You sent him a letter, and he died of a heart attack reading it."

Bob smiled. "Oh, yeah, the guy who cheated on his wife. Not my fault. He should have kept his zipper up."

Tim noticed Bob was sweating more now, wiping his forehead more often. He was afraid that the end was getting near. *I'm not going out sitting in a chair,* he thought. *No way.* He wanted to draw the man in closer, maybe give himself a chance to jump him. Bob was bigger, but he was younger.

"It must have really pissed you off when Gary Shellmack got the better of you over that busted transmission," Tim said. "Did you feel like a big man, writing him all those letters after you wrote him a fat check to fix your truck?"

Bob walked over and raised the gun up. "Let me tell you something about that tubby bastard. He's going to get his. I know a guy in his shop over there, and after I've sent a letter, Gary gets all pissed off. He won't take it out on anyone, but it makes him angry. I figure I can keep on doing that for as long as it takes to give him the heart attack that's just waiting for him."

Tim saw the barrel of the gun with the silencer attached move level with his eyes. It looked enormous, like the mouth of some deep, dark mineshaft. The glow of his laptop screen cast odd shadows. He steeled himself, and then a cell phone rang. Bob reached in his coat pocket and pulled out a flip phone. He stood in front of Tim and didn't move the gun as he looked at the phone. "Don't move or say anything. If you do, I promise I'll kill her first," he said, nodding toward Amy. The phone rang again, and he thumbed a button to answer it.

"Hello?" Bob's eyes grew wide, Tim saw. "Yes, Detective Coogan," Bob said. "I remember you."

Tim decided to act. He reached for the open Swiss Army knife lying on his desk under the rejection letter from the TV station. He barreled forward and hit Bob with as much force as he could muster from a sitting position. The big man went down, but Tim heard the muted gun go off, and Charlie screamed. Tim brought the knife down and stabbed Bob in the leg. The big man howled, and Tim felt hot blood splash across his face. He tried to pull the knife out to stab him again, but the plastic handle was slippery, and Bob squirmed away.

Bob still had a grip on the gun, and he aimed it at Tim's face. The reporter grabbed the barrel, and it jumped in his hand as the gun went off again, sending a bullet past his head into the darkened office. Tim brought his other hand down and punched Bob in the leg where the knife was lodged. Bob screamed in rage and pain. Tim lost his grip on the pistol, and Bob slammed it into his head. Tim saw stars dance before his eyes in the office darkness and felt Bob slip away from him.

"Tim," Amy screamed, snapping him back to reality. "Charlie's been shot!" He got up and looked at her. She was pressing a wad of napkins to the publisher's chest.

"Are you okay?" he said.

"I'm fine," she said, "but Charlie's bleeding."

"Where's Bob?" he said.

Amy pointed with her free hand. "He went down the hallway!"

Tim saw a flicker of light on the floor and realized it was Bob's cell phone. He picked it up. "Hello? Is anyone there?" he asked.

"This is Detective Coogan. Who is this? What's going on?"

"Coogan? This is Tim Abernathy. I need you and an ambulance at the offices of the *Hogan Shopper*. Bob Ellstrom just broke in here and tried to kill us."

"What?"

"Please hurry, okay? Charlie's been shot."

Tim looked into the dark hallway. The door stood wide open. Tim handed the phone to Amy. "Can you take care of Charlie? Coogan is on the phone, and he's getting us an ambulance."

"Yeah, what are you doing?"

"I'm going to see where Bob went," he said, and he ran down the hall.

• • •

Tim approached the doorway carefully and peeked out into the parking lot with a quick glance. The snow had picked up, and fat flakes were coating everything with a white blanket. He saw drops of dark blood in the snow leading away from the door and through the lot. He grabbed the snow shovel Charlie kept near the back door. Crazily, he recognized it as a model Tate sold at the hardware store.

He followed the blood trail. Edging around the side of the building, he peered toward the street. Blood drops the size of half-dollar coins were splattered on the sidewalk running up the side of the building to the street. Tim moved as quickly and as quietly as he could toward the sidewalk. He got to the corner of the *Shopper*'s offices and looked in both directions. He saw Bob on the right under a streetlight, leaning against the tailgate of blue pickup truck. The older man was bent over, pressing his hand against his thigh. Tim ducked back around the corner. He took a deep breath and considered the situation. He could wait for Coogan or another squad car, but if they pulled up and Bob decided to make a last stand, he might kill someone else before they got him. *He's got nothing to lose now,* Tim thought.

Tim raced back around the back of the *Shopper* and crossed behind the building next door. There was a narrow alley here, running between two shops. Tim moved through the alley, stepping around some garbage cans, and peered out onto the street. Bob was to his left, still leaning against the bed of the pickup and looking toward the *Shopper*'s front door. The sound of sirens filled the air, but Tim didn't know if they belonged to police or the ambulance he'd asked for. He didn't want anyone else harmed by Bob Ellstrom. Tim hefted the snow shovel and stepped around the corner of the building.

He rushed hard, the snow deadening his footsteps. He swung the shovel, but Bob heard him at the last moment and raised an arm to block him. The aluminum snow shovel glanced off him, and Bob fell to the snow-covered street, struggling to stay upright with his left arm on the pickup's bumper. Tim reared back again, and Bob tried to raise the gun but had trouble getting it high enough. Tim swung, connecting hard with Bob's gun hand. He saw the gun skitter out into the street.

Tim raised the shovel up for another swing, but Bob lay back in the street and raised one arm in a pathetic attempt to ward off the blow. Tim saw the snow under Bob melting and turning red where he'd been stabbed in the leg.

"Are you done?" Tim asked with the shovel raised up in the air.

Bob nodded. "I'm having trouble breathing. I can't catch my breath." A spasm shook his body, and he grabbed his left arm. "No," he said softly, almost whining. "This isn't fair."

"You killed people. Was that fair?"

Bob grimaced. "It's what they deserved," he said. "They all got what they deserved."

"No, they didn't. You're just angry and wanted to take it out on people. You told me on the phone you were going to die alone. Maybe you were right."

Red and blue lights flashed across the windows of the shops along the street, turning the night into a kaleidoscope. Black-and-white police cruisers stopped in front of the *Shopper*, and officers from three cars rushed to the front door. An ambulance was behind them, further down the block. Tim looked down at Bob.

"Help is here, Bob. The same people you sent all those letters to and terrorized are the same people who've come here to save your life."

Bob didn't say anything. Tim noticed his head had lolled off to one side and the emergency lights were reflected in his face. It didn't look like he was breathing.

"Abernathy!" someone called. Tim held his hand up to block some of the lights. Coogan and another detective ran up the sidewalk. "What are you doing with that shovel?"

Tim didn't realize he was still holding the shovel up like a batter at home plate. He lowered it and pointed at Bob. "This is the guy, Detective. Bob Ellstrom. He wrote the letters, and he killed Boyd and Frank and Frank's mother. He did it all."

"How is he, Lewis?" Coogan said. The other detective knelt in the snow near Bob, using two fingers to search for a pulse. He shook his head. Coogan spoke into a radio and asked for another ambulance.

Tim leaned on the shovel and watched as snow gathered on Bob's body.

• • •

Two days later, Tim and Amy were at the Hogan police station with detectives Coogan and Lewis. They were in separate interview rooms, Coogan with him and Lewis with Amy. Tim reached for his can of Pepsi and took a sip. He had run through the story three times as Coogan took notes.

"Are we almost done here?" Tim asked. "I want to get over to the hospital and see how Charlie's doing." Charlie was recovering from surgery. The bullet had gone into his chest and nicked a lung, but Charlie was strong.

Coogan's eyes came up off his notebook. "Yeah, we're done, but let me update you before you leave. We searched Bob Ellstrom's place."

"What did you find?"

"He had cameras all over the place. We've pieced together the timeline of Boyd and Frank robbing him and him leaving to kill Boyd. We also found all kinds of evidence indicating he was writing the letters you wrote the story about. The ribbon off the typewriter has hundreds of letters imprinted on it."

"What about the murders?" Tim said.

"We're working to match the gun he used to shoot Charlie with the Utzler murders. I have a hunch it will; they were both shot with a nine milllimeter."

"So he was behind the letters, and killed to keep that secret?"

"I think so," Coogan said. "The video seems to implicate him, and I think the state crime lab will match the marks on Boyd's body with the snow plow on his truck. I don't think there's any doubt he was the guy."

Tim nodded. "Was it a heart attack that killed him?"

"That's what it looks like. The stress of the situation probably caused it, and there were complications caused by you nicking his femoral artery when you stabbed him. Another couple inches to the right and you'd have sliced his balls."

"I don't feel good about that," Tim said, looking at the detective. "I just wanted to protect us, not kill him. Maybe if we'd figured things out faster he wouldn't have got the jump on us."

Tim stood up and Coogan did likewise.

"You can only do what you can do, Abernathy. You figured it out faster than we did." Coogan stared at Tim for a moment. "You know, guys like Ellstrom, they're cowards. They're scared of everything."

Tim smiled. "Tate Degman said something like that once."

"Well, he was right," Coogan said. "I mean, sure, Ellstrom caught a couple bad breaks, but don't we all? It's certainly no reason to become a murdering asshole. If I've learned anything at this job it's that no one gets out of life without a few scars."

Tim nodded and held out his hand. Coogan shook it.

• • •

Six months later, Tim and Amy stood in the cemetery in front of her family plot. They were looking at Boyd's marker.

"They did a good job, don't you think?" she said, kneeling down. "The engraving is nice and it's straight."

"Yeah," Tim said. He took a swig of water from a plastic bottle. "I'm sorry you had to go through all this, Amy. It's not fair."

She stood up, brushed the dirt from her knees and pointed to her dad's marker. "You know what he used to say about fair?"

"What?"

"Fair's a place you eat corndogs." She took the water bottle from Tim and sipped some. "I graduate in a few weeks, Tim and I have to tell you, I'm ready to leave all this behind me. I want to start over. I love my family, but I'm finally in a place where I can do what I want. I loved Boyd and he was all I had left, but loving him with all his problems was exhausting. I'm ready to move on."

"I can understand that," Tim said, "and as long as I get to be there for the new beginning, I'll be happy." He picked up the bucket of tools and they started back toward his pickup.

She snuggled in close, slipping an arm around his waist. "You better be there." She eyed the truck. "When do you get your new car?"

"Well, it's 'newer,' not brand new," he said. "Anyway, I trade in the old girl here on Tuesday. Gary Shellmack claims he has a nice ride picked out for me and will give me a heck of a deal. I feel kind of funny about it."

"You shouldn't," she said. "You figured out who was driving him crazy. If he wants to give you a deal on a car, take it."

Tim threw the bucket in the bed of the truck and strapped it in with a bungee cord. "I guess."

"Don't be shy about accepting accolades for your hard work," she said. "At the very least, you earned a discount on a used car. Not that you need it with your new job."

Tim rolled his eyes and smiled. "Weekend anchor at Channel 26. Between that and working full time at the *Shopper*, I'm back to having two jobs."

"Poor baby," she said. "Hey, are you hungry?"

He nodded. "Yeah."

"I'm starving. Take us out to Jupiter Joe's. I'll treat for bacon cheeseburgers."

"Yeah," he said. "That sounds like a good plan."

He dropped the little truck into drive and they moved toward the future.

Acknowledgements

Writing a novel is a difficult business, but the people around you make it easier. Tina, Wyatt, and Jacob, thank you for letting me steal time away from you to write this story.

This book also required expertise I don't possess, so it's a good thing I'm friends with Jim Newton, who provided valuable advice from a law enforcement perspective. Any mistakes in that regard belong to me misunderstanding his wise counsel.

Finally, thanks to Anne, Corinne, and Curtis at North Star Press for accepting this book and getting it published.